RUTH

RUTH

Marlene S Lewis

Matador
5 Weir Road
Kibworth Beauchamp
Leicester LE8 0LQ, UK
Tel: (+44) 116 279 2299
Fax: (+44) 116 279 2277
Email: books@troubador.co.uk
Web: www.troubador.co.uk/matador

ISBN 978 1848766 235

British Library Cataloguing in Publication Data.
A catalogue record for this book is available from the British Library.

Typeset in 12pt Perpetua by Troubador Publishing Ltd, Leicester, UK

Matador is an imprint of Troubador Publishing Ltd

For Alex and Kairee, with love.

CHAPTER 1

Friday 14th December 1956 had arrived at last. Fed up with boarding school, Ruth's final day couldn't come soon enough. She longed for the familiar lush, green landscapes of Papua with myriad flowering trees and vibrant, cascading orchids. And, of course, seeing Tommy. She hoped he'd missed her as much as she had missed him, and wondered if he had changed over the last year. Ruth knew she had changed. No longer beset by outbreaks of acne, her skin had blossomed. Her figure had also done what it should, by filling out in all in the right places.

The four-hour journey by train to Sydney from St. Margaret's Ladies' College seemed interminable. Ruth's interest in Neville Shute's latest novel couldn't compete with the pending trip home on a flying boat. Indeed, she might have been reading about her own life in *Beyond the Black Stump*. Even after six years of attending school on the mainland, the mountain vegetation still appeared foreign to her eyes. It had a lot to do with the shape and blue-grey colour of the trees; their branches weren't as densely leaved as trees back in Papua, and their trunks possessed a bare appearance. The sandy soil even resembled dust more than earth. Still, unlike most places west of the Blue Mountains, the eucalypt forest did bear some resemblance to the Owen Stanley ranges where she had grown up.

Pretending not to notice the two men who burst into the compartment, she stared at the pages of her book. The shorter of the two, plonked himself down on the seat next to her, and the other sat opposite. Dressed in well-worn dungarees and boots, she surmised they were jackaroos or shearers returning home. As soon as the men sat down, the smell of alcohol permeated the air; they had been drinking.

"So where are you off to, darlin'?" the one sitting opposite asked, then smiled conspiratorially back at his friend.

"To meet my father and do some Christmas shopping," she lied; hoping the mention of her father would cause them to lose interest.

"Christmas shopping, eh?" he said, turning back to his friend.

It worked. They began to speak about some lady, and then the taller one pulled his hat over his eyes and sprawled out along the seat.

Hopefully they'll fall asleep or pass out from the alcohol, she thought, as her mind turned to all the other girls who would probably be home by now. She almost regretted her decision to leave a day late, just to meet an uncle whom she didn't know. Still, she reasoned, her grandmother would be happy that she had waited to catch his flight.

Ruth was close to her grandmother, Eliza Madison. Kindred spirits in a way, they both shared a sense of disconnection from family ties. But visits were few. Eliza spent most of her time in the highland villages, documenting local customs and tribal histories. Ruth remembered her grandmother as always being interested in her and what she thought about things, which was in contrast to everyone else, especially her brothers and, more recently, her mother. It saddened Ruth that she didn't have a closer relationship with her mother. They hadn't always been distant, but since going to boarding school on the mainland, she had found her mother increasingly withdrawn.

"I reckon you should share ya chips, luv." The man next to Ruth eyed the bag of potato chips perched on her arm rest.

"Here you go," she said, holding out the bag, but instead of taking the chips, he grabbed her wrist. Shocked, she hastily withdrew her hand and the chips flew across the floor.

"Now, that's not nice. Anyone'd think ya don't like 'avin' ya hand held."

"I don't, and if you can't keep your hands to yourself, I'll pull the emergency cord," Ruth said bravely, as her insides knotted with fear.

"Hey, did ya 'ear that, Jack? She's go'na pull the cord on me."

The other man continued to snore.

"Crabby bitch, you're lucky it was only me hand I put on ya, miserable cow." His face twisted in disgust as he put his feet up on his companion's seat.

For a good ten minutes, Ruth sat wondering whether she should try to leave the carriage. Her holdall was on the luggage rack above the other man's head. To get to the door, she would have to climb over their legs. She decided to stay put and move if the ticket inspector came.

The air was heavy and sticky when the locomotive pulled into Penrith for water. Ruth drew-down the wooden shutter to block the sun that was streaming through the window. Eyeing the two drunks, she wished her brothers, Jake and Matthew, had been travelling with her. They were twice the size of these fellows, both over six feet tall. Ruth's brothers had preceded her to school on the mainland and, being older, had already finished their education. When they first went away, she had felt deserted. John Madison, her father, was rarely home, and her mother, Alice, was usually busy – or sick. Ruth had always depended on her brothers for company.

The colour bar in Papua between local, native families and the Australian administrators further compounded the isolation of many white children, although for Ruth, this turned out not to be an issue. As her mother's headaches and confinement to bed became more frequent, the servants let Ruth play with the native workers' children. This had opened up a whole new, exciting world for her.

Ruth jumped, the compartment door flew open.

"You two boys'll 'ave to move yourselves and let an old bloke sit down," the tall, well-dressed man ordered, as he pushed past the two sleeping men. He threw his bag up on the rack, making a loud rattle.

They both shot-up, bleary-eyed. "Where are we?" asked the one named Jack.

"Pulling out of Penrith, mate," the newcomer said.

The two young men swore profusely, grabbed their swags and staggered out of the carriage towards the exit. Ruth breathed a sigh of relief.

"Hope they weren't giving you any bother, Miss."

"They were okay, once they fell asleep," Ruth replied, wondering if he had detected her obvious relief.

"Looks like someone's been having a chip fight." The stranger looked at the scattered chips still on the floor.

"Yes, I dropped them," Ruth said, and began picking up the worst of the mess.

"I suspect you're off to visit relatives, eh?"

"I'm on my way home for the summer, to Papua," she replied, expecting this to invite interest.

"Strewth, you're a long way from home!"

Ruth smiled, but caught herself, she didn't want to appear too friendly; he could turn out like the others.

"Not long after my wife and I got married, we moved out West, to the grandparents' property. That was a world apart, too, in those days."

"I was born in Papua, so it isn't such a strange place really." But unless you've grown up in the islands, she thought, it probably would seem like the end of the earth.

"We didn't think we'd survive at first," the man continued. "I wouldn't change a thing now, though; life on the land is good, once you find yourself."

Ruth thought the stranger was interesting, but still would have preferred to daydream her way to Sydney. "Do you often travel to town?" she asked, filling in an awkward silence.

"No, I'm meeting my wife and son. His missus is in hospital, women's problems." The conversation stopped dead.

"I hope she gets better soon." Ruth didn't know what else to say.

"We're all praying, honey," the man replied, visibly upset.

Ruth gazed through the shutters at the passing trees in an attempt to stymie any further conversation about the man's family.

"I'm surprised to see such a young girl travelling alone; someone meeting you at the other end?"

"Yes, my uncle. We're catching the same flight."

"Ah, that's all right then, can't be too careful these days, luv."

Ruth wondered if he referred to all young women as 'young girls' or whether she did seem obviously young. She guessed it was because he was old, maybe he hadn't noticed how tall she was. Ruth was proud of her five-foot-eight inches height and developed figure. She was the envy of a lot of girls at school.

Opening the window shutter again to study her reflection in the glass, she scrutinised the mass of titian frizz cascading down her shoulders, and decided to put her hair up before getting on the plane. She wondered if her uncle knew that she was eighteen. It will be such fun meeting him, she thought, trying to imagine what he would look like.

The train accelerated across the plains on its approach to Sydney. Houses appeared with ever-increasing frequency and small suburbs punctuated the whistle-blows. Living in little boxes in a large city had always intrigued Ruth, but she imagined the claustrophobic conditions would be intolerable. She felt uneasy as the greenery faded behind her, revealing an almost continuous row of buildings and suburbs melding into one another with no clear division.

As the locomotive navigated the criss-cross tracks of MacDonnaldtown and Redfern, it slowed. Abruptly, point changes interrupted the rhythmic clickety-clack of the steel rails, and through a torrent of hissing steam, the train came to halt.

Ruth marvelled at the busyness of Central Station, and at how purposeful everyone appeared as they hurried by. It was too early to go to the flying boat terminal, so breakfast in the railway dining room seemed a fitting way to kill time.

Pushing through the early-morning commuters, she realised this was the most people she had ever seen in one place. To her surprise, she enjoyed the anonymity afforded by the crowd; just another face in a sea of hundreds.

She sat alone at an empty table for four. Ruth had always struggled with self-consciousness when eating in public, but decided it was a pleasant place to dine. The room was large and airy, with pristine white tablecloths. Each table had a vase of flowers and was set with the shiniest cutlery.

She opened her satchel and groped around for her grandmother's letter.

...he is a tall man like your father but older and slightly bald, so he'll look quite old to you... Eliza went on to describe how Ruth would recognise her uncle, Lindsay Drummond. She memorised the description and carefully refolded the letter.

Her grandmother had emigrated to Australia from Scotland with her first husband, James, who died of dysentery while trying his luck at gold mining. They had only the one child, Lindsay. After James' death, Eliza had continued prospecting on her own with the boy until she met up with Horace Madison. Horace had big dreams and planned to follow his quest for gold to New Guinea. When he proposed, Eliza accepted, having no other alternative. She couldn't go back to Scotland, destitute, and she knew she wouldn't last long on the gold fields, a woman with no man to protect her.

Before leaving for New Guinea, Eliza sent Lindsay to live with relatives back in Scotland. She had always intended to bring him back after a couple of years, but then she gave birth to a second child, John Madison. This put an end to their travels and they ended up settling in Papua. With a new baby demanding his wife's attention, Horace decided Lindsay should remain in Scotland and complete his education. He never did return, although Eliza endured the eight-week sea journey to visit him on a number of occasions.

"Mind if I join you?"

Ruth glanced up from her musings; the man from the train was standing next to her. "Oh, I thought you'd left."

"I missed the tram and decided to come back for some breakfast."

Ruth felt intruded upon. "Oh, I'm sorry; I have to rush to catch mine." She had heard a number of disturbing stories about girls coming to harm while travelling alone and thought a speedy exit was the best strategy. As charming as he seemed, it was disconcerting that he had followed her into the dining room.

"That's fine, luv, don't let me keep you. My name's William McGrath, by the way."

"Lovely talking to you, Mr McGrath; thank you for the company." Ruth started to walk away.

"Look us up if you're ever out near Collabine," he called out.

Ruth smiled back at him, knowing she would never be going there.

Finding the Rose Bay terminal turned out to be quite an ordeal. Unfamiliar with the route, she got off at the wrong stop and then had to run the rest of the way; all the while wondering if William McGrath was following. But she suspected her concerns had more to do with her own over-active imagination. When she arrived, hot and agitated, she discovered a mechanical problem had delayed the plane's departure; if you could call the bulky-looking vessel a plane. The body was entirely silver and had the appearance of a boat with wings stuck on top. It explained why they were called flying boats, but she hadn't expected such a distinct nautical shape.

The aircraft took forever to be repaired, and the terminal had little to offer in terms of entertainment. The suffocating air inside the waiting area added to Ruth's discomfort and her neck ached from briefly dozing off with her head crooked to one side. She began having second thoughts about taking this flight, when suddenly, the Tannoy burst into life.

"The launch conveying passengers for the ten-thirty flight to Port Moresby is now boarding." Ruth jumped up; the final leg of the journey home was finally underway.

As she approached the shiny, metallic vessel, she decided this was a far more romantic way to travel than by aeroplane. It reminded her of something you saw in a Tarzan movie, where they fly along jungle rivers, stopping along the way to let off explorers and news reporters. They even served hot meals!

Once on-board, Ruth surveyed the other passengers. She had been too excited to notice before, but everyone appeared to be wearing their Sunday best. Embarrassed, she tried to conceal her scuffed shoes under the seat in front and quickly put on her cardigan to hide a tomato sauce stain from a wayward breakfast chip. She had never been one for worrying much about her appearance, especially at school, where her curvaceous body and formless navy uniform were often at odds. At home, she mainly wore colourful sarongs with her hair tied or pinned up with flowers, like the native women. Make-up was a waste of time due to the humidity, although her mother always said she didn't need any with her rosy cheeks and brilliant, emerald eyes.

The Sunderland, now repaired, wasted no time at all in becoming airborne. According to the itinerary, this would have been a quick flight if it had left on time, stopping at Brisbane and Townsville before arriving at Port Moresby in the evening. Owing to the delay, the arrival time had been pushed forward to the morning.

For the first hour or so, the plane flew close to the water, which Ruth found exciting. But then it unexpectedly climbed higher and stayed at around ten thousand feet. After the initial novelty, flying above the New South Wales coastline became monotonous and she became bored – until delicious aromas drifted through the cabin. Her mouth watered when the hostess appeared with a nicely laid-out tray containing corned beef, boiled potatoes in a creamy parsley sauce and dainty baby carrots. Even dessert which, she noticed with glee, was strawberry blancmange!

The warm cabin became oppressive after dinner, and Ruth drifted in and out of sleep. Half dreaming and half awake, her thoughts turned to landing. She hoped her mother, Alice Madison, would be waiting for her, and they could spend a night in town. Before her mother's illness, they used to go to Port Moresby on shopping trips. Those were special times, shopping for clothes and books at Burns Philps department store, having lunch in the dining room under the punkahs, then in the evening, dressing for dinner at the hotel.

The war had taken a lot from Ruth's mother. Her own parents had refused to leave Papua when the Japanese invaded and they were found slaughtered just a few weeks before the war ended. On her return to Papua, Alice discovered her only remaining brother with both his legs blown away and dying of malaria. In a way, the delirium of the malaria had been a kindness, they all decided, as it provided some respite from the pain of his gangrenous limbs.

Like most civilians, Ruth and her mother had been repatriated to Australia before the Japanese landed at Basabua. Her father stayed on until the last minute, in case it turned out to be a false alarm. He thought he would be able to wait out the war, stockpiling the coffee harvests. He didn't plan on the invaders moving inland through the jungle.

When the administrators and business people returned after the Japanese surrender, they found a lot had changed. Even they had changed, along with their belief in British supremacy. More disturbing was the change in the local inhabitants. Perhaps it was resentment at having been caught up in the white man's war, or maybe something more fundamental, an awareness that in spite of all the distinct tribes, they were, in fact, one people; a colonised people. This had become increasingly apparent to Ruth as she arrived home each summer. Sometimes Papua seemed as foreign a place as the mainland. It was an uncomfortable realisation, not fully belonging to either place. She wondered whether she would experience that same sense of unsettled dissonance on this visit. Her main concern was for Tommy. She feared that he might become caught up in the smouldering undercurrent of political discontent that pervaded Papua.

The plane landed at Redland Bay, not far from Brisbane. Ruth glanced towards the doorway to see who was getting on but an elderly man, chatting to the hostess, blocked her view. Then something clicked, a sense of recognition. There stood Uncle Lindsay, the man who had always intrigued her by his absence – and the hushed tones with which his name used to be mentioned. He looked straight in Ruth's direction.

"Ruth!" he called, making his way to the empty seat next to her. "I'm so glad to meet you; Mum said you'd be on this flight."

She tried hard to be welcoming through a sudden attack of shyness. He was extremely dapper-looking in his stone-coloured safari suit, and he possessed the carriage of a much younger man.

"I'm sorry, Ruth. I'm Lindsay," he said as he surveyed his brother's daughter, "and what a treat it is to meet you. You look exactly like your photograph, only prettier."

All Ruth could do was smile. She wasn't at all sure how to navigate her way through this encounter. She blushed; everyone seemed to be watching.

"Your grandmother wired to say I'm to make sure you catch your connecting flight. Apparently there'll be no one at Port Moresby to meet you."

Trying to conceal her dismay at not being met at Port Moresby, she asked, "Have you come straight from Scotland?" She was at a loss for something more engaging to say.

"I've just had two lovely weeks in Brisbane." He squeezed her hand and smiled. "Don't worry, there's nothing worse than meeting long-lost relatives and trying to make conversation. I speak from experience."

She eventually relaxed a little. "I'm amazed that I've finally got to meet you. Gran's the one who always goes to visit you."

"Yes, I never wanted to go to New Guinea, although I did think about coming here to Australia after I finished university. But I got married shortly after I qualified, and with marriage and the war, I just didn't get around to travelling."

"Well, I'm glad you came." Ruth warmed to Lindsay. He seemed such a jovial and likeable character.

"Yes, I thought I'd better take a gander at the place my mother has loved for so long. Besides, I needed a vacation and your gran had a couple of legal matters to take care of in Brisbane. Her will actually; she has never made one. So it's a working holiday, if you like."

"Gran told me about your work and some of the cases." Ruth wondered what this obviously cultured gentleman would think when he arrived at her grandmother's village. "You know where Gran lives, don't you?"

"Yes, my dear, Mother has given me directions to her *haus*, as she refers to it."

"She lives in a village, quite remote."

"Yes, Ruth, your grandmother has always been positively eccentric, and if she lived anywhere other than a native village, I would have been surprised." He laughed.

There was a definite kindness and warmth about him; he had her grandmother's eyes, even the same creases when he smiled.

The two new acquaintances chatted away like old friends, until the lights dimmed for everyone to sleep. Ruth needed some quiet time to process her thoughts. She wondered how he had felt growing up in Scotland without his mother or father around. It seemed cruel, forsaking a child for a man. Maybe her grandmother believed his education was more important than being with her. Ruth imagined he probably missed his mother. She remembered her own feelings of abandonment after Jake and Matthew had gone to boarding school. Lindsay must have experienced an even greater sense of loss.

The monotonous drone of the propellers lulled Ruth into a semi-conscious daze, and her thoughts turned again to Tommy. They had grown up together and had always been close. She recalled how he used to play outside the plantation fence, and she would tease him. It had been such a delight when her mother agreed to let him come inside. Their friendship blossomed, although as far as the family were concerned, Tommy was and always would be just the native gardener's son. It was a harmless alliance which Ruth would eventually outgrow. As time passed, however, this failed to occur.

Their attachment became so troublesome to Ruth's father that he broke with custom and sent his daughter to the mainland for her secondary schooling. Normally only boys would be sent away. She wrote to Tommy every few weeks initially, but then her father found out and forbade her to write. Hurt by what she saw as a senseless intrusion into her life, she never did understand her father's actions and her relationship with him never fully recovered. She assumed he didn't have much regard for her feelings.

Ruth watched the sun steal its way into the aircraft from around the edge of the curtains, until she was distracted by the hostess readying breakfast. The cabin came to life again with passengers fishing through their purses and bags for make-up and combs, then rushing up the aisle to the toilets.

Looking down past the wing, Ruth wondered at the expanse of water, majestic and vast, a picture-book blue that extended all the way to the horizon. While Lindsay snored, she surveyed his face for further evidence of family resemblance. His nose had the same aquiline shape as her own, although his was larger, of course. She checked her reflection in the window. Her chin was round, his was square and firmly set. Probably from Gran's first husband, she thought; Dad's is more like mine.

Her attention turned back to the mottled water below with the tell-tale light-green patches of reef. The turquoise-blue expanse transformed into the purest crystal green as the plane banked around the contrasting white sands of Ela Beach. The ramshackle, stilted houses of Hanuabada stood out distinctly against the tropical backdrop. The village on stilts had been rebuilt following its destruction by the Japanese, but even now, eleven years later, remnants of war remained. Deserted planes, boats and heavy, rusting vehicles. Fleetingly, Ruth realised how close she and her family had come to the atrocities of war, something she hadn't contemplated before.

The Sunderland landed effortlessly on the smooth waters of Fairfax Harbour and as the cabin door opened, the warm, dry, familiar air rushed in. Embarking onto the wooden platform, Ruth luxuriated in the penetrating warmth of the sun and breathed in the recognisable sea-grass and salt aromas. Home at last, she thought and smiled.

A crowd of people had assembled at the gate, waiting to meet disembarking family and visitors. There were smartly dressed official-looking men, simply clad *haus bois* and *meris* ready to haul their family's luggage, drivers and eager porters, as well as entire families waiting to celebrate reunions. Ruth didn't recognise anyone; her uncle was right, although secretly she had hoped her mother would appear out of the crowd on this stopover.

She had little time to enjoy the scenery. Lindsay called her to the minibus that was waiting to convey them to Jackson Airfield. Okoro,

Ruth's home, was less than an hour away, once airborne. For Lindsay, the trip would be much longer; he had to continue on to Garua, where he would meet up with a guide to help him through the jungle to Eliza's village.

"I don't envy you, Uncle Lindsay; you have another ten hours' travel after I get off."

"Yes, I know, but your gran assures me she'll send a jeep to save me having to hike all the way; should cut a couple of hours off the trip."

Ruth glimpsed his smiling eyes again. She liked him; he had the same do-or-die attitude that characterised Eliza's approach to life.

The cramped DC-3 contained only two men, a woman in a white pantsuit, and piles of parcels. The lady traveller must be new to the territory, Ruth decided; she wouldn't have chosen to travel in white otherwise. The dirty cabin had electrical equipment stuffed under the seats and two large, covered cages at the far end.

Within minutes, the plane was banking away from Port Moresby to the accompaniment of honking and hissing noises as the altitude increased. New breeding stock, Ruth guessed, or someone hankering for a traditional Christmas goose.

"Penny for them…" Lindsay looked across and winked.

"Not much, I'm just wondering what my friends at school would think about how we travel here."

"I'm sure they'd love the adventure, Ruth; it's a remarkable place, from what I can see."

The plane moved out from behind heavy cloud, and Ruth noticed they were flying along a vast crevice of banked cumulonimbus. She half expected angels to appear; it reminded her of a Sistine Chapel fresco.

A sudden thud caused her to reel back from the window in fright. "What was that?" she shouted, more as a reflex than a question.

The other passengers looked across in stunned silence.

"Must have been a bird; can't be anything to worry about," Lindsay said, looking as though he were trying to reassure himself as much as anyone else.

The pitch of the engines had changed; it was higher and more laboured. The co-pilot entered the cabin.

"Ladies and gentlemen, we have an engine out; please remain seated. We will try to land at Kikori."

Ruth thought he looked nervous. The other passengers peppered him with questions.

"The plane can fly safely with one engine; just stay in your seats," the co-pilot tried to reassure them, but he was clearly agitated.

The remaining engine spluttered as if it were also going to stop. The woman on the other side began to cry and then became hysterical. Looks of horror crossed all their faces as the solitary propeller cut out. The cabin fell silent, apart from a strange, rushing sound made by the wind. The co-pilot ordered everyone to put on their safety belts.

"Stay calm, and put your heads between your knees," he shouted before hurrying back to join the pilot.

Ruth clung to Lindsay, who held her head tightly to his chest. She could still partly see out the window, but they had flown into a cloud. Ruth wondered how confident the pilot was of gliding through the ranges with no vision.

Another loud thud in the undercarriage caused the plane to lurch to one side. It didn't recover its pitch and remained at a skewed angle. The electrical equipment under the seats catapulted noisily to the opposite side of the aisle and an ear-splitting crack came from underneath the floor, as if something had snapped. The female passenger screamed; there were crashing and breaking sounds interspersed with the violent thumping of branches hitting the body of the aircraft. The sound of tearing metal reverberated through the cabin, followed by a ferocious gush of cold mountain air. Everything went black.

The remains of the DC-3 came to a thudding halt. Trees and vines had somehow broken the impact of the plane, preventing it from entirely disintegrating. The wingless wreck remained lifeless and silent.

"You should have asked Ruth to collect the package on her way," John said.

"Well, it's a bit late now. What time did you say the plane was due?"

"Jesus, Alice, that must be the tenth time you've asked in about an hour. Eleven o'clock. I've sent Tom and Billy to wait, in case it's early. Do you remember what to say about your trip to Townsville if she asks?"

"I was visiting Aunt Daphne; I wouldn't forget that." Alice had been rehearsing her trip details for over a week. No one was to know about her hospital stay, and to keep it a secret, John colluded with his wife.

"I'm going out to the strip. Put on some make-up and do your hair; she'll suspect something if you look like that." He left.

Alice would normally be hurt by the way John had spoken to her, but since returning from the hospital, she had somehow become immune to his commands. Bugger him, she thought, as she tidied up her hair.

"Matthew!" Alice called out towards the packing sheds.

"Yes, Mum, what's up?"

"I'm going to get changed, and then I want you to drive me out to the strip. Dad's already gone. We have to be there when she arrives." Alice's demeanour had suddenly changed; the excitement of Ruth's imminent arrival had quelled her annoyance with her husband. She was dressed and ready within minutes.

The jeep skidded on the muddy track as long, wet clumps of *Kunai* grass splattered across the windscreen.

"Don't worry, Mum, we'll get there before the plane." Matthew had taken the short route.

"Just make sure we arrive in one piece," Alice said, knowing it would make no difference.

The airstrip wasn't far but negotiating the muddy terrain required skill, something Alice wasn't entirely convinced that her younger son possessed. It took the best part of twenty minutes before the jeep pulled out of the vegetation into a large clearing.

"We even beat Dad!" Matthew declared, looking pleased with himself.

Within seconds, the other jeep arrived with a cross-looking John Madison at the wheel.

"You should be more bloody careful, Matt," he shouted as he checked Alice's appearance. "We'd better find the boys. I told them to come out over an hour ago."

"Masta, Masta!" The small group turned to see Billy Lamb running towards them with the two-way in hand. *"Balus em pundaun!"*

Alice's pidgin was good, but on this occasion, her mind refused to translate the ominous message. "Where are they, Matthew, still over the ranges?" she asked, looking at her son with fear dawning on her face.

"He said the plane's gone down, Mum."

CHAPTER 2

Ruth forced herself to take a deep breath and coughed violently, expelling mud and leaves from her mouth. She reached out into the darkness only to grasp a slimy, cool, smoothness between her fingers. A sudden rush of terror coursed through her, she couldn't see anything in the cold, earth-smelling darkness. Where am I? Where is everyone? She opened her eyes. Moonlight permeated through the jungle canopy onto the wet jungle floor. Water or some other liquid had soaked through her clothing where she lay.

Trying to make sense of her bewildering surroundings, she knew something was very wrong, but what? Native birds were chattering and bugs crawled over her exposed skin. She slapped at her arms and legs to knock away the insects. It was a nightmare from which she couldn't extricate herself. She grasped onto an overhanging branch and half lifted herself up. Something silver reflected in the moonlight; she craned her neck to appraise the object. An aeroplane wing.

"Oh, God, the plane!" she wailed, realising the horror of what had happened. Images flooded her mind; she began to flail her arms frantically to stop the imagined branches smashing into her. She screamed, and then collapsed back onto the ground, unconscious.

Through the malaise, she started to remember. Bits at first, like flashes of a movie. Her face pressed hard into a man's chest; the thudding sound of the plane hitting the canopy. Leaves, branches, insects smashing into her. It was dark, people were screaming. She tried to open her eyes but something pink obscured the light. Why can't I see? She lay, studying the pretty redness which came and went as she blinked. As she wiped away the bloody wetness from her face, the ruddy glow gave way to a luminescent haze of morning sun as it hit the mist. Or was it dusk? She couldn't be sure.

Her instincts told her she must move around to avoid going into shock. Terrified of what she might discover, she prepared herself to confront the carnage. She had to find out if anyone else had survived.

"Uncle Lindsay!" she called. No one answered.

Every part of her body hurt, either from the crash or insect bites. The prospect of dying from malaria or poisonous snake bites invaded her confused consciousness. With desperation, she clutched onto some branches and managed to stand. Debris surrounded her, but no other passengers. She collected dead leaves and bits of wood then piled them into a heap to build a fire. Something through the leaves caught her eye.

A bright, cherry-red glint against the dark green undergrowth, a handbag. The woman on the plane. Ruth forced her way through tangled branches to the bag. As she bent down to pick it up, she spotted something white in the bushes ahead. Calling out, she lunged towards the woman's legs protruding from behind a fern. The white pantsuit was soaked in blood about the shoulders and where the woman's head should have been, nothing, only blood-soaked leaves on the jungle floor. Ruth couldn't scream; her throat had contracted ready to vomit.

She retreated back through the bushy undergrowth to her pile of tinder where the woman was no longer visible. Opening the handbag, she found a cigarette lighter and within minutes, the damp mound of leaves was smouldering. She scurried around the forest floor, clutching handfuls of *gorgor* leaves to put on the flame. The plumes of acrid smoke might be enough to keep the hordes of voracious mosquitoes at bay.

As she stared at the flames, an overwhelming tiredness came over her, and she began to shiver. More than anything she wanted to sleep but was afraid that rescuers might come and she would miss them. As time passed, her tiredness became so compelling there was no choice but to lie down.

Ruth awoke to a noise, an intermittent droning. Insects, she guessed, but to make sure she cupped her ears in an attempt to capture the sound. But it had gone. She put more leaves and twigs on the fire before drifting back into a semi-sleep. She was woken again by the sound of something crashing through the vegetation, possibly wild pigs or cassowary. She sat up, ready to run. A sound like the repeated slashing of a bush knife came from beyond the wreck, and then a man's voice called out followed by the groaning of a jeep.

"Help, someone, please help me." Lights blinded her, as she squinted towards the vehicle.

"Ruth!" her brother Jake called as he ran towards her.

"Jake, oh, Jake, I'm so glad you're here." She threw her arms around his neck, relishing his warmth and his clean, familiar smell.

"Shhh, don't try to talk, you might be injured. Dad's almost here."

Ruth clung to his old chequered sports shirt. She was safe, Jake would fix everything. Another vehicle arrived, then others.

"Ruth!" John Madison leapt from the jeep to her side. "Ruth, you're alive, thank God!"

"I'm so glad to see you, Daddy. How long have I been here?"

"Two nights you've been missing; bloody difficult to find anything through all this vegetation. It's a good job you lit a fire, we followed the smoke. You stay here and don't move, we need to check the others."

Ruth cried with relief as the full reality of the disaster registered. It was as though her mind had been numb up to that point, somehow clouding her perception of the danger and perilous nature of her situation.

Distracted by voices shouting instructions and directions, she noticed the air becoming increasingly hot and steamy. Glancing up, she realised it was the sun filtering through the canopy, not the moon as she had thought earlier. John and Jake both shouted orders to the men, while her younger brother, Matthew, called-in their location and obtained passenger details on the two-way.

"There are seven of us and a goose, possibly two," Ruth explained.

"What?" Matthew said.

"Two crew, two men, a woman, Uncle Lindsay, me and a goose in a cage." Ruth was lucid.

"There's a man missing!" Matthew bellowed out to the others. Only four men had been located.

"The goose must have gotten away," Ruth said absently, as her attention turned to the empty cage.

"Forget about the bloody goose. Try not to talk and keep the blanket around you," Matthew ordered, as he left to join the others.

Only Ruth and a male passenger, it seemed had survived. A vine had decapitated the woman when she was thrown from the wreckage. Her partner was being cut free from a tangle of metal and upholstery, but he was failing fast. Ruth covered her ears to block out the gurgling sounds he made as he tried to get air into his lungs. The crew had been crushed beyond recognition by the dislodged prop shaft and the other man had become impaled on what appeared to be a broken seat. She tried to block out the horror of the scene by not looking but she could hear the gruesome details as the men spoke among themselves.

"Stoke up the fire, Matt," Jake said. "I can hear the chopper. When you've done that, get onto Okoro and let them know."

Matthew threw more timber onto the embers and doused it in petrol; a fierce blast rose upwards as the green branches burst into blinding orange flames. Ruth looked on as if she were watching some kind of horror movie.

"Okoro, come in," Matthew shouted into the hand-piece.

"Okoro, receiving," Alice replied.

Ruth sensed the distress in her mother's voice.

"Ruth's okay, Mum. We're waiting for the doctor."

"How badly is she hurt?"

"Shock mainly, and a few bruises. The doc's arrived, I better go..."

The force of the helicopter churned the canopy, releasing a downpour of water from the foliage. Mud and wet leaves covered everything.

"Matt! Where's Lindsay? Did you find him?" Ruth called, realising no one had mentioned his name, nor had she seen the men carry him out.

"He's the missing passenger, we're looking for him. Try to keep still and rest," Matthew rasped.

Ruth knew why Matthew sounded tetchy, he hated being ordered around and now her father and Jake were barking orders at him. "I don't want to rest. We were sitting next to each other; he can't be far. You realise who he is, don't you?"

"Yes, of course, Dad's half-brother from Ireland."

"Scotland. Look, Dad's waving; he wants you to do something. I'll be okay here."

As Ruth lay on a makeshift mattress of leaves, she thought about Lindsay and remembered his kind eyes. They'll find him, she told herself; he can't be far. She went over the last few minutes of the journey, trying to remember when they had become separated.

The doctor seemed to appear from nowhere. "Well, you're an extremely lucky young lady," he said, as he bent over Ruth to examine her.

"I'm fine, thank you." She flinched as the icy stethoscope made contact with her skin. "I'm worried about Uncle Lindsay. He was next to me; he should have been in the same place where I ended up."

"I'm sure they'll find him. We need to get you back to Port Moresby for X-rays."

"I'm fine; I can move everything, Doctor. All my bones seem intact."

"You're slightly concussed; we need to do some X-rays."

"We're almost home, I've been travelling since yesterday; I don't want to go back to Moresby."

"You do as the doctor says, Ruth," her father ordered as he walked over to join them.

"I'm okay, Dad. I know where I am and what happened; I just want to go home to Mum. Did you find Uncle Lindsay?" she said, intending to distract her father from the idea of going to hospital.

"The boys are still looking," he said, and walked back to the wreck. Ruth hoped she had got her way.

"I'm no doctor, Ruth, but if he says you should go to the hospital, you should. If you get sick, there won't be another chopper out today," Matthew called to Ruth, as he hurried to catch up to his father.

"I'm not changing my mind. We're only fifty miles out," she shouted back at him. Matthew always chimed in when he thought he was on the winning side. Ruth spotted the doctor and her father circling back towards her.

"I've been speaking with the doctor, Ruthy. Since you're adamant about going home he's agreed to let you go, on the condition you rest. He'll be calling to check on you. Sally and your mother can keep an eye on you as well. You promise to do as he says with no arguments?"

"Of course, Dad." Even if she did feel ill, which she didn't, there was no way she was going all the way back to Port Moresby.

The journey home in the jeep was turning out to be almost as rough as the aeroplane, Ruth thought, as she shoved Jake's discarded shirt between her tender ribs and Matthew's bony elbow.

"I wonder if he's been found yet. I don't understand how he could disappear." Ruth realised her own survival was probably due to Lindsay holding onto her so tightly. The possibility of him not having survived left her beleaguered with guilt.

"They'll find him; you just concentrate on yourself," John said, as they pulled into the clearing at Okoro.

There it stood, her home; the welcoming old Queenslander-style house with its grey, weathered, timber walls surrounded by an assortment of thatched outbuildings. And the trees; oh, how she had missed the trees and the thick, lush bushes of every imaginable colour green. Although after the last couple of days, the trees had lost some of their magic.

A small gathering of people caught her eye; she could make out Billy Lamb, the gardener, his two wives and his oldest son, Pups. Ruth scrutinized the crowd for Tommy.

"Miss Ruthy, I worry very much, but am happy now you come,"

Billy said, with his familiar toothless grin and a relieved expression.

"I guess I was lucky, Bill, a couple of scratches and a few bumps, that's all. Where's Tom?"

"He come later, he hunting."

Ruth smiled and rushed over to her mother.

"Ruth!" Alice cried, "I've been so worried, I thought I'd lost my baby girl."

"Mum, oh Mum, it was horrible, I didn't know if anyone knew where I was." They embraced, both crying with joy and relief.

Ruth noticed how pale and ill her mother appeared. She had lost weight, and her make-up wasn't quite right; she had too much rouge on her cheeks.

"You must still be in shock, Ruthy," Alice said, taking her daughter's arm. "I'll run you a warm bath and get some antiseptic for those cuts."

"How are you, Mum, you look pale?"

"Never mind me; I'll be fine now you're home."

As they walked, she clung to her mother's warm, familiar arm; at last she was safely home. Only a few days had she been lost in the jungle, but it seemed like weeks.

On entering the house, Ruth was surprised that the Christmas decorations hadn't been put up. They were always up when she returned from school. When she imagined going home at Christmas it was always a colourful, festive vision she pictured in her mind, even the outside of the house usually had decorations. Perhaps Mum was tired, she thought, remembering her mother's recent holiday to Townsville.

Sally, the housekeeper, made a pot of tea and arranged everything daintily on the well-scrubbed kitchen table. The shiny silverware and delicate china on the bare wood struck Ruth as incongruous, but she couldn't think of a time when a simple cup of tea had tasted so delicious. Too soon her enjoyment of Sally's ministrations came to an end as the smell of Dettol drifted into the kitchen. Her bath was ready.

Alice helped wash Ruth's matted hair and dressed her cuts and grazes. A tremor or nervous twitch momentarily distorted her mother's face. Ruth tried to remember if she had seen it before. She hadn't. Something wasn't right. It wasn't just her mother but everyone seemed different, as though there had been a big argument and they were all treading on eggshells.

Ruth realised that she must still be in shock, as her mother had said. Sally interrupted her thoughts with a tray of neatly-quartered sandwiches and a variety of sliced tropical fruit, which Ruth decided to eat in bed. She wanted to rest and then go to find Tommy, but after her snack, she fell into a deep sleep.

The sun filtered into her bedroom. She lay on the bed, staring at dust moats as they hovered in streams of warm sunlight; the light had a golden hue but wasn't overly bright. She supposed it must be late afternoon judging by the quietness of the house. I hope they've found Lindsay, she thought, still trying to work out why he wasn't anywhere near the wreckage.

In spite of a splitting headache and the odd sensation of being detached from everything, Ruth stumbled into the kitchen to make a cup of tea. No one seemed to be home apart from Alice, who had fallen asleep on the settee. It was a strange homecoming this year, no one hung around to talk and her mother appeared totally absorbed by her wounds; it was as though she had ignored the rest of her, like a doctor might treat a patient in a hospital. Perhaps I'm just imagining things, she thought, while making a glass of iced tea to take out on the veranda.

As she surveyed the gardens, a man walked purposefully towards the house. He must be at least six-foot, she thought, maybe more, and with the broadest shoulders. His complexion was swarthy, obviously of mixed race, part local and part white. Ruth floundered for a second. Surely not, he's too tall. It is!

"Tommy!" she called, running towards him. "Tommy! I missed you so much." She threw her arms around his neck. "I didn't recognise you!"

"You look different too!" His dark eyes resembled polished onyx against his light, olive-coloured skin.

Overcome with joy, Ruth hugged him tightly, as if to make up for all her months away. She realised he had changed much more than she; his lean, muscular body was that of a man. "My plane crashed about fifty miles out," she explained.

"I heard. I came as quickly as I could. I wanted to make sure you were okay," he said, drinking in Ruth's delight at seeing him.

"My head still aches a bit, and my legs are scratched."

"Didn't they take you to hospital?"

"They wanted to, but I insisted on coming home. The doctor humoured me in the end, but I had to promise to rest. I couldn't go back to Moresby after all the travelling and the crash. But tell me, what have you been up to all year?"

Talking to Tommy helped dispel the unreality of the last three days; Ruth was now excited about being home. Tommy always had a reassuring effect.

"Oh, you're awake; I must have dozed off while reading." Alice appeared on the veranda and cast an appraising eye over her daughter. "How are you feeling after your rest?"

"Recovering, I think, more the shock than anything."

"I better go home," Tommy said, appearing uncomfortable. "Dad will be looking for me." He quickly left.

"Tommy's grown very tall, hasn't he?" Alice said.

"Yes, I didn't recognise him at first. What does he do?"

"Jake couldn't find any work for him…"

"Since when did Jake start running things?"

"Well, your father's away a lot these days."

"Jake never did like Tom; Dad either, for that matter."

"Your father bought so much extra food for Christmas; we'll be eating like royalty until you go back to school." Alice changed the subject.

Ruth made a mental note to talk to her father about Tommy not being given a job. "You went to Townsville. I forgot to ask earlier, how's Aunt Daphne?"

"Oh, she's well, becoming quite frail now."

"You said in your last letter, you wanted to see a doctor about your headaches next time you went to the mainland."

Alice didn't answer.

"You did go, didn't you?" Ruth persisted, still annoyed at Tommy not being given paid work.

"Yes, I went, but he didn't say much, just one of those things apparently. Some people suffer from them and there's not a lot they can do."

Ruth wondered if her mother was telling her everything. She didn't look herself at all, especially her eyes.

Sally popped her head around the kitchen door. "The men are back, Mrs Madison."

"I have to check how Lindsay is…" Ruth bolted out to the driveway.

Jake was hosing off the jeep and Matthew was ranting about how no one ever listened to him. "How's Lindsay? Is he hurt?" Ruth said.

"We couldn't find him," Jake scowled, continuing to hose the vehicle. "There's a party out looking for him still."

"You didn't find him?" Ruth was incredulous. "He sat next to me; he's got to be there!"

"The plane almost disintegrated; he could have been thrown out miles back. Be patient; they're still looking," Matthew said, putting his arm on his sister's shoulder.

Ruth couldn't comprehend how he hadn't been found. "Did anyone contact Gran?"

"I've sent a message to the patrol office," Matthew answered. "Couldn't reach anyone out that way on the radio."

On hearing the news about Lindsay, Ruth became distressed and frustrated at being powerless to do anything. She kept thinking about him, lost somewhere totally alien, and with no food or water. She decided to go for a walk to clear her head. Without interruptions, she might remember some crucial information.

Walking towards the packing shed, she was met by Billy Lamb's motley grey dog. "Buster!" she called. His ears pricked, and he ran towards her. "Where did you come from?" As she bent down to pick up a stick to throw, footsteps crackled on the gravel pathway behind.

She turned; there was Tommy. "You gave me a fright! I thought Buster was on his own."

"I'm just shifting these weeds for Dad; his back isn't good anymore," Tommy said, looking pleased to find Ruth alone.

"I expected you to take over from your father."

"Don't worry, I can find enough to do. I went back to the Mission school this year; thought I'd try to keep up with you."

"Ha! I've done more schooling than I could ever need. All I seem to do is read, read and read. Remember those damn sums you used to help me with? Well, I can do them now." They both laughed, delighting in each other again after their forced separation.

"I'm sure they only sent me away because they thought we were too friendly."

"Perhaps it was for the best." Tommy looked at Ruth teasingly.

Ruth experienced a strange, not unpleasant, sensation. She wanted to hug him again but a conflicting mix of excitement and fear overcame her.

"Come on, Miss Madison, you better get back home or they'll come looking for you."

"I'll leave you to finish your work, but on one condition."

"What's that?"

"You come to visit me at the house tomorrow afternoon and don't run away if Mum is around."

"You drive a hard bargain. Once I finish helping Dad, I'll come up."

Life on the plantation had become dreary and miserable for Ruth. It was supposed to be Christmas, but everyone seemed more interested in their own chores and routines. Ruth found spending time with her mother difficult; she continually complained of headaches or tiredness, and wanted to sleep. The men worked all day on the plantation and her father grumbled if she interrupted them.

For company, she turned to Tommy. So reliant on his attention had she become that she thought about him constantly, reliving the feelings she experienced when she hugged him on her first day home. Ruth knew feeling this way about a boy was wrong, especially a local boy, but she couldn't stop herself and went to see him at every opportunity.

Almost a week had passed before any word from Eliza Madison reached Okoro. She radioed in to say she was travelling on foot with native trackers from her village. They intended to cut through the mountain trails and follow the path of the plane to the crash site. No official news arrived about Lindsay, only rumours among plantation workers of a cannibal tribe finding him. Cannibalism against whites hadn't occurred since before the war according to the police, but away from the capital, you could never be sure. Ruth refused to believe the rumour and waited to hear from the search party, but by Christmas morning, there had been nothing – even the authorities had stopped looking.

Everyone took their time getting to the veranda for Christmas breakfast. Ruth guessed they were all too worried about Lindsay. It was a family tradition to give their presents at this time, and in the past, they would all rush to the table and wait in anticipation. Sally always prepared the same special meal consisting of bacon, sausages, chops, tomatoes, fried bread, eggs and fruit crepes with cream. Sally's passion for making enormous meals always amused Ruth; Sally was one of the slimmest women she knew and ate like a bird.

As the crepes were served, Matthew rushed over to wind up the record player so they could listen to carols. It was time to unwrap their presents. Ruth was delighted that her father and brothers enjoyed her gifts of Old Spice aftershave. The school had taken the girls shopping in Bathurst before they broke up for the holidays; it was their only opportunity to buy gifts to take home. John Madison surprised everyone by treating 'the house' to a new Airzone wireless so they could hear the Queen's Christmas message, something they had missed last year after rain leaked in and ruined the old one.

Ruth received a shiny new gold wristwatch from her parents and was admiring how elegant it looked when she noticed her mother.

Alice hadn't opened her present, a tiny bottle of Shalimar which cost Ruth two months' pocket money. It used to be Alice's favourite. Maybe she has another headache, Ruth wondered, but decided not to say anything. Must be the shock of the crash still, poor Mum.

"So what are you doing after the holidays, Ruth?" Matthew asked.

"I'm hoping to do art at technical college if Dad will let me." Ruth glanced coyly in her father's direction.

"All those years studying to end up doing some airy-fairy painting course," Jake said.

"That's enough, Jake. Art is a good choice for a young lady. Although some secretarial skills would be useful, honey." He looked encouragingly at Ruth.

Ruth screwed up her nose at Jake and ignored her father's obvious preference for secretarial studies. All she had ever wanted to do was paint for a living: flowers, landscapes and people. Once married and settled down, she reasoned, a painting career could be continued. No one would complain about her going out to work and neglecting her family, as she would be working at home.

The small gathering all turned to watch Billy Lamb and one of his wives walking up the path towards the veranda.

"What do they want, John? Can't we have one day to ourselves without these people wanting something?" Alice said, stubbing out her cigarette.

Taken aback by the bitterness in her mother's voice, Ruth remained silent.

"Don't worry about it, Alice, it must be important or they wouldn't be here," John Madison said as he got up to go and meet them.

Matthew managed to divert the conversation to the guests, due out from Port Moresby that afternoon. Ruth tried not to think about how tedious that would be; entertaining Myrtle and Bert Johnson, a retired bank manager who only seemed to complain about the Territory but never actually left it, even for a holiday. As Ruth contemplated the guests' arrival, her father disappeared into the back of the house with Billy and his wife, re-emerging a few minutes later with a sack.

"More food on its way down to the village; I don't know what it is with your father. We'll end up destitute with everything he gives to that ungrateful pair." Alice glared at her husband as he bypassed the veranda and made his way back into the house.

"It is Christmas, Mum. They probably just collected some extra supplies," Ruth offered, trying to coax her mother into a more charitable mood. But it fell on deaf ears.

Alice lit up another cigarette and stared off into the distance. The boys excused themselves and left.

"I might go and find something nice to wear for this afternoon," Ruth said, feeling guilty at leaving her mother in such an angry state. She was also disturbed by her mother's tirade over Tommy's parents. After gently patting her mother's shoulder, she left to go to her bedroom.

As much as she tried, Ruth couldn't relax; her mother's behaviour and peculiar appearance kept playing on her mind. Alice had always been a glamorous, well-proportioned woman who dressed fashionably and took pride in her appearance, even on the plantation. Now, her clothes hung on her, and she seemed to have lost interest in her hair and make-up. She decided to ask her father or Jake if anything was wrong.

The kitchen clock chimed three just as the Cessna buzzed the homestead. The men left to go to the airstrip while Sally and Ruth rushed around putting up decorations. Alice had shut herself in the bedroom to get ready. Ruth ached to be with Tommy today, but there were too many people at the house. She had to be careful not to appear overly interested in Tommy otherwise people might get the wrong impression.

"What else can I do, Sally?" Ruth felt sorry for her, doing all the Christmas preparations on her own.

"You don't need to do anything, Ruthy."

"But I want to help. I'll make the centrepiece."

"Everything's on the draining board, apart from the orchids. I put them in the cool room."

Ruth enjoyed creating the table decorations, she and her mother used to make them every Christmas, a little tradition, just the two of them. Sitting down at the bench, she began to sort through the poinsettias, impatiens and orchids. She missed Alice telling her what to put where, but after a few minutes enjoyed the freedom to design it herself.

"Look, Sally, what do you think?"

"The prettiest one we ever had!"

Jake and Matthew burst into the kitchen, disrupting the quiet preparations.

"You'd better go and entertain the Johnsons. Mum's not out yet, and Dad's gone in to talk to her," Jake ordered.

"Goodness, Jake, you're just as bossy as ever. Why can't you talk to them? I never know what to say." When Ruth turned around, he'd gone. Asking her father or Jake about what was wrong with her mother would have to wait.

"Hello, Ruth darling, we were so pleased to hear that you're all in one piece," Myrtle said, through clouds of Sobranie cigarette smoke.

"Hello, Uncle Bert, Auntie Myrtle. Yes, I'm lucky. Only one of the other passengers survived, but he's in such a bad way they don't think he'll make it. And, of course, my uncle's body hasn't been found."

"It's such a dreadful place for transport, all this jungle and the mountains," Bert added.

Ruth realised she had triggered a barrage of complaints. "What would you like to drink? Daddy will be along shortly. He's just seeing after Mum; she was very tired."

"Yes, she looked tired when I saw her in Port Moresby last month," Myrtle said, looking concerned.

"I don't think she copes with the heat as well as she used to," said Ruth, hoping to stifle any more discussion of her mother's state of health. "Shall we go out to the veranda? Sally's prepared some hors d'oeuvres."

The veranda was beautifully set up with Chinese lanterns, fairy lights and large urns of native flowers. Sally had outdone herself with trays of stuffed celery, canapés of every variety, bacon wraparounds, dried beef rolls and a cornucopia of fruits. Millie, Sally's niece, had even been called in to help serve the food and refresh drinks. The only thing that spoiled the setting was the thundering rain.

"Sorry to leave you, Bert. I had to go down the cellar to get the wine," John Madison announced a little awkwardly as he joined the guests.

What a relief, Ruth thought; she was running out of things to talk about.

"Looks like the rain's going to set in," Bert said, as they glanced out through the trellis to watch the heavy downpour bucketing over the outbuildings.

"Oh my goodness, who on earth is that?" Myrtle said as her hand swept up to her mouth. "Oh, heaven's above, it's a white woman with no clo…"

Everyone stared in horror. There was Alice, sitting on an oil drum in the pouring rain, naked.

CHAPTER 3

Sally and Ruth had dried Alice and put her into bed before John Madison walked into the bedroom. His expression was hard to decipher, a mixture of embarrassment and annoyance rather than shock or concern. Ruth speculated this might not be the first time something odd had happened, but his demeanour discouraged her from asking.

"Here, Ruth," he said, "make sure she takes two of these every six hours." He walked out.

"Largactil," Ruth read out the name on the bottle. "Have you seen her like this before, Sally?" she asked, gently holding her mother's head up off the pillow so she could take the tablets.

"Some womans get funny when they no longer have babies, Ruthy."

"The change, do you think?"

Sally said nothing, just continued to wipe Alice's face with the warm flannel. Getting anything out of Sally was always next to impossible; she would die sooner than betray Alice in any way.

When her mother fell asleep, Ruth returned to the guests. She thought she caught the tail end of Myrtle saying something about sending Alice back to the mainland, but the conversation abruptly ended when she entered the room. Having been ushered in from the veranda, the party now sat in the dining room whilst Millie served them soup.

"I don't think I've ever tasted such superb bisque of lobster, Ruth," Myrtle Johnson said, without asking after her hostess.

"Sally uses sherry instead of white wine," Ruth remarked absently as she sat down.

A more bizarre situation, Ruth had never experienced. Everyone carried on as normal. She couldn't talk about her mother; it was as though the incident hadn't happened. The atmosphere was surreal and uncomfortable; business and politics were the topic of conversation. They all seemed to be making a particular effort not to refer to her mother. Then as the meal progressed, the polite chatter dried up, leaving long, awkward silences. The two brothers gulped down the remainder of their meals and excused themselves from the table, leaving Ruth listening to the tinkling of plates and cutlery. Her father was inebriated from drinking all afternoon which left him sullen and non-communicative, and the visitors looked ready for bed. Ruth had had enough; she needed to talk to Jake. She excused herself from the table.

Standing outside Jake's room, she could see the light shining from under the door; he was still awake. "I want to talk to you about something," she said, turning the doorknob.

"Can't you knock? What do you want?"

"What's going on with Mum?" She ignored his hostility.

"Nothing much, she's going through the change of life, been a bit strange for a while. It comes and goes."

"But she was out in the rain with no clothes on and when we brought her in, she was in a daze. That can't be 'nothing much'."

"She gets overheated, probably trying to cool down. Now I'm tired," he said, and turned to face the wall.

"I hope she's okay, I don't understand much about the change."

"She'll be right, don't worry so much," he said dismissively.

Ruth realised that he wasn't going to be much help. She suspected he was more upset about their mother than he was letting on. Jake had always been the same; it was as though he didn't know how to be upset, so he became angry instead.

"And what's this about having no work for Tommy? I'm sure you hate him."

"Look, Ruth, you're recovering from an accident; you should be resting, not thinking about stupid things. I've got nothing against Tommy, there's just not enough work for him."

34

"How can you say that? Poor old Billy will drop down dead soon, he's too old." Jake wouldn't care, though; she knew that, all he ever worried about was the business. The workers' well-being didn't matter to him.

"Goodnight, Ruth."

"You're the most frustrating person to talk to, Jake." She decided not to labour the point of Tommy's employment otherwise he might question her motives.

"But you love me still, eh?" He grinned; with his characteristically crooked, but lovable, smile.

"Goodnight, Jake." She marched off to her room wishing Tommy was around; he would listen.

The following morning, Ruth awoke to voices and bumping sounds along the hallway. She put on her dressing gown and peeked out of her door, only to catch the tail end of the Johnsons, with Jake trailing behind carrying their bags. They must have been more disturbed by her mother's actions than she had realised.

Alice's bedroom door was ajar; Ruth crept in. Her mother was sitting up in bed with an empty breakfast tray on the bedside, knitting. "Mum?"

"Come in, Ruthy. I'm having a day in bed today."

Alice looked normal enough. "How are you, Mum?" she asked, puzzled by her mother's apparent recovery.

"I'm well, darling; I'll be fine once I catch up on my sleep."

Ruth struggled to reconcile her mother's obviously well appearance with the scene the day before. Unsure of whether to raise the subject, she decided to mention only the medicine – maybe that would prompt her mother to talk about what had happened.

"Dad said you must take your pills every six hours, did you take them this morning?"

"Don't you worry about that, you're on holiday! Sally takes care of those things."

"Can we go for a walk sometime?" Ruth asked, not knowing what else to say.

"Of course, precious; in fact, I want to show you a little flower garden I've made behind the packing sheds. Sally and I planted all my favourites from home. Tomorrow morning after breakfast, I'll be up ready so we can go."

Still concerned, Ruth decided to confront her father. When she reached the kitchen, Sally was busy scrubbing the oven and the men had just left for work somewhere on the plantation. Annoyed, Ruth decided to walk to the village. The change of scenery might take her mind off the gloom at home, and hopefully she would run into Tommy.

After the heavy rain, the humidity had soared and with little breeze, the dank, earthy odour of the forest hung over the plantation. The village had expanded since the previous holidays; it now seemed overrun with unfamiliar children and animals. The palm leaf roofs had been exchanged for rusted tin which Ruth thought made them appear less attractive, shabby even.

"Hello, Essie!"

"Ahh, Ruthy, you come from school."

"Yes, on holiday. How have you been?"

"I's well, more old, but still good to work. Here, you want?" The old woman held up a ripe mango.

"You know I can't resist mangoes, thanks Essie. I'll have it for lunch." Ruth took the fruit and made her way to the river for a swim.

It had always been her favourite place to cool off; a peaceful, secluded area where the sparse canopy allowed the sun to shine through. The banks were covered with dark green moss and a profusion of ferns, all surrounded by overhanging vines and palms. Over the millennia, this part of the river had become more like a lagoon, having diverted away slightly from the main stream. Women washed their clothes in the faster moving sections of the waterway while children played and swam in the pools. Today, it was deserted; most likely the villagers were busy cleaning up after the rain. She sat at the edge of the stream and dangled her feet in the bracing water. Looking at her reflection, she tied up her hair with a strip of vine, allowing the breeze to catch her neck. Her appearance had almost become an obsession lately; trying to tame her wild hair and wearing closer-fitting clothes which emphasised her figure. She enjoyed Tommy's obvious pleasure when he looked at her, she found it exciting. Whenever she thought she might bump into him, she would make a special effort with how she looked.

Tommy often went fishing further up the river, so she decided to walk along the bank in case he was there. After a few minutes, she sat down, unable to stop thinking about her mother and the incident the day before. She knew something was wrong when she arrived home; her mother's eyes were leaden and her emotions seemed blunted – as though she had lost interest in everything, even her.

Coming home this year had been a total disaster, Ruth decided. No one seemed even slightly interested in what she did, or had to say. She imagined it must be how an overstaying visitor might feel, where their host neglects them in the hope they'll take the hint and leave.

Only Tommy, it seemed, enjoyed having her around. If not for him, she could spend a whole day without speaking to anyone. Her yearning to be with him was so intense she wondered how she would survive when she returned to mainland. She couldn't stop thinking about the overpoweringly blissful bodily sensations she experienced when they were close. At the same time though, these feelings scared her.

Ruth knew decent people frowned on relationships with locals, but Tommy was different. They had grown up together; they understood each other probably better than anyone else. Imagining being married to him, she delighted in how scandalous it would be and the shock on the Johnsons' faces. Perhaps they could go somewhere else to live; people might be more accepting on the mainland, or even in another country. The more she thought about Tommy, the more she wanted to be with him, close to him, enveloped in his strong, muscular arms.

Ruth peeled the juicy yellow mango and bit into the soft tangy flesh; a taste she associated with home and one she craved during the cold mountain winters while at school. She rinsed off the stickiness of the fruit and began to walk back downstream. Someone had jumped into the water. The sun glistened on lightly tanned shoulders as they bobbed in and out of the river. *Tommy!* Her pace quickened, she began to run, her pleasure so consumed her that she thought she would burst.

He glanced up and smiled as she approached. "What are you doing down here on your own?"

"I thought I'd come for a swim; the house was so hot and stuffy."

"You aren't very wet," he said, with a playful expression.

"I haven't been in yet, I wanted to eat my mango first." Ruth wished she could strip off and jump into the cool water the way she used to, but looking at Tommy now, with his manly physique, glistening broad shoulders and well-muscled arms, she felt self-conscious.

"You coming in now?" he said, his eyes even more enticing than on the day she came home.

She could barely contain her excitement. It seemed like fear but without the dread, and coupled with a curious tingling sensation that radiated throughout her body. "Turn around so I can get in."

"But I won't see you then."

"I know."

"You never used to worry about me seeing you."

"Well, I do now," she said.

Tommy's expression became serious, and then he turned away. Ruth experienced a rush of shyness as she removed her clothes before diving into the water for cover.

"Can I turn around?" Tommy said.

"Of course!" Ruth cupped a handful of water and just as he turned, she made a splash.

He retaliated; they both drenched each other before swimming into the shade. They grasped onto an overhanging branch to rest.

"I'm so glad you're here, Tommy, you're the only one I can talk to." Ruth explained about her mother's strange behaviour and how everyone pretended nothing had happened.

"They probably don't want you to worry."

"More like they think I'm too much of a baby to understand anything."

The sunlight caught Ruth's attention as it reflected off the water ripples. Like the sun streaming through stained-glass windows at church, it danced across Tommy's eyes causing them to sparkle. When he spoke, she noticed his white, perfect teeth; his lips were full and well-formed. The contrasting pink of his mouth and dark facial hair had a magical effect on her senses.

"Perhaps things are clearer after being away; I don't think anything's changed," he said.

"Maybe it didn't register before," Ruth's gaze fixed on his mouth, "although I'm sure Mum never did anything like that before, I would remember."

Ruth felt herself melting into Tommy, as if everything else had somehow paled into the background. Their lips met. She experienced a sense of disembodiment, as though she had become part of him; become one. Her excitement intensified; she thought her whole being would explode or reach a point where she was lost forever. The sudden sensation of losing control caused her to panic and she opened her eyes. She pulled away, just in time to catch sight of movement in the bushes.

"Tommy, someone's on the bank!"

He quickly turned to look. "I can't see anyone. Who was it?"

"I don't know, the light was in my eyes. Oh, Tommy, do you think they'll tell anyone?"

"Don't worry, my people won't say anything. Anyone else would have called out," Tommy said, putting his arm around her for reassurance.

"Oh, I don't care anyway, Mum and Dad don't care, why should I?" Ruth did care, but she was angry. Angry with her mother for being sick, angry with the plane for crashing and angry at society's rules and restrictions for forbidding her any feelings for a local man.

"Come on, Ruthy, you have to care. We need to be careful, or we'll get into trouble. I could be sent to prison."

"I'm sorry, Tommy, I never even thought about such a thing. It's just so damn hard living in this place with rules about who you can be close to depending on what colour they are. You're not black anyway."

"I'm black to the government, and that's what matters."

"Did you ever find out why you're so light when your brother, Pups, is dark?" This had always fascinated Ruth but with the easy-going adoption practices of the local people, losing track of your true ancestry was commonplace.

"It's *tambu*, you know I can't ask. Most likely a cousin in Moresby gave me to Mum and Dad, or maybe my real parents died. Don't matter anyway; Billy and Meka are my parents. Let's get dry and go back. If anyone says anything, we'll say you hurt your foot and had to lean on me."

They got out of the water and dressed. Ruth's inhibitions about Tommy seeing her naked had disappeared. She pushed her wet hair tightly back into her hat.

"I'm going to hold my head up high and dare anyone to say anything," she declared.

No one did say anything. Everything was the same as when she had left. Ruth wondered if she really had seen someone in the bushes. When she went to see her mother, she found her dressed and sitting on the bed looking through photograph albums.

"Mum, you look better!"

"I'm a lot better now. My headache's gone, and I think I might even have dinner tonight."

Ruth suspected her mother wouldn't mention the incident in the rain or the deranged, mental state she was in when she and Sally dragged her inside. And she didn't; it was as though she too had chosen to pretend it never happened.

Over the next few days, life almost returned to normal. The men of the family were away negotiating with the big men of the neighbouring Pagu village for more workers. Ruth and her mother spent the afternoons together talking about things that had happened at Okoro over the previous year: who had died, had babies and taken new wives. She was enjoying being home now and while they chatted, she painted watercolours of the gardenias and azaleas in her mother's new garden.

Ruth thought they were getting along so well that she decided to ask her about what had happened; this was something she regretted immediately. Alice said she had no idea what she was talking about and became upset. Ruth backtracked and said she had probably dreamt it all. The craziness of the conversation frightened her; she realised something was seriously wrong with her mother mentally. When she tried again to speak to her father and Jake, they told her to forget about it. Even more unhelpful, Matthew suggested Alice had been drinking, which was ludicrous; there wasn't the slightest hint of alcohol on her mother's breath when they had brought her inside. Ruth loved her brothers but in times of crisis, Jake sided with his father, Matthew's brain ceased to function and she would be shunted aside with her mother.

Alice became even more remote in the days following. Alienated and more alone than ever, Ruth's only way of dealing with the situation was to spend increasingly less time with anyone. She read, painted and went to visit some of the older women in the village; which helped at first. The situation at home was all too bewildering; being together as a family but not being able to connect with anyone, she thought she would go crazy.

Another week passed before Eliza's search party finally radioed through to Okoro. They had arranged to meet up with Ruth's father and brothers at the crash site. The news was dour; Lindsay, or his remains, had simply vanished. Depressed and confused, Ruth waited for her grandmother to arrive.

It was dusk when the muddied jeeps appeared at the far end of the coffee rows. She could see Eliza in the front seat of the lead vehicle; she looked pale and exhausted. As the jeep drew to a halt, Ruth opened the door for her; Eliza collapsed into Ruth's arms.

"I've lost him, Ruth."

"Oh, Gran, come inside." Ruth took her grandmother's arm and ushered her into the kitchen.

In spite of Eliza's obvious exhaustion, the men's conversation turned to analysing the search; the route taken and who followed which lead. Eliza didn't say much, Jake was doing most of the talking.

Ruth tried to imagine how it would feel to lose a child. Even though a grown man, she guessed Eliza still thought of him as her child. And now, it seemed, he was gone. All possible places to search had been exhausted; any chance of him being alive was slim, even if he did survive the crash.

Eliza became agitated with all the talk and excused herself to go for a shower. The whole, heart-wrenching business was depressing. The local authorities had given up, it was next to impossible to spot a single person beneath the canopy from the air, and the jungle was still largely unexplored so search parties into the deeper jungle were out of the question. There was little more that could be done other than wait to see if he turned up or was found by locals.

Ruth waited for Eliza to return, but she had gone straight to her room. Alice had gone back to bed and Matthew fetched cold compresses for her headache, which had returned following Eliza's arrival. Ruth went to find Eliza.

"Can I come in?" She knocked softly.

"Of course, Ruth, I'm only thinking. Such a waste of a good man, Ruthy, a top lawyer. He has a lovely wife, no children though; she owns a catering business. Poor dear, I hate to think how she'll cope."

"But you didn't find him, Gran. He might still be alive."

"I know he's dead, Ruth. I just know."

Ruth couldn't understand why Eliza had given up so completely. Maybe she had a sixth sense or perhaps there's some inexplicable way a mother knows when a child has died. Ruth held her hand in an attempt to bring some comfort.

"At least you're safe, Ruth. If I'd lost both of you..." Eliza's voice faded.

Ruth experienced an unsettling sense of guilt, as if she had somehow survived over someone more worthy.

It turned out to be a long night, with people walking up and down the hallway at all hours. By five in the morning, Ruth had given up on falling back to sleep and went to the kitchen. She found Eliza at the table, smoking a pipe; something she had taken up in the early days when cigarettes were scarce.

"Did you get any sleep, Gran?"

"Enough thanks, honey. You don't need as much when you get to be as old as me."

Ruth tried to think of what to say.

"Your mum said you'll be matriculating this year," Eliza said, as a trail of thick smoke streamed out of her nose.

"The results should arrive any day. I'm not expecting to do particularly well; I was always trying to catch up to the other girls. I only want to do art at technical school, so I should be okay."

"I expect most of the other girls went to proper elementary schools, you did home schooling. Don't worry; it's not the be-all and end-all of everything. You'll make a good artist; you've always had a flair for drawing and colour." Eliza held Ruth's hand.

"I miss being home when I'm at school. Well, I did but now I'm here, I'm not so sure. It's been horrible with the accident and Uncle Lindsay... Mum isn't herself either."

"I guess when you're away for a long time, life carries on without you. You probably feel a bit left out of things, eh?"

"I don't even understand Mum anymore. She was sitting outside in the rain on Christmas day with no clothes on, and we had visitors."

"Well Ruth, your mother's had a lot to deal with over the years; then the war, and going back to the mainland only to be dragged back here again. She's never taken to life at Okoro, too isolated I think. Besides, you'll be getting on with your own life soon, finding a nice young gentleman and settling down."

"I suppose so, Gran. I'll be nineteen in another month."

"I was already married at your age."

"I want to wait until I finish my studies before I think about settling down." Ruth imagined herself married to Tommy and enjoying life as an artist, painting tropical scenes for picture books.

"I might try to have a little more sleep, honey. We can go for a walk later when I wake up."

"I'd like that, Gran."

Eliza's visit turned out to be brief. After just two days, an argument involving Eliza, Jake and her father had erupted, and then Eliza caught a plane back to Garua. No one discussed what had happened, so Ruth had to make do with the snippets Sally shared. It was all about Jake not looking properly, or something he didn't check when he first arrived at the crash site. Matthew, as usual, was useless as a source of information. He said he never heard them arguing. Ruth feared she would go mad if she had to spend the rest of her life at Okoro. It seemed as though everyone lived in their own imaginary world and denied what was actually happening.

The continued absence of any news about Lindsay more or less confirmed what Eliza had already accepted: that he had perished. Alice's recurrent headaches now appeared permanent. Ruth was unhappier than ever and to occupy herself spent most of her time painting or trying to find excuses to go to the village in the hope of seeing Tommy.

As the weeks passed, Ruth began to look forward to returning to the mainland. She knew she would worry about her mother and miss Tommy but at least she would be busy. She wanted to talk to Tommy and work out how they could write to each other without anyone knowing. The previous night Jake had ordered him away from the house, so she now had to plan their rendezvous more carefully. Jake often displayed a hostile attitude towards him. When Ruth asked him why he didn't like Tommy, he always denied it. But to actually order him away, apart from being mean, clearly proved his ill feeling. Ruth wondered if Jake might suspect something, but couldn't think of any occasion where he might have overheard her talking with Tommy. It can't be that, she concluded, we're always so careful.

It was after six in the evening and already dark when Ruth slipped out. Alice had taken some pills for her headache and gone to bed early, and the plantation staff had finished for the day. They were to meet in the drying shed. A warm and comfortable hideaway with coffee bags to sit on; no one ever went there after dark.

"I'm glad you came, Tommy. Jake had no right to send you away last night, we were only talking."

"That's okay. Jake and I are always at odds, especially lately."

"He gets worse every year. Even Gran had some sort of argument with him before she left. It's been horrible coming home this year. If you weren't here, I don't know what I would have done."

Tommy moved closer to Ruth and put his arm around her, more for comfort initially, but it developed into a gentle embrace.

"I wish everything could be how it used to be," she said.

"I don't think we can ever go back, Ruth. We're both grown up now. You must move on with life, make the best of things."

Tommy explained how life had changed for him now that he was considered a man by his people. Ruth had tuned out; she was more engrossed in him and being together again. Having lost all sense of where she ended and he began, she nestled into his warmth, his smell and his deep, calming voice. She felt as though she were dissolving. Aroused by his closeness, she wanted him to kiss her again the way he did at the river. The excitement and need for him overwhelmed any sense of restraint.

Part of her knew she should move away and compose herself, but she didn't want to, nor was she able. Her desire to be one with Tommy had overtaken her ability to reason. She moved closer to him. He hesitated briefly before reaching out for her. Each kiss turned into another, and before Ruth could pull back from the pain, Tommy was deep inside her.

"I have to pull it out before it explodes," Tommy said, as he turned away and brought himself to climax.

"What happened? Why did you stop?" Ruth said, half relieved and half sorry because she had started to enjoy the sensation, once the initial pain had worn off.

"You might get a baby if I stay in." He tried to explain in between catching his breath. They lay together on the hessian coffee bags; holding each other tightly, trying to will away the prospect of their pending separation.

"I want us to stay together for always. I hate the thought of going back indoors," she said, half pleading.

"We can't stay, Ruth. We shouldn't have done what we did."

"Don't say that, Tommy. I wanted to do it." Tears welled in her eyes.

"Don't cry." He put his arm around her.

"It should have been special, like in the movies, but after you started it was horrible. I'm sore and bleeding and feel sticky."

Tommy tried to comfort her. He stroked her hair. "My pants are full of coffee dust."

After a short silence, Ruth began to giggle. The seriousness of their predicament dissolved, and they laughed and cuddled into each other. It seemed the most natural thing to do and if they were of the same race, it would have been. But what they had done was dangerous; the implications for them both would be dire, if caught.

"Ruth, we must go. You'll be missed, and they'll come looking for you."

Ruth checked her watch and realised she had been away too long. She became scared, as if the reality of what they had done suddenly dawned on her. I've just done the unthinkable, she thought, wondering if her virginity would still be intact. He did pull it out before anything happened, she tried to reassure herself. Retrieving her abandoned drawers and sarong, which she didn't remember taking off, she brushed away the coffee dust and tried to smooth the creases from her clothing.

"It's just so unfair," she fumed, "I want to be with you more than anything else."

"If I were white…"

"Don't say that, Tommy. I can't bear it. We'll find a way, we will."

"Come on, let's go." They seized a final kiss and left in different directions.

Arriving at the back door of the house, Ruth sighed with relief. The door was still locked so no one had come out looking for her. Once inside the kitchen, she realised the hall light was on. *Blast!* Her mother must be awake.

The house was eerily quiet. Ruth made her way to her room, tiptoeing past her parents' bedroom. She held her breath as she very gently closed her door. Looking at her dishevelled appearance in the mirror, she wondered if Tommy had noticed her messy hair. Wrapping her arms around herself in an embrace, she closed her eyes and relived the feeling of being in Tommy's arms. She undressed; the smell of her own dried bodily secretions mixed with Tommy's lingered on her skin. She filled the wash basin and reluctantly wiped away the physical traces of him, and the coffee.

Unable to sleep, her head buzzed with a profusion of conflicting thoughts. The intensity of her longing to be with Tommy became confused with feelings of guilt and shame at having given herself to him. She knew she had done wrong, but the closeness had felt so good and right. Being with him was the only thing that seemed real in her life.

She wondered if her mother knew she had gone out. Paranoia took over her thoughts as she imagined her mother was the person in the bushes at the river, or worse, one of her brothers. Unable to stand her disquiet any longer, she got up and made a noise, as if she had just woken. She banged the bathroom door and waited for her mother's usual, 'Is that you, Ruth?' There was no response. She crept to her mother's door and peered inside.

"Mum?" Alice's head hung in an unnatural position over the edge of the bed. She must be looking for something, she guessed. "Mum!" There was vomit everywhere. "Mum, get up!" She rushed to her mother's side and lifted her head back onto the bed. "Mum! Oh no, Mum, what have you done?"

CHAPTER 4

"Okoro to Madison two, come in, come in!"

When Tommy burst into the kitchen, Ruth was shouting into the two-way.

"Tommy, the misis… she's dead!" Sally managed to say as she sobbed into a tea towel.

Wide-eyed with shock and disbclicf, Tommy looked from Sally to Ruth.

"Mum's taken all her sleeping pills; I have to get hold of Dad," Ruth said.

"Madison two to Okoro, John here."

"Mum's taken all her Tuinal capsules, you have to come home."

"What? What's happened, Ruth?" He missed what she had said, or his brain refused to acknowledge it.

Ruth repeated herself, trying to control her breathing sufficiently to be able to talk.

"Get the doctor, I'm leaving now…" The sound of static punctuated his disconnection.

"I've called the doctor, Tom; he's on his way but she isn't breathing. I couldn't feel her pulse; I shook her and shouted but nothing…"

Sally walked over and embraced Ruth, as if to shut out a world too horrible to comprehend.

"I'll go and see her," Tommy said with a doubtful expression.

Ruth and Sally followed him to the bedroom. They waited in the doorway; it was too late for anyone to do anything.

Alice lay motionless with one eye closed and the other open. Snuggles, the old grey cat, was curled up on the bedside chair oblivious to Alice's lifeless body and the stench of vomit that infused the air. Tommy stopped by the bed to close the gaping eyelid and then calmly walked over to open the window. The two women watched him push the cat off the chair and shoo it into the hallway.

Tommy put his hand gently on Ruth's shoulder and said, "I'll go and get help."

"*Go kisim mama na bubu bilong yu*." Sally told him to bring his mother and grandmother.

"Get away!" Ruth yelled. "The cat's gone back in; you go that side and I'll chase him from here."

After helping Ruth evict the cat, Sally stopped by the bed and took hold of Alice's hand. "I'm sorry, Mrs Ally, I just make sure you comfortable." Sally carefully straightened the bedspread; a bright floral cretonne, Alice's favourite. "You can rest now, no more worry too much." She brushed cat hairs off the chair and bent down to pick up a crumpled piece of paper. She glanced at it briefly and looked back at Alice, before secreting the note into her apron pocket.

In shock, Ruth didn't notice the paper or the change in Sally's expression as they returned to the kitchen.

As the reality of her mother's death sunk in, Ruth became withdrawn and unresponsive. Sally helped her up and onto the couch. "You rest here, lovey, I'll make you some warm milk."

Tommy returned with his mother and grandmother, who sat with Sally as she told them what had happened. Alice had won the respect of the workers and their families. For many of the locals, she was the first white woman they had seen and they found her odd customs and genteel ways amusing. As well as their fascination with her, they enjoyed her gifts of second-hand clothing and the medicine she provided when the children were sick.

The small gathering finished their cups of black tea and began to sing softly, special songs for the dead and bereaved. Sally wouldn't allow anyone to touch the body until the doctor and masta arrived.

Tommy went to the parlour to be with Ruth. Her eyes were puffy and red. She stared hypnotically at the Tiffany table lamp; Alice's pride and joy, it had been shipped all the way from America. He reached for Ruth's hand and sat next to her in silence. It was well over an hour before she spoke.

"Tommy, why would she do such a thing?"

"Your mum must have been very unhappy. Sometimes there isn't a reason for what people do, not one that makes any sense to other people."

"I don't know how Dad will manage, especially the house, he's never had to organise meals or clean or anything. He might want me here now, to look after everything."

"You think you'd stay?" Tommy asked.

"All depends on Dad. I don't know, I can't think; my mind isn't working properly."

"You rest. No need to make any decisions now." Tommy squeezed her hand. There was nothing he could say to relieve her pain.

The pair were distracted by wooden chairs scraping across the concrete floor in the kitchen. The women were leaving. Sally remained at the table, exhausted and too distraught to move. Tommy's mother convinced her to go home to get some sleep. Hoku, Tommy's grandmother, assured her she would stay and look after Ruth until the men returned. Eventually, Sally agreed; she only lived next door. A few years before, Alice had insisted that John build a small timber cottage for Sally, so she would be close to the family.

The house fell into silence after the women left. Ruth watched Hoku walk towards the parlour. She stopped in the doorway.

"Tommy will sit with you, Ruthy. If you need anything, I'll be outside the window." Ruth wondered why she chose to sit outside the parlour window but thought she must have wanted to be close in case she was needed.

"What are you thinking about, Tom?" Ruth asked.

"You and your mum, and not being able to do anything; I feel guilty too."

"Why guilty?"

"Because of how close we are and what we did; and because nothing can really happen… we can't be together like normal people." Tommy's voice was barely audible and his features appeared drawn, wizened almost.

Ruth remembered the years they had spent growing-up together, discovering and enjoying the world. She cherished what they had. Even as youngsters, Tommy always delighted her with the best hiding places, the prettiest of flowers and the most succulent wild fruit.

"What will we do, Tommy? I want to stay here and be together with you and look after Dad." Ruth glanced up, waiting for him to say that's what would happen.

"We've got no future here, Ruth; people wouldn't allow us to be together. I'd be run off Okoro or shot, and your family would make life miserable for you. Even if we run away, where would we go?" He visibly swallowed hard to clear the lump in his throat.

"It's not fair; people don't know how we feel about each other. If they did, they would understand."

"Do you think so, Ruth?"

"No, I don't, but I want to believe they would." Ruth pressed her cheek against his arm. "I always thought life would be different to this; it all seems so out of control."

Tommy stroked her hair. He had no answers. A light tap on the window caught their attention.

"I go make breakfast 'case Sally late getting up. Go now, son, your papa going fishin' today – tell 'im I say he take you." The old woman sounded stern. Ruth guessed Hoku thought her grandson needed time away from the house. Or maybe from her.

The wait for John to return seemed endless. By the time the two vehicles pulled up at the house, a large crowd had assembled: plantation workers, their families, neighbouring workers and local villagers. John half jumped out of the jeep before it had fully stopped. He didn't speak; he ran straight to his wife, who by now had begun to exhibit a grey pallor. Gently, he held her hand and brushed aside a flyaway hair from her face. As he stared at his lifeless wife, his expression changed from disbelief to shock. He looked at Ruth with some indiscernible emotion in his eyes.

"She won't last long in this heat," he said. "Where's the bloody doctor?"

"He should be here in an hour or so; there was some emergency at Kerema."

The feeling of unreality that Ruth had experienced after the plane crash came rushing back. She was being thrust into another macabre dream where everything was horribly mixed up. As her mother lay in front of her, dead, she watched her father as he bent down and half lifted his wife into his large, muscular arms. Ruth thought her mother appeared delicate and tiny. Tears welled in her father's eyes. He began talking to Alice quietly at first, but then his voice escalated almost to shouting.

"Why, Alice? Why for God's sake?"

Ruth became panicky. The horror of the situation started to break through her defences. She rushed outside into the garden, retching, and then vomited. Tom and his father were returning from their hunting expedition just as she was being sick. Handing his father a trussed cuscus, Tom ran over to her side.

"Are you all right? I've been thinking about you all day," he said.

"I'm okay, Tom, it's the shock, and I haven't eaten. I must be strong for Daddy. He's not as tough as people think."

Jake appeared from nowhere. "You'd better come in, Ruth." He glared at Tom.

"I'll come in when I'm ready, Jake; you go in and talk to Dad."

Jake had always been jealous of Ruth's relationship with Tommy, or so Ruth assumed. He used to dote on his little sister before he and Matthew went away to boarding school. When they returned for the summer holidays, Tommy had taken his place. Ruth could sympathise with how he must have felt, but she couldn't understand why it still ate away at him. She knew Jake hated her being with Tommy, but right now, she didn't care. Their true feelings were hidden to the world, so a simple friendship shouldn't be anyone else's concern.

Heavy storms throughout the ranges further delayed the doctor. Ruth's father and brothers agonised over reasons for Alice's overdose, which annoyed Ruth. They were carrying on as if her mother had been entirely normal and the overdose was a total surprise. Finding one straightforward answer that explained everything would be impossible. Ruth's opinion was that her mother's motives were more complicated. If everyone were honest, they would have known that their mother hadn't been happy for years. Angry and frustrated with herself for not realising the extent of Alice's illness, and for not having done anything about it, Ruth went out to the veranda to be alone and to think.

The doctor's plane buzzed the house and touched down at dusk. She was still sitting outside when he reached the homestead.

"Ruth, is that you?"

"I'm sorry, Doctor, my mind didn't register," she replied, getting up out of the wicker chair.

"Don't apologise, you must be exhausted. On your own here when it happened, I heard?"

"The men had gone to Woitape. I went in to see why Mum never said goodnight and found her slumped over the edge of the bed." Tears flowed down Ruth's cheeks. The doctor put his arm around her shoulders and looked grimly at John, who had just emerged from the doorway with Jake.

"Evening, Jack. You better come through to the bedroom." John's words were barely audible.

Trailing behind the men down to the bedroom, Ruth thought her father looked like a little boy with his shirt hanging out, trying hard not to give way to his tears. Seeing him so vulnerable frightened her, he always used to be the one to fix things, make everything right. Now, he was totally lost and Ruth felt overwhelmingly sorry for him.

Alice looked peaceful, propped up on crisp white pillows. She could have been asleep if it weren't for her deteriorating pallor.

"If you'd like to wait outside, John, Ruth, I need to examine her to get a clearer idea of what's happened."

Ruth and her father returned to the veranda, Jake scuttled off to his room and Matthew returned to his bottle of scotch in the sunroom.

"Mum had two lots of tablets when I found her, that Largactil one from Dr Everidge and one from a hospital in Townsville. You didn't tell me she had been in hospital." Ruth waited for her father to explain.

"She didn't want anyone to know. We didn't want anyone to know." He hesitated. "She had shock treatment."

Ruth experienced a sudden, cold, sinking sensation. "I don't understand, why shock treatment? I thought they only did that in mental hospitals." Ruth knew her mother hadn't been well but going to an asylum had never even crossed her mind.

"She had bad nerves," John explained. "They got worse after we returned from the mainland but I thought she had got over them. The war finished her off I think; she lost everyone close." John stared off into the distance. "Perhaps coming back here after getting used to civilization again… probably everything all mounted up."

"When she was outside in the rain at Christmas, someone should have got the doctor. Everyone pretended it never happened. If we spoke properly to each other about her condition, she might not be dead now. I could tell she wasn't right, why didn't you talk to me?" Ruth cried.

"I should have spent more time with her, or sent her to stay with friends…" John blew his nose and coughed to suppress his tears.

The doctor emerged from the bedroom, still drying his hands. Ruth glared at the towel; one of her mother's favourite Egyptian cotton ones which she had sent from Melbourne. Alice allowed no one to use those. He must have taken it from the bedside chair. Ruth quelled the urge to seize the towel from him.

"I need to talk to you," the doctor said in a hushed tone, as he inclined his head towards Ruth's father.

"I'd like to listen if you don't mind, Doctor," Ruth interrupted.

John nodded in the doctor's direction. "She's stronger than the boys; she can hear what you've got to say."

"Well, like you said on the radio, she did take most of her tablets. She'd started to vomit up the barbiturate but it'd gotten into her lungs. Probably taken them over a period of an hour or so, some are more digested than others. From what I can tell, she intended to end her life, John. I'm sorry, but that's the only conclusion to draw."

They both looked at the doctor, as if expecting an explanation as to why Alice overdosed, but he offered nothing.

"Legally," he continued, "everything's straightforward, no need for an inquest. There's not a lot you could have done. They are one of the stronger sedatives."

"Did she go through much pain, Doctor?" Ruth wanted to know.

"Mental pain, I'd imagine, Ruth. Apart from vomiting, she probably fell into a deep sleep and simply stopped breathing."

Ruth could almost see her father's mind grappling with the doctor's explanation of his wife's demise. She was the one to break the silence.

"The cause of death needs to be recorded as accidental, Daddy." Ruth glared at her father with the expectation he would sort that out with the doctor. "I'll speak to Sally to make sure your room is ready, Doctor. You can use the front office for your paperwork." Ruth left.

Sleep was out of the question for Ruth, even after the medicinal brandy and milk that Sally had administered. With people walking through the house all night and knowing her mother lay dead in the bed next door, all she could do was think. She wanted to understand what had happened and repeatedly went over all the strange things she had noticed about her mother. She realised now that her condition hadn't simply been ignored, she'd even gone for treatment. What unsettled her most was how everyone had pretended that everything was normal and didn't mention it to her, even after the incident in the garden.

When the house finally quietened down, Ruth managed to doze off briefly. It was a fretful sleep; she would keep waking to remember afresh the horror of what had happened. To make sure she hadn't been dreaming, she would have to check that the doctor's plane actually was outside.

Nothing about the whole mess made any sense. Ruth's mind flooded with questions; she couldn't stop them going around and around in her head. Didn't the treatment work? Why did they send her home if she was still ill? If she had been unhappy for so long, why did she take her life now? Oh, Mum! Didn't she realise how strong the pills were? Maybe she knew she was losing her mind and couldn't cope. Ruth recalled the person she thought she saw on the riverbank when she was with Tommy, but then decided her mother couldn't have got back to the house so quickly. She went over everything that had happened since arriving home, conversations with her mother, conversations her mother had with family and staff. She puzzled over her grandmother's sudden departure but couldn't pinpoint any one thing which might have disturbed her mother sufficiently to end it all.

As if oblivious to the life-changing events of the day before, the first cheerful rays of sunlight filtered through the mist nestling the purple-grey mountain tops surrounding Okoro. A fresh, new day; cool and unusually quiet with little birdsong. The doctor's plane stood in stark contrast to the naturally subdued morning landscape with its bright, metallic yellow paint, almost glowing as the morning sun hit it. Ruth made her way to the kitchen, feeling as though she had done a round with Jimmy Carruthers. Her body ached, and her head pounded.

"Oh, Sally, what are we going to do?" she said, flopping onto a chair.

Sally hugged her, her own eyes swollen and her voice hoarse from crying. "I'm so sorry, Ruthy; it's a terrible thing to happen."

Ruth acknowledged Sally's concern with a firm squeeze of her hand. The two women knew words were pointless; they each understood the extent of the other's loss. Sally had been closer to her mother than most people; she was like a substitute mother to Alice in the early days, and often the only other woman Alice had to talk to for months on end.

The fly screen door banged open; it was Tommy. "How are you?" he asked.

"Tired, Tommy. Hoku and a couple of women from the village are washing and dressing Mum. Dad's arranged to have the funeral this afternoon."

Tommy's expression revealed his frustration. His face was taut with distress. It was clear that he wanted to pull Ruth into his arms and coax away her pain, but she was beyond his reach. Sally looked at them both; she understood the bond they both shared, although most likely not their physical involvement.

"I'm going to get some milk, Ruth. Your daddy and the doctor is up, they come for breakfast soon."

Obviously struggling with his impotence in the situation, all Tommy could do was reach over and gently touch Ruth's arm. "I'd better go; I can't be here when your dad and the doctor come. I'll be at the funeral."

Ruth discerned the ache in his eyes; she wanted to run into his arms, to feel them wrapped around her where she would be calm and comforted. With everyone around, they might as well have been oceans apart. The screen door clunked shut behind him.

Ruth couldn't handle being alone after he had left, and she didn't want to help dress her mother. It was becoming difficult to control her thoughts; she needed to distract herself.

"I'm going to get dressed, Sally," Ruth called out towards the dairy. "The pastor and the Johnsons will be here around midday."

Once in her room, her mind rebelled. Finding something to wear was too much of a demand. Any interest she had in her appearance had now well and truly been extinguished. She sat in front of the mirror, trying to focus on her unruly hair, but then she became irritated with the need to look respectable for the visitors.

"Why should I worry about looking proper when my mother's being buried?" she muttered angrily to herself. Her thoughts kept returning to what Tommy had said the night before and that made her even angrier.

What he had said was true though, she knew that. White girls never married native boys, even if they were light-skinned like Tommy.

The only interracial relationships anyone heard about involved white men living in sin with native women. She wondered what her mother would think if they married; she'd probably be horrified.

The small Cessna droned as it weaved its way between the final peaks of the ranges. The guests would be landing soon, which provided the motivation to dress and at least make some attempt to tidy her hair. Mrs Johnson wasn't really a close friend of her mother's. Ruth surmised that if she were, she would have helped when her mother went out in the rain; rather than being horrified and going home. Maybe her father had the right idea, she acknowledged, he should have sent her mother to Port Moresby or back to the mainland to live closer to her real friends. Dressed now and with her hair pinned up out of the way, Ruth went to the kitchen.

"The doctor will want lunch, Sally. I expect the visitors will, too. They'll be here in a few minutes. Cold meat and salad will have to do, with plenty of bread and butter. I'll boil the urn for tea and wash some fruit."

Ruth remembered she had to ask her father what the doctor had put on the death certificate. She went outside to find him only to discover everyone had gone. The workers and their families were no longer there, apart from a couple of men tidying up. Perhaps they were already at the grave site, she wondered, while forcing away a fresh lot of tears.

It was easier to stop the tears than allow them to flow. It was as though they were just the tip of something evil lurking beneath the surface, a smouldering blackness ready to consume her if she gave into them. Trying to hide her grief wasn't the concern. She feared that if she allowed it expression, she would never recover.

The gathering appeared sombre and surreal with everyone dressed in black; an obtuse contrast to the spectacular vibrancy of the landscape and bright, golden sunlight. Nothing much registered for Ruth until she felt her father's hand tighten on her arm.

"...we therefore commit her body to the ground; earth to earth, ashes to ashes, dust to dust; in the sure and certain hope of the Resurrection to eternal life..." the pastor read from his book.

John released a handful of earth which hit the coffin with a hollow thudding sound. Ruth stared at the soil in her own hand before reluctantly releasing it to join with her father's. The protective numbness which afforded her some degree of composure started to give way. Waves of intense fear and sorrow threatened to break through her defences. She wanted to scream and cry and call to her mother to come back. Matthew reached out and took her hand; the momentary alliance with her brother gave her strength. Her defences were re-established.

Looking around at the small gathering, she found it disturbing that of all the villagers, only Sally and Tom had attended. She broke with the party as they ambled back to the house to walk alongside Tom.

"Why did they stay away?" she asked.

"I think they just wanted to let you say goodbye in private, sort of respect," he said, looking at the ground.

"I can't believe the big men didn't come. Your dad and Sam were the first workers on Okoro; they're like family."

"They're old men; they probably don't want to see what's around the corner for them. I'd better go and find Dad; Jake won't want me up at the house."

His hasty departure annoyed Ruth. She hated Jake sometimes. Tommy could have stayed; he was just a friend for all anyone knew, and she needed him now. Tommy's guarded response and speedy exit made her wonder about the real reason why everyone had stayed away. She knew he was lying about the big men of the village. He didn't look at her when he said it, she remembered.

CHAPTER 5

After the funeral, Ruth spent most of her time alone, trying to come to terms with life without her mother. She painted mostly, it was easy to lose herself in painting; her own personal form of therapy. The spectacular colours of her natural subjects forced her to focus on the beauty inherent in life; this helped her restore a more balanced perspective on the world. John Madison and her brothers dealt with their grief by working harder, which involved them travelling away from the house to various parts of the plantation.

Her father had asked Ruth to sort through her mother's things and tidy-up. She managed to put off this job for as long as she could, as it was something she didn't really want to do. When she eventually got stuck into the task, she soon wished she hadn't started. Every item of clothing, knick-knack or piece of clutter seemed to have a memory attached. The most disturbing being old photographs, usually of happy times of the family together, all smiling happily. Birthdays, Christmases and end of school holiday barbecues; days that were now gone forever.

Although the sadness was hard to bear, a more disturbing aspect of Ruth's grief was the acute sense of loneliness. It would come upon her when least expected, like a sudden realisation that she was alone in the world. Then it would pass as quickly as it came. The men were just a radio call away but she felt deserted by them. Tommy dropped in whenever he could, but even he seemed to be keeping his distance. She missed the picnics, the swimming and the long walks they used to take together. It was companionship that she longed for and now regretted the stolen night they had shared, with the awkwardness and guilt she experienced afterwards. It was nothing at all like the dreamy, romantic bliss depicted in films.

The death of her mother had somehow changed Ruth's view of herself and her place in the world. It was a subtle shift, helped along by her school results, which came the day after the funeral. She had failed her matriculation. Under normal circumstances, the shame would have been too much to bear with her brothers making fun and teasing her about it, but no one commented. She didn't particularly care either. The only one who seemed remotely interested was her father, who said she must repeat her final year. If only her father would spend more time at the house, she thought, things wouldn't seem so black. She wondered if her mother had experienced the same sense of isolation, alone and with hardly anyone to talk to, too much time to think, too much time spent in your own head.

The isolation afforded Ruth plenty of opportunity to wonder about her relationship with Tommy. She suspected her need to be with him had been due, at least in part, to having been left alone by everyone. She also realised that being out of the house as much as possible must have been something the men used to do to avoid Alice's odd behaviour.

In spite of her second thoughts about going all the way with Tommy, she did love him still, although differently now. The shock of her mother's suicide enabled her to perceive the world with more clarity, especially the futility of her desire to be with Tommy as his partner, his wife. She reasoned that living for so long in relative isolation and attending an all girls' school, probably caused her to see him in an unrealistic way. He was the only boy she knew apart from her brothers. Even Tommy had said there was no future to their relationship. If he believed that, why did he go along with it? She suspected he had taken advantage of her, but then acknowledged it was she who did most of the pursuing. With so little to occupy her mind, her thoughts alternated between her mother and Tommy almost to the point of obsession. Then her holiday came to an end.

It seemed like any other day at first, but the bulging brown leather portmanteau by the door reminded Ruth that the big day had arrived. When her father told her she must go back to finish her schooling, she agreed; having considered the alternative. There could be no future at Okoro for her and Tommy, and she would end up having to take on her mother's role if she stayed. This was something she knew she could never do in spite of feeling sorry for her father.

"Morning, Ruthy." Her father sounded unusually chipper.

Sally's farewell breakfast filled the table, but Ruth wasn't hungry.

"Come and sit down, Princess. You'll be on the road a long time today." John motioned to the empty chair opposite.

The prospect of another plane flight should have caused Ruth some apprehension, but she hadn't given it much thought. She had been too preoccupied, trying to come to terms with the finality of her mother's death. Until today, she sensed her mother's presence about the house, as though she had been busy in another room or away visiting. Alice's absence was now very real and had to be faced. She also grieved for Tommy and the end of any hope for a future together.

"What time will you arrive in Bathurst?" John asked, between mouthfuls of heavily buttered toast.

"If I make all the connections and catch the mail train, about two in the morning," she replied, noticing he had stopped chewing. "Don't worry, the school bus meets the train."

"You shouldn't be travelling on your own all the way down there. I don't know why your mother chose that school and not one closer. I should send someone with you."

"Dad, I've done it three times before on my own. Besides, I'll meet up with other girls on the train."

"I guess this will be your last trip if you don't go on to do anything else," he said.

"I'd still like to go to art school after I matriculate."

"You'll probably want to start meeting young men soon, get married maybe and settle down."

"Oh, Dad, I'll worry about getting married later, I'm not in any hurry." Thank God, she thought, he mustn't suspect anything about Tommy.

"Masta Madison, Ruthy, it's a quarter to," Sally interrupted. The plane was due in fifteen minutes.

"Anyway, Ruth, you think about which art school you want to go to and I'll make some enquiries later on." He collected her bags, and they left for the airstrip.

As the plane taxied past the packing sheds, Ruth still hadn't spotted Tommy. To make things worse, heavy rain pelted down. Okoro always looked sad in the wet. She experienced a fleeting sense of dread as she remembered her last flight. Then the plane engine roared and reality struck – she was actually leaving Tommy, her mother, father and brothers. She wanted to fling her arms around them all and never let go; but it was too late. As she fought back the urge to yell at the pilot to stop, the shaky craft slowed, and then defiantly gathered speed before lifting off into the air.

The trip to Port Moresby and the connecting flight to Brisbane went according to schedule but the flight to Sydney was delayed. She missed travelling on the comfortable Sunderland, with only the one connection. Rummaging through her overnight bag for the Reader's Digest that she had taken from her mother's desk, a piece of paper fell to the floor. The handwriting was immediately recognisable.

Dear Ruth,

Sorry to say goodbye by writing but seeing you at the strip would be worse for me. I'm going to miss you. I missed you before, but this time will be worse. I know we can never be together as I want and now we both must find our own way in life. Hoku told me I must go away to Moresby to help my cousin with his market stall. It was Hoku that day at the river; she told me she saw us. I'll be going in a couple of days when Pups fixes his canoe. I should have told you at the funeral but didn't want to upset you more. The workers didn't come because Sam's cousin, Hiri, from Pagu village said the misis died because of payback for something Jake did. You know about the superstitions, probably nothing. I'll think about you every day and wish you were here.

Love, Tom.

63

Ruth was more confused than ever by what she read. She was relieved he hadn't simply forgotten she was leaving and felt ashamed that Hoku had seen them kissing. But she was sad as well. The letter confirmed that whatever it was they had together was now finished. And just to confuse her even more, the suggestion of payback. Why would anyone think it was payback?

Ruth spent most of the final leg of the journey staring out the window, lost in thought. No matter how hard she puzzled over her mother's death, what Tommy had said about payback made absolutely no sense. She decided to give up trying to work it out and focussed on what she needed to do to catch all her connections.

The increasing density of red roofs below caught her attention. Already, she could discern the suburbs of Sydney with the shabby, industrial inner West rapidly unfolding in the distance. In no time at all, the plane banked and the massive harbour bridge came into view. Brisbane seemed barely behind her when she stepped onto the tarmac at Kingsford-Smith.

Sydney was always humid, she thought, trying to ignore how sticky and flustered she felt while hurrying to catch a taxi. She arrived at the Central Railway Station with no time to spare. No chance on this trip for a leisurely meal in the refreshment rooms.

The double-engined train hissed and roared its way up the mountains. The foot-warmer seemed to have lost its heat and as the altitude increased, the carriage became chilly. After an arduous climb to Mount Victoria, the laboured locomotive negotiated the Ten Tunnels Deviation, before emerging at Lithgow with its blazing platform lights.

Ruth tried to avoid looking outside to lessen the unpleasant glare. Not far to go now, she thought, realising that she hadn't managed to get any sleep. By the time the train pulled out of the station, some of the other girls in the cabin had woken up, but no one appeared in the mood for conversation. It was late, cold and the beginning of another full year away from home.

When the weary locomotive chugged into Bathurst, Mr Styles,

the caretaker, and Miss Dunne, the housekeeper, were waiting with the old green omnibus.

"Come on, girls, don't keep Mr Styles waiting," which really meant Miss Dunne was tired and wanted to get back to her bed.

Once they came to the end of the bitumen road, the ride to school became bumpy and uncomfortable. Rain had created corrugates along the dirt road and it appeared Mr Styles drove over every possible ridge. The school's high sandstone wall and prison-like iron gates loomed up from behind a rise; an ominous vista set against an eerie, moonlit sky.

Ruth wondered what this year held, as the bus drew to a halt by the side door.

By the following morning, she found herself thrown back into the regimental routine of boarding school. It seemed as though she hadn't been away. A number of her classmates were also repeating the final year, so making new friends wasn't a pressing demand. In spite of the enforced structure to her life now, Alice's death was still raw and she often woke through the night, crying for her mother. Through the day, she made a special effort not to appear upset, but something fundamental had changed in Ruth. She realised that returning to school might have been a mistake; she experienced incongruence with the world around her, as though she had outgrown her friends and being at school.

"How are you, Ruth?" asked her roommate, Greer Andrews. Greer had lost her own mother to consumption a couple of years before. She understood Ruth's grief, as well as the pressure at school to act as if nothing had happened.

"Not too bad, thanks, Gre, but I haven't had my things since Christmas."

Greer looked at Ruth. "Nervous tension can cause that you know. Mine stopped after Mum passed away and the doctor said it was due to the upset and not eating. Don't worry, you'll be wishing them away again soon enough."

"I just want to be somewhere else. I can't settle."

"It's hard trying to be normal when inside you feel anything but normal."

"I'm glad you understand, Gre, I don't think anyone else could; all they want to talk about is what they did on their holidays."

"Did you hear about Susan Tiggins? She ran off with her mum's baker. Her family has disowned her even though she's no longer with him, can you imagine? She's staying with an aunt in Woolloomooloo. Felicity received a letter from her, but don't say anything, no one's to know."

"No, of course not. Poor thing, I wonder what made her run away with the baker, of all people."

"The butcher would have been better, Felicity said, he owns a farm as well as a shop!" Greer quipped.

The two girls laughed.

"Come on, let's hurry," Ruth said, "the dinner bell will be going soon."

As the weeks passed, things became worse instead of better. Ruth had altogether lost interest in her lessons and was becoming increasingly concerned about her absent periods. She knew she couldn't be expecting because Tommy had withdrawn. Her fear was that something was wrong with her body, some sort of disease that might cause her periods never to return.

Ruth found herself taking refuge in the needlework room each afternoon; here, she could sleep without anyone knowing. Sleep was the only respite from the troublesome thoughts about her mother and her still confused feelings towards Tommy. At an intellectual level, she understood the folly of her infatuation, but her emotions defied reason. She knew she would always love him and hoped to have her own plantation one day, and then the world could go to hell!

The breakfast bell was ringing which meant Ruth had missed the wake-up call. She rushed to get up but fell back on the bed from acute nausea. She swallowed to stifle the urge to vomit.

"You okay, Ruthy?" Greer's head craned through the doorway.

"Yes, I think so, Gre; just a bit off colour this morning."

"Probably those ghastly sardines we had for dinner last night. It only takes a whiff of them to make me heave. Shall I get Sister?"

"No, I'll be down in a minute. You go, no need for us both to get into trouble." Ruth reluctantly dressed and made her way to the dining room.

Sister Agnes was waiting at the door, chastising latecomers as they arrived.

"Sorry, Sister, I wasn't feeling well."

The smell of poached eggs and burnt toast hit Ruth even before she had reached her seat. With her stomach heaving, she made a quick exit to the toilets. The cool, clinical odour of carbolic soap provided immediate relief, and her nausea subsided.

"Have you been sick, Ruth?" Sister Agnes asked, appearing from nowhere.

"No, Sister, just a bilious attack but it's passed now."

"If you aren't well, I'll send for the nurse to come over. She's down the road today at the old people's home. Best she checks you over. Were you eating properly over the holidays?"

"Yes, I think so, Sister, but I haven't been completely right since I came back. Perhaps I need more fruit or something."

"Well, you'd better go back to bed and rest. I'll send for nurse."

It did not take Nurse Johnson more than a couple of minutes to diagnose the cause of Ruth's sickness. "She is expecting, about ten weeks I'd say, Sister."

Sister John, the headmistress, maintained a poker face. "Of course, no one else needs to know. I'll speak with her father and we'll handle it from here. Thank you for coming on such a cold day." With that, Sister John dismissed the nurse and turned to Sister Mary, her secretary. "Sister, go and fetch Ruth Madison immediately."

Ruth suspected something might be wrong by the look on Sister Mary's face. The complete absence of conversation as they marched down to the office confirmed her suspicion.

"Come in, Ruth, sit down." The headmistress pointed to a chair. "The nurse came to see me after she examined you, Ruth. I know she told you that you have a stomach upset, but I'm afraid there's something more."

A sudden rush of adrenaline hit Ruth's stomach. I do have a disease, she guessed. She wanted to run; the serious look on Sister John's face was ominous.

"You're expecting," the nun announced.

Ruth thought the diagnosis must be so terrible the nun couldn't bring herself to say it and had to ask, "What am I expecting, Sister?"

"Gracious, Ruth, you're expecting a baby."

"A baby! I'm expecting a baby, Sister?"

"Yes, Ruth, a baby. You've been up to no good, it seems, and now you'll suffer the consequences. You're the third girl who's gotten herself into such a predicament."

Ruth had to keep telling herself this conversation was happening, and that she really was sitting in Sister John's office being told she was expecting a baby.

"I can understand how you might be shocked, Ruth, and to be honest, so am I. If you're sensible, it doesn't need to be the end of the world; after the baby, you can finish your schooling at one of our Sydney schools. Of course, you must never tell anyone about it; your condition needs to remain a secret."

"No, Sister. I won't tell." Ruth said, confused. "Not tell anyone?"

"I don't know, Ruth. You're a bright girl but you can be dense on occasion. When you've had the child and return to school, you're never to talk about it. People will think you're a harlot and your life would be intolerable. This is a shameful thing, Ruth, and the fewer people who know the better."

Ruth didn't follow much of what was said; her mind raced off on its own with a string of questions. How could I be expecting? Tommy pulled it out; he said we'd be safe. But I wasn't safe, I'm going to Sydney to have a baby and then I'm going to a different school.

"What about my father?" she asked, almost too afraid to imagine his reaction.

"I'll contact him. I'll require his permission to send you to Sydney but he won't disagree with me, of that I'm sure. Go and get some rest. I'll try to get you away before Friday. Remember, Ruth, not a word to anyone before you go. This can't reach the other parents, they'd be wondering what sort of an institution we are running here. Will you promise me that?"

"Yes, Sister." Ruth returned to her room.

Oh God, what have I done? Kept going around inside her head. She closed the door behind her and threw herself on the bed. Lying with the window open, she could hear the other girls outside playing while they waited for lunch. This can't be happening, she told herself; the nurse must be mistaken.

Her mind raced back to the days spent with Tommy and the night that they 'did it'. Tommy had told her that if he didn't finish inside, nothing would happen. Ruth was panic-stricken. What would her father and brothers say? Would they know it was Tommy? What would happen to him? She cringed at the thought of everone talking behind her back. How did she get into such a mess? The things her mother had told her about not trusting what boys said must have been right. "He told me I'd be safe," she cried, and buried her face in her hands.

Ruth felt utterly wretched, like a criminal, leaving school in secrecy to board the five o'clock train. The cold, early morning fog against her face somehow confirmed the reality of her disgrace. Only a couple of weeks ago she had travelled all the way back to school with the prospect of art college at the end of the year. Now, she was leaving to go to some sort of convalescent home in Sydney.

Such a thing had never happened to anyone she knew. She wondered how she could be sure that she was doing the right thing. As hard as she tried to make sense out of the situation, she couldn't. For now at least, she would have to trust Sister John and go along with the arrangements.

When the train pulled into Central Station, the bitterly cold, wet weather had conspired to make her feel even worse. The buildings looked grey and unappealing; the people who seemed so busy and fascinating before, now appeared cold and disapproving. *Did they know?*

Her connecting train was due to arrive but even if she missed it, the hurried letter to her father had to be posted. It would not be difficult to guess Tommy's part in her condition, but this one last disgrace might just save him from her family's wrath.

Would her father believe she had met a boy and thrown away her virginity while waiting for the flying boat to leave Sydney? To make the ruse sound more believable, she described how they had met some time ago and had been writing to each other. She hated herself for lying to her father. Making out she was some kind of trollop was even more mortifying, but there was no choice. Tommy could end up in prison if she told the truth.

She found the pillar box and thoughtfully pulled the letter from her satchel. Airmail should only take a week or so; she pushed the article through the slot.

It was a rush to catch the suburban-line connection but she made it, arriving just fifteen minutes later at her destination, Ashfield. A busy station it turned out to be and rather pretty. Red, flowering geraniums cascaded from planters hung along the platform, and the woodwork had recently been treated to a fresh coat of ivy-green paint.

"Ruth!" An Irish accent, stronger than Sister Mary's, hailed from behind.

Ruth turned to see an expectant face looking in her direction. "Hello, are you Sister Rose?" Her escort to the convent was a short, rotund woman with flushed cheeks and dressed in a brown habit. A foreign sight compared to the crisp black and white of the school sisters.

"Aye, I'm Sister Rose. The Reverend Mother sent me to meet you," she managed to say in between breaths. "Well then, lass, let's make a start, we can stop on the way for a rest."

Ruth thought she seemed friendly in a funny way.

"Have you done laundry before, Ruth?"

What an odd question, she thought. "No, not really, someone does the washing for us at home, but I did my own smalls at school."

"You'll get used to things soon enough; you're a strong looking lass," the nun reassured her.

"Do I need to do my own washing?" Ruth enquired, intrigued by the nun's odd conversation.

"Yes, of course, but I mean the work, the laundry. We do the laundry for some of Sydney's best hotels, didn't they tell you?"

"No, they didn't tell me much at all only that I'm coming to Sydney to go to a rest home."

Sister Rose laughed, rather too loudly. "It isn't a rest home, lass. It's a convent, and we also run a commercial laundry. Many lasses, like yourself, stay and work with us. In your case, you'll be staying until you're all sorted out and then you're back off to boarding school. You're lucky, Ruth; very few have the option of returning to school and a normal life."

Panic set in; Ruth experienced the familiar cold, empty sensation in the pit of her stomach. She had many questions to ask, but kept quiet; she was afraid of the answers.

When they arrived, the convent looked uninviting and stark in spite of the meticulously maintained gardens. The back of the grounds were fenced off with a combination of wooden palings and barbed wire. The main sandstone building had an imposing entrance. Inside, the floors were polished wood with holy pictures along the walls.

"Sit there, lass. The Reverend Mother will be seein' you in a minute. You can call her Sister Ignatius." Ruth sat on the wooden bench as instructed. Sister Rose disappeared down the corridor.

The heavy wooden door opened and a nun in a white habit beckoned her to enter. Behind a large, inlaid, blackwood desk, sat Sister Ignatius.

"Well, Ruth, I see you made it here all in one piece. There are no other girls from the country, or from the islands for that matter; they are all city girls. Many have no families or are here because they've gotten themselves into trouble, like you. While you're here, Ruth, misbehaviour of any sort won't be tolerated, so make sure you behave yourself from the start. You'll be given a bed in the seniors' dormitory, two per room, and we provide your meals in return for work in the laundry. The wake-up bell goes at a half past five, and you must be dressed and at the chapel by a quarter to six. After which, the girls follow Sister Rose to the refectory for breakfast. We don't speak until after breakfast; the morning is a time for reflection."

Ruth's head spun; meeting Sister Ignatius hadn't been what she expected – nor was the convent. Working didn't bother her but the hours seemed harsh compared to school, and she worried about how she would manage with her constant tiredness and morning sickness. Before she had a chance to ask any questions, Sister Rose had been summoned, and they were marching up a flight of stairs and down a narrow corridor to the dormitory.

"Leave your bags 'ere, lass, and I'll be taking you to meet Sister Philomena; she'll be showing you what to do."

Ruth had been hoping for a snack before being put to work, but it seemed this was out of the question.

As they retraced their steps and then walked down another corridor towards the laundry, the interior decoration rapidly deteriorated. White walls with beautifully framed pictures turned bare and off-white. The Persian carpet runner disappeared as they turned the corner and then the parquetry floor gave way to concrete. The laundry walls were a mixture of grey, fibrous asbestos and old brick, no paint at all, and the girls looked dishevelled; almost like characters in the Dickens' annual her grandmother had given to her one Christmas.

"What's ya name, luv?" one of the girls enquired, only to be told to be quiet by a supervising nun.

"Sister Philomena, this is Ruth Madison; she'll be with you in the laundry for a few months. I've shown her where she'll sleep, and she's to be put on folding first; she's come to us straight from school."

Sister Philomena nodded dutifully to Sister Rose, while casting an appraising eye over Ruth.

"I'll see you after morning prayers tomorrow, Ruth," Sister Rose called out as she walked away.

"Thank you, Sister." Ruth experienced a surge of apprehension;

the only friendly face had now left.

The girls worked like automatons, Ruth observed; apart from occasionally stopping to wipe the sweat from their faces or to drink water. Some appeared quite young, but the majority must have been around her own age. Two were in the advanced stages of pregnancy. They didn't look at all friendly, but neither did the sisters. Ruth found the whole arrangement disturbing.

After a strange afternoon, learning to fold sheets in silence, a bell rang and Sister Philomena ordered everyone out to the showers. Cold water and one disfigured lump of un-perfumed soap made its way along the line of girls.

"You better stick with me, Ruth. I'll see ya right," said the girl with whom she had been working. "It's a horrid place, but we get by; ya just 'ave to play ya cards right."

It didn't take Ruth long to realise that her fellow laundry workers were unwanted, had been in trouble with the authorities or were deemed to be in 'moral danger'. Ruth had never heard of such a term before but discovered this latter category was the one to which she belonged.

The following days dragged, but Ruth soon grew to accept the long hours and hard work. The dreadful food she objected to most. Shirley, her fellow folder, had only recently turned sixteen. Her own mother had put her into the convent for fighting with her stepfather. Shirley claimed he used to look at her while she bathed, and worse, play with himself as he watched. Ruth was coming to the realisation that unfairness didn't only apply to her own life.

"So what's this Tommy do, Ruth? Is he a black fella?"

"Sort of, but not entirely, I think he was adopted, maybe a cousin in Port Moresby had him to a white man. His father takes care of our vegetable gardens; he used to be Dad's leading hand early on. Tommy lives on the plantation but spends most of his time fishing and hunting."

"So he's sort of just suntanned looking, is he?"

"Yes but his eyes are dark and his hair is black and curly."

"Sounds lovely, living with servants, but I don't think I could get used to living in the jungle. Anyway, don't suppose I'll ever get the chance. I hope someone nice adopts his baby though, would be a shame to get someone 'orrible."

"What do you mean, adopt my baby?"

"Well, isn't that why you're 'ere? Have the baby, give it away and get on with your life?" Shirley said coldly.

Ruth thought for a moment. That must have been the plan. Everything made sense now. The baby was to be adopted. Ruth didn't know what to say, she was too shocked.

"Well, you can't exactly take a baby to school with ya. Do you 'ave anyone back 'ome who'd look after it?"

"No, only my grandmother but she's too old. No, no one, but I don't want to give my baby to anyone."

"Poor darl, you work out what you want to do, and I'll help ya. You better not let the nuns know you're having second thoughts, I think they make money out of people adopting. Anyway, let's get some shut-eye. Night, Ruth."

"Night, Shirl."

Ruth's thoughts raced; she couldn't sleep. Sister John didn't just mean the travel and accommodation arrangements would be taken care of, she meant finding someone to take the baby. She gently held her abdomen as if to comfort her unborn child. Tears welled in her eyes, and she had to bury her face into the pillow to muffle her crying. When her tears subsided, she looked around at the stark room. Glancing at her roommate, she wondered what sort of horrible world she lived in. Shirley seemed to fall asleep as soon as her head hit the pillow, she noticed; must be worn out from all the work.

Ruth grabbed her handkerchief from under the pillow and blew her nose. Well, that might be their plan, she thought, but it certainly isn't mine. *No one is taking my baby!*

CHAPTER 6

"Shirley, Ruth, help me get her to the infirmary," Sister Philomena yelled. "Sister Rose, fetch Sister Theresa." Elizabeth Jenkins had started to have pains the previous night but wouldn't let anyone tell the sisters.

The girls knew immediately what was happening. Sister Theresa used to work at a city hospital, as a midwife.

"I told her it wasn't wind, didn't I, Ruth?" Shirley said, proud of her right diagnosis while everyone else was wrong.

Ruth and Shirley helped the patient onto the bed. Sister Theresa returned as quickly as she had left, accompanied by two postulates with buckets of steaming water. Ruth looked on with dread.

"Back to the laundry, you two! Sister Philomena, take these two back to work." Sister Theresa had a voice like a drill sergeant.

Sister Philomena had to pull Ruth's arm; she was transfixed at the sight of her co-worker writhing in agony and calling for some man. And the buckets of boiling water, whatever did they do with them? Ruth wondered, too scared to ask.

Back at work, the girls had trouble concentrating on their folding duties with Elizabeth's intermittent screams resonating through the corridor. Ruth remembered similar screaming coming from the workers' quarters at Okoro. She surmised giving birth must be the same for all women: excruciatingly painful. The idea of being in so much pain, surrounded by strangers, was a terrifying prospect. Ruth wished her mother were still alive; she wouldn't have left her alone to deal with this.

By the time the girls had finished their showers, the screaming had stopped and everyone settled into a more relaxed mood. After prayers, Sister Rose unexpectedly appeared.

"I've got something for you, Ruth: a letter from your father."

Ruth eyed the open letter with delight, but as she tried to imagine what he had to say, her excitement turned to trepidation.

"Reverend Mother censors all the post," the nun said apologetically, as she gave Ruth the opened letter.

Ruth smiled and put the envelope into her apron, she'd read it in private.

When the girls reached their room, Shirley was almost as excited as Ruth. "Come on, Ruth, what does he say?" Never receiving any letters of her own, Shirley wanted to share Ruth's news.

"Nothing much, Shirl. Well, nothing pleasant, only that he's disappointed and ashamed of me, and that I'm to do what the sisters say. He then says I'm lucky Mum isn't around to hear about what I've done and that my bothers are ashamed of me too, especially Jake, who said he wants no more to do with me. Dad said I'm only to write after I start back at school." She guessed that meant after the baby had been given away.

"Is that all?" Shirley wanted to know every detail.

"Apart from telling me not to write or talk to anyone else back home." Which meant Gran and Sally, Ruth suspected.

"I guess he's ya dad, he can be angry; but your brother sounds like a right ponce."

"He's trying to show Dad how wonderful he is and how dreadful I am; he's always like that," she said, trying to conceal the quiver in her voice. She never wanted to hurt anyone.

The following morning was crisp. The girls' breath resembled clouds of smoke, as they hurried to the chapel. When they arrived, Father O'Grady had come up from the church to lead prayers. The girls guessed they would miss breakfast; he never stopped talking until way past the time for work to start. They huddled together to keep warm; thankful to be able to close their sleepy eyes again – so long as they didn't completely fall back to sleep, or there would be hell to pay.

The silent prayer had only just begun when one of the congregation started to snore. Eyes slowly opened to see Sister Ignatius marching down the aisle to intervene, when a piecing scream came from the back row. The girls and their minders all turned just as Angela Williams, on the end pew, passed out. Elizabeth Jenkins was walking up the aisle – her white, starched nightie was covered in bright-red blood with darker, carmine blobs splattering onto the floor as she walked.

"Quick, she's cut her wrists!" Sister Rose called out as she grabbed her, and in what seemed like one continuous movement, ripped the hem from Elizabeth's nightie and began wrapping it tightly around her arms.

Prayers had to be abandoned. The girls were too distressed. "Quiet, girls; move along to the refectory, no more talking," Sister Ignatius ordered.

The solemn gathering disbanded and the girls walked out in single file, looking downwards to avoid stepping in the trail of blood. Some cried; others were too scared to look.

"She'll be sent to the loony-bin now," Shirley informed Ruth.

"I'm getting out of here, Shirl," Ruth whispered. "I'm not ending up like her." Ruth understood only too well the emotional distress Elizabeth must have been going through. She realised now the depth of her mother's despair; to be so miserable that killing herself seemed the only thing to do.

The incident haunted Ruth over the following days; it could easily be her own fate if made to part with her baby. Who knew what could happen to a woman's mind if forced to give up a child? She loved her baby, even though it was yet to be born; she cherished the life growing within her. It would be someone to love and never have to say goodbye to.

After the horror of Elizabeth Jenkins' attempted suicide, and prompt removal to Callan Park Mental Hospital, life at the convent gradually returned to normal. Ruth had settled back into her routine of waking, working and sleeping – when not bothered by nightmares of incarceration in a lunatic asylum. She loathed her situation but decided to accept it, at least for the time being.

"Ruth!" Sister Rose's familiar voice bellowed above the automatic mangles.

"Yes, Sister?" Ruth said, rather alarmed. Sister Rose never came to the laundry without a reason.

"Ruth, I need a girl to help me in the kitchen, and I thought you'd be perfect. You can come with me now and help with dinner."

Delighted at having been chosen, Ruth looked forward to the break from folding but she would miss being with Shirley. Even though her roommate was younger, Ruth admired her ability to deal with whatever life threw up at her. She always managed to see the funny side of things and make Ruth laugh – as difficult as it was to find anything to laugh about inside the convent.

"We need to prepare three meals a day," Sister Rose continued, "which is actually six, because the sisters have different food to the girls. Nothing grand, mind, but we have lots of salad and cold meat in summer."

Ruth discerned a guilty tone in the nun's voice as she told her about their wider choice of menu.

"The kitchens are always kept locked to remove temptation and reduce the risk of any nasty business. One of the girls got in last year and stabbed Sister Philomena with a fork. So, lass, this is a position of trust I'm putting you in, working here with me."

How could anyone stab a nun? Ruth thought. The possibility of such violence further convinced her of the need to get away. Some girls were clearly delinquent from the things they had bragged about, and not much would be needed to end up on their wrong side. She hoped they wouldn't view her move to the kitchen as a betrayal.

Ruth had never seen such a large kitchen. Pots and pans hung from racks, there were two enormous black Metter's fuel stoves and, much to Ruth's delight, freshly baked bread cooling on the table. Ruth salivated at the sight and smell of the hot crusty loaves and the fresh vegetables piled up on the draining board.

"You can help yourself to one piece of fruit a day, but be discreet, and don't let on to anyone or we'll both be sweating it out in the laundry," said Sister Rose.

Ruth enjoyed working in the kitchen, although with two wood-burning stoves going and all the doors locked, the work wasn't light duty by any means. It did, however, give her access to the vegetables and fruit she had been craving and, indeed, needed.

The daily routine for Ruth had now changed to a succession of short shifts alternating between the laundry and the kitchen. The other girls didn't seem to take issue with her being in the kitchen. She put this down in part to her friendship with Shirley, who seemed to get along well with the worst of the girls. The variety of work and the additional rations made life at the convent almost enjoyable.

In spite of the improvements to her life, Ruth was still as determined as ever to keep the promise she had made to Shirley and to her unborn child. She had no intention of ending up like Elizabeth Jenkins. And working in the laundry was proving to be useful. She often came across money which had somehow gotten mixed in with the linen. Unnoticed tips, maybe, or careless diners with more money than sense. It would come in handy once she escaped.

As the weeks passed, she got to know Sister Rose a little while they worked together; in fact, she had become quite fond of the old nun. Especially after discovering it was her own fruit ration she had given away. Her relationship with Shirley had also developed. Ruth loved having a friend with whom to share her thoughts and plans. It was like having a sister, something she had always yearned for.

"Well, Ruth, what did you decide, after all?" Shirley looked across from the other bed.

"I'm not giving my baby away. I'm keeping him, or her. I don't know how yet, but we're going to be together."

"They'll take it anyway. You're under twenty-one, and even if you weren't, they'd still do it."

"Oh, Shirley, would they do that if I said I wanted to keep the baby?"

"Bet ya life they would. No one has ever kept their baby."

Deep down, Ruth knew Shirley was right. "I must get away, Shirl, and soon." The idea of running away was terrifying, but it would be a preferable fate to the alternative.

"Where will you go?"

"I've got no idea, apart from an address of a girl from school. She got into trouble too." Sue Higgins was the only person Ruth knew in Sydney and even then she wasn't a proper friend, just a classmate. She felt sick at the thought of having laughed at the girl's misfortune when she had first heard.

"I'll come with you. I've lived 'ere all me life. We'd have a better chance together," Shirley said optimistically.

"You can't put yourself at risk for me, Shirley, but it's sweet of you to offer."

"Sweet, nah, just sick of this place, and looking after you gives me an excuse to get out."

"You're almost two years younger than me; I should be the one looking after you."

"Yeah, you're older, but you're clueless," Shirley said, but then tried to sound more tactful. "Not smart about life, I mean. Everyone knows if a bloke pulls it out, you can still get lumbered. He should have used a franger, a rubber."

"Heavens, Shirley, you certainly understand all about those things. All I ever got to find out was what I heard from the other girls at school, and from seeing the animals back home."

"Oh, well, not to worry, but I do know Sydney like the back of me 'and, so I'll come."

"You really want to come with me?" Ruth said feeling relieved, even though she didn't want Shirley to get into trouble.

"Yeah, why not? It'll be a cinch now you're in the kitchen."

"How does that make a difference?"

"The butcher and greengrocer deliver to the back door of the kitchen, so Rosy must have a key. If you get the key, we can walk straight out."

"What about the door into the kitchen from this side?" Ruth said.

"You'll have to see where she keeps the keys."

Ruth felt a sudden pang of guilt. She didn't want to betray Sister Rose's trust; but she had little choice.

"I'll watch her in the morning, although it's open when I arrive. I'll try to be early." Ruth smiled, more reassured at having made a definite plan to leave. Surviving outside, though, would be tough.

Now that she knew for sure she would be leaving, Ruth found working in the kitchen a confusing ordeal. She was torn between doing what was right for herself and her sense of loyalty to Sister Rose. Getting away was the only chance for her and her child to to be together. Yet the thought of betraying the nun caused her a great deal of angst. Of all the adults in her life, Sister Rose had never once appeared condemnatory or shown disdain. They often chatted while they cooked, and in many ways, Ruth found their conversations comforting.

"I might be a nun, Ruth, but I'm also a woman. I understand that Elizabeth wanted to keep her baby, but sometimes what we want isn't possible. Her family wouldn't support her. What would she do for money and a roof? Besides, she'll eventually want to get married and what man would want her with another's child?"

Ruth remained silent. It seemed as though what the sister was saying about Elizabeth equally applied to her own situation. Has she guessed that I'm planning to escape? she thought. "Do you think it's right to give a baby away, Sister?"

"Oh, Ruth, it must be best for a baby to go to a good home, but whether it's right, I don't know. I think in that situation you'd need to pray to the Lord for guidance and follow his direction."

"How would you know what he wanted?"

"Goodness, Ruth, so many questions. You'd know in your heart what God wanted you to do, lass. Now we must get on with the sisters' dinner; they're having salad and corned beef tonight."

Ruth felt better after listening to Sister Rose talk about Elizabeth. It somehow helped her overcome any feelings of uncertainty about leaving. Like Sister said, she knew in her heart that keeping her child was the right thing to do, so that must be what God wanted, too. Ruth decided Sister Rose would understand why she had to run away and that made her decision easier. The two girls planned their escape for the following night.

"After everyone's been asleep for an hour or so, we'll throw our bag out the window and make our way downstairs to the kitchen. Just make sure you get the keys," Shirley instructed, sounding excited.

"I'll bring them. They're kept in an empty Arnott's tin next to the biscuit barrel. I'll get them while Sister's eating, before wash-up," Ruth said.

Ruth awoke the following morning with a mixture of excitement and foreboding. She found the prospect of leaving to start a new life heartening, but the possible difficulties they might encounter didn't bear thinking about. If adopting out her child wasn't part of the deal she would have chosen to stay, but her unborn baby deserved to have its own mother. She believed that no matter how difficult things might become, no amount of difficulty would warrant giving up her child. She was over her misgivings; thinking about her baby gave her courage. The time had come to make a move.

After dinner that evening, her plans were going like clockwork. Sister Rose had gone to the breakfast room to have her meal which left Ruth alone. She had just picked up the Arnott's tin when Sister Ignatius walked in. Ruth's stomach churned.

"I wanted to say thank you, Ruth. You're doing a grand job here with Sister Rose. She even gets to sit down and enjoy her evening meal now."

"Thank you, Sister." Ruth said, trying to hide her agitation. Now she had to endure a lecture about washing-up and germs. Sister Rose would overhear and come to join in the conversation, and that would be the end of the escape.

"Yes, Sister, I always carbolic the floor after supper's been washed-up." Ruth was beside herself but managed to contain her annoyance.

"You'll go far, Ruth, after this situation is behind you." The Reverend Mother glanced at Ruth's bulging stomach, then left.

Sister Rose mustn't have heard, Ruth decided, as she looked at the nun still eating her meal. She rushed back to the tin and carefully prised off the lid, careful that it didn't make a pop sound. She grabbed the spare keys. With precision, she put the tin back, matching up the base with the ring mark on the shelf.

"Now, time to wash the dishes in *hot* water," Ruth said under her breath, and smiled.

As she went upstairs to her room, she felt light and cheerful inside, a state of mind she had almost forgotten. She had even enjoyed evening prayers. They seemed to hold a particular significance for the impending escapade.

"Forgive me, my gracious God, and protect me always as I set out on my life's journey. Blessed Virgin Mary, our ever loving mother, pray for me. St. Joseph, my valorous guardian angel, and all the saints in heaven, pray for me."

A bright, full moon illuminated the street below.

"We'll throw the bag out the lav window in case the nuns spot it going past their bedrooms." Ruth couldn't help thinking how clever Shirley was.

The girls made their way to the toilets and after taking great pains to open the window without it squeaking, lowered the bulging overnight bag down to the ground on a string of joined bandages. With that completed, they crept down the hall to the back stairs. A door banged in front of them. They froze.

"What shall we do, Ruth?"

"It must be Sister Philomena. She probably went to spend a penny. We'll wait a few minutes to make sure she's gone back to bed and then keep going. We can't stop now we've started."

Nothing would hold Ruth back now. She motioned to Shirley, who seemed to have lost her nerve. They tiptoed down the rest of the hall to the safety of the steel staircase, which, unlike the main wooden one, didn't creak.

The kitchen door was a welcome sight; once through it, they would be free. Ruth pulled the keys from her pocket and opened the door. Shirley stared in awe at the shelves full of food, before making a beeline for the biscuit barrel.

"Shirley, leave them! We've got to get out." Ruth didn't want their escape foiled over a biscuit. She nervously dropped the keys but recovered them and within seconds, moonlight was glaring in through the back door. Once outside, they ran to the side of the building to collect their belongings.

It all seemed too easy, Ruth thought, with a sense of apprehension. They hurried down the road, all the time looking behind to make sure no one had followed. As they turned the corner, she stopped to look back at the convent and bade farewell to the gloomy-looking building, and the refuge it had provided. She also thanked it for the opportunity to meet Shirley, for without her friendship, things may have turned out very differently.

They arrived at the train station, trying their hardest to appear like night workers on their way home.

"All aboard, last train to Central," the stationmaster called before blowing his whistle. The night air had a chill, they were glad to get into the warmth of the carriage. As the train pulled out of the station, both girls anxiously peered through the window. No one had come after them.

The trip to Central Station took only twenty minutes. They were both tired and wanted to sleep. Reluctantly, they had to leave the warm train for the cold, windy Sydney streets.

"Be careful!" Shirley grabbed Ruth's arm. "There's a copper. Wait till he gets round the corner."

At that moment, Ruth realised the perilousness of the venture she had embarked upon. Being pregnant was one thing; having escaped from a home for wayward girls and having no home to go to could see her end up in prison. Keeping within the shadow of the station colonnade, they stealthily made their way down towards Broadway.

"We'd better get to that friend of yours pretty soon, or we'll end up in the clink with all these coppers around," Shirley said, confirming Ruth's fears.

"She lives in Woolloomooloo. I've got the address." Ruth located a piece of folded exercise paper that she had secreted away in her brassiere. "Riley Street," she said.

"Gawd, that's back the way we came. Come on, let's go." Shirley was eager to find shelter, getting caught by the police was just part of it; you never knew what could happen once they had you locked up.

They took the back streets to avoid running into any more of the constabulary. As the cover of night dissolved into a bleak, grey dawn, freezing winds gave way to rain. Nipping in and out of doorways to keep from getting soaked, their journey to Woolloomooloo seemed to be taking forever.

"I hope they don't mind us calling so early," Ruth said, as she knocked on the door. The downstairs lights came on, slippered feet could be heard shuffling up the hall towards them.

"Yes? Who are you and what do you want?" A tall woman with her hair in curlers stood in the doorway.

"My name's Ruth, I'm a friend of Susan's. I wanted to say hello while I'm in Sydney. We went to school together."

"You look more like urchins than school friends. Anyway, she isn't interested in seeing anyone, especially at this ungodly hour. You'd better run along." The door closed with a bang. Ruth and Shirley stared at each other in disbelief, then dread.

"What shall we do now?" Ruth asked.

"I've got an aunt who lives in Surry Hills but I haven't seen her in years. Maybe she'll let us stay for a while," Shirley said, looking hopeful.

"Let's find some food first, I'm starving and my feet are sore from these damn shoes. And I want some tomatoes."

"Tomatoes?" Shirley looked perplexed.

"I keep craving them. Since I've been in the kitchen, I've had one on toast every day for breakfast." They burst into laughter and went to find a delicatessen.

Armed with a small brown loaf, two tomatoes and a can of bully beef, the escapees made their way to Belmore Park. Ruth found a tap and washed the blood from the broken blisters on her heels, then set about massaging the balls of her numb feet. Hidden between a wall and a row of bushes, they made a hearty breakfast. The rain had stopped, and out of the wind, they found the watery morning sun to be warm.

"I've got to shut my eyes for a while, Shirl, or I won't be any good for the walk to your aunt's." They arranged the camellia bushes so no one could see through the gaps. Propped up against the wall, they both fell asleep.

"Get away! Shoo!"

Ruth's eyes shot open to find a big black dog sniffing at the can of bully beef and Shirley trying to scare it off without making too much noise.

"There are people in there!" a man's voice shouted. "Here, Rover!"

"What are they doing?" replied his companion.

"Up to no good I'd say!" The men's voices were getting closer.

"Ruth, stand up quickly and try to look normal." Shirley had a plan, she turned towards the men. "You should keep that dog of yours on a lead; scared us both so much we had to run into the bushes!" she admonished.

One of the men called the dog and the other started to apologise.

"We should report this, you know. Come on, Ruth," Shirley continued.

"What about the bully beef?" Ruth said.

"The dog licked it, we don't want it now." They made a hasty exit along the cobbled path as the intruders continued to call out apologies.

"If Auntie Joyce is home, we can stay for tonight and look around for work tomorrow."

"I hope she's home," Ruth said, at the same time wondering what they would do if she weren't.

Ruth could barely walk by the time they reached the top of the hill and Auntie Joyce's street.

"Look, the door's open!" Shirley squeezed Ruth's arm and ran the last few steps. She knocked briskly on the dilapidated green paintwork.

"Jesus! Who's that banging?"

The sound of a woman's voice was a relief, but Ruth couldn't help thinking how rough she sounded. It was a narrow, old house with peeling paint on the walls. The door swung wide open to reveal a large red-headed woman.

"Shirl, what are you doing 'ere? Come in! Aren't you supposed to be at that place in Ashfield?"

Joyce was a loud, brash-sounding woman, but she seemed friendly and Ruth was grateful for the invitation to stay until they were 'on their feet' as Joyce said.

As much as Ruth wanted to get a job, Shirley insisted that in her condition, it was out of the question. Shirley made up her mind to find a job herself first and then Ruth could start looking after the baby arrived.

A few days later, Shirley told Ruth that landing a first job was turning out to be more difficult than she had imagined. She could hardly give the convent as a reference and they all asked about previous work. A whole week of looking hadn't been fruitful, not even the promise of anything. Then out of desperation, Joyce agreed to lie to the landlady of a hotel in Fitzroy Street. She told the woman her niece had just turned eighteen and needed work to help with her keep, or she'd be out on the street. It worked! Shirley was offered a job cleaning guest rooms, but only three days a week; barely enough to keep them in food.

"Now I've got a job, we can save up and get a room," Shirley said, overjoyed at having money and the prospect of finding their own room to rent. Ruth tried to look optimistic, but guessed four pounds a week wouldn't get them far.

"I feel useless, not being able to work."

"Don't worry, you won't always be expecting," Shirley tried to reassure her, but Ruth was uncomfortable having to rely on someone else for her keep.

Ruth tried to pay her way initially, by cleaning and cooking. She even broke into the money she had saved from the laundry to buy treats. By the end of the third week, her savings were almost gone and she was miserable.

"Come on, cheer up, darls, you're doing a lovely job with the house, and the cooking's as good as a pub meal."

"Thanks, Auntie Joyce, but I can't keep living off you and Shirley; besides, I want to save some money for when the baby's born. I'm going to look after my baby properly. All I have at the moment is two pound ten left from what I found at the home."

"If you want to work that bad, I might be able to find you something, but it won't be anything like you're used to, luv."

"I don't care. What sort of work?"

"Do you know what I do for a living, Ruth?"

"You work in a restaurant, don't you?"

"That's what I tell everyone but the money they pay wouldn't buy me smokes, let alone the electric and gas bill. I entertain gentleman."

"That sounds exciting, what sort of entertaining?"

"Gawd, Ruth, go wash your face; you can come and meet me boss. And if Shirley asks, it's a restaurant, promise?"

"Okay." Ruth had only ever known life on the plantation and at boarding school. The sordid side of city life was something she'd never heard about before, let alone had any contact with.

When Joyce explained more about the nature of the business where she worked, Ruth had to hide her disgust. The worst part was that no other business would take her on while expecting, especially now that her condition was becoming obvious. With no money even for food, she couldn't afford to let her moral revulsion get in the way. So long as she didn't have anything to do with the men, she reasoned, it would provide a way out of her current money-less situation.

The desperation of her situation made Ruth a keen student. By the end of the first week, she had mastered her job of glass-washer at Lil's Starlite Bar. The large, airy bar at street level and thriving gaming room in the cellar distracted attention from the busy bordello upstairs. Ruth had an attractive face, according to Lil, and was soon transferred to work the reception desk upstairs.

"Just make sure you wear loose-fitting clothes and don't walk around in front of the clients and you'll be right," warned Lil.

After the initial shock, Ruth was surprised by how quickly she adjusted to the move upstairs. She had managed to cultivate a veneer, a persona even, which was impervious to the moral corruption of her surroundings. She constantly reminded herself that she was doing this for the baby, so they could be together, and that it wouldn't be forever. The other girls found it amusing that the first person the clients should lay eyes on when they entered the brothel was expecting a baby. After a while, Ruth found her condition useful because the customers lost interest in her once they noticed her increasing girth, apart from one older man.

Ali had emigrated from Turkey; he was a sophisticated-looking man in his mid-forties. He told Ruth he was a new Australian and had come to Australia to start life afresh following the devastation of war in Europe. He would loiter near the reception area, waiting for opportunities to talk to Ruth. At first, she enjoyed talking to him until he began asking to meet her after work. He was attractive, with thick, black hair which was going a little grey at the temple. He wasn't overly tall and had light skin and dark eyes which gave him a striking appearance. Ruth guessed he must do some sort of physical work; his physique was rather athletic compared to other customers around the same age. He never said anything vulgar like many of the other men but would talk about life in Australia or back home in Europe. She was almost tempted go for a meal with him but then realised he more than likely wanted something other than just friendship. Even if she were the sort to meet up with strange men, she wondered how he could possibly find an eight and a half month pregnant woman desirable.

"You leave my girl alone, Ali, she's not interested in old men."

Joyce would periodically try to dissuade him from talking to her.

"He's okay, luv," Joyce said, "probably married with ten kids and just looking for a bit of fun. They like to come to these places, no complications, the girls don't want any more from them."

Ruth puzzled at the motivations of the men who frequented Lil's. She often wondered if the regulars ever fell in love with the women they came to see, especially the ones who insisted on seeing the same one each time. Although still uneasy with working in such a place, she was grateful for their immoral ways. It provided her with a means to put money aside for when her baby was born. She knew she was being two-faced but decided it was unavoidable; her child's welfare came first.

It had been announced that a police raid was to occur, and the top-floor girls had all been sent home early before the police arrived. At one time, Ruth would have found this intriguing but she was quickly learning that hypocrisy and corruption existed everywhere, not only back home in Papua. Ruth and Joyce were walking home together after the 'raid' and had stopped to buy their supper – a big parcel of fish and chips wrapped in newspaper. As they came out of the shop with their mouths watering, Joyce grabbed Ruth's arm.

"Coppers! They're at me door. You go up here and wait while I see what they want." Joyce directed Ruth into the narrow night-soil lane which ran along the back of the street, then boldly strutted off towards the police.

"Damn!" Ruth shouted and then covered her mouth, hoping the sound hadn't travelled. She had slipped in dog excrement. Looking around for something to scrape it off, she bent down to get a twig but recoiled immediately at the severity of a snapping sensation through her abdomen. A rush of panic came over her. She leant against the wall, trying to calm herself, when she noticed a warm feeling travelling down her legs. God, no, something's happened! Managing to stifle her reflex to shout out, tears welled in her eyes; partly out of frustration, but mostly out of revulsion for the surroundings into which she would soon be introducing her child. At that moment,

Joyce returned looking pleased with herself.

"They were asking about you and Shirley, but I said I hadn't seen Shirley since her father died and I don't know you. I think they believed me. Ruth, what's wrong? Come out into the light."

"I slipped, and wet myself with the fright."

Joyce realised straightaway what had happened. "More like your water's broke, luv. We better get you home and cleaned up."

After having a warm shower, the pain seemed to go away but Joyce told her to lie on the bed anyway. Ruth accepted that the inevitable was about to happen and although initially terrified, she now experienced a sense of calm.

"When you've had the baby, Ruth, we'll find our own room and move out. After the police coming once, they might come again."

"You're right, Shirley, we'll get a room. We can say we're sisters."

"Eat your oranges; I'll bring ya some more tomorrow."

"You're a dear friend, Shirley."

"You're not bad either, Ruth. I'm going to sleep. Have to do fifteen rooms on me own tomorrow. The other girl won't be in; she fell over a bucket and twisted her ankle, silly cow."

The pain, when it returned, was immobilising. Ruth's contractions were coming regularly, but in between she recovered sufficiently to chat with Joyce. She learned of her tragic life raising two of her dead sister's children with next to no money. A child herself almost when her sister died but she eventually managed to buy her own home – all on her own, with no man for support. It gave Ruth confidence that she would also survive.

Seventeen hours had passed; the birth seemed no further along. "Gawd, Ruthy, I'm getting worried; I'm going to get Aggie from next door." Joyce disappeared.

Ruth lay there, weary but relieved; it will soon be over, she thought. After what seemed like hours, Joyce returned with her friend from next door. An elderly woman in a tatty red dressing gown.

"Don't worry, Ruth. Aggie used to be a nurse, she knows what to do," Joyce reassured.

"Joyce, you should have called me sooner. I thought she was just starting. Deep breaths, girly," the woman commanded. "Let me check what's happening." The tatty dressing gown belied an accomplished midwife. "The cord's around the neck, Joyce."

"I had no idea, Ag." Joyce looked on in horror but the wily midwife maintained her calm. Aggie's hand deftly slipped the cord over the head and out to the side. "Push, Ruth, push now, as hard as you can," shouted the midwife.

After nearly eighteen gruelling hours, Ruth finally gave birth.

"Ten fingers and toes, and feels about nine pounds; a healthy boy!" Aggie announced.

CHAPTER 7

Ruth had been pining for Tommy since the birth. She was miserable and desperately missed her mother and grandmother. Tommy should at least know he's a father, she told herself. He should be here with us. But deep down, Ruth knew the futility of these sentiments, and that made her even more miserable.

Apart from learning how to breastfeed her baby, she spent most of the following week in bed or on the settee, trying to come to terms with the significance of the birth and what it meant for her future. There would be no art school, no big christening or going home for family reunions. Above all, though, Ruth understood that her convalescence must be short-lived. Her sole means of support consisted of thirty-two pounds and ten shillings from wages and tips she had managed to save. The money at Lil's had been good, but she didn't want to return. Starting out life with his mother working in such a place would be doing her son a further injustice.

Ruth's body recovered quickly from the ordeal of the birth. Aggie put it down to being young and fit. After just a couple of weeks, Ruth was keen to restart her life and try to make a home for her son.

"Shirley, in a day or so, I want to start hunting around for lodgings. Do you still want to get a place together?"

"Of course I do. I even saw something the other day, not too far from here, with two rooms."

Ruth longed for her own place where she could set things up for the baby without being in anyone's way.

"It's a boarding house in Devonshire Street, with two adjoining rooms upstairs. Four pounds a week."

"It sounds perfect, Shirley. I found a couple advertised in the paper too. I can go and inspect them and if they're any good, you can come after work to look."

"I'm going to miss you two girls when you go," Joyce said, bending down to straighten the baby's blanket.

"We won't be far away," Shirley reassured her.

"You've always got a place to stay here; you remember that if you're ever stuck."

"We will, Joyce," Ruth said, with tears welling in her eyes. "And I'll never forget how kind you've been."

"Don't be daft, just doing what any woman would do for a couple of kids down on their luck. Oh, and before I forget," Joyce withdrew her hand from her apron pocket, "take this, luv, put it on when you're out and about. People can be mean you know."

Ruth studied what Joyce had given her. A plain gold band. "A wedding ring," Ruth said, surprised.

"Just tell any nosey parkers you're married, or a widow; either will do. Save you the shame of explaining yourself. And if they mention the littlun's olive skin and dark hair, say your husband's European."

"Thanks Joycey, I didn't think about that."

He probably is a bit darker than normal, Ruth thought. At that point, she realised her life was going to be even more complicated than simply finding a job and somewhere to stay.

The first accommodation Ruth inspected turned out to be a converted shed, basic but private, and separated from the main house by a long garden. An elderly couple owned the house. They appeared keen initially, but when Ruth decided not to heed Joyce's advice and told them she had no husband, had a baby and wanted to share with another woman, they were horrified.

Ruth had expected them to be sympathetic and was shocked by their hostile reaction; they had seemed such a benign old couple. On reflection, she probably would have reacted the same way herself twelve months earlier. But now, she was desperate to find somewhere to live. She couldn't stay with Joyce forever, and her son needed a home. When she arrived at the next house, she decided to lie; Joyce's ring was a perfect fit.

"So does your husband send money regularly?" the landlord asked.

"Yes, monthly, but I want to find a part-time job as well. We're saving for a house," Ruth reassured him.

"Well, maybe that'll be all right, unless the baby keeps everyone awake. How old is he?" The man looked into the pram, then backed away. "He's a half-caste ain't he?" he said indignantly. "Got something in him, I bet. Sorry love, you can't stay here, we run a respectable place. Try one of the boarding houses."

The door slammed shut before Ruth could think of something to say. She couldn't help noticing the disgust on the man's face as he looked at her. She could accept people being critical of her own unmarried situation, but she was furious at the man's reaction to her son. Ruth decided there and then that if that's how people were going to play this game, she would play it better. They wouldn't deprive her son of a roof over his head. Ruth's hurt and shock turned to anger; she resolved to use whatever means necessary to ensure her son had a home.

Next on her list, the Devonshire Street rooms, the ones Shirley had spotted. The clean, white Federation terrace with its manicured flower garden appeared even less likely to be welcoming, but she pressed on.

"Mrs Kyriakou." Ruth practised pronouncing one of the names she had heard at Lil's. The neatly printed notice that Shirley had spotted still sat in the corner of the window. Ruth crossed her fingers.

"Good morning, I'm interested in seeing the vacant rooms."

"Just the three of you?" the woman asked. Ruth guessed she had assumed she was married.

"Me, the baby and my sister. My husband works away in Western Australia." Many of Lil's customers worked at the mines, only to return once or twice a year.

"You'd better come up and take a look, although I'm not sure about the baby; I have a lodger who does shift work. How old is he?" Mrs Robertson peeked into the pram and then turned to face Ruth with a reproving expression.

"My husband is from Cyprus, Mrs Robertson." The apparent pride in her tone disarmed the woman.

"Oh, well, I mean he does have lovely dark eyes. I just assumed he would be Australian. I guess what you do is your business, but I wasn't expecting foreigners."

"My husband only returns to Sydney once or twice a year, and when he does, we usually go away for holidays. Rest assured, Mrs Robinson, there'll only be the three of us to contend with." Since she had started work at Lil's, Ruth had developed a talent for manufacturing alternative biographies for herself.

The walls were a pale lilac colour and spotlessly clean. At the top of the stairs stood a gigantic, Chinese-looking jardinière containing an overgrown aspidistra. The white, newly painted woodwork contrasted tastefully with the long, purple chintz curtains. It would be a dream come true to live in such a clean place and to have her baby grow up in pleasant surroundings. She hoped Shirley would like it and that the landlady would let it to them.

The rooms would be perfect, Ruth thought, as she walked home. Even the stove's out on the landing, which will be cooler in summer. So excited was she at the prospect of starting life afresh in her own place, she was on pins and needles until Shirley walked in the door.

"There are a couple of places which might suit us, Shirl. The one you found, if we can convince the woman the baby won't be any trouble, and a private hotel in MacDonnaldtown. Yours is four pounds a week and the one in MacDonnaldtown is three, but that only has one room and nowhere to cook; the toilet's outside too."

The girls decided they couldn't do without a stove, not to mention the luxury of an inside toilet, so the Devonshire Street residence won out. It was closer to Joyce's house and Shirley's work, which had now increased to four days a week. Ruth reasoned the proximity to everything would be better for her too when she found another job.

Convincing Mrs Robertson of the baby's good nature wasn't difficult once they showed her the first month's rent. They moved in the next day.

Ruth found the move bewildering at first, having little idea about caring for a baby. Being the youngest in her family, there had been no younger siblings, but she had seen the native women with their picaninnies, and Aggie had given her a list of instructions to follow. In spite of her lack of experience, she marvelled at how naturally everything came once she stopped worrying. It must be instinctive, she guessed.

"Stewart's going to be his name, Shirl. I've decided against Thomas."

"Stewart's a nice name, Ruthy. Will his father like it?"

"I hope he does, although he doesn't even know he's got a son at the moment." Ruth lost focus momentarily as she tried to imagine how Tommy might react if she just turned up and presented their son. He'd probably be as shocked as she was. "Oh well, I don't know where he is anymore, I can't even write to him at home. I'm going to find out what jobs are going tomorrow, and how much a babysitter costs."

"Don't rush things, Ruth, you aren't strong enough yet."

"I'll be okay, Shirl." Ruth pressed Shirley's hand and smiled.

Ruth felt optimistic and confident now; she was determined to find work. Like Aggie said, her body had readjusted quickly but she guessed her new found exuberance stemmed more from fear of ending up destitute than a good constitution.

Most days were spent trudging around the industrial areas pushing the old pram Joyce had given her. She called on factories mainly, hoping to find one that needed workers. There weren't any openings for married women it seemed and Ruth was wondering if she might have more luck saying she was a widow. Joyce came to the rescue again and offered to babysit during the afternoons, which freed Ruth to go job-hunting without Stewart in tow. Joyce was good at babysitting, Stewart seemed to like her, but finding someone suitable on a more permanent basis was going to prove difficult.

As the days passed, Ruth became increasingly desperate about the lack of available work but rather than feeling defeated by her fruitless efforts, she become more ardent in her search, venturing further afield each day. After visiting almost every factory and warehouse within walking distance, and completing all sorts of aptitude and ability tests, she was finally offered a position as a ceramics decorator. Her spirits soared. If she couldn't go to art school this would be nearly as good. They made a range of luxurious items such as vases, ash trays and cabinet plates, and although most of the work involved only filling in colours, they had told her that if she did well, she might be promoted to the drawing section. The job paid six pounds seven shillings a week, which didn't leave much to save but was enough to live on, at least for the time being.

The girls and Stewart settled into a comfortable, albeit hectic, routine. Joyce and Aggie worked out an arrangement where they would mind Stewart for four days a week for ten shillings each. This left one day, which Shirley wanted to do until her work became full-time.

Life finally seemed to be falling into place. The girls found living in their own bed-sit liberating and enjoyed their independence. They even had a little money left over each week once they had paid for everything. The months passed by quickly and in no time, it seemed, a special day had arrived – 25th October 1958. Stewart's first birthday, and nine months since they had moved out on their own. Ruth wanted to celebrate the double anniversary with something special.

Work at the factory finished at three on Fridays, so after collecting Stewart from Aggie, Ruth made a special trip to the butcher's to buy some corned silverside.

"I'll make parsley sauce to go with the meat, new potatoes and peas, and strawberries with cream for dessert." Stewart looked as if he understood. This was going to be the best meal they'd had for ages. Ruth beamed; she felt as though she wanted to skip all the way home.

Shirley usually arrived from work first, at around two in the afternoon, so it was unusual for her not to be home. "Perhaps she went to see Joyce. You lie there and watch Mummy make the dinner." Ruth propped Stewart up on their only armchair. Halfway through shelling the peas, she heard women's voices downstairs and then footsteps coming up the polished wooden staircase.

"Ruth! Ruthy, it's Auntie Joyce."

Ruth put down the peas and rushed to the door. "Joyce! What a surprise!" It was then she noticed the serious expression on Joyce's face. "Is everything all right?" She knew immediately that something was wrong.

"It's Shirley, luv, the coppers took her. A guest at the hotel caused some sort of raucous and the police got called. They interviewed Shirley as a witness but then they took her away."

Ruth could feel butterflies building in her stomach. "Did you go and see her at the police station?"

"Yes, I've just got back; been there all afternoon. They're sending her back to the home."

"Can they do that, after all this time?"

"Apparently they can. She went before a magistrate and he ordered her return until she turns twenty-one or her parents take her. They won't, though, not her stepfather anyway. I tried to tell the magistrate she could live with me, but he said she couldn't if I didn't have a husband or a respectable job."

"I can't even go to visit her," Ruth managed to say between waves of panic and mounting tears.

"No, luvy, you must keep going on your own now, for the baby's sake."

Joyce was right; nothing else could be done.

The weeks following Shirley's arrest proved difficult for Ruth, juggling Stewart between Joyce and Aggie and feeling guilty because they had to give up their housie-housie afternoon on Fridays. But then Mrs Robertson surprised her by volunteering to mind Stewart on Shirley's day.

"I don't mind, Ruth, he'll be company for me, only until Shirley comes back from your mother's, though."

"You're very kind, Mrs Robertson." Ruth was grateful and wished she didn't have to keep telling lies. She had told the landlady that Shirley had gone home to look after their mother who was sick. I'll tell her the truth one day, she promised herself. It made the lie seem less deceitful.

With Shirley gone, Ruth found she had to supplement her wages with some of her savings each week. No matter what she went without, they never quite had enough money. Initially, she thought she would try to live on potatoes only – fried, boiled, baked, roasted and mashed. This would stretch the housekeeping to ensure Stewart had all he needed. After only a week of this, she became ill. Ruth realised then that she needed to look after her own health better if they were going to survive. Remembering Sister Rose's stew, she made her own, making sure she saved most of the meat for Stewart. Joyce helped her with some recipes for cheap but nutritious meals and sometimes they would all eat together as this worked out even cheaper.

In spite of the financial strain, everything went relatively smoothly for the next nine months, but Ruth had learned that when things were going well, that was just the time to expect them to go wrong.

On a cold, wet, June afternoon, the charge-hand came over to the workbench where Ruth sat finishing off a pile of cabinet plates.

"How are you going with the flowers?" he asked.

"They're fine, but I'm finding the new colours don't fire as well as the others." She suspected he hadn't come to discuss the latest transfers and wondered what was coming next.

"Ruth, our sales weren't as good as we hoped last summer. You're a good worker, but the boss wants to cut the women's hours down. I've been told to reduce your roster to three days a week now instead of five. Maybe in the summer, things will pick up."

Ruth fought hard to control her reaction. Two days' less pay each week would leave her with only enough for rent and babysitting.

"I guessed you had bad news. The other girls have been talking about lay-offs for a couple of weeks now. I suppose there's nothing I can say, if you don't have enough work." She struggled to make her voice sound normal.

"I'm sorry, Ruth, but you'll be the first to get more hours when things pick up. You're one of the quickest painters."

Ruth managed a weak smile.

It was as though her world had fallen apart. As she walked home during a late afternoon downpour, warm tears mixed with icy rain; her whole body and mind were crying. Life for her and Stewart was about to become much more difficult.

Her greatest fear was losing Stewart if she were unable to provide for him. She imagined the police sending her to prison, or back to the home like Shirley, and poor Stewy being pulled out of her arms to be adopted out to strangers. When she arrived home, exhausted and depressed, Mrs Robertson greeted her.

"What's wrong, darling? Has something happened?" Ruth had no interest in talking to anyone; she was beside herself with worry. Now she was going to have to lie again, Mrs Robertson wouldn't understand her crying over losing two day's work when she was supposed to be married.

"I'm fine, thank you, Mrs Robertson; just missing my husband. I'll be fine."

"You poor thing, is he due to come back soon?" Ruth wanted to burst out crying but managed to muster sufficient restraint to maintain the façade. It was a relief when Mrs Robertson let her go. All she wanted was to be alone with Stewart, and to close her door on the world outside.

"What a mess I've gotten us into, Stewy." Ruth hugged Stewart close to her, noticing anew his sweet, milky smell. He was going on two but still had his baby ways, which Ruth loved. Within minutes, he had fallen asleep and looking down at his perfectly smooth, innocent face, Ruth realised she had to do whatever it took to ensure they were never parted.

"You must never be hurt by this damn muddle I've created," she said softly. "Don't worry, Stew, I'll make everything all right." The next day, she went straight to see Joyce.

Joyce's face lit up. "Come in, darl, I don't usually see you on the weekend."

"I need my old job at Lil's back. Well, just for a couple of nights through the week. They cut my hours back at the pottery and we can't survive on what I earn now. I've looked in the paper but there's nothing going for women, not unless you can type."

"Life's hard without a man, eh, luv? If you're sure, I'll speak to Lil tomorrow night when I go in."

"Thanks, Joyce; I don't know what we'd do without you."

"No need to thank me, honey, you go and enjoy the park with Stew. I'd come with you but me feet are aching bad today."

Knowing she was going back to Lil's, Ruth expected their Saturday afternoon in Prince Alfred Park to be miserable. She laid out a blanket for her and Stewart and noticed a clump of gardenia bushes; they reminded her of the day she and Shirley had escaped from the convent. So much had changed since then, she reminisced; it was probably good she wasn't aware how difficult things would be when they'd run away.

Lying on the grass with Stewart asleep on her arm, Ruth felt strengthened as she watched the large cumulus galleons drifting gracefully across the bright azure sky. Lil's wasn't what she wanted for herself, but at least for now, the money would ensure she and Stewart survived. If that's what it's going to take, she thought as she looked at Stewart, then that's what I'll do.

Joyce's visits to Devonshire Street usually meant something serious, but today, Ruth was expecting news from Lil.

"Come in, Joyce. I'll put the kettle on; sit down."

"He's sleeping good these days, luv, he hasn't stirred." Joyce straightened Stewart's blanket. "I don't have any good news for you, Ruthy; I spoke to Lil last night and she doesn't need anyone at the moment. When you left, she gave Rosy May your shift."

Ruth's heart dropped like a heavy weight. "I guess I was silly thinking she'd just put me back on; of course she would have found someone else when I left." Ruth tried to sound reasonable.

"She did say, though, that if Rosy or any of the girls downstairs got sick, you could fill in, but that wouldn't be regular work like, unless one of them left."

"That was good of her but I can't wait around on the off-chance."

"You know, Ruth, I saw your old admirer at work last night, Ali. He was asking after you." Joyce looked as if she were going to say something further but changed her mind.

"Go on, tell me; what did he say?"

"You're a good girl, Ruth, but life is hard and sometimes you need to make sacrifices." Joyce managed to articulate what she wanted to convey without actually putting it into words.

"So what are you saying, Joyce?" Ruth had to be sure she understood.

"He said I was to tell you he wants to help you out. He overheard Lil and me talking."

Ruth remained silent, remembering the conversations she had had with him while working on reception. And his constant requests to join him for a meal after work.

"I told him you probably wouldn't want his help, but I'd tell you anyway."

"I should be shocked, Joyce, but I'm not; maybe I've grown up a bit lately," Ruth said thoughtfully. "It might be a way out for now; nothing else seems to be working. The factories are full, I don't type, cleaning doesn't pay enough and I can't go home." She took a deep breath. "Tell him I'll let him know by Wednesday. I want to think it through." She surprised herself by the ease with which she was willing to consider the offer.

"He's one of the nicest ones who come in, luv; at least he seems that way," Joyce tried to reassure her.

The sense of optimism Ruth had experienced in the park on the weekend had turned into mild melancholy by Tuesday afternoon. Her resolve to do whatever became necessary to survive was about to be tested.

Since Joyce's visit on Sunday, the possible arrangement with Ali was all she thought about. She had only been a receptionist while working at Lil's, nothing to do with the actual sexual goings-on. To be involved in such exploits seemed humiliating and dirty. She realised she was being hypocritical after having already worked in the business. Being an unmarried mother was bad enough, but to become what to most people would be considered a prostitute was totally repugnant and foreign. In one last frantic attempt to find respectable work, Ruth ventured further afield – even travelling by train to the factories around Granville and Bankstown. But nothing came of it.

Tuesday evening arrived. Only one day to go before she had to give Ali her answer. This time tomorrow, she thought, I'll be in the worst possible situation that any woman could be in. I've become like Doctor Faustus, only worse; I'll be selling my soul for money!

Ruth went straight to Joyce's to collect Stewart after work on Wednesday.

"Hello darl, how was work?" Joyce said, as if Ali was the furthest thing from her mind. Joyce always managed to bring her back down to earth. She never focussed too much on the bad things life threw at her or others, she just dealt with them as best she could and got on with life. She seemed only to acknowledge what really mattered and didn't dwell on what she saw as incidental, however bad that might seem at the time.

"Not bad, thanks, but my feet are sore from running up to the Savoy. Mabel at work told me they were looking for waitresses, but they're paying less than half what I get at the pottery, and it's only on call," Ruth said, sounding deflated.

"Bugger of a life, eh luv? You need to find yourself a man and settle down. Oh, this came for you today. Aggie was home. A nun, of all people, dropped it off."

Ruth examined the crumpled envelope. "A nun?" She noticed the address of the convent in Ashfield. "That means they know where I am." Ruth panicked.

"She was a stocky woman with an Irish accent, Aggie said. Apparently Shirley told her I'd pass the letter on if I saw you. She said to tell you she'll pray for you and your baby."

"Must have been Sister Rose. None of the others would come all this way to drop off a letter. I wonder how she got it off the Reverend Mother, unopened."

"Perhaps she pinched it," Joyce said.

"Surely not," Ruth said, but when she thought about it, maybe she had!

On the way home, Ruth recognised the writing on the envelope. It was her grandmother's, although rather than excitement, she felt uneasy. After her father's last letter, she assumed the family wanted no more to do with her. "Probably nothing exciting, Stew," she said, putting it back into her coat pocket.

After putting Stewart down for the night, Ruth curled up on the bed, staring at the letter propped up next to the bedside lamp. Part of her wanted to forget about everyone at home, but another part longed to be reconciled. Had the letter been from anyone else she might not have opened it, but of all her family, her bond with her grandmother was strongest.

My dearest Ruth,

I'm not sure when or even if this letter will reach you, but I thought I'd send it on the off-chance.

I can't begin to tell you how sad I am, knowing you're alone on the mainland. I wanted to come and find you when I heard, but was told everything was taken care of and that I shouldn't interfere. I'm hoping everything has been taken care of and you are well.

Your father and brothers are doing fine with their new coffee crops. Your mother's passing affected Matthew the most I think. He wants to go back to the mainland to start up on his own. He kept in touch with a girl he met while at school so that might have something to do with his wanting to go. Your father is managing but he's aged a lot. As you know, he and your mother used to argue, but in a way, I think it kept them both going. Jake is a different story.

He's turned into a very angry man, and for the life of me, I don't know where it all comes from; no one else in the family is like that. By the way, that young boy you used to play with when you were little, Tommy, I think. He moved to Port Moresby apparently and met up with one of my house girl's cousins, Hane, do you remember her? Your dad gave Tommy's father's job to Sam; he said Billy was too old now. Anyway, that's all the village gossip.

Ruth, I'm not going to ask a lot of questions, I just need to know you are well. Did you keep the baby?

Well, my love, if this letter reaches you, please write back. I'm enclosing twenty pounds for the birthdays I've missed.

Gran

Ruth's attention fixed on the news about Tommy, especially the girl he had met up with in Port Moresby. She remembered that he had liked Hane when she came to Okoro with her grandmother one Christmas. Ruth experienced a rush of emotion like panic and anger all mixed together. Looking across the room at Stewart, tears traced their way down her cheeks; her chest ached, as if her heart were about to break. The pain was not so much for her but for Stewart; he would never know a normal family life and might never even know his father.

Eliza's letter helped Ruth realise she had to make the most of her life now. If she returned home, the only possible place to go would be to her grandmother's village. Seeing Tommy would be almost impossible if he was living in Port Moresby and if married, there'd be no chance at all. No, she reasoned, Stewart is better off here. He couldn't grow up in a village; he might contract malaria or some other dreadful disease, and with no schools, he'd have no education.

Ruth decided to write to her grandmother and tell her about her life, although she would have to maintain the lie about Stewart's father to ensure Tommy's safety. If only her grandmother had written sooner, she lamented, she could have asked for some money to tide her over until the pottery returned to normal. It was too late now, she realised, with the slow post, especially to the village.

By the time Ruth arrived to collect Stewart from Joyce the next day, her mind was made up.

"So, Ruthy; today's the day. I'll be seeing Ali tonight and I told him you'll have an answer for him. Did you give it any thought, honey?"

"Yes, Joyce, I've thought about little else, to tell you the truth." Ruth paused to enjoy one moment more of freedom before agreeing to the Mephistophelean contract. "Tell him yes, Joyce. I'll meet him."

CHAPTER 8

Eliza's money bought Ruth a little time; she decided to spend another week searching for proper work before taking Ali up on his offer. She was learning that life for an unmarried woman with a child was precarious and unpredictable. A couple of pounds meant the difference between retaining your self-respect and living in the gutter. The planned arrangement with Ali could be delayed, but the possibility of not finding work before Eliza's money ran out remained. To turn Ali down now and possibly alienate him would be foolish. She decided to go ahead with the meeting as planned. Best not burn my bridges yet, she reasoned.

Friday evening came around far too quickly. The rendezvous was to take place at the Savoy café. Ruth wore her best beige gabardine costume with a tubular skirt. She had bought the outfit from the Salvation Army depot to go job hunting. A conservative style, exactly the impression she wanted to convey; she steered clear of anything that resembled what the girls at the brothel wore. After dropping Stewart off at Aggie's, she walked briskly to the café. In the rush to get the meeting over with as soon as possible, she ended up arriving almost an hour early.

The Savoy had an entirely different clientèle to the hotel of which it was part. The moderate prices attracted office workers who boarded in town during the week and it provided a welcome alternative to pub counter meals. As Ruth walked into the dining room, she wavered; it was packed. She spotted an empty side cubical and promptly sat down only to notice it was self-service. Embarrassed, she had to get up again and walk to the servery. She took a tray and moved along the shiny, stainless steel counter. Her mouth watered as the lady handed her a plate of fish and chips, but she declined the bread and butter to save twopence halfpenny. Parched from walking, and her gathering nerves, the sturdy silver teapot and matching milk jug were too hard to resist so she put them on the tray.

Once over her initial nerves, she began to enjoy the meal, savouring every piece of the thick, flaky white flesh. Dining in such pleasant surroundings made her question again the need to be taking such drastic measures in her quest for survival; nothing seemed quite as grim as when sitting at home, worrying. While pouring her tea, she contemplated leaving, but a man's voice interrupted her ambivalence.

"May I sit down?"

Ruth glanced up to see Ali with a cup of coffee and a biscuit on a tray. He wore a well-cut sports jacket and, with his tan and Brylcreamed hair, appeared younger than she remembered. His formal way of speaking hadn't changed any; she guessed he must have had a well-spoken English teacher back in Turkey.

"How are you?" he smiled and sat down opposite.

"I'm well, thank you. I was just having dinner." All the rehearsing of conversation openers was now redundant.

"I'm pleased you agreed to meet me, I missed you when you left work."

"I found another job after I had Stewart, which suited me better until they cut my hours."

"Yes, Joyce told me about the hours, and I thought here is my chance to see you again!"

The man's enthusiasm caused Ruth to feel a little guilty. She almost wished she could reciprocate. "I must be honest, Ali, since agreeing to meet you my grandmother has sent me some money so my circumstances now aren't as dire." At least not for a couple more weeks, she thought.

Ali's expression didn't change. Maybe he didn't understand.

"The original reason for our meeting," Ruth ventured, "no longer exists but I thought I'd meet you out of courtesy as I had already made the arrangement."

"Whatever the reason, I'm happy. I liked you when we first met. Your bright green eyes and big smile. Unlike the other girls, you seemed lost and I wanted to make sure you were all right. My wife and children are in Turkey, so I've got no one to look after here."

Ruth thought he seemed a kind man, and his level of sincerity caught her off guard. She wasn't sure how to respond.

"Finish your tea and we'll go for a drive," he said.

"A drive? I'm not sure I want to go anywhere." Ruth's sense of self-preservation kicked in.

"Don't worry, Ruth. Joyce knows me; she knows we're meeting so I'm not going to kidnap you. We can go to Bondi and watch the sea."

Ruth relaxed as she began to realise that Ali wasn't the mercenary monster she had assumed, well at least not so far. His perfect manners impressed her, and he genuinely did seem concerned about her well-being. Thinking of him as an insurance policy had been easier when he hadn't been such a real person. His directness did surprise her though, especially when talking about his wife and children. He maintained no pretence of courting. Whatever they were, or would become, he was very married. The thought of a wife and two children waiting for him caused Ruth a degree of uneasiness, but she reasoned that so long as they remained just friends, their association didn't appear overly immoral.

Ali did most of the talking. Ruth was too far out of her depth to say much. He explained how he no longer worked in the mines and now gambled for a living. Reasonably successfully too, Ruth thought, if his shiny, new Chevrolet Bel Air were anything to go by. He genuinely did seem quite decent; but she wondered how long this would last.

The drive out to Bondi in such a fancy car was exciting until 'Mack the Knife' came on the car radio causing Ruth to grow tense again. They pulled up along the esplanade and stared out to sea. She couldn't help but marvel at the sunset, a frieze of golds and reds against a faded, ice-blue backdrop.

"Have you been here before, Ruth?"

"No, only to Manly on a school excursion." Ruth felt more confident now. "Let's go for a walk."

"Of course, let's walk along the most beautiful beach in the world."

"A beautiful beach maybe but not *the* most beautiful," she said, smiling.

Ali looked curiously at her. "You know of one more beautiful?"

"Yes, Ela beach in Port Moresby. I grew up in Papua." Ruth enjoyed his interest.

They chatted and walked for a good couple of hours. He spoke a lot about himself and his life before the war. Ruth found the conversation interesting but her mind often drifted to times she had spent with Tommy, when they walked along the riverbank together at Okoro.

They stopped for a soda, by which time the sun had gone down. Ruth wanted to be back with Stewart. She felt guilty leaving him with babysitters when she wasn't working. Ali agreed to take her back to town.

When the car pulled up outside the Savoy, an awkward silence came between them. As she went to get out, Ali caught her hand; she jumped but didn't pull away.

"I've enjoyed our evening, and seeing you again."

"I did too, Ali. The change did me good. Thank you." Ruth withdrew her hand.

"Maybe next Friday we can meet again?" Ali appeared hopeful.

Ruth hesitated, but then she agreed. "Yes, I'd like that. Shall we meet here at the Savoy again?"

"We'll meet here, but then I'll take you somewhere better for dinner." He smiled.

Ruth couldn't help wondering if his kind demeanour were a ploy or whether he genuinely was as pleasant as he appeared. She did enjoy his company, and that was the reason she agreed to see him again; it just seemed the natural thing to do.

"I'll see you next week then," she said, and left.

Ruth arrived home just after ten-thirty. She put Stewart to bed and made herself a cup of tea. She went over everything that had happened. It turned out differently to what she was expecting; she enjoyed meeting him. She wondered if that made her even worse; although they didn't do anything. Ruth tried to justify the liaison, to diminish the inward sense of defilement she experienced. She wondered if she had further betrayed her family by seeing Ali. Even though nothing physical had occurred yet, she had initiated the arrangement and was in the process of following through. Should the need arise.

As if to ease her guilt, she went to her handbag for a hanky to wipe off the pillar-box red lipstick Joyce had cajoled her into wearing. She didn't even want to wear make-up, she remembered reprovingly, as if make-up made the situation worse. Her purse was already undone; she lifted the flap to discover a folded ten-pound note. The reality of her evening out dawned on her immediately. *He still thinks he's buying me!* She felt sick, offended and angry. But the more she thought about the evening, and it being her only possible means of maintaining a home for Stewart, her anger began to dissipate into something less threatening – a blend of embarrassment and resignation. She did enjoy going out with him, more like two friends, she concluded.

At the pottery on Monday, she was still distracted by her evening with Ali. She wondered if any of the girls at Lil's liked the men who paid for their services. It was confusing; the meeting had started out, at least in her mind, as a business arrangement but then it metamorphosed into something entirely different. What that was exactly played on her mind all the way to collect Stewart.

Turning the corner into Joyce's street, a police car pulled out from the kerb right in front of the house. Her heart raced. She sidled along the footpath on the other side of the road, pretending to be a passer-by, but she couldn't contain her distress.

Her thoughts raced out of control. If they've taken Stewart, I'll give myself up to get him back, but what if they put me in prison? After what seemed like ages, the car turned the corner. She ran across the road and banged on the door.

"Come in quickly, Stewy's fine," Joyce reassured. "He's next door with Aggie. The coppers came; they're looking for you. Your father got the Port Moresby police to list you as missing."

Ruth's worst fears were being realised. She couldn't stay in case they returned. "I'm going, Joyce," she said in a panic, rushing around to collect Stewart's things.

"I don't think they'll be back today, luv. I told 'em I've never even met you, let alone had you staying here. I'm a good liar when I have to be, but I'm not sure what the nuns told them."

"I'll go home and think. Dad said not to write to him, but maybe I should. I'll ask Mrs Robertson to take care of Stewart tomorrow."

The police visit had cast Ruth's life back into turmoil. As soon as life settled down, something new happened. She decided that she should write to her father, but after reading his last letter again, she couldn't bring herself to. She hoped Eliza would receive her letter quickly and convey to her father that she was well. Hopefully Eliza wouldn't give him her address.

She worried herself into such a state that she couldn't leave the house. Her imagination ran out of control, she even thought she heard the police downstairs talking to Mrs Robertson. When Friday arrived, she had to force herself to go and meet Ali; perhaps talking to him might help put things into perspective.

"If you want to be safe, Ruth, you should move away and start afresh somewhere else."

Ruth knew Ali was right. Her grandmother had her address now, and with the police involved, she might be forced to give it to them.

"I know, perhaps I could get another job out in the suburbs."

"Of course you could, but I said I wanted to help you. I haven't changed my mind," Ali said.

"Yes, I understand that, but I need to get a job to support myself. I don't want to live off you. In fact, I have your ten pounds here." She put her hand into her purse, but Ali caught her wrist.

"That was a gift for you and your son. Keep it." He relaxed his grasp.

Ruth hesitated but his expression turned serious. "Well, I guess if you insist, just this once." The whole situation made her feel uncomfortable, but she tried to be gracious. "The hardest thing for me will be getting accommodation. I'm unmarried with a child which makes it almost impossible to rent anything. I can't say that I blame them; I probably wouldn't want to let my place out to someone like me either. If I had a place to let out."

"Ruth, listen to me. What you've done isn't so bad. I'm sure if circumstances were different you would have married the father."

Ruth remembered Tommy, and although she had been angry with him since receiving Eliza's letter, a surge of tender feelings brought a lump to her throat.

"Yes, I would." She swallowed hard, forcing her mind to let go of Tommy. "For now, though, I have to deal with the mess I've got myself into. You're very understanding, Ali. I don't expect this is the sort of evening you had in mind." Ruth smiled. They both laughed.

"If you like, I'll come with you to find a place. We can say we're married. I won't live with you of course; it'll be your home. I might have to put in a few appearances, though, to look good."

"It would certainly save a lot of trouble lying to everyone to convince them I'm reliable and decent. Let me think for a day or two. I'm not even sure where I could go."

The prospect of moving again and pretending to be married to Ali made her miserable. Her entire life had become a lie. She thought she might be better off just staying where she was and hoping the pottery work increased. She could save up and move later on. If Joyce and Aggie came to the flat to babysit then there would be no way the police would spot her.

After a couple of uneventful days, she had convinced herself that she didn't need to move. Her procrastination went on for nearly three weeks, and in spite of Aggie and Joyce not wanting to go to the flat to babysit, life almost returned to normal.

Ruth was beginning to enjoy her work at the pottery again, and spending time with Stewart on her days off. She had also reconciled herself to the strange relationship she was having with Ali. She appreciated spending Friday evenings with him, going to new places and dining out on food she had never even heard of before. The company of a man brought a much needed balance to her life; she wished she had met him under different circumstances.

Walking against the cold wind to Aggie's robbed Ruth of what little energy she had left. The pottery had had a rush job on and it was almost seven o'clock by the time she turned the corner into Joyce's street. Just a few doors away from her destination, she noticed a flickering orange glow in the window and wondered why Aggie had candles burning. The street lights were on, so the power hadn't been cut. Looking more intently, she became aware of smoke drifting upwards from around the window. She ran towards the house, there were flames inside.

Banging on Aggie's door proved useless. She grabbed a loose brick from the wall and frantically smashed out the window. As she climbed inside, she was met by a wall of heat and smoke. Pulling the curtains down off the rail, she half covered herself, then seized the smouldering rug from the floor and threw it onto the blazing settee so she could get to the sitting room door. The smoke stung her eyes; her throat and chest burned as she coughed. She ran into the hallway and down to the bedrooms. Aggie was in the first room, asleep.

"Aggie, wake up!" Ruth screamed, not waiting for a response. She charged into the next room, searching for Stewart.

Screaming Stewart's name as best she could with the choking fumes blocking her airways, she continued desperately through the rest of the house but couldn't locate her son. She pulled all the bedding from the linen closet and rushed back to smother the flames. Stewart had to be there somewhere. Someone started hammering on the front door, just as Joyce appeared from the back.

"Stewart, I can't find Stewart!" Ruth shouted hysterically. Joyce grabbed Ruth's arms to get her attention.

"He's safe; he's with me, asleep. Where's Aggie?"

"Oh, God, thank God! Oh, Joyce, I thought… Aggie's in there, I think she's asleep." Ruth ran towards the front door; she had to see Stewart. As she put her hand on the doorknob, the door exploded open and the hallway filled with men. One burley fireman took her arm and pulled her outside.

"Come on, luv, this way."

"I've got to get my baby!" Ruth struggled free and ran next door.

Another fireman led Joyce and Aggie out to the kerb while the rest proceeded to hose down the sitting room.

"Oh God, the baby!" Aggie screamed. Joyce grabbed her to stop her rushing back inside.

"Stewy's fine, Aggie, I brought him in to me when I came home; you were asleep."

"I must've dozed off, I don't remember." Aggie dissolved into tears.

Ruth knew the commotion would alert the police.

"Joyce, I'm going home. Stewart and I are both in one piece. I'll come around tomorrow." She surreptitiously disappeared amidst the confusion and gathering onlookers.

Once home, she flopped onto the armchair but the smell and taste of smoke were still thick in her throat. Her chest was raw, and she noticed a blistering burn on her hand from Aggie's door knob. Curdled blood had soaked through her skirt from a gash to her leg. It must have happened while climbing through the window, she guessed. Holding Stewart tightly to her; she studied his face and a contented warmness came over her which momentarily obliterated the pain of her cut and singed body.

"So long as you're okay, my angel, that's all that matters."

By the time of Ruth's next meeting with Ali, she knew she had no choice but to take up his offer. The incident with the fire had been a close call, and now Eliza's money was running out.

"Tell me what happened," Ali said.

"Aggie had been drinking and dozed off. It was sheer luck Joyce came home early and took him in with her. I'm just as much to blame, though. I knew she drank. If I hadn't gotten us into this mess, I wouldn't need anyone to look after Stewart."

"I think the sooner we find a place, the better. I'll be free tomorrow. We can check out what's available. You can be Mrs Nesin for the day." Ali smiled.

Early the next morning, Ruth was more optimistic as she sat in the comfortable front seat of the Chevrolet. Despite their unconventional relationship, she was grateful to Ali; he seemed more like a friend or older brother. She guessed, in time, he would be calling in his debts, and although the prospect bothered her, it didn't seem anywhere near as shocking as it had originally.

They stopped at the Savoy for a cup of tea and to go through the to let section of the newspaper. A house not too far out of town sounded just right; close to a train station and within walking distance of the industrial areas along Parramatta Road. They called the agent for an appointment and had to go to see them straightaway.

Ruth could sense Ali's affront as they spoke about the property. The real estate agent was patronising and obviously had a problem with migrants. The whole process was belittling; almost having to apologise for oneself. Still, she decided, being 'married' to a foreigner was a preferable predicament to being an unmarried mother. At least he hasn't slammed the door in our face, she thought, thankful that Ali was doing all the talking and not her.

They inspected one property but discovered an infestation of German cockroaches, which were next to impossible to get rid of. The second house they viewed was the Federation bungalow that was advertised. It had a decent size yard and was much cleaner. Located in Croydon, it was close to a train station and the paintwork and lino appeared almost new. The backyard contained a hoist and the laundry even had a boiler. Ali drove back to the agent to sign the lease before anyone else applied. Stewart had already discovered the back garden and played contentedly in the grass. Ruth tried to act positive but inside she was concerned about the cost of the rent.

She was still trying to work out if she could afford the house when Ali returned. Apart from the rent, moving into a proper house was exciting, she was happier than she had been for a long time.

"I've taken care of the lease," Ali said.

"You're a kind man, Ali, but I'm worried about the rent and how I'll manage."

"Let's sort everything out first and then we'll worry about money. I've paid a month in advance, so there's no hurry."

"I hope it hasn't left you short."

"I must get back to town now." He ignored Ruth's money concerns.

"Oh, okay," she said, surprised and a little disappointed that he wanted to rush off. She rather enjoyed being Mrs Nesin. "Yes, all right. I must give Mrs Robertson notice, so I might get a lift back with you if that's all right."

Arriving home, she realised how miserable the place looked. All her sad memories rushed to the fore – Shirley getting caught, work cut-backs, the police and, more recently, the fire. She made herself a cup of tea and sat on the floor with Stewart.

"Well, Stewy, I just have to find a way to pay the rent now."

The following Thursday, Ruth caught the train back to Croydon to check what she needed for the house. The train station was next to a small row of shops and luckily one of them sold second-hand furniture. As she rummaged through the stock for something reasonable, she spotted a bed that had an innerspring mattress, a cot, wardrobe, two armchairs, a mat for the sitting room and a small dining table with four chairs.

"I can give you those for twelve pounds, delivered, Madam. Local delivery, though."

"I'll take them; we're not far up the road." After shelling out the twelve pounds, Ruth realised she had been impulsive. If she couldn't find work, or if the situation with Ali didn't work out, she'd be camping on the sidewalk with all her new furniture.

"Well, we're stuck now, Stew. It has to work out," she said as they walked up the road.

To celebrate, they stopped at the milk bar to buy a paddle pop each. They savoured the cool lolly-ice as they walked slowly home. The delivery van pulled up just as they arrived.

The two hefty men who came with the truck had the furniture indoors within minutes. After they had left, Ruth rearranged everything to make the rooms look more homely, but no matter where she put things, the house still looked bare.

"Look what Mummy has here!" Ruth took two parcels from the pushchair. She tore off sheets of crumpled newspaper to reveal two floral vases and held them up with glee.

"They've got firing cracks, but they don't leak. Come on, let's go and find some flowers." They went out into the garden and collected two handsome bunches of gladioli mixed with watsonias.

"It's a start anyway, Stew; at least we're away from the police."

Ruth left her job at the pottery and spent every morning looking for a new one. The next-door neighbour offered to mind Stewart, and once the woman gained her husband's permission, it was arranged. Being married certainly made finding accommodation easier, but it was a disadvantage for securing employment. Ruth discovered she had to revert to Miss Madison if she wanted a job. Married women, it seemed, didn't get a look-in. Fortunately, a lot of large factories were located in the area, and finding work turned out to be relatively easy. The wireless factory in Ashfield was taking on people to keep up with the demand for television sets. Ali didn't agree with her working right away, but she was adamant, she didn't want to be dependent on him. Although in many ways, that was already the case.

Ruth and Ali increasingly spent more time together. Instead of going out for meals, Ruth would cook dinner at home and afterwards they would go for a walk or listen to *Blue Hills* on the wireless. When Ali pressed her for more than just friendship, physical intimacy seemed more like a natural progression than anything indecent. Ruth found she enjoyed the closeness and feeling of being cared for. Ali proved to be a gentle lover, and in spite of their unusual arrangement, she was convinced it was lovemaking and not just sex. Their time together provided her with a release, it was the only time she was able to let go and forget the mess which had become her life.

Gaining work at the factory had been a godsend, she enjoyed soldering wires into television sets, and the speed of the assembly line gave her little time to think about anything else. The other girls were friendly, and although the work was fast and repetitious, it wasn't difficult. With bonuses, she made eleven pounds in her first week.

"Yeah, not bad, darl, but those lazy bloody men over there get half that again," said Val, a widow supporting a family of four.

"It doesn't seem fair, but my last job paid less," Ruth smiled back, unsure if she had said the right thing.

"I don't know, you young girls should 'ave more fight in you," Val said.

Ruth smiled. Her reclaimed unmarried status must have been convincing.

"I'm not that young you know, Val. I had my twenty-second birthday a few months back."

"Gawd, love us and save us, you'll be left on the shelf if you're not careful." Val chuckled.

Walking down the street on the way home, Ruth spotted Ali's car parked outside the house. As she got closer, she saw he was leaning on the car, smoking. He appeared older than usual today. She had never thought much about their twenty-year age difference. He still had his striking looks, not overly handsome but not unattractive. It was his caring nature and masterful way of dealing with life that she found attractive.

"You aren't due until tomorrow," Ruth said, pleased to see him all the same.

"I'm going to be busy, so I thought I'd come over today."

"Oh, how come you're busy on a Friday?" Ruth quizzed. Their Friday evening rendezvous had been as regular as clockwork, until now.

"Something's come up, that's all. We can talk later."

"I don't have anyone to take care of Stewart tonight."

"He can come. I've got everything we need. We'll go to the drive-in and for a walk along the beach afterwards. *Gigi* is on; you wanted to see that when it came out."

"I'll go and fetch Stewart from next door."

In the excitement of going to *Gigi* and with Stewart playing-up through most of it, any chance to talk to Ali about the sudden change in his plans didn't present itself. He never mentioned anything again, so Ruth let it go.

Eight months had passed since moving into the house, and although Ruth judged her life to be less than ideal, it had become manageable and stable. Stewart's third birthday seemed to arrive out of the blue.

"I thought we might go to Luna Park and have a picnic, if you're agreeable," Ruth said.

"Sounds good. I'll go and get some petrol and come back." Ali appeared distracted; Ruth wondered if she'd overstepped the mark with the Luna Park plan. He did rather like to be the one who arranged everything.

"If you'd rather not go or prefer to go somewhere else, that'll be fine." Ruth tried to appease him.

"No, Stewart will enjoy the park." He turned to leave but turned back to Ruth. "We must talk later. I wanted to talk to you a few months ago. But I have to now."

"Oh, would you rather tell me now?" Ruth suspected something ominous. Butterflies began to churn in her stomach.

"No, later will do," he said.

They arrived at the park in high spirits although Stewart started to cry when he saw the immense, laughing face at the entrance. They had fairy-floss and toffee apples and decided on hot dogs for lunch in place of their picnic. Ali looked bored by the time Ruth and Stewart had laughed their way through the Mirror Maze, so Ruth insisted they all go on the River of Caves together. This seemed to cause Ali to withdraw into himself even more. She was worried, but had to make an effort to appear light-hearted so Stewart would enjoy the day. When they found a place to sit for afternoon tea, conversation between Ali and Ruth had almost dried up. She could stand it no longer.

"Ali, can we talk about what you want to tell me? We've hardly spoken since we got here."

"We should finish eating first and wait for Stewart to fall asleep."

"I can't eat. I need to know what it is. I've never had a more uncomfortable day."

"I'm sorry, Ruth, I just thought we'd enjoy the day first."

Now, Ruth definitely expected something unpleasant.

"You know, Ruth, I thought if I paid for your company everything would be easier, no complications, for either of us. We didn't end up doing it that way, though, did we?

"No, and I didn't want it to be that way. It was difficult enough accepting your gifts of money, especially when I got the house. I'd never have taken anything if I'd not been stuck."

"What I wanted to tell you Ruth is that my wife and children will be arriving next week."

Ruth experienced a sudden sinking sensation. She couldn't speak.

"I know it's a shock, but things don't have to end. We can still spend time together."

Ruth knew her life was about to be torn apart again. She had always known this day would come, but she hadn't been concerned in the past, he rarely ever mentioned his wife and children. Maybe their being in another country made them less real. A torrent of emotion began to build within her.

"I can't talk about it now, Ali. Would you take us home, please?" Ruth was determined not to burst into tears, even though that was what she wanted to do more than anything else.

CHAPTER 9

After driving home from Luna Park in silence, Ruth told Ali she didn't want to see him again. Ali agreed easily, and although his agreement was no surprise, his complete lack of protest hurt. She wondered if he ever had any interest in her other than as a paid companion.

Unlike when she and Tommy had parted, there were very few mixed feelings and emotional turmoil. Ruth realised that although she had grown close to Ali over their time together, she wasn't in love with him. The only thing that really worried her was losing his emotional support and having another adult around for company.

The initial dread of being alone soon gave way to a sense of self-reliance. Ruth discovered she could function remarkably well on her own, and rather preferred having only Stewart to consider. Her work at the factory seemed secure with plenty of overtime, and the babysitting arrangement worked out well. The sitter had a son the same age as Stewart, so he enjoyed going next door each day, although he was always thrilled when Ruth called to pick him up.

Ruth's life had become stable and predictable since moving to Croydon. She now felt as though she was providing her son with a proper home, although birthdays and Christmas were difficult with no other family at hand to share the celebrations. Christmas this last year looked like it would be a disaster with no Ali, but Joyce and Aggie saved the day by arranging a festive lunch and inviting some of Joyce's elderly neighbours. They doted on Stewart and delighted in his amusing antics, which made the day a happy one. Ruth loved Joyce and Aggie, but she worried about not having any real relatives for Stewart to become acquainted. Luckily, her relationship with Eliza had started to regain ground. Her address no longer needed to be a secret now that she was over twenty-one. No one could force her to do anything, so writing to her grandmother wasn't a problem, but she remained estranged from her immediate family.

"Stew, the postman's been!" They raced each other to the mailbox to remove the protruding letter. "It's from Gran." Ruth showed Stewart the blue and red airmail envelope with the green, *klinki* ply mill stamp on the front. "Klinki is a pine tree, darling; they use it for making plywood."

Stewart examined the little picture, fascinated.

"When you're older, I'll take you to meet Gran and show you where I grew up."

Eliza's letters often contained a small sum of money which Ruth ferreted away for emergencies. With Ali no longer in her life, the small nest egg provided a sense of security. Ruth knew she couldn't rely on Eliza should any major difficulties arise, with the mail to and from Papua still as slow as ever. Besides, she wanted to be responsible and self-sufficient now. What she needed most was to find a way of saving money on a regular basis until her nest egg was sufficient not to have to live in fear of financial emergencies. When her workmate Val told Ruth about her younger brother moving into lodgings, she had an idea.

"My boys share a room between 'em, so I couldn't squash any more in. You're close to the station which is handy. You'll need to get another girl, though, or the neighbours will be talking."

"Sounds like a good idea; I might put a note up at the milk bar," Ruth said.

"You can always try, luv, see what happens."

That evening, Ruth drafted a small advertisement and, on her way to work the next morning, asked the shopkeeper to put it on his noticeboard. A shilling didn't seem much to pay if it meant finding a boarder to help with the rent.

On the following Saturday, two men called at the house, which disappointed Ruth as she had specifically asked for a lady. She informed them that the room was taken. Every weekend turned out the same. The only female who enquired was an older woman wanting a paid housekeeper position.

"Four weeks now, Val, and all I've had is men."

"Half your luck, luv!" Val laughed.

"You know what I mean." Ruth smiled, half-disapprovingly.

"You left yourself open, darl, but yeah, it's a bugger. What'll you do then, maybe take on a bloke? P'raps if you got a real oldie no one would think anything."

"I don't know, it's 1961 but people seem stuck in the Dark Ages."

"That's 'cos you're young. We all think people are behind the times when we're young."

Despite Ruth's better judgement, she decided to show the room to a man on the following Sunday. Ralph appeared to be in his early forties; he lived in Katoomba with his elderly mother. He seemed respectable; he worked as a signalman at Central Station and needed somewhere to stay during the week. He said the three pounds ten shillings a week that Ruth wanted was reasonable, so they both agreed there and then.

"Do you think I should meet your husband before moving in?"

"No, he works away but doesn't mind me making decisions when he's not here." Ruth remembered Ali hadn't collected any of his belongings, so the façade appeared feasible.

"Well, if it's okay with you, Mrs Nesin, I'll move in next Saturday."

"Sounds fine to me. There's a single bed and a wardrobe, but you're welcome to bring anything else you need."

Happy with the arrangements, she planned on using the deposit to buy Stewart a more comfortable bed and put his old one in the spare room for Ralph. The only thing that troubled her now was the need to lie again. She was one person to half the people she knew and someone else to the other half.

The situation got off to a good start after the initial discomfort of having a stranger in the house. The extra money helped with the rent and Ruth managed to save a few pounds each week. Ralph returned home to his mother each weekend, which particularly suited Ruth; she could relax and enjoy time alone with Stewart.

The new male boarder intrigued Val and some of the other women at work. "So how's your fancy man going, darl? You haven't mentioned him for a while."

"He's not my fancy man, Val, but he's well. He pays his rent on time and goes home to his mum after work on Fridays."

"What's he like, then?" Val almost salivated for some juicy gossip.

"Well, if you must know he's about forty, going bald, about five-ten with a big stomach."

"Not Rock Hudson, then?" Val quipped.

"Goodness no, he's got broken teeth in the front and smells sweaty most days."

"Gawd, luv, no wonder he goes 'ome to his mum on the weekend. Any of the neighbours said anything yet?"

"No, I told the lady next door that my cousin had moved in, and I haven't mentioned anything since."

"You wanna hope they don't bump into each other when you're not home or you'll come undone," Val said with a grave expression.

"They won't; he's gone at the crack of dawn and doesn't come home until late."

"Oh, well, just watch yourself, luv; nothing worse than nosey neighbours."

Ruth looked forward to weekends; she and Stewart would go out and do things together and then come home and work on little projects without anyone around. Saturdays were their favourite; they would dress up nicely and go to the shops. Once the grocery shopping was finished, they would go to the milk bar for elevenses. After milkshakes and sharing a jam and cream match, they would go to feed the ducks at the park with bread crusts that Stewart had saved through the week. At almost four now, Stewart was becoming much easier; he could walk most of the way home, so Ruth was able to fill his pushchair with shopping.

"Stew, post!" Stewart ran to collect the letters from the box. They put the groceries away and sat down to read Eliza's news. "Come on precious, sit with Mummy and we'll see what Gran has to say."

A thicker letter than usual, but Ruth's attention went straight to the middle of the first page.

...from what I've heard, that Tommy of yours has become involved with troublemakers in Port Moresby who are pushing for independence. Rumour has it that the UN is coming back again next year because they aren't happy with the progress...

Ruth experienced a mixture of emotions. She was happy that Tommy had become involved with a cause likely to bring a better deal for his people, but she worried; political things could be dangerous and independence would happen eventually regardless of what people did. Even her father expected such a change and had often complained to her mother about how bold and cheeky the workers had become compared to how they were before the war.

The next bit of news concerned Matthew, who had married. He and his wife lived on the mainland at a place called Carradale.

...Okoro bought him out, so he had enough money to buy into a sheep property. Well, we paid him his share. As you know, ownership is between your father and me, although he manages everything. Speaking of your father, he hasn't come around any yet, still can't bring himself to write to you. I told him what a fool he was being but of course he doesn't listen to me. I think Jake influences him a lot. These days Jake seems to think he's the boss as much as your father.

Matthew coming to live on the mainland delighted Ruth, but her grandmother's obvious disinclination towards Jake continued to be a puzzle. She guessed something had happened between them, but she'd never had an opportunity to ask, or rather, didn't think it her place to ask.

Ruth spent the following few weeks wondering whether to write to

Matthew and finally decided she would; if he didn't reply, at least she'd know where she stood. Surely he's gotten over everything by now? Although, she realised, her situation would appear ten times worse back home; it was still behind the mainland in terms of people's views and outlook. Ruth decided she could manage without her family, but deep down she wanted some sort of reconciliation for Stewart's sake.

"You seem deep in thought this evening."

Ruth jumped. She hadn't heard Ralph walk through the door. "Oh yes, just reading a letter."

"From your husband?"

His intrusiveness surprised Ruth. "No, from my grandmother."

"You don't have a husband, do you?" Ralph's eyes narrowed.

"What?" Ruth thought she had misheard.

"I said you ain't got a husband, have you?" His tone became hostile.

Shocked by his outburst, she couldn't get her words out. Then she became angry. "What I have and don't have is my business." She stood up and went into the kitchen. As she nervously wiped down the clean draining board, she wondered if she'd imagined what he'd said.

"You shouldn't leave your letters around for people to read. Looks to me like some kanaka called Tommy is the boy's father." Ralph had followed her into the kitchen.

"How dare you refer to Stewart's father in that manner and you had absolutely no right to go fishing in my room. My letters are in the dressing table; you must have gone through it."

"Come on, Ruth, I don't care who you are or who the boy's father is, I just don't want all this bullshit."

Ruth could smell alcohol on his breath. "You've been drinking. I don't want to talk about it anymore."

"No, I guess you wouldn't. I'm going to bed, I'll go home tomorrow instead of today." He went to his room.

Ruth was still trembling with rage and disbelief when Stewart came in from the garden. "Come on, Stew, let's go out and get some fish and chips."

While walking home, she decided that Ralph had to leave. His aggressive outburst made her almost too frightened return home. If not for work, she would have gone to stay with Joyce until he moved out.

The next morning, Ralph had left for Katoomba. Ruth spent the rest of the day preoccupied. How dare he, the gall of him! Apart from indignation, she was still furious. By Sunday morning, she had calmed down sufficiently to write to Matthew. No sooner had she begun than there was a knock at the front door. Checking from behind the curtain, she recognised the car. It was Ali.

"Come in, what a nice surprise! Take a seat." What good timing, she thought; they hadn't seen each other since the day out at Luna Park.

"I'm surprised you're so pleased to see me after our less than affectionate goodbye," Ali said with a smile.

"Of course I'm pleased; must be over six months." Ruth's throat constricted, and her eyes welled up with tears.

"Ruth, what's the matter?" Ali put his arms around her.

"I'm only being silly. I'm upset. I had a disagreement with my boarder."

"You've got a boarder? Another girl, I hope."

"Actually, it's a man. Only one lady answered the advertisement and she was after a job. He seemed all right until last night." Ruth explained what had happened, although she didn't reveal precisely how hostile Ralph's behaviour was.

"You should have told Joyce to get some money from me if you needed help."

"I'm managing. I wanted to put something aside for Stewart in case anything cropped up."

"So you've thrown him out?" Ali growled.

"I will when he comes back; he's gone to his mother's for the weekend."

"I'll get rid of him for you."

"No, I'll speak to him. I want the pleasure of telling him to go." That wasn't the real reason; she just didn't want to fall back into depending on Ali again.

"Always Miss Independence, eh? Well you make sure you let Joyce know if you need any help."

Ali's visit cheered Ruth up, and Stewart always brightened when Ali was around. His visit helped take the edge off the incident. By the evening, Ruth knew exactly what she intended to say to Ralph and looked forward to having the house to herself again.

"I don't know, Stew, life's hard, eh darl?" she said, tucking Stewart into bed. In spite of everything, the day had been productive. After Ali had left, she and Stewart weeded the garden, got all the washing done, and dry, finished her letter to Matthew and packed her lunch for the morning. As she walked over to lock the back door, she heard footsteps. Quickly latching the door, she went to check the windows. As she reached the front door, a key went into the lock. Damn, he's back early, she cursed to herself. The door opened and there stood Ralph, glaring with a strange expression on his face. She thought he was an ugly man with his inflated opinion of himself and broken front teeth. Apart from being overweight, his excess weight concentrated around his middle, like a barrel.

"You're back early," she said, unable to hide her annoyance. He wasn't due until after work on Monday evening.

"Sounds like you don't want me here." He closed the door and sauntered past Ruth towards the kitchen. He took a bottle of Resch's Ale from his bag and poured a glass. The glass must have been warm; the froth overflowed down the side and plopped onto the lino.

"I'd rather you didn't drink in the house, Ralph, and tomorrow I think you should leave." The hairs on the back of her neck prickled. She had been confident initially but now she was nervous; it was an effort to keep herself from shaking.

"Now I wonder why you want me to leave? Maybe something to do with your refo friend who drove off a while back?" he said, with a self-satisfied smirk.

"You've been sneaking around spying on me; it was you I heard outside!" She tried to contain her anger, Stewart was asleep.

"Good job I did, otherwise I wouldn't know what sort of a slut

I'm boarding with." His face morphed into a distorted sneer. "You've got a kid to some kanaka, and now you're rootin' refos."

Ruth was frightened now, the pit of her stomach turned ice-cold from panic. Ralph moved towards her and grabbed her arm. He twisted it up her back so she couldn't move. He glared into her face, so close she could smell the partially digested beer on his breath. The pores around his nose were large and black from dirt; his bulging eyes looked red and fierce.

"Why are you so quiet, Mrs Nesin? Can't think of anything to say?" He pushed her backwards, pinning her against the bench-top with his torso. Ruth tried to push him off with her leg, but he pressed closer. He put his mouth over hers and with his free hand ripped her blouse open. He briefly let go of her twisted arm, and she smacked him in the side of the head. He retaliated by pushing his knee into her stomach. She managed to free her arm again and grasped a handful of his hair and began to twist it. He punched her in the chest and as she bent over, winded, his other fist pounded into her face.

Ruth's mind was working independently of the assault on her body. She tried to think of things she could do to get him away from her, but they were all too risky. If she managed to run out into the street, he would be alone in the house with Stewart. If she screamed for the police, she could be dead by the time they arrived. If Stewart woke up and came in, he'd be in danger. Escape wasn't possible. She decided her only option was to go along with him and pretend she was enjoying it; hopefully, he'd finish and fall asleep, or leave, and Stewart would be safe.

Blocking out who he was, she forced herself to grind her crotch on his knee and make sounds as if aroused.

"Ah, I knew you liked a bit of rough, you mangy slut. I'm going to root you senseless, whore!" Ralph undid his trousers and then lifted Ruth's skirt. He pulled the crotch of her knickers to one side and forced himself into her. Ruth was numb; her mind had disconnected from what he was doing.

After a short silence, she realised he was no longer trying to beat her into submission but now focused on relieving himself. Her ploy was working. Her disengaged mind retreated into a dark, safe place, where half-formed memories of people in her past drifted in and out of focus interspersed with images of Stewart, curled up safely in his bed asleep. Ruth realised Ralph had finished; he was doing up his trousers.

Lying on the floor, looking up at the ceiling, Ruth became aware of something obstructing her vision. She reached up; it was her cheek, swollen out of shape as if dislodged from her face. Exploring inside her mouth with her tongue, she detected the salty taste of blood. Her bottom teeth had punctured her lip. Gradually, as feeling returned to her beaten body, she became aware of a stinging warmness in her pubic area; she had lost control of her bladder. Her head began to throb and a sudden wave of nausea swept over her. She was cold and started to shiver. The front door banged closed. The house was suddenly quiet.

"Stewart!" she called, dragging herself to the bedroom. She pushed his door open; he was safe, curled up and still asleep, as she had imagined. She staggered to the bathroom to clean herself, to rid her body of Ralph's disgusting odour.

After scrubbing her skin until the shower water turned cold, she went to her room and collapsed on the bed.

"Mummy, Mummy, wake up!" Stewart pulled at her nightie.

The harsh sunlight caused her eyes to squint, which set off a severe, shooting pain in her cheek; then the terrifying memories rushed back. Trying to sound as normal as possible while keeping her face buried in the pillow, she tried to reassure Stewart.

"Mummy hurt herself last night, precious; my face is all puffy, so don't get a fright."

"I want to see." Stewart lifted the sheet which half covered Ruth's head. "Oh, Mummy, it's sore." He hugged his mother. "I'll cuddle you better, Mummy."

Someone knocked on the door. Ruth's body reacted, as if preparing for another onslaught. *God no, he can't be back.*

"Ruth, are you home?" a man's voice yelled.

"Uncle Ali, Mummy!"

"Go and open the door, Stew." Ruth daren't move; the pain in her ribs was excruciating.

"Jesus Christ! What's happened? Lie back." Ali eased Ruth into a more comfortable position and propped her head up on the pillow. "I'll get a flannel."

He reappeared a couple of minutes later with a bowl of Dettol in warm water and began gently washing her face.

"Mummy hurt herself, Uncle Ali." Stewart pointed to the swelling.

"How about you go and play, while I wash Mummy's face? I'll get you some breakfast in a minute."

Ruth was reassured by Ali's presence, she knew Stewart was safe now; Ralph would be dead if he returned while Ali was here.

"Don't say anything, Ali; I know what you must be thinking." She didn't want to be reminded of Ali's earlier offer to get rid of Ralph.

"I was right though, eh?"

"You were." Ruth cringed as the antiseptic penetrated the tear in her lip.

"When I've given Stewart something to eat and got you cleaned up, I'm taking you both to Joyce's. No disagreeing or arguing; you're going. I'm not leaving you here."

"I won't argue; I can't stay here now, he might come back." Ruth felt defeated.

"That bastard's stuff is still in the spare room. What time does he come home?" Ali asked.

"About six usually, but I don't think he'll be back today."

"I'll feed Stewart and then we're off. Tell me if there's anything you want to take."

It seemed like only minutes before Joyce and Aggie were helping Ruth through the doorway.

"Gawd, love us, I hope someone teaches that mongrel a lesson. Come on, luv, sit yourself down, I'll put the kettle on," Joyce said as she disappeared into the kitchen.

"Stewy's having a nap, luv," Aggie said while tucking a blanket around him. "I've got some lamb stew in my fridge. He can have it for lunch when he wakes up. I'll mash it up to hide the carrots."

"Thanks, Aggie, he's only had a bit of cereal." Ruth's shock abated slowly, but aching pains continued to gnaw at her body.

"Here, I've put extra sugar in; help settle ya down." Joyce passed Ruth a mug of steaming, sweet tea.

"Did Ali leave?" Ruth asked. She didn't notice his departure with all the attention she was receiving.

"Yes, darl, had some business to take care of, he said." Joyce had that look as if she knew something but wasn't telling. Ruth half guessed he would go back to the house in case Ralph turned up. Normally she would have objected, but now she was glad.

"I just hope Ali is all right," Ruth said.

"Don't you worry about Ali; he knows how to look after himself," Joyce reassured her.

"Well I hope he kills the bastard," Aggie added.

"What are you going to do about work, luv? You want me to go in and talk to them?"

"Would you mind, Joyce? I can't go in looking like this."

"Leave it to me. I'll go in the morning."

By the end of Ruth's second week of nursing her wounds, most of the swelling and bruising had gone. It wasn't the physical assault so much that tormented her, but her total powerlessness to do anything to stop him. And the fear of being pregnant. Aggie said she could send her to an old doctor friend if necessary, but for the time being, she found it easier not think about that. Her main worry was her job.

Joyce informed the factory supervisor that Ruth had fallen down a flight of stairs. He was sympathetic and said he would hold her job open. Although relieved at this news, Ruth had been toying with the idea of moving away from Sydney and starting afresh somewhere else. Nothing she had done since coming to Sydney had turned out well or lasted for very long. Not only was she living from pay packet to pay packet, but rents were so high that she couldn't afford to live anywhere decent without having to take in a boarder. The horror of Ralph's attack also kept repeating itself inside her head; if he hadn't left when he did, she kept thinking, Stewart might have been hurt.

While laid up recovering from the assault, Ruth had the opportunity to take stock of her life. She realised that she had been living from one crisis to the next and was at the mercy of whatever came along. If she was going to ensure Stewart had a secure future, she had to act quickly, and now seemed as good a time as any to make the necessary changes.

Flicking through the *Sydney Morning Herald*, the range of jobs available now for women came as a surprise. Back home in Papua, few women worked outside the home, but here in Sydney things were very different. She glanced down the page to a large advertisement for trainee nurses and wondered if she would be accepted. The more she thought about it, the more her interest piqued.

On the following Monday morning, Ruth squeezed into her beige costume and caught a bus to the Prince of Wales Hospital, where she completed an application. Three weeks later, a telegram arrived, calling her in for an interview.

"You look smart, luv, that blue brings out the auburn in your hair," Joyce said, appraising Ruth's navy pencil skirt and matching tailored jacket.

"I couldn't wear the same outfit twice. Aggie gave me some dye, one of those new cold water ones."

"That old costume came up a treat. Make do, mend and dye should be the new motto!" Joyce laughed. "Here, luv, you can borrow this." Joyce handed Ruth a peacock coloured silk scarf.

"It's beautiful, Joyce, thank you, I've never seen such rich colours." Ruth carefully tied the scarf elegantly on the side of her neck. "Not quite Grace Kelly but close enough." She smiled into her compact, making sure she had no lipstick on her teeth.

On the bus to the hospital, Ruth had to keep taking deep breaths to quell her butterflies. She tried to imagine every possible question so she had answers ready. When she arrived, she joined a row of nervous girls sitting on a bench along the corridor. When they called her name, she walked in confidently. She had learned over the last few years how to just 'act the part' when in a difficult situation.

As it turned out, the interviewers didn't ask many questions. Their only concerns, it seemed, were her medical history and why she wanted to become a nurse.

"I've always wanted to be a nurse and help people, ever since I was little." The two interviewing sisters looked pleased, so Ruth didn't bother adding the real reason, that being a nurse would provide steady work and an opportunity for her and Stewart to move away from Sydney. The only other in-depth questions related to childhood illnesses she had suffered and then the interview concluded. Ruth couldn't wait to get back and tell Joyce and Aggie.

"So how are you going to manage, living in the nurses' home with Stewart?" Joyce asked, looking puzzled.

"I said I'm a widow with a child to support. If I told the truth, they wouldn't have considered me. They didn't question it," Ruth said.

"I suppose if they're as short of nurses as they say on the wireless, they might not be too bothered about checking references."

"One of the other ladies is married, although her children go to school," Ruth added.

"Funny how times change, luv. No one used to go out to work after they got married. I guess the war's changed a lot of things."

"I'm glad it did, Joyce, otherwise I'd be stuck in a factory for the rest of my life." Ruth smiled.

"Here comes Aggie. She'll tell you plenty about being a nurse, eh, Ag?"

Ruth and Joyce watched as Aggie collapsed into a tired bundle on the faded floral armchair.

"Strewth, it's hot today! How are you, luv?"

"Better now, thanks, Aggie."

"That's good; best to put it behind you now. I realise it's hard, but if you don't, it'll eat away at you. You've got Stewy to think about. I just hope Ali gave him a good sorting out. A nurse, eh? Where will you go?"

"I haven't been accepted yet, but if all goes well, Lincoln or Wagga Wagga."

"An old friend of mine lives out at Lincoln, Martha Jones; we served in Malaya together."

"I'll pay her a visit if I get there, Aggie, say hello for you."

"Yes, you do that. She'll babysit for you if you pay her something. We're all as poor as church mice since we came back, hardly got any compensation."

Only a week had passed when a letter arrived from the hospital. Ruth's application had been successful and she was to be posted to Lincoln Base hospital. She jumped up and down with joy. They were all thrilled, but after a few days, the reality of her new adventure hit home. Although strangers really, Ruth didn't realise how sad she would feel at the prospect of leaving Joyce and Aggie. In many ways, they had become her family.

The sombre drive down to Central Railway Station took only a few minutes. Everyone was subdued, even Aggie, who always had something to say about the length of skirts getting shorter and shorter. Even the long grey platform looked sad, with just a few people getting ready to board.

Ruth had mixed feelings; she was pleased to be going, but incredibly sad at having to say goodbye. If Joyce hadn't taken her in, she would probably be back at the home and have been forced to give up Stewart. And Aggie, if it weren't for her know-how and swift intervention at the birth, Stewart might have ended up dead. And Ali, as odd as their relationship was, he had been there for her during tough times.

Through welling tears, Ruth gazed at the small gathering waiting at the carriage door. Joyce had organised the farewell party: Aggie, herself and Ali to drive. Momentarily, Ruth's perception shifted and she sensed that same surreal feeling that she had experienced at her mother's burial; like participating in a movie of some kind, half real, half dream. She knew nothing would ever be the same, from this point onwards.

"Well, luv, don't forget to write and let us know how you're doing," Joyce said, through her tear-soaked handkerchief.

"You be careful, Ruth, and if you get stuck, let Joyce know so I can help." Ali held Ruth's hand. Almost a shake.

"I've written to Martha, so she'll be expecting you to visit; don't lose the address." Aggie bent down to plant a big kiss on Stewart's cheek.

"You've all been so very kind. I promise to write." Ruth and Stewart disappeared into the carriage.

As the train pulled out of the station, the small party waved goodbye. Ruth waved back but could barely make out who was who through her tears.

CHAPTER 10

The first few months in Lincoln were gruelling and hectic. In addition to finding suitable accommodation, getting used to hospital shifts, looking after Stewart and studying in the evenings, Ruth missed Joyce and Aggie. In spite of this, though, she was determined to make a success of her life.

When Martha Jones told Ruth her eyesight had gone and she would be unable to mind Stewart, she was about to despair, but then Martha's daughter, Joan, quickly came to the rescue. A middle-aged woman, Joan had a tribe of children of her own. Stewart took to her bright, jovial disposition straightaway, which dispelled Ruth's reservations about leaving him with yet another stranger.

Apart from Joan's babysitting offer, the only good thing to happen in those first months was the return of Ruth's menstrual cycle; she could now finally try to put Ralph out of her mind. Aggie had been right about the ordeal having the power to consume her if she dwelt on it, so she made a conscious effort to focus on other things when the memories began to intrude. She knew, however, that the terror of that day would never leave her.

A prosperous town, Lincoln had become the main centre for stock sales and other business in the far west of New South Wales. The size of the place surprised Ruth, with its wide streets and beautiful park just across from the station. The only drawback had been the heat, but she soon acclimatised and actually found the dryness preferable to the humidity of Sydney. Always tired and having little time with Stewart made life a drudge, but she maintained that the move away from Sydney had been for the best.

Working as a trainee nurse turned out to be an exhausting vocation. One ended up with all the ghastly jobs and was ordered around like a skivvy, but Ruth managed. It wouldn't be that way forever, she kept telling herself.

"Nurse, would you dress the wound in cubicle seven? You can go for lunch afterwards," Sister commanded, before disappearing into the next cubicle.

"Good afternoon, how are you?" Ruth said, observing the male patient who had had an infected burr wound lanced.

"I'll be right, once I get home; doesn't hurt much now, just a bit sore," he said.

The man's face was obscured as he was lying on his stomach. Ruth tried to make small talk while cleaning the infection site, but her patient didn't seem interested.

"All done, and with the antibiotics, you should be fighting fit in no time," Ruth said, catching a glimpse of his face. "Oh!" she exclaimed, staring at him until she realised how rude she must appear. "Sorry, forgive me; I thought I recognised you."

"No worries, darl, maybe you're thinking of me dad or brother; they've been here before."

When the man left to collect his prescription, she was more convinced than ever that she knew him from somewhere. It played on her mind for the rest of the afternoon until she picked up Stewart.

"Hello, Joan; has he been any trouble?" Ruth collected him religiously, fifteen minutes after her shift finished, the time it took to wash her hands, change her shoes and briskly walk through the park to Joan's.

"As good as gold. I let him fall asleep in the pushchair so he wouldn't have to wake up to go home." Joan was in her late forties and had lived in the country all her life. She had a matronly figure hidden behind her well-worn apron. She probably had a pretty face when young, Ruth thought; she had the deepest blue eyes, framed by lovely long lashes. Her husband worked away for extended periods of time, shearing. If he drank his wages, which happened all too frequently, there would be no food money, so the babysitting arrangement helped sustain both women and their children.

"I'm off all day and night this Saturday, so I'll bring him back around four on Sunday?"

"That'll be fine, love. You have a good rest. Don't know how you manage those long shifts."

"Case of having to, I suppose. Ah well, see you Sunday."

It was a warm night as she walked home. The hotel patrons had spilled out onto the footpath to catch the breeze. "Gawd, Stew, we've got to walk past that lot." Workmen celebrating the end of the working week. "If only they wouldn't call out. Come on, Stew, let's get a move on." She pushed Stewart along, as if in a hurry, hoping they would ignore her as she passed.

"'ow ya goin' luv?" An old man sitting on the pub steps glanced up at Ruth.

"Evening, ma'am, nice night, eh?" said a younger one, doing a better job of sounding sober.

Ruth half smiled and kept walking.

"Excuse me, Sister! You just finished work?"

The voice sounded familiar. Ruth took her eyes off the pavement, only to see the mystery patient with a beer in his hand, smiling. "Hello, Mr McGrath. Yes, I'm on my way home, and you should be too! Didn't Sister tell you not to drink with the penicillin?"

"Only having the one, luv. Helps the digestion." His disarming smile was almost convincing.

"Well, you'd better make it your last, or you'll be back at the base."

"Maybe that wouldn't be such a bad thing." He eyed Ruth with a devilish grin, making her uncomfortable.

"Goodnight, Mr McGrath." In a flummox, she pushed Stewart along even harder, making sure she looked where she was going so as not to trip.

Arriving home after a long day always filled Ruth with a sense of joy; only Stewart and her together, in their own quiet house. As tired as she felt, it was a good tired. Her life had direction now, and all the hard work had a purpose.

After putting Stewart to bed, she had a shower and made herself a cup of tea. On the back veranda, she flopped down onto her only household luxury, a padded easy chair, and took the redirected letter from her apron. It was from Mr Matthew Madison.

Dear Ruth,

Great to hear from you, Sis, what a surprise! I'm married now and own a sheep property out at Carradale, it's called Carraroona. We stayed in Sydney for our honeymoon; I had no idea where you were staying. I'm glad I moved here. I hated it at home with Jake and Dad so involved with their coffee 'empire'. You know Jake, he thinks he owns the place; no one else gets a look in. Still, he's welcome to it; I have all I need here. Next time I'm in Sydney I'll look you up. It would be good to visit and catch up properly. Write back soon,

Matt.

And that was all! Ruth stared at the miserly eight lines which comprised her brother's first contact after five years. At least he wrote back, she thought, deciding to write and tell him that she was no longer in Sydney. The letter was typical of Matthew, very matter-of-fact, no animosity or probing questions. She guessed that must be what happens when people grow up, no one cares about what has happened in the past. Well, apart from her father, she remembered, puzzled more than hurt now at his continued refusal to be contacted.

It was a clear night, and although it was getting quite late, Ruth was mesmerised by the stars and bright, almost full, moon. I wonder what sort of farm Mr McGrath works on, she thought.

The next six weeks were the hottest Ruth had ever experienced, either on the mainland or back in Papua. The temperature soared into the hundreds and remained there until one morning she awoke to no sun. Drawing back the curtains, the sky resembled an inky-black cauldron.

"Come on, Stew, let's get dressed and out before the rain hits."

They had only made a hundred yards or so before the downpour started. A few scattered drops at first, making large, dark blotches on the ground, then the pace quickened causing a cacophony of metallic hammering as the rain hit the corrugated iron roofs.

Ruth arrived at work, soaked. "Good morning, Mrs Anderson, how are we today?" Ruth asked, feeling a little sorry for the woman who had had no visitors since her gall bladder operation.

"I'm good, now the rain's come. I thought we wouldn't get rain this year but just look at it!"

Ruth glanced towards the open window. "Yes, it's been a tinderbox these last few weeks." The distinctive smell of bush rain drifted in through the window; wet, red earth laced with aromatic eucalyptus.

The change in weather brought an almost palpable change in the patients; they had become talkative and cheerful. Ruth's mood also shifted. A sense of release, a certain optimism, as though some oppressive burden had been lifted and replaced with a newfound sense of hope.

It was almost lunchtime when Ruth finished the beds. She agonised over whether to go to the canteen or brave the rain to go shopping. She hadn't been able to afford a fridge, so food shopping had to be done almost daily.

"Nurse Madison!" Matron interrupted her deliberations.

"Yes, Matron?"

"You need to go to Outpatients straightaway. A Mr Casey for you, something to do with your son being ill…"

Leaving Matron in mid-sentence, Ruth ran; her panic was so intense, her legs almost gave out.

"Joan sent me up to tell ya Stew's got a temperature and looks a bit crook," George half smiled.

"God, I thought he might have had an accident."

"Sorry to scare ya. I think he's coming down with something, you know what kids are like."

"Thanks for coming all the way up in the rain, George. I'll ask Matron if I can leave early. I should take him to the doctor."

143

"He'll be right till you get 'ome; if he gets any worse, Joan'll take him."

"I thought you were at Wirrambeena?"

"The rain, luv; too wet for shearing. I'll be 'ome annoying Joan for a week or two," he said with a laugh.

"Tell Joan I'll pick him up as soon as Matron lets me go."

Luckily, Matron had been in a good mood all day, not having had any emergencies. Ruth hurried as best she could down the road against the wind. The previously dusty, unpaved footpath now flowed into the street, turning it into a large brown stream. A shortcut through the park would be the answer, she thought.

"Bugger!" she shouted, cupping away water from the puddle in which she stood. Her foot had sunk into the mud and came out without her shoe. After thrusting her hands into the slush to retrieve it, she decided to trudge back across to the street and walk under cover of the shops.

"Hey, you're getting wet!" a man's voice called loudly from behind.

Ruth half turned to compliment the man on his observational powers, when she realised he was the septic burr patient. She nodded in acknowledgement and kept walking; he ran to catch up to her.

"I'm sorry, I can't stop. I have to take my son to the doctor."

"Sorry to hear he's sick. Let me give you a ride; my ute's at the corner." He pointed.

"He's at the babysitter's, and then I want to take him up to Dr Dempsey." Ruth had no intention of passing up a lift. If Stewart was sick, the last thing he needed was to be out in this downpour. Mr McGrath appeared a decent sort, and Lincoln was a country town after all, you never read about bad things happening out this way. They got into the car.

"I'm not a Sister yet, by the way, I'm still in training." Ruth tried to make light conversation.

"Jesus! Still training and they had you practising on me!"

She thought he was serious for a second, but then he laughed; they both laughed.

"Here," Ruth pointed, "the weatherboard house. I'll run in and get him." She wanted the man to stay in the vehicle, so she wouldn't have to explain who he was; but she needn't have worried. George came rushing out with the pushchair and quickly offloaded a hot and sleepy Stewart into Ruth's arms.

"G'day, Lachie," George said. Apparently the two men knew each other.

"G'day mate, just being a taxi driver for the Sister here. You get rained out?"

"Yeah, been raining on and off for a week out at Wirrambeena, set in now."

"It's a bugger out that way in the rain. Anyhow, mate, better get the Sis' and her bub up to the quack."

George shoved the pushchair under a tarpaulin on the back.

When they arrived at the surgery, only one other person was waiting. Ruth wanted to thank Mr McGrath for the lift so he could go, but Stewart was already sitting comfortably on his knee.

"My daughter got sick last year, tonsils. Been right as rain since she had the op."

"You've got a daughter?"

"Sure do, my little princess, Jessica, all of eight. Only the two of us now since Evelyn passed on."

The poor man, Ruth thought, not knowing what to say apart from being sorry to hear about his loss. The doctor then called Ruth and Stewart into his room.

"I'll give you a ride back." Ruth didn't have time to agree or refuse.

"Well, Mrs Madison, he has an ear infection and it's caused his ear drum to burst. Nothing much to do now apart from clearing up the infection and keeping him out of draughts." So much for being a nurse, Ruth thought, annoyed with herself for not picking up on what was wrong with her son. She thought he just had the grizzles.

"I told ya he'd be right, didn't I?" Lachlan said, looking pleased.

"You did, and I'm sorry I caused you so much inconvenience, Mr

McGrath." Ruth wanted to go home to be alone with Stewart.

"Call me Lach, or Lachlan, Mr McGrath's too formal. You're not causing me any inconvenience either, let's get you both home."

The rain had slowed to a constant drizzle by the time they reached Ruth's small, rented cottage.

"You've been a big help, thank you, Lachlan…" Ruth intended to go straight in, but she hesitated.

"I'll be in town until the rain dries up a bit. Want to meet me for dinner one night?" Lachlan asked.

"Goodness, I might have a husband waiting for me indoors." His forwardness was a surprise.

"You aren't wearing a ring!"

Ruth wished she still had the one that Joyce had given her in Sydney.

"No, I'm not, you got me there," she half smiled. An awkward silence prevailed while she struggled to find something to say. "I'm working all week but thank you for offering. I really must get Stewart in now."

"Okay, Sister, you go and look after the boy. I'm sure we'll meet again before I leave."

The rain continued off and on for another two weeks. Many properties were waterlogged, and some of the outlying villages were in flood. The farm workers and shearers stayed on in town until the ground dried sufficiently to return to work. In spite of the inconvenience, rain was always welcome in the bush, unlike in Sydney, where everyone complained.

When the rain did eventually subside, Ruth returned to having lunch in the park. On this particular day, however, there seemed to be a grasshopper invasion; they were everywhere. As she turned to walk away, she spotted Lachlan coming towards her, waving. She was unconvinced this was another coincidence; he had 'just happened' to be at the park during her lunch-break three times already this week. He said he still had business in town, but she wondered how much actual business he managed to do.

"Ruth, what are you up to on the weekend? I want to take you out for dinner."

"I'm working all day Saturday, and my brother will be visiting for a couple of days." Matthew had telegraphed to say that he was coming to Lincoln to pick up a new ram. "I haven't seen him for a few years." Ruth didn't want to appear rude by saying no to Lachlan again, especially after him being so helpful when Stew was ill. "Perhaps you'd like to call Sunday afternoon? We're having a bush picnic in the garden."

"Grouse! I'll bring some chops." Clearly the invitation delighted Lachlan. Ruth guessed he viewed it as progress from lunches in the park.

When Saturday arrived, Ruth and Stewart waited anxiously for Matthew's utility to pull up out the front. Ruth experienced a combination of exhilaration and dread; she was thrilled at the prospect of seeing him, but after the disgrace she'd brought upon the family, she was apprehensive. She wondered what sort of awkward questions he might ask, but then realised Matthew probably hadn't changed much and would more than likely carry on as if nothing had happened.

When the car pulled up, they both rushed outside to meet him, and all her fears and reservations melted away. There he stood, her brother, a grown man, tall and filled out in the shoulders. He had a bronze suntan and was almost handsome, Ruth thought, but he still had the same quizzical frown she remembered. He was as happy to see her as she him. He was visibly moved when Stewart kept calling him Uncle Matthew; he had never been an uncle before.

It wasn't until the evening, after Stewart had gone to bed, that the conversation turned to Ruth's forced exile.

"I'm sure if you'd written home, someone could've done something." Matthew was shocked to hear of what she had endured. Some things she kept to herself.

"Well, Dad told me never to write to anyone until I had everything sorted out, which meant getting rid the baby, but of course I couldn't do that. I guess he tried to help in his own funny way by letting the nuns send me to the convent. I accept that I did the wrong thing by everyone, but I'd never part with Stewart."

"I'm glad you kept him too, people can't go giving kids away. Must have been damn hard on your own, though."

"I made some good friends; they helped."

"You're better off here on the mainland, Ruthy. You know what it's like at home with all their old-fashioned ways."

"I know, but I'm surprised Dad hasn't come around yet."

"I'm sure he would but with Jake yapping in his ear all the time, he's probably confused. Jake's gone a bit loopy lately. He's obsessed with Okoro, thinks people are trying to take it away from him."

"You mean he thinks I'm some kind of threat?"

"You, me, the locals, anyone who has an interest."

"Surely he wouldn't be so mercenary as to stop Dad from writing to me. I never had anything to do with the running of the place, even when Dad and I were on speaking terms."

"More to do with ownership, I think, like who'll get it when Dad and Gran eventually pass on. Anyway, not my concern now; they bought me out and I have my own place here."

Ruth could tell Matthew was happy now that he was out of Jake's shadow. He had come into his own now, married and running a property. Jake's paranoia still bothered her; she wondered if her mother's mental problems might be genetic.

Showing Matthew around Lincoln made Ruth realise that her life wasn't so much coming back together as being recreated. It was a matter of learning to fuse the new with the better parts of the old, especially her relationship with Eliza, and now Matthew. Maybe I can never restore my life to how it used to be, she thought, I'll just have to create a new one.

Sunday, Matthew's last day in town, and Lachlan was expected over for the backyard picnic. More than a little uncomfortable at the idea now, Ruth wondered what Matthew would think of her inviting over a strange man whom she didn't know. Especially after confirming that Stewart's father really was someone she had met in Sydney on the way back to school. Tommy's safety remained a major concern. Still, having made the arrangements with Lachlan, there was little she could do.

Lachlan arrived on time with the promised chops and some beer. After the introductions, the men went out to rake the coals and put the meat on the griddle. Stewart was in his element having other males around. He had a terrific time rolling around on the grass and getting thrown up into the air. Matthew took to Lachlan just as easily; they were both farmers and shared many of the same interests. The day turned out to be one of the best times Ruth could remember.

"Last two beers, who wants one?" Ruth held up two cold bottles of Resch's dinner ale. At that moment, she froze. Looking at Lachlan as he glanced up from the table, she realised from where she knew him. The train trip to Sydney, when returning home for the holidays.

"What's up, Ruth?" Lachlan said.

"I just realised who you reminded me of. Remember, I said I recognised you from somewhere? I met a man on the train to Sydney on my way home from school once. He said he came from Collabine and was going to see his son's wife in hospital."

"Bill? Was that his name? December '56?"

"Yes, William." Everything fell into place. Lachlan was the son whose wife he was going to visit.

"So you met me old man; what a small world!"

Ruth didn't want to get into any details of Lachlan's wife's illness, it wasn't the place, so she quickly changed the subject. "How is your father?"

"My old man passed away a couple of years back now."

"Oh, I'm so sorry." Ruth wanted to kick herself for asking.

Lachlan must have picked up on Ruth's discomfort and guided the conversation away from his family. "There ya go then, Ruth. I'm not a stranger anymore. You knew me dad! Now me and the little fella here are going to finish off these chops before the flies cart them off."

Ruth felt differently about Lachlan now, he was no longer a complete stranger. Having met his father somehow afforded some respectability to their friendship.

Matthew left early Monday morning with his prize ram sitting up proudly in the cage on the back of his utility. Lachlan had also left Lincoln early to return to his property, Bryliambone, and Ruth, reluctantly, went to work. In many ways, her world had changed that weekend. Since running away from the convent she always believed that one day she and Stewart would return home. She realised now that the home she had always envisaged was nothing more than an outdated memory.

"Maybe what Matthew said was right, Stewy. You'll be five this year; I need to decide where home is going to be." Ruth hugged Stewart, but he squirmed. "I guess you'll be too big for cuddles soon, eh? Come on; let's get you over to Auntie Joan."

With no more rain for months on end, the only opportunities for Lachlan to come into town were provided by breaks in the farm calendar. Whenever he did manage to get away, he would spend most of his time with Ruth and Stewart. They had grown comfortable with each other, both having had sufficient time to heal their past wounds.

In spite of the long breaks in between visits, their relationship had proven to be enduring. The distance suited Ruth; her reluctance to become seriously involved was never challenged while most of his time was spent at the farm. It had nothing to do with not liking him; she did. He was caring, understanding, funny, mature, established and attractive. Not handsome in a movie star sense, but solidly built with a strong jaw line and thick, shiny, dark brown hair. Wholesome looking. No, the problem didn't lie with him; it had more to do with Ruth's own opinion of herself. She still partly blamed herself for Ralph's assault; she guessed if she had behaved differently around him, things might not have become so ugly. Not that she could actually pinpoint anything she had done, it was just a feeling that she must somehow be partly to blame. Another thing that kept playing on her mind was what Sister Rose had drummed into her about men not wanting to marry 'second-hand' women. Ruth believed this; it made sense.

April, halfway through autumn and the weather was still hot and dry. Ruth and Stewart were to meet Jessica at the weekend and Stewart was beside himself with excitement. Ruth became increasingly tense as the day approached. It was Lachlan's suggestion that they should meet, but she couldn't help wondering if the meeting would change the pace of their relationship. Until now, she was comfortable knowing that she held the reins of the relationship, but meeting Jessica was a significant step, and one she hadn't initiated.

"They're here, Mummy." Stewart jumped down from the window and ran to the door.

Ruth's apprehension had disappeared by the time she reached the door to greet them. "And this pretty little girl must be Jessica." Ruth gave her a gentle hug. "This is my boy, Stewart, Jessica; shake hands, Stew." Ruth couldn't help noticing the pride in Lachlan's face, he glowed as he watched his daughter. She wondered if her own father had been as proud of her when she was young.

"I thought we'd go to the Bushman's Carnival over the river," Lachlan said.

"That'll be exciting. Stew's been talking about it all week." Ruth wanted to go too, she had never been to a carnival before, and all her patients had been saying how much fun they were.

Lachlan was already dressed for the day with his moleskins, boots and Akubra. Ruth thought he looked like an American cowboy when she first saw him wearing his hat but was now accustomed to the way men dressed in the country. Stewart had made such a fuss about the hat that Lachlan had bought him one of his own.

The event turned out to be a memorable occasion for Ruth; they all thoroughly enjoyed themselves and the weather was perfect, sunny with just enough breeze to keep the flies away. Ruth was fascinated with the cattle and the skill of the riders, and the children fell about in hysterics at the antics of the clowns. Ruth couldn't help noticing how much Stewart and Jessica enjoyed being with each other. For the first time in eighteen months, she almost called in sick so they could all spend Sunday together. But she didn't. She rushed off that evening in time to start her night shift.

Ruth hadn't seen Lachlan since the carnival and although it had only been a few weeks, she missed him. She had missed him before but never so soon after a visit. On returning from work to collect Stewart, Joan invited her in for a cup of tea and some freshly baked scones, which she was just taking out of the oven.

"God, they smell nice, Joan." Ruth's eyes lingered on the fluffy golden delights with the butter melting into pools quicker than Joan could spread.

"Ruth, I've known you going on two years now and I'm worried about you. All you do is work and spend your spare time with Stewart. You should go out with friends and meet people."

"I don't like leaving Stewart. Besides, I've been out with Lachlan. We went to the carnival not so long back."

"Yes, I know. So what's happening with you and Lachlan? I can't work it out."

"Goodness, Joan, you're too nosy!" Ruth smiled.

"I know, but I'm stuck here all day with six kids, seven, if you count George; I rely on other people for excitement." They both laughed.

"I didn't really take him seriously until a couple of months ago. Well, maybe until I met Jessica a few weeks back. I think I was just glad to have someone to talk to, and a man to visit and play with Stewart. At the carnival he started talking about the four of us in a way he hadn't before. I thought perhaps we should see a bit less of each other."

"Jesus, Ruth, why ever would you want to see less of him? He's a good man, not to mention a good-looker with his height and lovely dark hair. I wouldn't want to let one like that get away, if it were me."

"He is a good man," Ruth acknowledged. "I didn't want to lead him on at all, but then for some inexplicable reason I asked him around for dinner when my brother was here, and things sort of carried on from there."

"Sounds like fate to me, especially after you met his father."

"You think so, Joan?"

"Take my advice, Ruth. He's about as good as they come."

Ruth knew Joan was right, but Lachlan's goodness had never been the issue.

As the weeks passed, Ruth's reservations about becoming involved with another man waned. She had begun to embrace the notion of building a new life for herself and trying to put the old one behind her. If Stewart was to have a proper home, then she needed to stop living in the past.

The wheat stripping season had arrived and Lachlan's visits to town had become less frequent. In his absence, Ruth became acutely aware of the loneliness that had taken over her life. Increasingly, she found herself anticipating his visits, but she acknowledged it wasn't just out of loneliness. She cared deeply for Lachlan; they had a special understanding, something she put down to the losses they had both experienced. When he came into town now, he always brought Jessica. The four of them seemed to have been practising being a family for some time, although no one actually said that. It came as no surprise then when Lachlan raised the issue of marriage.

"So how come you've left the crop half stripped?" Ruth asked, concerned.

"Well, I didn't really; my workers do the actual stripping. I do the carting mostly."

"Oh, I see." Ruth didn't see; she wasn't expecting him for two more weeks at least.

"How long did you say before you finish your nursing?"

Something's plainly wrong with him today, she thought. "Well, as you know, I'm enrolled now, so that leaves about another year to eighteen months before I can go for registration."

"Quite some time then, if you go on to become fully trained."

Ruth couldn't help noticing the silly expression on his face, sort of like an amused puppy. His big brown eyes were playful, yet he appeared serious; nothing about him seemed right today. Ruth was about to ask the real reason why he came and why the sudden interest in her nursing, when he took her completely by surprise.

"You should leave, now you've finished the first part. You'd be much happier on the property, I reckon."

Taken aback, she wasn't entirely sure what he meant, but he appeared serious now. "So what are you saying, Lachy? I'm not following you at all today."

"I want you to be my wife, Ruth. Will you marry me?"

Ruth dropped the tea towel. Her mind refused to process anything and went blank for a second. She was about to ask if she had heard him properly when he took her into his arms.

When her brain had recovered sufficiently to utter a coherent reply, she looked him in the eyes. He undoubtedly was everything Joan had said. "Yes, Lachlan, let's get married."

The weeks up to the wedding sped past in a blur for Ruth, what with work, arranging invitations, deciding on buttonholes for the men, her bouquet and buying the dress.

"Mrs Ryan's ordered all the food for the reception. She'll put on a good spread." Lachlan seemed to have an army of willing helpers.

"I expect she'll want some assistance." Ruth didn't have a clue when it came to catering for large numbers.

"She'll be right; she's getting paid. Did you invite all your people?"

"Yes, my brother and his wife, two friends from Sydney and my grandmother. All five of them."

"I've only got a few family too; the rest are mates and their wives, neighbours mostly."

Ruth found the prospect of her own wedding exciting once she got over of the shock; the complicated arrangements, however, seemed daunting. She had little idea about weddings, never having attended one before. Another issue playing on her mind was all the strangers who would be there.

"I can guess what you're thinking, Ruth, but stop worrying; they'll have already done their gossiping by the time the day comes." Lachlan laughed.

"Well, I guess they'll have to take me as they find me."

"That's me girl!"

With all of Ruth's pre-wedding anxieties and insecurities, Eliza's arrival was almost as jubilant as the wedding itself. Matthew and his wife, Barbara, arrived the day before Eliza and were put up at the Imperial Hotel. Ruth wanted Eliza all to herself, at home. Apart from catching up with all the news, she desperately needed to talk and spend time with someone she knew and who knew her; she missed her mother, especially now.

"He's a grand boy, Ruth, you've done yourself proud." Eliza and Stewart were equally fascinated with each other. "You know, Lindsay never had any children to carry on the line. Stewart is my first great grandchild." Ruth hadn't thought of Lindsay for a long time. When her eyes met Eliza's, she realised Lindsay had been her first-born child and how devastating his death must have been.

"I can't imagine how I'd cope if anything happened to Stew."

"Well, my love, when you lose someone, you have two choices; let it kill you too, or find a way to keep going. Of course, you never get over the loss; you learn to keep living in spite of it. But look here, no getting all maudlin, there's a wedding tomorrow! By the way, I have a letter here from Sally. She said I'm to make sure I put it in your hand personally, so here you go."

"How is Sally?" Ruth brightened. "I feel dreadful never writing to her but Dad forbade me to write to anyone."

"She's aged a lot these last few years. I think she must be older than I originally thought. Your father's put on two other women to help her now. I don't know how she ever managed the house on her own after your mother became ill. Speaking of your father, he was almost going to come down with me, much to Jake's consternation, but then he changed his mind. Perhaps you should write him a letter; might be the push he needs."

"I will, I'll send him a photograph of the wedding." Ruth wondered what she would say in the letter.

"Well, I'd better go to bed, Ruth, or I'll be dozing off during the ceremony tomorrow."

Ruth was also tired but too anxious to sleep. Picking up Sally's letter, she peeled it open to reveal two pages of mismatched writing paper. She recognised Sally's hand immediately but her attention shot to the second paragraph.

...because I'm old now, I must give this letter to you. If I was younger, it could wait until we meet again. On the night the misis died, it was on the floor in her bedroom. She was writing to your aunt in New Zealand. I didn't know what to do, so I kept it until now.

Ruth's stomach churned as she anxiously unfolded the second sheet.

The boys from Garua had been talking to some of ours and I overheard one say that the trackers found the spot where Lindsay had crawled from the plane but his tracks disappeared after Jake's vehicle arrived. Jake was first on the scene, and when the others reached him, Lindsay had vanished. The boys said that Jake had done away with him.

Ruth stared at her mother's half-written letter in disbelief, *... Jake had done away with him.*

CHAPTER 11

30th June 1963: the big day had arrived. Ruth awoke from a hellish night of fitful sleep and nightmares about Jake. The possibility of his being responsible for Lindsay's disappearance seemed too incredible and frightening to contemplate. She forced her mind to focus on getting ready. I'll deal with it after the wedding, she told herself; maybe then I'll pluck up enough courage to ask Gran what she thinks.

Small by country standards, the wedding party comprised Matthew and Barbara; Joyce and Aggie (Shirley had to work so she couldn't come); Lachlan's two cousins, Hazel and Kathleen, and their husbands; Joan the babysitter; Stewart, Jessica and Eliza. Ruth wanted only a small, intimate gathering at the courthouse. The rest of the guests went straight to Bryliambone for the reception.

The solemnity of the event struck Ruth when they arrived. The courthouse was an austere Victorian building made of sandstone; the imposing front portico towered above most of the surrounding buildings. The ceremony was to take place inside the grand reception room, just as intimidating, with dark wood panelling and massive ornate vases of wattle. Everyone wore their smartest and most formal outfits; a wedding in the country provided one of the few excuses to dress up, so everyone outdid themselves.

Joyce took charge of Stewart and Jessica, as the happy couple walked to the front of the room to face the clerk. Eliza and Kathleen's husband acted as witnesses, which pleased Ruth; having Eliza's blessing was important. The lady playing the piano stopped abruptly without finishing the piece, and the ceremony began. Only minutes later, the whole thing was over. They signed the register, and after a few photographs, found themselves standing outside in the sunshine.

The ceremony turned out to be something of an anti-climax, Ruth thought, after all the worry about what colour dress to wear, whether the children should attend and the weeks of soul-searching which had preceded the occasion.

"How do you feel?" Lachlan asked, with a stunned look on his face.

"I'm not sure; I didn't think it would be over so quickly. I feel different, though." Now married, Ruth's sense of apprehension and concern about whether she truly loved Lachlan seemed irrelevant.

"I'm glad we had the littlies with us; sort of made them part of the occasion," Lachlan said. He had insisted they attend.

"Yes, they both seem happy. I hope Stewart will be all right travelling out to Bryliambone with Matthew and Barbara. He doesn't know them that well."

"Ah, stop worrying. He'll be six soon. It'll do him good to be with other people for a while. He'll lose his shyness when he gets to Bry; plenty of people there for him to mix with."

Ruth experienced a sudden pang of guilt. Being married meant Stewart would have to get used to sharing his mother's attention. This would be a major change for him, especially with starting school in the New Year. Still, she reasoned, having a father and sister would more than compensate.

Bryliambone was a few miles north of the township of Collabine, a three-hour drive from Lincoln. Normally a tedious trip, the monotonous landscape had come to life for their special day. Dusty red paddocks had given birth to a covering of emerald green grass, thanks to more rain. The normally brown sheep were cream-coloured without their coating of dust; even the mulga and ironbark were alive with white cockatoos and pink-breasted galahs. As they drove past the gates of Lachlan's parents' property, Ruth thought the run-down house looked sad. The station had been vacant since Lachlan's mother passed away. With Lachlan fully occupied with Bryliambone, the place had become neglected.

"I didn't realise you had two properties until I came out here last month."

"Just one originally, Bry's a subdivision. Something to do with leases and land purchases years ago, when we were all squatters. When Dad died, he left the Bry subdivision to me; Mum continued to manage Derrigeribar. Bobby took exception to the arrangement and took me to court. I had to buy him out."

Ruth realised this must be why Lachlan had to mortgage the property.

"When he went to live in Sydney," Lachlan continued, "he said he never wanted anything more to do with the place."

"Sounds as though everyone has family problems of some sort," Ruth said, thinking about her own family situation.

"He owns a real estate business in the Big Smoke, never could stand hard work. Josh is another mad bugger, refused to take anything at all from the folks, wanted to prove he was as good as the old man. He owns Gallerun, the citrus farm I told you about."

"He's the reclusive one, eh?"

"Yeah, sort of; weird bunch, us three. One's money hungry, one doesn't wanna know ya, and me… hey, look, there's the homestead!" Lachlan pointed to an assortment of rambling green tin roofs nestled amongst a copse of ironbark.

Ruth spotted a group of people spilling out of the buildings. With some apprehension, she said, "I'd better take a deep breath and smile."

"You'll be all right. Come on, darl, I'll carry you over the threshold." Lachlan pulled on the handbrake and dashed around to Ruth's side of the car.

"Ladies and gents, say hello to me missus, Ruth!" He swept Ruth up in his arms and, with great theatricality, carried her through the doorway to an ear-piercing chorus of cheers, whistles and a shower of rice.

The introductions went better than Ruth had anticipated; everyone seemed friendly. They cared a lot about Lachlan she realised; his happiness had somehow bought her acceptance from this group of strangers. Or so it seemed, until everyone's attention abruptly turned to a raucous melee outside.

"Jessica twisted my arm!" the boy cried, as if his arm had been severed.

"Daddy, he called Stewart a half-caste," an indignant Jessica protested, as the crowd recoiled in stunned silence.

"I think we should go and find some ice cream," said Lachlan's younger cousin, Kathleen, as she hustled the children away.

Ruth wanted to rush over and put her arms around Stewart. To tell him that the boy was just an ignorant yokel who knew no better, but she resisted. As hard as it was, Stewart would need to find his own way in the world, and she wouldn't always be around to comfort him. She watched as Jessica ran off with the two boys to get some ice cream. A child wouldn't just come out and say such a thing, she reasoned; he must have overheard his parents talking. Returning to her husband's side, Ruth smiled graciously. But she couldn't let the incident pass.

"Kids!" she said, loud enough not to be missed by the other guests, "they repeat everything they hear at home." The party resumed, but not before Ruth's steely gaze caught the boy's mother's sheepish eye.

"Good on ya, luv. You got her good and proper, cheeky cow. I bet they been saying all sorts before they got 'ere," Joyce said.

"I hope they don't all turn out to be like them," Ruth said.

"Some of them seem nice. I was talking to Mabel over near the salads. She said that woman and her husband turn up for anything where there's a free feed," Aggie said.

"Lachlan said they only got an invite because they were at the club on his bucks' night. He got drunk and invited everyone!" Ruth said.

"Oh well, that's men for ya, luv; even the good ones have their moments."

"You always make me laugh, Joyce, I'm so glad you came."

"A bullock train wouldn't have kept us away." Joyce gave Ruth an extra big hug.

Eventually, most of the guests left. A few stayed over, either to sober up or to prepare for their long trip home. Joyce, Aggie and Eliza retired to the guest quarters and were looking after the children so Ruth and Lachlan could spend some time alone.

The way the day turned out pleased the newlyweds but they were glad it was over. They had neglected each other all day. Now they could be together, their own time to celebrate.

"How did it go, do you reckon?" Lachlan asked.

"I think everything went well, apart from that ghastly pair and their rotten kid."

"Yeah, sorry, I didn't realise they were at the club when I invited everyone."

"Never mind, but it made me think, I'm going to have to make a conscious effort to prepare Stew for that sort of thing."

"He'll be right, he's only got dark features; his skin's no darker than mine."

"Well, I'll think about Stew another day," Ruth said, gently planting a kiss on Lachlan's cheek.

"Yeah, let's think about each other for a bit." Lachlan pulled Ruth close into his arms and kissed her on the mouth.

"Come on, let's go to bed," Ruth said, disentangling herself from his ardent embrace.

The return of the rains had delayed much of the scheduled work on Bryliambone over the last few months. Now that the weather had finally cleared, the honeymoon would have to be postponed. Not rushing off to some exotic destination straightaway suited Ruth. She wanted to make sure Stewart settled in, as well as spend time with Joyce, Aggie and Eliza, who were all staying on for a few days.

"I was so happy for you when I heard you were getting married. Aggie and I worried ourselves sick the night you and Stewy left on the train," Joyce said.

"I told you we'd be okay. Tell me about Shirley's job, I'm dying to know what she does," Ruth asked, keen to learn more about her former collaborator.

"Well, as you know, the sisters taught her how to type so we managed to get her the job on the railways. They made having a suitable job to go to a condition of her getting out early. She does typing and filing, that sort of thing. We asked if she could take a week off to come here, but they said she had to work for a year before taking holidays."

"That's understandable, I suppose. I'm just happy she's doing so well. I'll send her some photos when they're ready."

"Who are you two talking about?" Aggie appeared with a plate of savouries.

"I was just telling Ruth how worried we were, the day she left on the train."

"We were, luv; all on your lonesome with no friends out this way. Speaking of trains, we think we saw that scoundrel at Central, big bugger in a rail uniform, biggest scar down the side of his face you've ever seen."

"Aggie! That's all in the past now; she doesn't want to know."

"Ralph, you mean?" Ruth said, experiencing a wave of nausea.

"Yes, luv, looked like the same fella, from what you told us. Ali got him you know, knocked the living daylights out of him from what I heard," Aggie said.

"I'm glad he got him. He deserves more than a scar on his face," Ruth said, momentarily lost in her own personal terror. "I only hope he never puts anyone else through what he did to me. He's an animal."

"Enough about the likes of him, now. Let's try some of Aggie's corn dip," Joyce said, determined to change the subject.

As Bryliambone returned to normal after the festivities of the wedding, Ruth's guests readied themselves to leave. One of the jackaroos drove Joyce and Aggie to Lincoln railway station, which left Ruth a couple of hours to spend alone with Eliza before the plane arrived to take her to Sydney.

"If I'd known the trains were so good, I would have travelled down with Joyce and Aggie," Eliza said.

"They are good, but this way you won't have to worry about catching a taxi to the airport."

"Only the wealthy used to fly, but everyone goes by plane these days. By the way, any messages for Sally?"

"No, only to say thanks for her letter and that I'll send some photos of the wedding when I get them developed. I don't think Dad would begrudge me sending her a few snaps." Ruth wanted to tell Eliza about the contents of her mother's note but couldn't find the right words. When reading what her mother had written it seemed real but articulating it made it sound nonsensical and fantastic. She wondered if her mother's illness had caused her to imagine the things that she had written.

"I've never pressed you about Stewart's father, have I?" Eliza said, looking directly at Ruth.

"No, and I'm grateful for that, I –"

"I don't want to know, Ruth, but I will say, for the boy's sake, you might need to revisit all of that one day. We all need to understand our roots, Ruth; we can never be fully whole otherwise."

"You're turning into a *puripuri meri* in your old age, Gran." Ruth smiled, but what Eliza had said was true, he did have a right to know the truth.

"An old witch, eh? No, Ruthy, just been around a long time."

"Don't worry, Gran, I'll do what's right for Stewart." She had a strong suspicion her grandmother had worked out the identity of Stewart's father. The fact that she never mentioned anything suggested she had either guessed the truth and realised the danger of it, or she believed the ruse and found it too embarrassing to mention. The latter was unlikely.

"I'd always hoped you'd find a good man and settle down, Ruth. You've a chance to put everything behind you now. Do you love Lachlan?"

Eliza's barrage of questions surprised Ruth, it was as though she had been saving them all up for the last minute.

"I believe I do. I'm just not exactly sure how love should feel. It isn't the same as before; different, less urgent, if that makes any sense."

"It does, and I think that's a good thing. Real love isn't only about urges and feelings, it has to be balanced by other things; otherwise there'd be no future to a relationship. Perhaps the more urgent feelings are something different. I don't think it's real love."

"Come on, ladies, we have to drive down to the strip." Lachlan appeared from nowhere. The plane had arrived early.

Eliza's pending departure reminded Ruth of the time she had left Okoro. There had been so much she wanted to tell Tommy, her father, even her brothers. Then the moment disappeared, and the time to say anything was gone. So many things left unresolved.

The small, single-prop plane revved its engine and bumped off along the strip before lifting off sharply over the perimeter fence. Ruth couldn't think of how to tell Eliza about Sally's letter, but realised it might have been for the best. If her mother had been imagining things, why bother upsetting her grandmother?

The plane soon became a speck of silver against the blue, cloudless sky. Ruth wondered when, or even if, she would see Eliza again.

"Don't look so miserable, love, maybe we'll go up to visit one day." Lachlan put his arm around his wife.

"She's getting old now. I don't imagine she'll come here again. Going to and from Garua is like going on a major expedition."

"Certainly likes doing things her way, eh?"

"Always has, I think." Ruth and Lachlan turned towards the homestead.

"Come on, wanna come and lay some fox baits?"

"Yes sure. Why lay baits?"

"The lambs, darl; bloody foxes eat anything, especially lambs and chickens."

Ruth spent the following months trying to find a place for herself to fit in at the farm. Having a housekeeper and other staff removed many of the household chores which would normally occupy a wife.

In spite of feeling somewhat misplaced though, marriage and living back on the land had been transformational for Ruth. She had not only regained her emotional strength but had a whole new perspective. Life now was all about moving ahead as a family. Any guilt she harboured about Stewart's impoverished start in life had been replaced by a newfound confidence in his future. He and Jessica clicked from the moment they met and were now inseparable. Both children must have been lonely for the companionship of another their own age, although a shared interest in lizards and collecting bugs helped.

Life at Bryliambone had evolved into a comfortable, albeit hectic, routine, which centred on the seasonal workings of the property. Ruth's days comprised making breakfast for Lachlan and the foreman, packing lunches for everyone, taking the children into town for school, cleaning and doing the laundry with Mrs Ryan and, later in the afternoon, helping prepare the dinner. Weekends were usually spent assisting Lachlan with odd jobs around the property to save on overtime costs. Their favourite pastime was taking a picnic down to the creek on Sunday afternoons. Apart from bed, the Sunday picnics were the only private time they had together.

"I think we must be the luckiest people of all, having this to ourselves," Ruth said, surveying the lush, green, grassy banks of the creek which meandered through the middle of the property.

"Yep, this is as good as it gets, I reckon."

"Stewart's never been as happy as he is now. Starting school and living out here with Jess was what he needed."

"It's been good for Jess, too. I didn't realise the difference it would make." Lachlan lapsed into a pensive silence.

Ruth sensed he might be thinking about his first wife, and although he would never say, she knew he still loved her; but she allowed him those feelings.

"I think they both needed someone else around, someone their own age to talk to," Ruth said.

"That's for sure. They would have been old before their time with only us for company. I always had brothers to muck around with."

As the autumn of 1965 heralded its arrival with cooler winds and shorter days, financial pressures began to mount. The untimely rains led to a succession of missed or waterlogged plantings and Ruth became frustrated at not being able to contribute more. She wondered how she could help save money. Mrs Ryan was a far more capable housekeeper, she conceded; so after getting under the woman's feet for nearly eighteen months, she came to a decision. Ruth announced to Lachlan over dinner one evening that she would be working with him, helping out with the day-to-day running of the property. Any other man would have taken issue with such an announcement, but Lachlan's own mother had run Derrigeribar successfully after his father's death. So Lachlan's response surprised her; he suggested she give it a go.

Initially, the men didn't take Ruth seriously, and even Lachlan cringed when he heard his wife giving the men orders; but in time, she proved she could hold her own. The turning point came when the roustabout went to hospital with a snake bite. Ruth got up on the boards and worked alongside the men until the last sheep was shorn. They said she could throw a fleece 'as good as Jack Howe' once she got the idea. It turned out to be her rite of passage.

As the weeks turned into months, Ruth and Lachlan forged a strong working partnership as well as a solid and happy marriage. Lachlan's initial reservations about being in each other's company all day proved groundless. Ruth understood men well. Thanks to her upbringing, she was adept at maintaining the boundaries between their work and personal lives. For Ruth, the best part of any day was coming home and just being Lachlan's wife.

"Some mail came for you today, love." Lachlan put the discoloured, brown envelope on the table.

"It's a wonder it got here, the envelope's all but disintegrated," she said, noticing the Papuan stamp. "My father, Lach! It's nearly two years since I wrote him."

"Yeah, just after the wedding," Lachlan said, sitting down with an expectant expression on his face.

"Must have got lost. The post mark's nearly six months old." Ruth tore open the weathered envelope.

"What does he say?" Ruth's family intrigued Lachlan; her father's continued lack of communication baffled him.

"He says he's sorry for cutting me off for so long, and that he couldn't handle the thought of his little girl being 'in the family way'. Weird, he goes on to say he could deal with the guilt more easily if he had nothing to do with me. I wonder what he means. Maybe he thought he was to blame in some funny way."

"Sounds bloody mad to me. If Jess ever got into trouble, I'd be furious at first, but I'd get over it."

"Perhaps he was just slow in coming to terms with what I did. He says he found my letter in Jake's ute twelve months after the post date. When he confronted Jake, they had a fight."

"They're all mad, your lot, I'm sure. You reckon he's okay alone with Jake?" Lachlan asked.

"I don't know. Matthew said he received a letter from him a couple of months ago, and everything seemed fine; although they don't talk about anything much, well, only farm stuff."

Lachlan shook his head, "Maybe living in the jungle makes them the way they are."

"Oh no. Dad says Gran had a stroke not long after she returned from the wedding. She never mentioned anything. I thought her letters had become a bit odd," Ruth said, holding the letter up to the light to decipher the faded script.

"She must be reasonably okay. That would have been nearly two years ago."

"Well, yes, I guess, apart from disjointed letters and repeating herself a lot, I thought it was old age."

"I'd be more worried about the old fella if Jake's not giving him his mail. That sounds bloody queer."

"Unless he just forgot, but then Dad says it was opened."

"Jake might be more of a nut than anyone thinks."

"I'll talk to Matt again, just in case. I certainly can't mention anything to Gran now with her condition. I wonder what Matt will make of this; he thinks Mum wasn't rational when she wrote the letter Sally gave me."

"If they had proper telephones in that godforsaken place, you wouldn't have to rely on letters," Lachlan said.

"They will soon, according to Gran, although she told me that a couple of years ago. Would certainly be a lot easier to just pick up the phone, eh?"

After calling Matthew to discuss the letter, Ruth's concerns about Jake seemed hysterical. Matthew assured her that Jake wasn't foolish enough to jeopardise his inheritance by doing anything to his father.

Reassured for the time being, Ruth's attention returned to the business of Bryliambone. Wheat stripping time had arrived, and Lachlan was working long hours to get the crop off and away to the silos. Ruth looked forward to when he finished. Once the trade cattle were put out onto the stubble, she could start preparing for Christmas.

"What's wrong, Mum?" Stewart said, squeamishly peering through the toilet door at his mother retching.

"Go away, Stew, nothing, just the heat." Ruth knew that wasn't it.

"Jess and me are going to find Baxter."

"I," Ruth called back at him.

"You, what?"

"Jess and I. Don't worry, just go and find the dog." Baxter was Lachlan's early Christmas present to Ruth, a black Kelpie, but he had changed allegiance and was now Stewart's playmate.

After missing her second period, Ruth was certain it wasn't the heat making her sick every morning. She was expecting again.

"That's great news, love, how far along?" Lachlan beamed as if one of his prize merinos were in lamb.

"Don't look so pleased with yourself. You should try being pregnant in this damn heat. Only six or eight weeks I suppose." Ruth smiled.

Having more children was something she wanted; it was the timing she objected to.

"Well, no more work for you. Jeez, I'm happy, love. What a beaut Christmas present!" Lachlan jumped up out of his chair and embraced his wife.

"I'm happy too, Lachy. I think a baby will be good for us, the children too."

With Christmas and a new baby around the corner, spirits on the farm soared. Lachlan seemed to have a spring in his step. Both Jess and Stew were being extra well-behaved and Mrs Ryan even looked as though she had a smile on her face – although, Ruth suspected, *she* might be the one who was being more agreeable.

Lachlan's delight at having another child filled him with a renewed zest for life, and for Ruth; he could hardly keep away from her. He finished work early most days and would call in throughout the day to check on her. In the evenings, he would sit next to her on the old couch and hold her hand. It was like courting again, Ruth thought.

"A registered letter arrived today," Ruth said, as Lachlan plopped down onto his favourite armchair to open his mail. "I had to sign for it. You should have seen the postman's face, if looks could kill. I told him to leave any registered mail at the gate in future. One of us can sign when we go to town. I made him a cuppa; he mellowed a bit then." Ruth looked up at Lachlan, who had gone quiet. Immediately, she knew something was wrong. His face had turned pale.

"What's wrong?"

"Nothing, darl; nothing to worry about." Lachlan sounded terror-stricken.

"It must be something. Come on, Lach, what's up?"

"The bank... I can't believe it. The bloody bank wants to foreclose."

CHAPTER 12

Ruth's reaction to the threat of foreclosure was to start planning rescue strategies, but she had to stop herself. So used had she become to solving her own problems, that she almost overlooked the fact that she now had a husband. She realised her priority must be to provide support to Lachlan. His sense of what it meant to be a man depended on him maintaining a sense of mastery over what life threw his way.

"You'll think of something, Lachy; things will turn out okay." She massaged his neck while wondering if he would let her apply for part-time work in town.

"I can't lose the place; the farm's been in the family for four generations. That sort of history doesn't just end."

Ruth understood only too well; she remembered people back home talking about losing their farms once the country gained independence. Nothing is permanent, she had learned, but Bryliambone was far from a lost cause; Lachlan just needed time to come up with something.

By the third day, Lachlan's depressed and withdrawn state had Ruth worried. She had never known him to be without a joke, a smile or his optimistic view of life. Maybe now would be a good time to mention getting a job, she thought. But then he surprised her.

"I have to go to town and talk to the bastards, find out what they're playing at," he growled.

Ruth knew this to be a healthy sign. As with her, a certain degree of anger, or fear, was necessary to propel him into action.

"I'll do lamb for tea, honey." A full roast dinner with Yorkshire puddings always made him happy. She leaned over and kissed him on the cheek.

Once he'd left, the house was noticeably quiet. Mrs Ryan had gone to town and the children were out playing. Grateful for the solitude, Ruth could process her own thoughts about the possibility of foreclosure. It seemed an odd time to contemplate their marriage, but faced with the prospect of losing the farm, she realised just how much she did love Lachlan. Like Eliza said, love was something which grew over time, especially when that involved working through difficult times together.

"Where's Dad?" Jessica stuck her head through the window.

"He went into town, honey. He'll be back for dinner."

"He didn't ask if we wanted to go," she said, looking deflated.

"That's my fault. I told him you two were busy playing."

"Oh, we've got no comics," Jessica whined.

"Christmas isn't far away; you'll have plenty of new books to read. Will you do me a favour, Jess?" Ruth swiftly changed the subject before her voice alerted Jessica that something was wrong. The last thing they needed was the children or staff worrying about Bry's financial woes.

"Hmm, I suppose," she said, with a quizzical expression.

"I need some mint. We're having lamb for dinner."

"Is that all?" She disappeared into the garden, much to Ruth's relief. Jessica was adept at deciphering emotions.

By the time Jessica returned with what appeared to be half the herb garden, Mrs Ryan had arrived back from her monthly shopping expedition. Ruth was glad of the distraction.

"Are Joyce and Aggie coming up for Christmas?" she asked, cursorily checking off the Christmas grocery list.

"No, not this year," Ruth replied. "They're going to spend the day at the beach; Shirley has offered to stay home to cook the dinner, a special treat they arranged earlier in the year."

"What a shame. I enjoyed having them here last year; I don't think I've ever laughed so much."

"They're certainly good for a laugh, especially Aggie, with her yarns about being a nurse in the old days." Ruth wondered how she would get through Christmas, knowing they might lose the farm.

Christmas on Bryliambone had always been a grand affair, starting on Christmas Eve and finishing the day after New Year's Eve. Christmas Day was traditionally reserved for family and the few permanent workers who stayed on over the break. The days before and after were usually open house for neighbours, contractors and whoever happened to stop by. It was the cockie's wife's duty to greet and feed everyone; reputations were made and broken on the welcome given to guests over the festive period.

Lachlan's utility finally pulled up outside. Leaving the washing-up, Ruth rushed out to meet him.

"How did you go?"

"Bloody vultures. They'd see us out of a home and livelihood for ten grand."

"Is that what they're demanding?"

"I'm giving them the wheat sales. That'll take care of the outstanding repayments, but Jess won't get to boarding school this year, and I'll have to put a couple of blokes off."

"We'll manage. I can help, and I don't think Jess will mind staying at school in town for another year." Ruth relaxed a little; in her mind she had already been rehearsing the family's forced move into town.

"Keep 'em off our backs for a while, maybe give me time to put in extra winter crops."

"I'll make sure we don't overspend at Christmas."

"You'll be right, love; we can afford Christmas." Lachlan managed a smile although Ruth could tell he remained troubled.

Christmas was the one occasion each year when everyone took a break from their daily toil and spent time with friends and loved ones. Ruth decided not to let their money problems interfere with everyone's enjoyment of the holiday, especially the children. She put extra effort into creating a cheerful atmosphere around the homestead with homemade decorations, festive culinary treats and small gifts of food and handmade items for the workers. Jessica made Christmas cards while Ruth embroidered tea towels. Stewart volunteered to wrap up the presents in some bright green paper Ruth had bought to cover school books.

"Mrs Ryan left the cranberry sauce off the list, so I might pop into town tomorrow morning." Ruth really wanted to see the doctor to ease her mind about the pregnancy. Lachlan worried too much when it came to 'women's matters', so the best policy was not to say anything, especially now with all their financial worries.

"Sure, love, I've got the beer already so I'll be right."

Collabine was the closest town to Bryliambone and boasted a well-stocked general store, a baker, a greengrocer, two banks and four hotels. Small, but well-serviced, and only a forty-five minute drive.

When Ruth arrived, the main street was astir, which she expected really, being the last shopping day before the holiday break. The hotel patrons overflowed onto the street, and judging by the procession of cars outside the general store, she guessed few, if any, Christmas goodies would be left.

I wonder if currants would do, she thought, pushing open the fly screen door. There were quite a few empty shelves over near the condiments corner, but then to her delight she spotted not only a couple of jars of cranberry sauce, but also a tin of Scottish shortbread sitting on the counter. She couldn't resist. They had always been her favourite. For some reason, shortbread was one of the few biscuits which never spoiled on the journey to Papua, so they were a mainstay in the biscuit barrel back home.

Buoyed by her shopping success, she made her way across to Doctor Fuller's surgery.

"He went to the hospital, Mrs McGrath. You'll catch him if you hurry." The doctor's wife used to be a doctor, too, but after a stroke, gave up practicing to be her husband's receptionist. Although it was very sad, Ruth was grateful in a way. If the woman hadn't been rushed off to hospital following her stroke, Lachlan would have had no need to go to Lincoln with his septic burrs. They might never have met.

"Thank you, Mrs Fuller." Ruth had never quite worked out whether she should still be addressed as Doctor.

The hospital entrance appeared deserted. Ruth walked gingerly along the corridor. Four elderly patients occupied two of the rooms, so she guessed there must be staff around somewhere.

"Excuse me, may I help you?" A flustered voice echoed though the ward.

"Yes, I'm after Dr Fuller; his wife said I might find him here."

"He's finishing up with Mrs Reiss; you can wait if you like. I'll let him know you want to see him. Mrs McGrath isn't it?" The matron disappeared out of a side door just as a buzzer went off.

"Nurse, nurse, I need a pan." A distressed voice rattled from the room behind where Ruth sat waiting. She spotted a stack of bedpans on a shelf across the corridor and took pity on the patient whose strained voice conveyed a sense of urgency.

Within seconds of her selfless deed, Ruth could hear someone else rummaging through the tin pans.

"Oh, you have one already!" The matron appeared, half surprised and half annoyed, having run back down the corridor to get the pan. "You can go in now, Mrs McGrath; the doctor will see you."

A short, wizened-looking man, Doctor Fuller had a full head of snow-white hair and appeared well past retirement age.

"What brings you in today, Mrs McGrath?"

"I'm expecting, I think. Well, I'm pretty sure." Ruth reluctantly climbed onto the table.

He prodded and poked briefly before announcing, "Everything seems to be in order. If the date you gave me is correct, you're about twelve weeks along, give or take a few days."

Ruth smiled to herself as she drove up the main street on her way home. Matron seemed rather benign after she recovered from the bedpan flurry. As it turned out, she was short staffed and had worked a double shift. It had been a pleasant trip, the doctor had confirmed what Ruth expected, that the pregnancy was going well, she had a large tin of Scottish shortbread sitting on the passenger seat, open, and to top it off, the store had cranberry sauce! In spite of the anguish over the mortgage, Ruth decided she was looking forward to Christmas.

By mid-morning on Christmas day, celebrations were in full swing. Matthew and Barbara had arrived with gifts, the children were playing with their new toys and Lachlan, Matthew and Mr Ryan had decamped to the veranda with a crate of beer, so as not to 'get in the women's way'. The temperature was over a hundred degrees outdoors but Ruth and the other women were immersed in the kitchen, tending the roast turkey and side of pork; the kitchen was more like a hundred and twenty.

"You know, Mrs Ryan, it's so much hotter out here than back home, yet everyone insists on all this Christmas cooking."

"Madness, eh? A remnant from colonial days, I think, when folk tried to copy people back in England. What do you normally eat at Christmas?"

"Cold meat and salads mainly, although sometimes we used to have roast duck or chicken. We had a lot of fruit and tropical desserts. My favourite are fruit juice cocktails with crushed ice, no alcohol though." Ruth salivated at the thought of a tangy mango and lime juice cocktail. She tried to imagine what her father and Jake would be doing, until interrupted by Mrs Ryan, who was still focussed on the conversation.

"I don't know, wouldn't be Christmas without the turkey and all the trimmings."

"True; the children certainly enjoy all the festive goodies," Ruth agreed.

As she continued to baste the slowly browning bird, it occurred to Ruth that most of what she had ever wished for in life, she now had: a loving husband, children, a home and a few good friends. Remembering how determined she had been to provide Stewart with a secure home, she was pleased with how everything had turned out. She concluded that the best way to live life was to have a dream and stick to it, no matter what difficulties got in the way.

175

The spectacular Christmas lunch fulfilled everyone's expectations of what Christmas should be. There were sweet and savoury treats aplenty, laughter, high spirits and that elusive feeling of well-being which everyone works towards creating at Christmas, but so rarely achieves. Ruth could vaguely remember only one or two Christmases as a girl that came anywhere close to this wonderful day.

As the bright, harsh afternoon sun gave way to a kinder, diffused eventide, the noisy homestead fell into silence. The children slept on the couch and the staff had migrated to the shearing sheds to continue with their own celebrations. The family guests had overeaten and retired to their rooms for a rest, leaving Ruth and Lachlan on the veranda alone. A half-hearted breeze wafted past, laden with the rusty aroma of the parched plains. Shadows were already long on the ground, and frogs and cicadas provided a vocal backdrop for the rapidly approaching night.

"Beautiful out here, eh?" Lachlan said, climbing into the hammock.

"I'm always amazed by how clear the sky is. We get a lot more cloud and rain back home. Even when it's not raining, we have mist."

"I wish we had some rain here, haven't seen any since our wedding."

"Seems like such a long time ago now, when you were chasing me all over town."

"Ha! Who was chasing who?" Lachlan laughed.

"Cheeky thing, if you hadn't figured out where I went for lunch, I would never have set eyes on you again. How did you guess anyway? I never did ask."

"A mate told me, I think." Lachlan wasn't a good liar.

"You think? Was it George?"

"Not directly."

"You sneaky thing! You asked George to find out off Joan!"

"Sneaky? I'll have you know that bit of information cost me a killer. It was a straight-out business deal."

"You gave him a sheep for my whereabouts? You're more despicable than I thought!" Lachlan's ingenuity delighted Ruth. "Well, now you're in a good mood."

"Oh no, what's it going to cost me?" Lachlan gently pulled Ruth closer to him.

"I went to the doctor's yesterday."

"Is something wrong?"

"Hang on, everything's fine, but I thought I'd go and get a check-up, just to make sure. Anyway, I got speaking to the matron. She told me they'd advertised for a nurse but hadn't received any applications. I said I'd speak to you, and if you agreed, I might be able help out." Ruth didn't actually mention Lachlan to the matron but thought it best to add that if she wanted his agreement.

"What? You want to work at the hospital? You're married and expecting."

"They take married women now, with the nursing shortage. Only be for a month or so, and after work I can pick Stew and Jess up from school; it'll save me making two trips each day. Won't be more than a few hours a day and it'll bring in some extra cash." Ruth's reasoning was hard to resist.

"Jeez, love; you certainly have some funny ideas. The money won't make much difference. We owe thousands."

"Well, I can buy things for the baby."

The silence was palpable while Lachlan considered the proposition. She suspected he'd be wondering if people would think he couldn't afford to support his wife, or that it would be like advertising their financial troubles, or worse, she had taken a job to get away from him.

"If that's what you want to do, I guess it's okay with me. Just to help out until they get someone, though, and only for as long as you can manage."

"I'll start next week then." Ruth turned in the direction of an intruding wail. "What's that?"

"A bird," Lachlan said, with an odd expression.

"What sort of bird, and why the funny look?"

"A curlew, honey."

"And the funny look?" Ruth smiled.

"There's a blackfella legend about them; you hardly ever hear them out here."

"A bad luck thing?"

"Yeah darl, they reckon if you hear one someone close to you has died, or will die. Now, never mind the bloody bird, I've got some good news too."

"What's your news?" Ruth said as a cold shiver ran down her back.

"On my way home from town yesterday, I called into the silo…" Ruth cut him off.

"I wondered why you took so long. I thought you must have had some floozy hidden away."

"Nah, don't be daft, got no time for floozies!"

"Go on, tell me the rest."

"I got talking to old Jack Hennessey and he said his sister in Queensland was crook, but he couldn't go and visit because of the crop stripping. I said I'd do it for him if he wants to get away."

"Take on his stripping contracts?"

"Yeah, finish the wheat and make a start on the lucerne."

"Won't you wear yourself out? What about the mulesing? I can help with most things but I can't even stand to look at that."

"Don't worry about the mulesing. If I do the harvesting, we'll have enough to pay Bill and his boys to come out and do it." Lachlan smiled; he had solved the cash flow problem until the winter harvest.

Ruth admired his resourcefulness, but he already did the work of two men. "You're a good husband, Lach. Not many men would be willing to take all that on." She turned her head abruptly. "There it is again. Do you believe in what they say?"

"What? The tale about the curlew? Just superstitious rubbish." He threw his beer can in the direction of the bird. The sound stopped.

"I think it's gone. Hope you didn't hit it."

"Bugger the damn bird. Come on, darl, let's go to bed."

The guests drifted home over the following couple of days, and the children occupied themselves with the spoils of Christmas. Ruth and Lachlan made the most of the remainder of the holiday by spending time down at the creek, swimming and relaxing.

"We never did get away on our honeymoon, eh?" Lachlan said as Ruth lay with her head resting on his arm.

"No, but I don't mind. I'm happy here at Bry. I'm content now."

"Maybe after we get the bank out of our hair we can go somewhere. Coolangatta sounds good."

"That'd be exciting, but we don't have to hurry." Ruth looked up. "Here come the kids." She watched as they approached.

"No chance of a kip now…"

After being her own boss on the farm, returning to nursing came as something of a shock for Ruth. It took a few days but she soon adapted; the best part of the whole arrangement was the daily ritual of taking the children to the swimming pool after school. By the time they left to go home, the worst of the day's heat had passed. Ruth enjoyed the work and having time for some fun with the children. Unlike her previous pregnancy, her morning sickness only lasted a few weeks, and now her energy level and sense of well-being seemed to know no bounds.

"Wouldn't you rather be at home, Ruth? I think I would, given the chance," Matron asked.

"It's only for a couple of months, but no, I enjoy having female company again. It's all men at Bry, apart from Mrs Ryan." Matron and Ruth got along well. Matron was delighted at having an extra nurse and Ruth increasingly came to rely on her wages; Lachlan's pay for the contract work often took weeks to come through.

The drive to and from Collabine each day was no longer the drudge it had been before she started work. The morning rush was tiresome, but Ruth enjoyed the time she spent with the children after school. She even enjoyed the boring drive home now. Once the main street had disappeared out of sight, it was like being in the middle of nowhere. With no rain for nearly two years, the lush green plains had turned to washed out shades of brown and beige. The dusty landscape appeared lifeless apart from drifting salt bush and the occasional willy-willy.

Stewart often fell asleep on the back seat out of boredom, while Jessica read, although she had to remember to look up occasionally or she would get car sick. Today, the trip was particularly onerous because they had to pull up to change a tyre. This was on top of three hours overtime at the hospital and having to stop at the general store for supplies. The gates of Bryliambone were a welcome sight.

"Whose car is that, Mum?" Stewart pointed towards the homestead.

"It looks like Uncle Matthew's, but I don't think he'd visit without calling first," Ruth said.

"The radio aerial looks the same as his," Jessica added.

Driving across the cattle grid a little quicker than was comfortable, Ruth could see it was Matthew. "I wonder why he's here," she said, and stuck her head out the window to say hello.

"You better send the kids in, love," Lachlan said, with no trace of a smile.

"Matthew, what's happened?" Her voice strained.

"There's no easy way to tell you, Ruthy. I received a letter from Jake this morning. Dad's been in an accident."

"Oh, God, what sort of accident? Is he hurt?" Ruth instinctively knew the answer before asking.

"It happened almost four weeks ago; he was driving along the river road at Okoro and somehow went off the edge."

"What? He knew the place like the back of his hand," Ruth said, experiencing a sudden sinking feeling in her stomach. Then she remembered her mother's letter.

CHAPTER 13

In spite of the torrent of air from the massive fans, the ward was stifling. Only the one patient tonight, Mrs Johnson, who had fallen ill at the school fête. A touch of heat; nothing too demanding. Ruth clipped back her chart; it was time for a tea break.

The hospital was a rambling old weatherboard building with rooms opening onto a long, shared veranda. The extensive gardens and shrubs made it a pleasant place to work. Ruth manoeuvred an old wicker chair over to Mrs Johnson's window, put her cup of tea on the rickety wrought-iron table then slumped onto the chair. She revelled in the sensation of relief as her feet were unburdened of their load then experienced a pang of guilt as she wondered if Stewy and Jess were in bed. Ruth had volunteered to do Friday nights as a favour to Matron so she wouldn't be on the ward alone.

Apart from the guilt over leaving Lachlan and the children, working at the hospital had helped dispel, at least in part, Ruth's preoccupation with her father's death; especially the frustration at having received the news so many weeks after the funeral.

How could the real cause of the accident ever be established if he were already buried? Ruth obsessed over this question. She had raised the subject of Jake again with Matthew. He still clung to the view that Jake had nothing so sinister in his make-up to do anything to harm their father. Writing to Eliza was out of the question; judging by her letters, she had deteriorated further. There was no point upsetting her, unless actual proof presented itself. Even then, her grandmother might not fully comprehend. She couldn't even write to Sally in secret, now that she had lost her sight. There always seemed to be something in the way of getting to the bottom of things.

Relying on Mrs Ryan to cook for the children on Fridays had become another source of annoyance for Ruth. She loved cooking for her family and missed out on that pleasure now that she was working. The wages she received made up a little for the missed family time. It provided a much needed boost to the housekeeping and afforded them the occasional treat. She wondered how they would manage as her pregnancy advanced and she had to stop working. The original agreement had been for only a few weeks, but that had already turned into three months. She had promised Dr Fuller and Lachlan not to work beyond the sixth month.

A light breeze drifted along the veranda, heavy with the fragrance of the gardenias bordering the driveway. It reminded Ruth of Joyce's Jungle Gardenia perfume, which she had worn at the wedding. Ruth recalled again the time she had first met Lachlan. Sheer luck really, when she thought about it; Dr Fuller's wife having a stroke, Lachlan's burr injury turning septic and going to Lincoln Outpatients, they…

The ambulance roared into gear, noisily interrupting her reverie. Red lights flashed, and the bell blasted, as the vehicle sped off down the road.

Ruth rushed inside to prepare, just in case the patient came back to the hospital. Night-time emergencies usually went to Lincoln. It was always disconcerting when the ambulance went out. Being a small community, it was often someone you knew. Dr Fuller appeared from the back door.

"Oh, good evening, Doctor. I guess the emergency must be coming here if you've been called. Someone from town?" Ruth quizzed him.

"Ruth…" At that moment, Sergeant Riley walked through the door. The two men exchanged a doleful glance.

"Sit down, Ruth," the sergeant directed staidly. "There's been an accident at the silos."

Ruth immediately thought of Lachlan; he had been at the silos all week with the sorghum harvest. Her eyes darted from the sergeant across to the doctor. It was obvious from the sergeant's demeanour that something terrible had happened; waves of cold fear flowed through her entire body. It was as if the two men were talking from somewhere off in the distance; she heard the policeman describing how Lachlan had been changing the bearings on the Bedford when a jack gave way. He kept talking, but her mind had stopped comprehending, … jack… gave way… time of death… nothing anyone could do… The words kept repeating themselves in her head. An intense, cold blackness began to envelope her. She wanted to scream, she wanted to run to Lachlan, then grey, hazy blotches invaded her vision and a paralysing numbness hit her legs.

"Give me a hand, she's passed out," Matron ordered.

Ruth became aware of disembodied voices. They were talking about Mrs Ryan and the children. In her muddled state, the voices sounded distorted and terrifying. She sat up abruptly.

"You fainted," Matron said, seeing the confusion on Ruth's face.

Ken Oates, the ambulance driver, walked into the room.

"I want to see Lachlan," Ruth said, as if nothing had happened.

"I think you should stay put, Ruth. You're in shock," the doctor said, obviously concerned by her apparent spontaneous recovery.

"I don't want to rest, I want my husband." Ruth knew Ken Oates would have brought Lachlan's body back in the ambulance.

"Come on, I'll take you through." Dr Fuller took Ruth's arm.

Lachlan lay on the infirmary table, still clothed and looking as though he were asleep. Ruth ran to his side, searching his face through her tears, desperate to glimpse some recognition in his eyes. He was still warm, but his skin looked pale. He possessed a relaxed appearance but his lips were darker than normal. She recognised the same purple tinge that she had seen on her mother's lips.

"Oh Lachy, why now? Why now?" Ruth embraced the lifeless body, pressing tightly against her husband, as if to force life back into him. "Can't you do anything? Did you try to resuscitate him?" she pleaded.

The doctor could only reassure her that everything possible had been done.

As she lifted her head from Lachlan's motionless chest, she wondered what sort of agony he must have gone through before passing into unconsciousness. Matron gently ushered her back to the staff room.

"I have to go home," Ruth said, now alternating between despair and mechanical coldness.

"I can take you if the doctor agrees, Mrs McGrath," Ken Oates offered.

"I'll come out in the morning," said the sergeant. Ruth seemed not to hear as she looked past him towards Ken.

"Can we go now? I must get home to the children."

Ruth said nothing for the duration of the journey home. She was mentally paralysed. Ken seemed to understand and didn't press her. The car turned slowly onto the dirt track leading up to the house. As they approached, the station lights were all on and the men had gathered on the front veranda. Mrs Ryan helped Ruth from the car. Mr Ryan and the farmhands looked on in silence. There was nothing to say.

"If you need anything, give the wife or me a call," Ken called, as Charlie Ryan ushered Ruth through the front door.

"Sit down, love." Mrs Ryan placed a cup of sweet tea on the table and then burst into tears.

"Has anyone told the children?" Ruth asked.

"No, they're still asleep; we wanted to wait until you came home."

"Let them sleep; another few hours won't matter." Ruth got up from the table and went to the door; the men were still hanging around, talking about what had happened. She audibly took a deep breath, before addressing the small gathering.

"There isn't a lot to tell you other than what you've probably already heard. Lachlan was working on the truck when the jack gave way; they tried to get him out; the wheel rim came down onto his chest. They did their best..." Ruth lost track of what she was saying. "...they did all they could. Just ask Mr Ryan for anything to do with work." As she turned to go back in, the robotic façade began to crumble.

"I need to be alone, Mrs Ryan. I'll be in my room."

Ruth stared at the empty double bed and recalled the day her mother had died; that unreal sensation of being in a nightmare and unable to wake up. The room seemed empty and strangely unfamiliar, the silence of it was something she could almost feel. She experienced again that terrifying sensation of being alone in the world and exposed to the whim of fate; as though some omnipresent aegis had been stolen from her. Picking up Lachlan's folded, blue-striped pyjamas, she buried her face into them. She could smell him, his musky mix of sweat and soap; she sensed his warmth and strength.

Baxter came rushing into the room, agitated and whining. Ruth reached down and touched his ear.

"Lachlan's gone, Bax," she said, as tears rolled off her chin. Baxter placed his muzzle on her knee. "We must tell Stewy and Jess." She sat thinking of what to say to them, Jessica in particular, who had already lost her mother.

Breaking the news to Jessica was the hardest thing Ruth had ever had to do. The depth of Jessica's pain was terrifying; she didn't know how to comfort her. Ruth had learned to hide the outward expression of intense feelings while growing up. Now, confronted with Jessica's raw, unbridled agony, she felt scared and out of control.

The days following the accident seemed like a blur, each terrible day seemed to coalesce into the next. Jessica's behaviour was a concern; she hadn't eaten anything and was becoming increasingly remote.

"Come on, Jess, I'll feed you; you must eat to get though the next couple of days."

"I don't want to get through them," Jessica said, her fixed gaze not moving from the pillow.

"I understand, Jess; believe me, I do. What would Dad say if he knew you weren't eating? He'd be worried." After a few minutes, to Ruth's relief, this seemed to have an effect. Jessica began to sip at the soup that Ruth spooned to her taut lips.

Visitors started to arrive for the funeral and the house and spare rooms quickly filled. Ruth was glad of the guests for Jessica's sake, but for herself, she would rather they had all stayed away. The funeral itself was the most difficult. As well as trying to come to terms with her grief, she had to deal with her husband's body being carried, prayed over, transported and finally buried by people she had met only once or twice. She kept reminding herself that they thought they were helping; it was the only way to keep her anger in check, and the desire to tell them all to go home.

Stewart turned out to be the one who provided Jessica with the comfort she needed. They would go walking together, away from the house for hours at a time. There existed that special connection and understanding that only children share, a sort of knowing; an ability to experience each other's world.

A whole month passed before the station settled back into any kind of routine. The mourners had all gone, Lachlan had been laid to rest, and Ruth was alone trying to make sense of everything. A task made more difficult by intermittent bouts of panic when she remembered Bry's financial woes. The last cost-saving measure involved cancelling all but the legally required insurance policies, those that covered the workers. Not Lachlan.

Jessica's depression continued to trouble Ruth. As the weeks went by, she seemed only to want to be with Stewart. It was as though she had disengaged from everyone else. Ruth realised that if she were going to help Jessica recover, she would need to find a way to overcome her lack of connection with her. The strong maternal feelings she had for Stewart didn't easily transfer to Jessica. Ruth had also been careful, perhaps overly so, not to appear as if she were trying to take the place of her real mother.

"So how come you and Stew haven't been helping me with the garden this week? I picked the last of the tomatoes today; we had so many, I made them into purée."

"No real reason, I just want to be somewhere quiet."

"It's a lot to deal with eh, Jess?" Ruth put her arm around Jessica's shoulder. "Your father's accident has been hard for all of us, but I can only imagine how devastated you must be."

"I've got no one, it's as if they've just gone and left me."

"Oh Jess, come here, darl." Ruth gathered Jessica into her arms and embraced her while she cried. Ruth guessed her shock had been so great she hadn't been able to cry properly.

"He shouldn't have gone, why did it happen? Why did he need to cart other people's sorghum? Why? I just want to know why he left me." Witnessing Jessica's anguish was heartbreaking, but Ruth knew her increasing anger was a good sign; it boded well for her recovery.

"I can't tell you why, Jess, who knows what God's plan is for our lives? There might not even be a reason why, things just happen and we must keep going."

"Life isn't fair, it doesn't make any sense, I don't even believe in God anymore."

"I guess all we can do, Jess, is keep the ones we love alive in our hearts; to live our lives in a way that would make them happy. That's what I'm going to do. Your father wanted us to have a home that no one can ever take away, one where we feel safe. I'm going to make his dream happen."

"You think that's what he wanted?"

"I know that's what he wanted, precious, that's why he was carting for Hennessey, to pay the bank so we could stay on Bry. Your father hoped the farm would continue for generations to come."

"And you're going to do that for him now?"

"For all of us, Jess, I promise you that. I might not be able to take the place of your mum and dad, but I can try to make their dreams for you come true."

Ruth acknowledged that she might never be able to provide Jessica with all she needed emotionally, but she vowed to at least realise Lachlan's wishes for the family: that the next generation of the McGrath family would always have a place to call home.

With a renewed sense of urgency, Ruth decided that she must

tackle the farm accounts. She was aware of the critical nature of their finances, especially now without Lachlan's contracting fees, but she had to find a way.

"Do you need anything else, Mrs McGrath?"

"No, thank you, Mrs Ryan. I want to go over the books again before going to bed."

"I'll see you in the morning then." The housekeeper disappeared, leaving Ruth with the task of trying to extract some sort of viability from the debt-ridden enterprise.

"If we don't eat for the next year, Bax, and don't pay any of the men, we might break even." Baxter turned his face to Ruth as if he shared her concern. "Let's just hope the sorghum price is good. Come on, let's get some sleep."

The maturing sorghum crop and shearing season forced the people of Bryliambone back into a near normal routine. Ruth's advancing pregnancy had caused her to change from horseback to riding a tractor.

"Lachy would have me shot if he knew you were out here still," Mr Ryan said.

"You mean with me expecting?"

"Well, it is a bit of a worry."

"Yes, I appreciate your concern, Mr Ryan; maybe I should try and stay at the house a bit more." Ruth understood that she had to be careful. The last thing she wanted was to lose Lachlan's baby.

"I can manage this lot; I've run the place on my own before."

"Of course you have." Ruth recalled her meeting with Lachlan's father on the train, when all of the McGraths were in Sydney keeping vigil over Lachlan's first wife. It was Charlie Ryan who ran the show while they were away.

"You carry on, Mr Ryan; I'll be up at the house with the books." She might not be able to physically run the property anymore, but she could plan a survival strategy.

Repeatedly going over the accounts was a dismal task, trying to find money where there was none. Apart from ensuring the best outcome for the family, Ruth appreciated how concerned the workers were about their jobs, especially the permanent ones who lived on the station. It didn't come as too much of a surprise when Mrs Ryan broached the subject.

"I don't want to seem selfish, Mrs McGrath. I know you've had a lot to deal with, but we're all worried about what will happen to Bry."

"Everything will work out, Mrs Ryan. We have a good sorghum crop and I'm hoping to put more land under wheat. I just wish this baby would hurry up, so I can get back to work." Ruth's conscience pricked, giving Mrs Ryan a false sense of security, but she hadn't fully decided which course of action to take yet. The most promising in the long run, seemed to be the most painful in the short term.

Ruth went to bed to escape her worries, but this turned out to be futile. Apart from the unbearable heat, her mind raced out of control, dissecting every possible way forward and the inherent consequences for all concerned. Tossing and turning, she frantically rearranged her arms and legs in the bed to find a cool spot but gave up in despair. A long, tepid shower helped her body relax, although her mind remained unsettled. Positioning the fan directly over the bed and spraying the sheets with cold water from the ironing spray, she readied herself for a second attempt at sleep.

The air from the fan against her face brought back memories of being with Tommy. When the weather became unbearably hot back home, they would run off to the river together to escape the heat and humidity. Drifting in and out of sleep, she was aware of the overpoweringly fragrant jasmine plant beneath the open window, annoying at first, but intoxicating when combined with the warm, sultry night air.

Ruth peered outside and spotted her brother Matthew, running for his life with their mother in close pursuit; he'd caught another python, which he'd released in the kitchen. Ruth laughed with delight. Her mother hated snakes; she would shut herself in the bedroom until Sally caught the reptile and held it up to the window to put Alice's mind at ease.

"You shouldn't laugh!" Jake bellowed through the doorway.

"You're no fun at all," she called back, experiencing a rush of guilt at having taken so much delight in her mother's fear.

Turning back towards the window, she noticed it had turned dark. Ruth recognised the plain white curtains; she was in her bed at boarding school. She felt scared and wanted to cry. Her vision blurred as she stared towards the corridor lights; tears erupted through her best efforts to suppress them. Clutching a handful of nightgown to wipe her face, she noticed her swollen abdomen. A wave of nausea swept over her and the icy coldness in the pit of her stomach gave way to panic.

"God! I'm so scared, what can I do?" she screamed.

"Mum! Wake up!" someone called out from way off in the distance.

"Wake up, open your eyes, you're dreaming," a girl's voice shouted.

Ruth opened her eyes, startled. Stewart and Jessica were sitting on the bed, looking at her in shock.

"You must have been dreaming," Jessica said reassuringly.

"Jess, Stewy; yes, I must have been, one of those crazy mixed-up ones," Ruth explained as she got up to do something in order to make herself feel normal. "Let's go and have a midnight feast, eh?" Ruth led the way.

They made Milo with cold milk and opened a packet of Iced Vo Vos. "I think we might be in for a storm by the looks of things." What Ruth observed from the window worried her; a storm could ruin a mature crop. "Come on, bring your drinks; we'll sleep in my bed and listen to the rain." Ruth enjoyed the sound of rain on a tin roof when cuddled up in bed. It conjured up a cosy, safe feeling.

The children fell asleep almost as soon as they got into bed. Ruth still couldn't relax; the wind seemed to be getting stronger. A crashing sound signalled that a sheet of corrugated iron had become dislodged, probably from the chicken pen. Peering out the window, she spotted a metal bucket blowing noisily across the driveway. A number of flickering lights approached the house; Mr Ryan and some of the hands, she suspected. Hastily putting on her coat she went to the kitchen door.

"Looks like we're in for a rough night. I've just heard on the radio that hail has hit about ten miles north," Mr Ryan announced, looking grim.

"You think it'll come this way?" Ruth said, almost too scared to hear his answer.

"The wind's blowing in this direction; but it keeps changing."

A bolt of lightning cracked overhead, followed rapidly by a barrage of thunder; the storm was almost upon them.

"Come inside, nothing we can do now," Ruth said, as gusts of wind battered the windows, causing them to rattle. A deafening crash hit the side of the house. She rushed to look; a fallen tree branch half covered the veranda. The light pizzicato of raindrops on the iron roof that they enjoyed earlier had now turned to violent hammering.

"Mum, the noise woke us up." Stewart looked dazed.

"Come here." Ruth gathered Stewart and Jessica close to her.

The worst of the storm lasted about twenty minutes before petering out into silence.

"The moon's out now; we'd better check the damage," Mr Ryan said, as he left to get the men. Ruth suspected that the news wouldn't be good.

"You two stay here," she said. "I'm going to have a look." Pulling her coat around her, she ran out of the house to the water tower. From the top, most of the farm could be seen. As she awkwardly clawed her way up the side of the tower, carefully protecting her stomach as she went, she surveyed the sorghum paddocks.

"No, not the crop! You've taken my mother, my husband, my father and now our bloody livelihood. Why? What have I done?" Ruth screamed as she stared aghast at the vast patches of flattened, tangled crop. Crying and beating the side of the tower in anger, she implored the Almighty to show compassion, at least for the children. By the time Mr Ryan returned, her rage had commuted into defeated acceptance.

"Not good news," Mr Ryan called out, just as Ruth reached the ground.

"I know. We'll drive around at first light, see what we can salvage. Go and get some sleep." Ruth went back to the house, beaten and miserable.

The damage turned out to be worse than anyone had imagined. Practically none of the crop was salvageable and what could be sold would be severely downgraded. When Matthew called, Ruth was too depressed to talk to him. He turned up mid-morning to offer moral support and to help out if needed. Ruth just wanted to sleep. She was mentally exhausted and had been having pains. Tiredness she guessed, too soon for labour.

"I just need to rest," she told her brother. Matthew obliged by taking the children to the pictures to see *Mary Poppins*, and then out to Carraroona for the night.

The sound of more rain woke Ruth; the time on the clock was two-thirty in the afternoon. The weather had turned chilly; she went looking for jumpers for the children to wear when they came home but stopped when she reached the hallway. For a moment, she was lost in thought, then turned around and came back to the kitchen.

"It's no good, there's no choice." She quickly combed her hair, grabbed her coat, put Baxter in the back of the utility and drove into town.

It was just over an hour later when she arrived at the stock and station agents.

"Good afternoon, Mr Hayes."

"G'day, Mrs McGrath, come and sit down." The man's eyes fixed on Ruth's swollen abdomen.

"I've thought about what you said, Mr Hayes, and have decided to go ahead and sell Bryliambone."

"I must say I'm rather surprised, Mrs McGrath," he said, lighting up a cigarette.

Ruth felt no need to defend her decision and didn't reply.

"Well, as you're aware, the property itself is in good shape. You'd make enough from the sale to get the bank off your back as well as make a fresh start for yourself."

"I'll leave all that in your hands, Mr Hayes. I want to focus on Derrigeribar, now that I've made the decision."

"You'll have your work cut out for you there. Apart from the weeds, the homestead is in need of a lot of repairs from what I remember."

"The house is run-down; I anticipate it'll take a while before I'm able to move in properly," she said, realising it might be sooner rather than later if there was a buyer for Bry.

"You could run a profitable concern if you manage the place well, but you'd need to outlay some capital. How much, of course, depends which way you want to go; crops, cattle, sheep –"

"Cotton, I want to grow cotton," Ruth said, trying to rein in the agent's suggestions.

"Cotton? No one's done that out this way."

"No, I need to do a bit more research."

"Pity the bank wasn't willing to help you out more with Bry."

"I know, but I can understand, a woman with no experience and expecting a baby."

"Bit of a gamble, I guess. Cotton, you might make a go of it, been quite successful up near Moree. Let me know if I can help. If you like, I can put a manager on Bry for you; take off some of the load."

"I'm putting Charlie Ryan in charge until it's sold. Maybe the new owners will keep him on. He's a good leading hand."

"You just let me know if I can be of assistance."

"I won't take up any more of your time, Mr Hayes. You've been very helpful."

Ruth's only emotion when she stepped out of the agent's door was an intense sense of foreboding. Forcing her attention away from the negative feeling, she reminded herself that if her plans were to succeed, she had to start straightaway.

Before returning to the utility, she stopped at the general store to buy a new thermos and a pair of gum boots for Stewart. By the time she put the vehicle into gear, her mood had lifted from one of fearful apprehension to a newly dawning sense of purpose and optimism.

193

"Home now for an early night, Bax. We've got a big day tomorrow."

The rain had stopped by the following morning and the sun tentatively groped its way through breaks in the overcast sky. Ruth mentally ticked off what she had packed: water, the Thermos, sleeping bag, dog biscuits, sandwiches and some fruit.

"Let's just hope it doesn't turn into a disaster, Bax. Come on, in the front. You can navigate."

The familiar buildings which had been home quickly disappeared behind the tree line. Derrigeribar adjoined Bry, but with the rain, the bitumen road was the safest way to go. Once out of the property, it was clear just how much rain had fallen. The back road to Lincoln looked flooded, and the usually dry, dusty track into Derrigeribar had what appeared to be canals running along each side. Paddocks of crops along the road had turned into swamps, and those that were not fully submerged looked like rice paddies. Ruth appreciated the beauty of the rain; within hours of a downpour, new grass shoots would appear from the sodden soil, an affirmation of life's ability to regenerate and begin again. If only it wasn't so destructive. As she turned off the bitumen onto the dirt road to Derrigeribar, any remaining apprehension evaporated. The children will have a home, Lachy!

"Hold on, Bax!" A bumpy ride for most of the journey, but beyond the gate, the ground became more even. The large wooden sign next to the mailbox looked incredibly well preserved, it simply said: Derrigeribar. "Only a couple more miles," Ruth called out to the dog. He barked, looking as excited as his mistress.

The track to the homestead wound around past a creek and then turned sharply to the right. The soil was dark brown, almost black, as a result of the rain. The well shaded house sat in front of a stand of ironbark. As she drove closer, the grand frontage surprised her; it was a Queenslander style homestead, set on a sandstone base in place of wooden stilts.

"God, what's that?" She slammed on the brakes. A large, thick brown snake was wrapped around the top of the gate. Baxter barked eagerly.

"Quiet!" Ruth shouted as she examined the reptile from the safety of the driver's seat. "I don't think it noticed us, Bax, it seems very still." As she opened the door, Baxter bolted across the front seat and began to bark again. The reptile's head appeared squashed.

"Looks dead but come away. I never thought of damn snakes; I hope there's none in the house." Not taking any chances with the gate, Ruth carefully heaved herself over the fence instead. "Good job Mr Ryan didn't catch us doing that, little one," Ruth said, gently patting her tummy.

Baxter ran around the veranda, sniffing, while Ruth hopped over broken floorboards to unlock the door. A layer of brown dust covered everything inside, like icing sugar on a cake. She glanced up at the high ceilings and was pleased to see only a few cobwebs. The empty house made an eerie impression. All the furniture and ornaments were as Lachlan's mother had left them when she moved into town, obviously expecting to return from the convalescent home. She had kept a tidy house, with everything neatly placed. The kitchen was welcoming and well appointed; a large deal table sat in the middle of the room where three generations of McGrath women had fed their families. Ruth imagined the sound of children running through the house, with the smell of bread baking in the fuel stove. Family pictures adorned the sideboard, with one of Lachlan and his brothers in the centre. A wave of sadness came over her as she remembered she would be alone on this adventure. The sound of creaking floorboards distracted her. She made a mental note to get those checked.

There were six bedrooms in all, plus a large sleep-out. The bedding was probably rotten, she surmised, looking at the dust-covered pillows. She returned to the veranda for some fresh air and checked one of the chairs for spiders as she glanced over towards the snake to make sure it hadn't moved.

"Come and sit, Bax, we'll share a sandwich before we start cleaning…"

There was a loud crack as the chair leg broke through the rotting veranda. Ruth fell to one side, and as she tried to stop herself, her leg went through the broken boards. She half screamed before the sound ended abruptly with a thud. Her head crashed against the foundation. Dark red blood trickled down the sandstone block, pooling on the aged, sun bleached timber flooring.

CHAPTER 14

Ruth decided it was the most beautiful day, as she picked wild blackberries while walking along the river's edge. The sun blazed overhead, warm but not hot, and the grass appeared greener than usual, more lush and vibrant against the opal blue sky. In the distance, Stewart's laughter rose above the chirping cicadas; she guessed he and Jessica must be playing a game with Lachlan. It felt as though she had been walking for miles and she wondered how far along they were.

"Stew, Lach, my leg's aching, how much further?" No one answered. Surely they weren't so far away that they couldn't hear. The sky had started to cloud over; she didn't want to get stuck in a downpour.

"I'm going to rest a while." She had had enough and found a grassy patch to sit down on. At least I won't starve, she thought, rinsing a handful of the shiny, ripe berries in the stream.

As the sun filtered through the lofty river gums, it was warm on her face. She finished off the deliciously sweet berries and reclined on the grass. She closed her eyes; her tiredness was compelling.

Excruciating stomach pains forced her awake; she hastily glanced at the blackberry bush for evidence of herbicide dust. "Lachlan!" she shouted, trying to stand, but she couldn't move. "Lachlan, I'm sick." Her annoyance turned to anger, "I'm not playing, you lot, I'm ill! Lachlan, Stew, I need help!"

"Just keep still, luv, you'll be okay." The disembodied male voice barely penetrated Ruth's distress as the arresting pain returned.

She screamed out in agony as her body contracted. "God, help me… what's happening?" As she forced open her eyes, she half expected to see a wild pig tearing at her torso. Instead, utter shock; a man was holding her hand and wiping her forehead. There was blood, and worse, most of her clothing had disappeared.

What's happened to me? Who is this man? Where am I? Ruth's mind flashed back to the horrors of the house in Croydon, and with every ounce of strength she could muster, she endeavoured to struggle free.

"Steady on, missus, you've had a fall and right now you're having a baby."

Ruth discerned no hint of malice in his expression, as she tried to make sense of what he had said. Baxter stood next to him, looking at her. It was unusual for him not to be barking at the stranger. Slowly, the pieces started to fall into place and she recalled her trip to Derrigeribar.

"Your leg went through the veranda; you must have hit the wall as you fell. No major damage."

As the man continued to talk, her memory kicked back in. "I need to get to the doctor; I can't have my baby here."

"Bit late for that, darl…"

Before the man had finished, the familiar waves of contracting pain took over Ruth's body. The break between contractions didn't provide sufficient respite to sustain any meaningful conversation. Unlike Stewart's birth, this delivery appeared to be almost spontaneous.

"Well, well, a good job I reckon, considering all the fuss. A baby boy!"

The baby cried as the stranger deftly cut and knotted the cord. Ruth held her new son close to her, losing herself in his distress at having arrived in such a chaotic, foreign world.

"We'll need to get word back to Bry," the man said.

Ruth watched as he cleaned up; under normal circumstances such a predicament would be highly embarrassing, but right now, she didn't care.

"You seemed to know what to do," Ruth managed to say.

"Horses, sheep, women, all basically the same," he said very matter-of-factly.

Between bouts of sleep, Ruth's eyes followed the stranger as he swept the worst of the dust from the floor around her. A tall, solid man, older than Lachlan, with greying temples. Then she realised: he must be Joshua, the brother who 'doesn't want to know anyone', according to Lachlan. The resemblance was striking.

"Excuse me," she mumbled.

The man turned, raising his eyebrows in much the same way as Lachlan had.

"You're Joshua, aren't you?" Of course he is. She remembered the photograph on the sideboard.

"That's me, luv... and you're Lachie's wife?"

"Yes, that's right." Ruth wondered how he knew.

"I guessed who you were, I recognised the ute."

"Lachlan told me about you; I expected you to come to the funeral."

"I was out the back of Cunnamulla when all that happened."

"I see." Ruth's attention returned to her son and the sadness of him never knowing his father. Baxter's loud barking interrupted her brooding.

"They've come out looking for you, darl." Joshua went outside to meet the vehicle.

"Is Mrs McGrath inside?" Ruth heard Matthew ask.

"Sure is, mate, come on in." Joshua led a relieved, though puzzled, Matthew into the house.

"Jesus, Ruth! You had us worried. I wish you'd told us about coming here; didn't find out till Toby Hayes called to speak to you. You've had the baby?" Matthew said, looking uncomfortably at his sister, who remained only partly covered.

"We're both fine, Matt, apart from falling through the veranda; bit unexpected that was, but everything's right." Ruth tried to make light of her fall; the last thing she needed was a lecture. "Joshua's been wonderful."

"Joshua, Lachlan's brother?" Matthew's eyebrows arched, causing a deep furrow.

"Yep, that's me. Pleased to meet you, mate." The men shook hands.

"He checks on the place every now and again; not sure how things might have turned out if he hadn't called in yesterday," Ruth added.

"I don't know, Ruth; you don't half get into some funny situations. We'd better get you back home."

Being confined to bed only added to Ruth's annoyance at not being able to get on with her work. She felt miserable as well; Lachlan was on her mind constantly, and how he would never get to see his only son. To make things even worse, she'd broken the news to everyone about Bry going up for sale and the atmosphere in the house had become unbearably tense. Their reaction hadn't been sympathy, but more one of betrayal and resentment. Matthew sat on the bed trying to convince her that they would eventually appreciate the wisdom of her decision; Ruth wasn't so sure. Jessica had taken the news badly. She had promised Jess that she would make sure they kept their home. Now here it was, up for sale.

"How's your leg, Mum?" Stewart looked surprisingly happy.

"Getting better thanks, Stew. How come you're so chirpy today?"

"I was talking to Jess about going away to school and she said we might not be going now."

"At least not for another year, Stew; the two of you can help me get the old farm up and running first."

"What will Willy do while we're working?"

"Sleep, I hope!" Ruth smiled.

"Is that his real name?" Stewart wanted to know.

"Yes, Dad and I agreed on William for a boy. It was your grandfather's name."

"You'll have your hands full with three at home. What happened to boarding school?" Matthew asked.

"I can't afford it now. They can go to the school in town for another year."

"They don't seem too bothered," he said.

"No, they're not, they think it's wonderful. When are you and Barb going to start a family?" Ruth changed the subject. There would be plenty of time to worry about her own troubles when everyone had gone.

"Barb wanted the farm to make a bit more money before having children, well, so she said."

"It's a pity you two live so far away; you should move here and we can get Derrigeribar up and running together. I'm sure Barbara would like the company." Ruth's thoughts raced ahead, making plans for the dilapidated farm.

"If things were different, I might have thought about moving closer."

"Different, how?"

"I've signed up. That's why I'm here."

"I don't follow. What do you mean?"

"Barb threw me out."

"What are you talking about? How can she throw you out? And signed up for what?"

"The RAAF, Ruth. I've signed up for the Air Force. I'm to report in Sydney in two weeks."

"I don't understand, you're married. You can't get called up."

"I volunteered, something I've wanted to do for a while."

"What a stupid thing to do," Ruth blurted. "Why would you volunteer now of all times? You'll end up being sent to Vietnam. No wonder Barbara's mad, not that she has any right to throw you out. She's probably scared you'll get killed in some godforsaken foreign country."

"Come on, Ruth, you're reacting as badly as she did. I want to join the Air Force; I think it's a good thing."

"I don't know, Matt, perhaps I just don't understand how men can view war and fighting as a good thing. I hope my boys never need to go to war. You do what you need to do; it's your life I guess." Ruth realised she wasn't going to win any arguments today. "Damn this leg, I want to get up and do some work. Give us a hand, Matty. I'm going over to Derrigeribar to work on those boards before anyone else falls through them."

The arrival of a telegram cut short Matthew's two weeks; he had to leave for Sydney a week early. Ruth had every intention of trying to talk him out of going, but with everything else happening in her life, she never seemed to find a good time to sit and talk. Bry had a buyer, the Ryans were offered new jobs out near Bourke and the school holidays had finally ended. After just a week of the new routine, it seemed to Ruth as though she was spending all her time travelling backwards and forwards to school. Trying to make Derrigeribar habitable had to be done in between trips. Luckily, William had turned out to be a good baby, rarely crying, unless he was hungry.

The day to leave Bry came around almost too quickly, but Ruth guessed they would never be entirely ready. She wondered if perhaps subconsciously she had been putting off the actual move, leaving it to the last minute as she had. The busyness of moving, with the cleaning, the packing and making notes for the new owners, had kept her mind occupied and prevented her from acknowledging the emptiness that now existed in her life.

They sat on the front steps, a family of four now, looking out across the weedy paddocks. No use tilling or planting anything, she had told Stewart. The prospect of leaving conjured up all sorts of feelings. Sadness at leaving behind a home and loving memories, a sense of relief at having resolved the problem with the bank and fear at the prospect of taking everything on single-handedly. Only one parent, no doting grandparents, Matthew in the Air Force, too far away for friends to visit, one disaster after another; she wondered if she would ever be able to provide the children with what they needed to grow up with a chance in life.

"Will we come back again?" Stewart asked, trying to make sense of the bewildering changes in his life. He was too young to remember the move from Sydney. For Jessica, it was a move away from the only home she had ever known.

"I'm sure we'll visit the new owners from time to time, Stew. Derrigeribar will be our home now, though, at least until I make enough money to buy it back."

Ruth wanted to leave everyone with a little hope. She guessed that when Derrigeribar was all fixed up, they'd like it as much as Bry. But of course the memories wouldn't be there, not the happy times they had spent together with Lachlan. Ruth put her arms around both their shoulders. "It'll be an adventure; you, Jess, Will and me, making a new home. Come on, we've got a lot to do. Let's make a move."

"Can we sit in the back?" Stewart asked.

"So long as you don't hang over the side," Ruth said, as she secured the carrycot along the bench seat next to her. "No sniffing, Bax, or you'll be walking!"

The over laden vehicle wormed its way along the track towards the bitumen road. Ruth locked the last gate and hurried back to the utility. Pulling out onto the road, she glanced quickly into the rear-view mirror. Bryliambone had all but disappeared behind a cloud of red dust.

Years of accumulated grime had to be cleaned from the house before Ruth could even contemplate the state of the paddocks. She made the most of her daily trips to and from school by spending her days in the town library, arranging consultations with stock and station agents and visiting the agronomist at the research station.

To grow cotton, according to the experts, the land needed to be cleared and levelled to a particular incline, which would allow for even watering and drainage. There was then the problem of actually getting water to the crop, which Ruth solved by taking a gamble on dry-land cotton. The creek always contained some water, if the rain didn't come. She made a special effort to ensure the children understood what was happening so they would feel involved. And more importantly, want to help.

"What happens when the men finish, Mum?" Stewart had been studying the tree-stippled scrub as it was transformed into a vast flatland. He seemed overwhelmed by the prospect of working such a large area with his mother alone.

"That's when I start doing some work. Once all cleared, it has to be cultivated before we can plant."

"With machines?"

"Yes, matey, all machines up to that point, but then we have to keep chipping the weeds out."

Ruth realised how much she had missed having Stewart all to herself. He had been a collective responsibility on Bry. He was a proper little man now.

"Are you sad, Mum?"

"No, darling, just thinking about you and me and what we've been through these last few years. You were too young to remember when we lived in Sydney. Life was difficult then too." Stewart hugged his mother and tears welled in her eyes. Sadness, joy, fear; the actual emotion was too complicated to pinpoint.

The following weeks were unrelenting. Ploughing the uneven ground was taking longer than Ruth anticipated, and William had developed the annoying habit of wanting to be fed at the end of each lap. Reluctantly, Ruth decided to withdraw Stewart from school for a while and tutor him at home in the evenings. Jessica's best friend's mother had offered to let her stay in town through the week, which gave Ruth an extra three hours' work time each day.

Stewart's new job was to entertain his baby brother who, for some reason, had become cantankerous. Probably not enough attention, Ruth thought guiltily, but with Stewart now babysitting, she was free to drive the tractor. After an initial period of protest and indignation at doing a 'woman's job', Stewart seemed to take a shine to his new career.

"Mum! Mum, someone's here!" Stewart called. A dust-covered utility had pulled into the homestead driveway.

"Who is it, Stew?"

"Don't know, I'll go and investigate."

"No you won't, we'll all go; jump in the ute while I get Will."

Joshua was waiting for them on the veranda. From what Lachlan had told her about his reclusive tendencies, she hadn't expected to bump into him again. As they approached, Ruth sensed her cheeks flush; he had seen her at her worst. God no, she thought, he's seen all my private bits!

"My word, you've certainly recovered, Ruth!"

"Hello, Josh. This is Uncle Joshua, Stew," she said, trying not to think about William's arrival into the world.

"Hello," Stewart said, staring at the ground.

"This is Daddy's brother, Stew. Do you remember him telling you about how they used to go yabbying in the creek?"

"I thought I'd come and check on you; make sure you're all right." Joshua didn't appear the least bit uncomfortable.

Darn it, Ruth thought, it wasn't any use being embarrassed now. "Been busy but things are going well. How's your citrus?"

"Got another lot coming off in about a month; good crop this year."

"Come inside, I'll make some lunch." Ruth normally loathed unexpected visitors but on this occasion she was glad of some adult conversation.

"You had a pile of mail in the box," Joshua said as he dropped a bundle of yellowing letters on the table.

"I haven't checked for a couple of weeks. I wasn't expecting anything." Ruth eyed the handwritten letter from Sydney.

"A mate of mine from out near Moree grows cotton. He's going to irrigate this year; they weren't getting good enough yields."

"I was hoping to get by for a couple of years without paying out extra money."

"They've put the new dam in now you know, but you'll need to apply for a licence."

"I'll get round to it soon." Ruth didn't mention she had virtually no money to eat, let alone to buy water licences. "Now tell me more about what you do, I was hardly in a state to make conversation the last time we met."

"Not much to tell really; worked like a dog out in the scrub for ten years, then bought Gallerun."

"Didn't you miss home?"

"Not at first. I wanted to show the old man I could do as well as him. I guess pride kept me from coming back."

"I shouldn't be prying..."

"That's okay, always been a bit of a black sheep. Never got along with the old man much. Lachy was always Dad's favourite. All seems a bit daft now."

"Funny things, families; I used to think mine was the craziest, but they all seem to have their moments." Ruth smiled. He was a rough character in comparison to Lachlan, but he had a certain charm.

"Well, you came back; there must be something about the place."

"Yeah, it's peaceful here and has good memories. When we were kids, we'd all sit around this table for dinner. Where you're sitting now used to be my seat. Mum used to bake the best bread and she'd pile it up, still warm, in the middle of the table here." His eyes glazed over as he stared at the centre of the scrubbed kitchen table.

"Come on, I'll show you the plans of what's going on so you don't get lost the next time you visit. I'm only putting in the one paddock of cotton, the land from the creek down to the second dam, about four square miles."

"Lot of bloody hard yakka if things don't work out."

"I'm not expecting a miracle. If I make enough to cover costs with a bit left over, I'll be happy. I want to add sorghum next year and wheat the year after. It'll take me all that time to get the rest of the land up to scratch."

"You should run sheep out on the west paddock; they'll do well."

"I'll need men on the property if I run livestock. I want to get all the crops going first."

"You seem to know what you're doing."

"I'll tell you in June if I know what I'm doing, we'll find out how many pickers I can fill."

Ruth enjoyed Joshua's company, so much so that she asked him to stay the night to save driving in the dark. Stewart was the happiest he had been since Lachlan's accident, and even William went straight to sleep after dinner. Must be the sound of a man's voice, she guessed; probably makes them feel more secure.

Dinner was a special effort, roast leg of lamb with mint sauce and baked vegetables. When she was making the gravy, Ruth realised just how much she missed Lachlan, not only having someone to cuddle up to and do things for, but the partnership. It was exhausting taking on everything alone, being everything to everyone and having no one to talk to about anything.

"I'm off to bed now; the little fella's worn me out," Josh said, looking exhausted.

"Okay. I'll just go through the post and I'll hit the sack as well."

Joyce's letters were always newsy, but this one was only a page long. Ruth guessed something must be wrong.

"Oh Joyce, poor Aggie!" Ruth said aloud. Aggie had been diagnosed with lung cancer. As she read further, she could sense Joyce's fear beneath her overly optimistic tone. Joyce went on to say she was expecting the disease to go into remission. Reading between the lines, Ruth suspected it was probably too advanced.

Ruth's own recent losses had numbed her to some degree. All she could feel was a resurgence of her own sense of misery and loss. The next letter in the pile was from the bank, but that held no surprises; just enough money to scrape by on for the next six months, if they were lucky. She knew that if the cotton didn't pay, she would have to go back to nursing and living in town. You've made it damn hard, she thought, surely you're still not punishing me for Tommy? Ruth often found herself pleading with the Almighty for answers, although she was beginning to wonder if such an entity existed. If it did, he definitely wasn't the benevolent father she had learned about at school.

Bacon and coffee aromas drifted into the bedroom; Ruth threw on her dressing gown and hurried into the kitchen.

"Sorry, Josh, I should have been up over an hour ago."

"That's okay, thought I'd make us all some brekkie. I might give you a hand with the tractor if you don't mind me hanging around."

"No, not at all. You can stay as long as you like if you're going to drive the old Fergie for me." Josh's offer was a pleasant surprise. He was a lot like Lachlan she realised, his features of course, but also his laid-back way of doing things.

"Hope you got through that pile of mail before it got too late."

"Yes, didn't take long; bills mainly, apart from a bit of sad news."

"I'm sorry, I should've left it in the box," Joshua said with a waggish smile.

"No, it's okay; someone I know in Sydney is ill and I don't think she'll recover. The midwife who delivered Stewart, actually; she helped look after him as well while I worked." Ruth wondered if she might have said too much but realised the town gossips had probably already filled him in on her past. Joshua didn't look up from his tea.

"You should probably go and visit if she's that ill. You might regret it if you don't."

"It's not just Aggie; Joyce, her best friend, is taking it hard. She took me in when I arrived in Sydney and had nowhere to stay."

"Go then, I'll look after Stew. You can get the train down."

It hadn't occurred to Ruth to go to Sydney.

"I don't think I should leave everything here, unless it was just a lightning trip down and back. I guess if I caught the mail train tonight, I could be on my way back tomorrow evening."

"Sounds like a mad rush, but if that's what you want to do."

"You really don't mind me going?" Ruth said enthusiastically.

"I wouldn't have offered if I minded; better see what the little fella thinks first, though."

"I'll be good, Mum; I can help Uncle Josh drive the tractor." Stewart was delighted by the idea.

"So long as you promise to help and not get in the way."

"I will, I'll help with all the work and do what I'm told." Ruth cringed at the prospect of leaving Stewart, but maybe spending time with another male might be good.

"Okay, you can stay and I'll go to see Auntie Joyce. She hasn't met William yet. He might cheer her up."

Being chauffeured to the station was a treat for Ruth; a small thing in itself but it meant a lot. It brought back memories of Lachlan.

"I'm grateful for all this you're doing, Josh."

"Ah, well, I never did much for anyone when they were around. Now there's hardly any McGraths left."

Ruth suspected he felt guilty about deserting the family, especially leaving his mother to manage the farm alone.

The Western Mail was due to pull out of the station. Ruth hastily made her way to the compartment and looked out the window at Stewart and Joshua. She always had trouble saying goodbye to Stewart, even just going to work. The whistle blew.

Brave face, Ruth, she told herself, and waved goodbye.

CHAPTER 15

The train rolled into Central Railway Station. The cityscape had lost much of its former charm. The childlike notion of a new and exciting world beyond the jungle of Papua had long faded for Ruth; the city appeared cold and heartless. To her surprise, buses now took the place of trams. During the few years that she had been away, many things had changed. After some confusion, she found a bus which stopped just a few doors down from Joyce's.

"Ruth! Come in; come in, what a surprise!" Ruth disappeared into Joyce's ample hug. "And who is this little possum?"

"This is William. He's come all the way down to meet you. How are you, Joyce?"

"Bearing up, thanks, luv. They took Aggie to St Andrew's hospital last night. She was having trouble breathing. We can go up to visit later."

"Yes, I'd like that, but I'm worried about you, Joyce. She's your best friend."

"We've known each other for nearly forty years and been neighbours since just after the war. I'll miss her, Ruthy, never had any other real friends, only Ag."

Ruth put her arm around Joyce's shoulder. God, life's hard when you get older, she thought. "I'll take a quick shower and then we'll go up to the hospital. I can only stay for the day; I left Stew with his uncle."

"You're a good girl, Ruth; you shouldn't worry about me, you've got such a lot to contend with yourself."

"Don't be daft; knowing Aggie was so ill, I had to come to make sure you were all right."

"I'll manage. It's life, after all." Joyce wiped away a tear with the end of her pinny. "Happens to us all, eventually. Anyway, look at this big healthy bub! Goin' to be another good-looker, I reckon."

"You wouldn't believe the state I was in when I had him. I'd fallen through the veranda at the old farm and knocked myself out, only to wake up in labour."

"I can remember when you had Stew. You fell over up the alley and kept telling me you'd wet yourself, remember?" The two women could still laugh in spite of the tragic circumstances which had brought them back together. "After the hospital, we'll go to Shirley's. She only lives around the corner, next to Mrs Robertson's place, where you both used to live."

"It'll be good to visit Shirl. Neither of us seems to get the time to write regularly. She been keeping well?"

"Health wise, as fit as a fiddle, but she was going out with this no-good fancy boy there for a while, another fly-by-night. Doesn't have much luck with men that girl, like her mother. If I've told her once, I've told her a hundred times, find one who's plain-looking with a good, steady job; but no, she goes for the good-looking ones. Makes no difference what I say."

"I'm sure she'll meet the right one eventually, Joyce."

"Well, she wants to hurry up or she'll be left on the shelf. Anyway, let's go up to the hospital."

The walk to St Andrew's hospital in Darlinghurst affirmed Ruth's decision to leave Sydney. Apart from the dead-end life she used to have, the number of cars, buses, people and the noise had become unbearable.

"You should come up to the farm for a break, Joyce. Might do you good to get away from all this chaos."

"Not like it used to be, eh? It gets busier by the week. All the new migrants, too many of 'em, I reckon."

A cloud of apprehension descended over Ruth as they approached the hospital. Death and loss had taken their toll, and although she wanted to be a support for Joyce, she felt uneasy. To make matters worse, William had woken up and started to cry. As they pushed through the large hospital doors into the foyer, he became cranky and his cries were unremitting.

"I should have woken him up for a feed before we left," Ruth said, flustered.

"No, you can't do that anymore. They say you're to feed them when they want feeding. I'll ask the nurse to find you somewhere private. I'll pop in and see Ag and you can come in when you're finished."

Grateful for William's outburst; Ruth had a chance to collect herself before seeing Aggie. With William cradled in her arms, she sunk back into the deep, padded, leather chair and luxuriated in the warm, golden sunlight which streamed through the window. She nodded off briefly, only to wake with a start. Joyce was standing over her, creating a shadow. Something had happened, her face was ashen and stunned-looking.

"Joyce?"

"Oh, Ruth, she passed away last night. In her sleep, the doctor said." Joyce slumped onto the chair opposite.

Ruth expected a more tearful show of emotion, but Joyce appeared more stunned than distraught. "I'll get you some water," she said, carefully putting the sleeping baby into his pram.

"No, I'm all right, luv, a bit shocked, that's all; the doctor said he'd sent for her husband. I've known Ag most of my life but never had a clue about any husband."

"Do you think they made a mistake?"

"Don't think so. He's coming to make all the arrangements, apparently. I've left my name and address with the charge nurse. The least he can do is come and talk to me before he goes ahead with anything. She told me she wanted to go to Rookwood Cemetery."

Ruth leant over and hugged Joyce; words seemed pointless.

"Anyway, luv," Joyce continued, "no good sitting here; let's get back home." She stood, ready to leave.

Neither of the women had much to say as they braved the chilly wind back to Surry Hills. Apart from the shock of discovering Aggie's mysterious husband, her passing didn't seem unjust, or even unexpected for that matter. She had been ill for some time and was in her mid-seventies. She smoked like a chimney and had drunk heavily since before the war. It was still terribly sad, Ruth thought, especially for Joyce.

Joyce's tatty, blue front door was a welcome sight as the rain started to bucket-down. Returning home to Derrigeribar had been on Ruth's mind since leaving the hospital, but she felt sorry for Joyce and didn't want to leave her straightaway.

"Shirley finishes work at three today, so she'll be home soon. We'll go round after I've made a cuppa," Joyce said.

"If I can find a phone box, I might call home on the way."

"Try the station when we go; they've put in a lot of new ones."

"I thought I'd stay and go to the funeral with you if I can get hold of Josh to let him know."

"Stewy must be missing you by now, luv."

"He'll cope, Joyce, although I'm not so sure about Josh. He doesn't have any children of his own."

"Come on then, let's go up to Shirley's, we'll stop at a phone on the way." Joyce brightened at the prospect of her guests staying over.

Ruth remembered the streets as if she had never left. As they walked past Mrs Robertson's house, her first reaction was to pop in and say hello, but then she changed her mind. Having left behind her dreadful life in Sydney, she really had no desire to revisit the past. Mrs Robertson had been kind, Ruth remembered, and she always intended to tell the woman the truth about her circumstances one day. But maybe things were better left as they were.

Every telephone box either had a queue a mile long or someone engrossed in deep conversation, so they arrived at Shirley's flat without having made the call. Annoyed at not finding a phone, Ruth started to worry about her decision to leave Stewart for longer than planned.

"Ruth!" Shirley threw her arms around Ruth's neck.

"You're looking well, Shirley." Ruth's antipathy melted. It was delightful to see Shirley again.

"And this must be Master William. What a cute little face!" Shirley said, taking William from the pushchair. "Come through to the kitchen; I've made a fresh pot of tea."

"My feet are killing me," Joyce said. "We walked all the way from the hospital and then up Rupert Street trying to find a telephone, and finally up all your stairs." She collapsed into an oversized wicker chair and then burst into tears. The reality of Aggie's death had hit home.

"Come on, Auntie Joyce, sip some tea." Shirley tried to console her. "You wanted to make a telephone call, Ruth?"

"I better call home before they go to bed. I want to check that Stew and Josh are okay."

"Mrs Payne downstairs has a telephone; she won't mind if you make a call. Come on, I'll take you down."

"I'd rather use a public one for a trunk call, Shirl."

"Don't be nutty. So long as you give her the money, she'll be right."

Ruth remembered just how resourceful Shirley was, always knowing the quickest and easiest way to do something.

Privately tucked away in a cupboard at the end of the hallway stood the telephone. Mrs Payne and Shirley disappeared into the kitchen.

Ruth lifted the heavy black receiver off the cradle and dialled. She wasn't expecting a woman to answer. "Hello, who is this? What number is this?"

"Is that you, Ruth? This is Barbara. Joshua asked me to stay until you came home."

"Barbara, would you put him on, please?" Ruth tried to contain her anger at her sister-in-law; apparently making herself at home while she was gone. And why did Joshua tell her to stay?

"Sorry, Ruth, but he's in town with Stewart at the hospital."

A sudden jolt of panic hit her insides. "What happened?" Ruth demanded.

"Stewart was bitten by a snake, a brown one. Joshua said he sucked out most of the poison, but Stew got sick, so he took him to the hospital."

"God no… not Stewart!" Ruth pleaded. "Collabine or the base?"

"Lincoln base, they have all the anti—"

"I'll be on tonight's train." Ruth hung up the receiver. "Shirley, I have to go; Stewart's in hospital." Ruth left a dollar next to the telephone and rushed upstairs to tell Joyce.

Within seconds, they were all bustling down to the station. Ruth and Shirley were trying their best to hurry, William cried hysterically in the pram and Joyce was limping; they arrived just in time. All Ruth could think about was Stewart and the painfully slow journey home. As they said goodbye, a distressed Ruth invited the two women to Derrigeribar for a visit, but in the rush, no one set a definite date.

Sensing his mother's distress, William continued to cry until the train started its ascent into the mountains. When he finally fell asleep, Ruth began to cry out of sheer frustration. She had nine more hours to go with nothing to do apart from worry.

Calm down, Ruth, he'll be okay; she tried to talk herself out of the terrifying visions of Stewart lying unconscious in hospital. Then the compartment door opened. An elderly lady entered and sat in the seat opposite.

Blast! Ruth thought, sitting up and trying to compose herself.

"Are you okay, dear?" the passenger enquired after a few minutes' silence.

"Yes, thank you." Ruth had no interest in conversation.

"This is such a slow trip, stopping at every station. I'm going all the way and then on to Coonamble. How far are you going?" The woman persisted.

"Lincoln," Ruth blurted out but then realised she sounded short and rude, so reluctantly she told the woman about Stewart's bite.

"They can be such aggressive creatures, brown snakes. They stand their ground if you get in their way. He'll be fine if he's at the hospital. They use anti-venom nowadays."

Ruth's nurse's training had taught her about snake bites, but she also knew the damage they could cause if the anti-venom wasn't administered in time.

"When we first moved out to Coonamble, my daughter was bitten by an eastern brown. Poking it with a stick, silly girl, only four she was, and not a hospital in sight in those days. Luckily, I had darkies working at the homestead; they knew what to do. I thought I'd lost her, never seen anyone bitten by a snake before, only heard all the dreadful stories about them. We'd always lived in Sydney until my husband inherited the family property. They were certainly hard days then. You never saw the men for weeks at a time when they were out working."

Ruth's annoyance with the woman gradually eased. She was grateful for the company and her stories helped take the edge off her distress.

When the pinkish-orange morning sunlight streamed through the wooden shutters; Ruth realised she must have dozed off. William began to stir, so she quickly rearranged her shawl in order to feed him before any other passengers came into the cubicle. The last leg of the journey seemed to take forever, but after nine hours and ten long minutes, the train chugged into Lincoln station.

Everything seemed to have conspired against her on this trip: Aggie passing away, the dreadful weather, the painfully slow trip home and now the footpath ran out halfway along the road to the hospital. The pram wheels kept locking on the uneven gravel; it reminded Ruth of when she got her foot stuck in the mud, the time Stewart had an ear infection.

She deposited the pram in the foyer and, with William in her arms, made a dash for Admissions.

"Ruth!" a familiar voice greeted her. "I bet you were frantic all night on the train. He's in Paediatrics, bed twelve. I'll come down after my shift if you're still here." Ruby had a permanent morning shift on Admissions and Ruth could always rely on her to know exactly what was happening with everyone.

He must be all right, she thought; Ruby would have said something otherwise. Half walking and half running along the corridor to the children's ward, she spotted Stewart in the bed near the door.

"Oh, Stewy! My poor little man." She leaned across the bed and kissed his forehead. He immediately began to stir and opened his eyes.

"Mum!" He reached up for a hug. William also reached out as if to hug his big brother. Ruth wiped away tears; she was overcome with joy and relief. Stewart seemed well enough, apart from being a bit pasty-looking.

"Uncle Josh!" Stewart's eyes averted.

"G'day Ruth, I hoped you'd get in this morning," Joshua said, with a look of relief.

"I couldn't get here quick enough when Barbara told me. I was imagining the worst all night."

"He's okay now. The doctor said he can go home this morning. They kept me in too; reckon I absorbed some of the venom when I sucked it out his leg."

"Goodness, I don't know. I go away for two days and look what happens. And what's the story with Barbara? She answered the telephone."

"I'd better leave that up to her to tell."

"You can tell me on the way home. I've had enough surprises to last me a while."

It was a relaxing drive home with Joshua at the wheel. A warm, sunny day, bright blue sky and a fresh breeze. One of those days that forces you out of any intellectual preoccupation and into contact with the reality of life, a quirky mainland phenomenon that Ruth put down to the harshness of the light.

After the madness of the night before, Ruth couldn't wait to get home. With Stewart safe, she mentally vowed never to go away again. But then remembered, he would be going off to boarding school in a year or two.

"There'll be no work today. You two can join the sick parade for a couple of days," Ruth announced, half expecting them to protest, but Stewart and Joshua remained quiet. "So, what's the matter with Barbara? She never visits unless it's Christmas or there's a funeral."

"She said she didn't know how to get in contact with Matthew," Joshua said, looking uncomfortable.

"Go on, that can't be all." Ruth was keen to know why Barbara had come looking for Matthew after having thrown him out of his own home.

"Strewth, Ruth, you want all the gory details. She told me she wants a divorce but doesn't know how to get in contact with him."

Ruth remained silent until she had satisfied herself that she wasn't hearing things. "A divorce? Why would she want to tell him about getting a divorce when he's away fighting a war? She's such a selfish woman; I'm sure she has the same contact information as I do. Maybe Matthew's letters didn't reach her. I don't know, I'll worry about her later. Let's just get you two home and settled first."

Derrigeribar was a welcome sight as they drove along the dirt track towards the homestead. The first thing Ruth noticed was all the work Joshua had done. Miraculously, the paddock was now level and every inch painstakingly turned. It gave Ruth a burst of enthusiasm; she wanted to get straight back to work. But first, she had to deal with Barbara.

"It wasn't just his enlisting, he never discussed it with me; I had no say," Barbara snapped.

Ruth thought she looked shrewish; and guilty in a funny way. "Well, I don't know, Barbara. He's a man, and they do odd things sometimes, especially where fighting and wars are involved. I couldn't understand it myself, but what can you do?"

Ruth was annoyed at what sounded like Barbara's dissatisfaction with married life and her mental acrobatics to try to make Matthew's departure to Vietnam look like desertion.

"I mean, he just decided to go and wouldn't listen to anything I said. I don't understand how he could leave me on the property all on my own." Barbara tried her best to elicit Ruth's sympathy.

"To be honest, Barbara, everything you're saying sounds quite selfish and petty; you have a manager at Carraroona! If you want a divorce, that's up to you and Matthew. I've got far too much to worry about here. Come on, Bax."

Ruth waited for the dog then barged out the door. Climbing into the old Ferguson, a rush of guilt came over her. Barbara had obviously been a spoiled child who clearly hadn't grown up. Maybe it was bad timing; she realised that she should have been a bit more sympathetic. Oh I don't know, what can I do anyway? She thrust the tractor into gear and sped off.

Barbara left almost as unexpectedly as she had arrived. Joshua returned to his citrus crop, which left Ruth alone to make a start on planting the cotton. Two days were all she managed before William came down sick. Dr Fuller said it was just a bug, but his continued vomiting nearly caused her to miss the critical soil temperature for sowing. The decision to use the money set aside for a new tractor was hard made, but it was either employ a couple of men to help, or end up with a scraggy crop. Unexpected emergencies, she had learned to accept, but what surprised her was the rain, it came almost on cue!

Stewart's tenth birthday came and went and in no time November had arrived. It was make or break time, and they had to continuously chip away the weeds from the young cotton seedlings. Ruth's day in the field started at first light. She would go back to the house at eight to make the children's breakfast and return with the two boys for another four hours of work before breaking for lunch. She had progressed from chipping two rows at a time, to being able to cover sixteen. The most effective way to work, she discovered, was to secure William in a *bilum* and carry him on her chest like the village women back home. Thus freed from his childcare duties, Stewart was also able to help with the chipping.

"There's another patch of burrs ahead, Mum." Stewart had declared himself the Bathurst burr spotter, the prickliest and woodiest of all the herbaceous invaders.

"I need some water before I get stuck into that lot; must be a hundred-and-twenty degrees out here today," Ruth said, melting onto the ground and trying to position herself under the shade of a large castor oil bush, another woody weed. "Was this frozen, or did you just fill it up from the tap?" To Ruth's annoyance, the water was almost hot.

"The frozen one's down the other end," Stewart said sheepishly, but then William started crying.

"Come on, Stew, let's go up to get the mail and have a *cold* drink. We'll eat lunch at the house today; I put fresh lolly ices in the freezer last night." Stewart's eyes lit up.

Mail deliveries had been few and far between over the last couple of months, but today the postman had outdone himself – one handwritten letter from Sydney, one early Christmas card from Eliza, which was almost unreadable, and, of course, the usual bundle of bills.

"Good news, Stew! Joyce and Shirley want to know if they can come to stay with us for Christmas. I'll ask Uncle Josh to come as well. It'll be nice having visitors."

"I hope they bring presents."

"Goodness, Stew! Just be happy they're coming to visit."

"I want a train set and a robot," he declared.

"Oh, I told Father Christmas you wanted a new hoe so you could keep up with me doing the chipping."

"A hoe? That's a horrible present!" Stewart looked deflated.

"Well, if you want a train set *and* a robot, you'd better be especially good."

"I will, Mum; I'll be so good, you'll think I'm a new Stewart!"

"Oh, Stewy, you're the only Stewart I want." Ruth smiled and leaned across to give his shoulder a squeeze.

Endless days of hoeing up and down cotton rows ensured that November quickly passed into December. Ruth's work had been meticulous, not one errant weed was visible across the entire paddock. At last, the cotton would have a chance. Now it was time for a well-earned break and a trip to Lincoln to collect her visitors.

Ruth put on her blue gingham dress to go into town. The material was light and cool, and the drop-waist always flattered her figure. Checking herself in the mirror, she almost didn't recognise the woman staring back at her. No amount of make-up or Pond's cold cream would hide the ravages of months of working on the cotton. Her hair had become stringy and parched, her skin was a ruddy brown and the few freckles she used to worry about had multiplied, even joining up together in places. What a mess, she thought, it's a good job Lachie can't see me.

"Come on, Jess, hurry up or we'll have no time for Christmas shopping." Since staying with her friend, Jessica had become obsessed with her appearance. Ruth tried not to be annoyed, but every time they wanted to go somewhere they would end up waiting for Jessica. "There are only paddy melons and kangaroos to show off to, you know."

"I might see someone from school in town." Jessica was indignant.

"If you hurry, we'll call into Mrs Moretti's and get your hair done."

"Really? Can I have a Dusty Springfield beehive?"

"All that teasing and lacquer will make your hair brittle, Jess. How about a nice bob? It'll be cool for the summer."

"I'll think about it," she said, unconvinced.

After a painful hour in the hairdressers, rocking William so he would stay asleep and cajoling or bribing Stewart to sit still, they were back on the road. Ruth could hardly contain her excitement as they drove to the railway station. Apart from not having seen Joyce and Shirley since Aggie passed away, she couldn't wait to show them around Derrigeribar. The cotton was already two feet high and bushy, thanks to timely rains, and the house was now comfortable and clean. Although pleased with her efforts, she had learned not to tempt fate too much by revelling in her success. She always remembered the lesson she had learned in Sydney: when everything is going right, that's just the time to expect it to start going wrong.

"Stewart! Wind the window up!" Jessica shouted. A gust of hot wind had blown the entire left side of Jessica's new bob across her face.

"I'm too hot. I can't breathe," Stewart said, innocently looking out the window.

"You can both get out and walk if you don't cut out the squabbling." Ruth half closed her window to reduce the through draft. "We'll fix it before the train comes, Jess." Ruth glanced at her wristwatch, making sure there would be enough time. "I'll park near the Ladies', did you bring a comb?"

There was a good twenty minutes to remodel the windswept bob, even enough time for lemonade at the refreshment rooms. They had just finished their drinks when the station bell rang. Within seconds, the Central West Express was hissing along the platform.

It was like a reunion of long-lost kin. Ruth could never have imagined how close she would become to complete strangers; they were more like family. Both children were instantly enveloped by Joyce's ample arms, until Stewart recoiled as a big, red, lipstick kiss was planted on his cheek. Shirley looked as though she was ready to burst with excitement and Ruth, she simply basked in the heartwarming glow of being surrounded by people she loved.

"Wow, it looks like the real country, like in books," Shirley said. She had never been away from Sydney.

"It is the real country, Shirley," Joyce chided.

"You'll love it," Ruth said, "especially Derrigeribar. It's like a miniature town with all the outbuildings. No one there, of course, only us."

Joyce had seen the more remote parts of the country while in the Women's Land Army during the war, but Shirley was entranced by the vastness and picture book contrasts of vibrant crop fields set against dusty scrublands.

The normally long drive home seemed to take no time at all. As they turned into Derrigeribar, Shirley and Joyce were both in awe.

"My goodness, Ruth, I had no idea," Joyce said, craning her neck so as not to miss anything. "The other place was huge, but this goes on forever."

The property looked spectacular, with its endless, even paddock of cotton, the homestead vegetable and fruit gardens and the rambling array of sheds and barns.

"How many people work here?" Shirley asked.

"Two, Stewart and me," Ruth laughed. "I do most of it with Stew's help, although I had to put a couple of men on to help with the planting. Will was sick and I couldn't get out to do anything. Lachlan's brother, Joshua, helped out too, with the cultivating mainly."

"And Stew does all his schooling at home Joyce was saying."

"Yes, but we can usually pick up the School of the Air from Broken Hill, which helps. He'll go to boarding school in another year," Ruth added, to let them know she intended to make up for any shortcomings in Stewart's education.

Shirley was more overwhelmed by the sheer vastness of everything than bothered by Stewart's school arrangements. "It's unbelievable, Ruth. I couldn't imagine having a place like this. Maybe Joyce and I can stay and give you a hand after Christmas? I've got four weeks off."

"You don't want to spend your holiday working. I'll be fine; I only need to watch it grow now."

"I'd love to help out. It will be good to do something other than typing, and it would give Joyce a break from only having her cat to talk to. Can we, pretty please?"

Ruth easily agreed. Having other women to talk to would be a treat after so many months alone.

Christmas Eve arrived, and the kitchen came to life. Clouds of steam were swirling up around the ceiling, tantalising aromas seeped out of the stove and a cornucopia of produce lay on the draining board waiting to be prepared. Cooking on a wood range was a novelty for Shirley, who had only ever used gas, but when dinner went from one turkey to two, along with two legs of pork, a ham and enough roast potatoes, pumpkin and green vegetables for fifteen people, her sense of adventure turned into trepidation. Joshua, the Ryans and five of the redeployed jackaroos from Bry had descended on Derrigeribar for

Christmas. Luckily, Mrs Ryan brought the plum pudding and three cold, cooked chickens. The men brought beer, cases of which filled every crevice of both refrigerators and overflowed into hastily constructed Coolgardie safes, which hung on the veranda.

As Ruth watched everyone enjoying themselves, she remembered how last Christmas had passed almost unnoticed, or had been blotted out of consciousness as everyone grappled with Lachlan's accident and the fate of Bry. This year, everything had begun to heal. Lachlan was missed, of course, but life had to go on, something everyone acknowledged and made an effort to ensure. Lachlan's absence was formally acknowledged with a toast, but he remained in the background, especially for Ruth and Jessica. Visitors helped, their festive spirit rubbed off, compelling everyone to join in and enjoy the celebration.

It seemed like Christmas was over in a flash. No sooner had Ruth said goodbye to her guests than she was back chipping out weeds. This time, however, she had help.

"You know, Ruth; I must have lost at least a stone," Joyce said proudly, as she appraised the top of her arms.

"It's the constant walking. You'll go back to Sydney looking like Twiggy."

"Gawd, save us, I could never be that slim! Shirley's blossomed these last few weeks, though. I've never seen her looking so well, eh, Shirl?"

"What's that?" Shirley glanced up from the monstrous castor oil bush with which she had been wrestling.

"I was just saying how much this country living agrees with you," Joyce shouted, as she stepped in to attack the other side of the bush.

"Apart from having blisters on blisters and no nails left!"

They all laughed. It was the happiest Ruth had been since losing Lachlan.

"Here comes Stew. I wonder why he's left Will on his own." Ruth marched up the row to meet him. "What's wrong? Why did you leave Will?"

"Will's okay, he's asleep in the playpen. You've got a telegram; they phoned it through."

"Hurry up then, what did it say?" Ruth barked. After Stewart's snake bite, she had become fiercely vigilant about the safety of all her children.

"It's Uncle Matthew. He's been wounded; they're sending him home."

"What?" Ruth heard, but her mind needed time to process the information.

"Uncle Matthew, he got shot, and they're sending him home."

CHAPTER 16

Ruth had heard nothing from the RAAF since the telegram two weeks before. More worrying, she'd received no word from Matthew. He was always terrible when it came to writing, but the thought of him being unable to write because of injuries was a different matter. Maybe no news is good news, she hoped, throwing herself into an all-out attack on another outbreak of bollworm.

The only way to rid the crop of the insidious grub was to spray. This involved driving up and down the cotton rows all day and night until completed. After two days straight, the job had taken its toll on Ruth. By the time she got to bed, she could feel her body still moving to the motion of the tractor. Even worse, she had absorbed the poison through her skin and was nauseous.

"You look bushed, Ruth." Joshua had come by to check on how things were going.

"I've never been so tired in my life. I fell asleep on the tractor last night and ended up in the creek. If it weren't for the furrows, I'd have flattened half the cotton."

"You need to put someone on or you'll be dead in another year or two," he said, with a concerned frown.

"I will, after this first crop." Ruth suspected from Joshua's expression that he thought she must be trying to prove something, rather than doing the work from necessity.

"When Lachlan had the accident, he had no insurance and the bank wanted to foreclose on the mortgage. You know Lachy had to pay Bob out, don't you?"

"I didn't until old Charlie Ryan told me at Christmas. I had no idea he had no insurance, though. You must be skint."

"Almost, but I've got enough to strip the crop and to survive until we get a payment."

"I can give you a hand—"

"No thanks, Josh. If I can't succeed on my own, I'll quit and go back to nursing. The children can go to a government school. We'll manage." Ruth knew Joshua had noble intentions but after almost prostituting herself to Ali in Sydney, relying on a man again for money was out of the question. Joshua looked perplexed; she realised she had been tactless.

"Thanks for offering, Joshua; I appreciate your concern. I just think if I can't make the farm work, I have to accept that and find another way to make a living."

"You're a tough nut, but I understand. If you do get stuck, though, give me call before you go moving back to town."

"Matthew will be home soon. Once he's recovered, he can help out, if he doesn't go back to Barbara."

"Yeah, Stew said he's coming home. What happened?"

"I don't know. They didn't give me any details other than that he's recovering from a bullet wound. They mentioned early June, but nothing definite."

"Poor bugger, he'll probably need Barbara when he gets back."

"Well, you'd think so, but I haven't heard from her either since she was here last. Matt never mentions anything about her, but then he never says much at all in his letters."

"Ah well, you never know. She might come running when she knows he's back," Joshua said.

"Yes, no point worrying, I guess. I need all my energy to get this crop sorted out." Beneath the surface, she did worry about Matthew, but the family's future was at stake. There was only one chance to make this venture work, or lose the lot forever.

March 1971. Weeks of searing summer temperatures had brought the cotton to readiness sooner than Ruth anticipated. Defoliation of the crop was now complete and each of the bolls had split open, revealing their fluffy white contents. The paddock took on a magical appearance, like a snow-covered fairyland. Ruth almost allowed herself to rejoice in what she had achieved but any sense of triumph was soon overshadowed when she worked out how much the picking contractors charged. The original quote hadn't included transport costs. The machinery had to come from Wee Waa and then the cotton carted to the ginnery. She had no choice but to pay.

Once started, the two hungry stripping machines worked non-stop, devouring the crop until every last boll had been ripped from the bushes. Ruth found herself bewildered by the disappearance of her cotton; months of preparation, sowing and tending the crop had ended in just a few days. The paddock appeared ravaged – dead foliage, stripped plants and stray cotton scattered through the rows. It was as though there had been a death.

Curled up on the couch, Ruth consoled herself with a couple of days' rest and enjoyed some uninterrupted time with the two boys. Jessica had finally gone off to boarding school, as Lachlan had wanted. The house was peaceful. Stewart and William played outside mostly, giving Ruth the chance to read *Airport*, a new book which Shirley had sent. On the second day, the shrill sound of the telephone interrupted her relaxing interlude.

"Matthew! How are you? Where are you calling from?"

"G'day, Ruthy, I'm okay. At Richmond, just been demobbed." He sounded well.

"They said you're coming here. Is that right or are you going out to Carraroona?"

"I'll arrive at your place about mid-morning tomorrow; plane to Lincoln then a truck."

"We can pick you up from Lincoln if you like."

"Nah, they can take me out… anyway, better go; another bloke's waiting and I want to call Jake while I've got the phone."

"Call Jake? Where is he?"

"At Okoro. He's got a phone now, paid to get a line connected to the Sogeri exchange, couple of months back."

"I never knew." So surprising was the news about the telephone line, she forgot all the things she had wanted to ask, especially about his injuries. Hopefully they're all better now, she thought, making her way down the hall to fix his room.

Excitement filled the air the following morning at Derrigeribar. Stewart polished his coin collection to show Matthew and Ruth had the main oven full of bread. She cleaned and tidied the house from top to bottom while Joshua killed a sheep so there would be plenty of fresh meat.

Matthew's transport pulled into the drive just after midday, a shiny green Land Rover truck with a red cross blazoned across the side. Ruth was alarmed, she had assumed he had recovered from his wounds and wasn't expecting an ambulance. Rushing out to the vehicle, she noticed Matthew grasping at crutches as he awkwardly alighted. She floundered for a second as she stared at the dusty ground where he stood, then rushed forward to hug him. He had lost a leg.

"Cadged a lift with some army buddies, good blokes they are." The pair waved as the vehicle disappeared into a cloud of red dust.

"Come on, Matt, let's go in. Stew's been up since five waiting for you to arrive."

"Uncle Matt!" Stewart bolted through the doorway. "Jeez, you've had your leg shot off!"

"Stewart!" Ruth reprimanded.

"He's okay," Matthew said, smiling at Stewart. "Sure did, mate, blown off by a bloody gook!"

Stewart was fascinated and, to Ruth's further annoyance, he wanted to know all the details. He remained wide-eyed as Matthew recounted how, after crawling through the jungle to evade enemy fire, he had the misfortune to walk into a booby trap.

Matthew's homecoming provided a welcome break from the relentless schedule of farm activity, but as the weeks passed, Ruth began to wonder what he intended to do. He had been home for nearly a month and hadn't mentioned returning to Carraroona, or anything about Barbara for that matter. She realised his injuries must be making him depressed and worried this might complicate his recovery. She decided he needed a push.

"So what do you plan to do?" Ruth said matter-of-factly, as she glanced up from her ironing.

"Barb wants a divorce, so I'll probably sell up. If I can keep enough for an old Ceres or even a Pawnee, I'll be happy."

Ruth stared at him, dumbfounded; not only by the apparent ease with which he intended to relinquish Carraroona but also by his desire to buy an aircraft.

"Why do you want an aeroplane?"

"I want to start up an aerial spraying business; will do well with all you cotton farmers springing up out here."

"Surely you can't let the property go so easily?"

"If I fight her, I'll end up with nothing after paying solicitors. If I finalise it all quickly, I'll be able to get on with my life. No good trying to get back together. Once Barb found out we couldn't have kiddies, everything went downhill."

Ruth tried to remember if he had mentioned not being able to have children before. She couldn't. "Couldn't anything medical be done?"

"The doctor she went to didn't seem to think so, and Barb wasn't interested in adopting. Anyway, I want my own kids, a son to carry on after I'm gone."

Ruth didn't want to pry into their medical situation but guessed Barbara was the one with the problem. She still had a sneaking suspicion that another man lurked somewhere in the background. *She couldn't look me in the eye when she spoke about Matthew,* Ruth recalled; *she appeared guilty in an odd way.*

"So you'll what, let her take you for desertion?"

"Seems to be the best way out. I just won't go back."

"I don't know what to say. You're being too reasonable, if you ask me. Still, I suppose you're not asking me, eh?"

"Nope." And that ended the conversation about divorce. Not unlike Ruth, once he had made up his mind, Matt relegated the subject to history.

The cotton harvest turned out to be a spectacular success. The yield exceeded all expectations, which made up for the impurity penalties and the extra transport costs. The crop provided Ruth with the money she needed to replant as well as buy a small mob of sheep. The main challenge now would be repeating the success the following year. This year's rain had been sheer luck.

The new Burrandong dam, which Joshua mentioned, was providing reliable water to some of the surrounding properties. Ruth decided her safest bet would be to buy into the scheme and obtain a water licence. Growing irrigated cotton would ensure her agricultural endeavours continued. Once again, the old Ferguson would have to wait another season to be retired.

"You did it then?" Joshua smiled, more out of relief than pleasure.

"Seems so. I banked the cheque last week! I had to keep looking at it to make sure I wasn't imagining things. My water licence came through too, so next year I won't have to gamble on rain."

"That calls for a celebration, I reckon." Joshua lifted up a large bottle of orange juice. "I've gone into juice now, bought myself a processing plant." He poured two large tumblers.

"Well, the gods must be smiling on us at the moment; even Matthew's happy," Ruth said, taking a sip of juice.

"Has he decided what to do yet?"

"Barbara's going to file for a divorce at some point. Matt's taking all the blame and giving her a huge chunk of the property. He's out looking for a plane this week, wants to start up his own crop-dusting business."

"Good on him."

"He reckons with his defoliation experience in Vietnam, he shouldn't have any trouble."

"He can do mustering in the off season." Joshua said thoughtfully, intrigued by the potential uses of a plane.

"Yes, he probably could. Are you going to be here for Christmas?" Ruth asked.

"Hadn't thought that far ahead, but yes, if that's an invitation."

"You don't need an invitation, you're always welcome. Besides, it'll be Matthew's first Christmas home and Stewart's last before going away to school." Ruth's mood abruptly changed.

"A proper school will be good for him, Ruth; can't be around women all his life. The little place in town won't prepare him for much, nor will home schooling."

"I know. I'll miss him, though."

Ruth knew she had clung onto Stewart longer than was good for both of them. He would be fourteen by the start of the next school term; any longer and it wouldn't be worth the trouble of sending him. She enjoyed chatting with Joshua. He helped her to view things from a different perspective. Stewart going away to a proper school made a lot of sense, but the separation would be a significant adjustment for both of them. She decided that busying herself with work was the best way to deal with her sadness.

The better than expected returns afforded Ruth the luxury of using contractors to excavate the irrigation channels. She then panicked about wasting money, so the contractors ended up being her only extravagance. Matthew's mechanical skills were put to use readying the reluctant Ferguson for one last cultivation, and Ruth even cut her own hair to save money.

Matthew had his good days, and he was depressed on others. Adjusting to single life with one leg was proving more challenging than expected. He was happiest when flying his new Pawnee, where his physical restrictions were of little concern.

"I've invited Shirley and Joyce up for Christmas," Ruth said, looking up from her sewing. "They were a big help last year; gave me a hand with the chipping. The Ryans are coming too, but with only two of the boys; the other three got married."

"Hmm," Matthew grunted.

"I've been thinking about buying a television, I couldn't afford one before. It'll make a change from listening to the wireless."

"Stew will like that. He's been going on about wanting to see the Yanks land on the moon. They're taking the Lunar Rover on the next mission"

"Yes, he's space-mad at the moment. We all stood outside the electrical shop watching the first landing. I'll have a look when I go into town, find out what sort of price they're asking." Ruth hoped the prospect of having a television might give Matthew something to look forward to as well.

Apart from the excitement of ordering the television set, the workload over the following months was gruelling and constant. In addition to replanting the cotton, Ruth cleared and planted a further thousand acres. When not working on the rows, she was out repairing fences, until her hands became so cut and sore that she had to stop for a couple of days to allow them heal. Fencing, she decided, would be the first job to be contracted out when she had enough money. Matthew helped with the tractor work when he wasn't spraying or away on business, but it was Joshua on whom Ruth had come to rely. Not so much for help with the work but as a companion, a mate. Someone with whom she could share her ideas and dreams for the future. She found Joshua's belief in her judgement and ability to run Derrigeribar reassuring, which boosted her confidence.

The December school holidays soon came around and, in no time, Christmas was upon them. As the three children watched the delivery man erecting the mast to attach the aerial, they decided it was the most exciting thing that had ever happened. The solid walnut cabinet sat proudly in the sitting room, waiting for the necessary connections to bring it to life.

"When the man's got it going, make sure you don't sit too close. It might damage your eyes," Ruth warned, as she made her way to the car. Collecting Shirley and Joyce from the train station couldn't compete with the excitement of watching the television being installed, so Ruth went alone.

The long, solitary trip into Lincoln provided plenty of time to think. What Josh had said about Stewart going away to school was right. He must go; it's the only way he can complete his education and make a life for himself, she told herself, trying to feel excited. Instead, she experienced a confusing rush of emotions, excitement and pride that Stewart would soon be making new friends and having new interests, but also a profound sadness. It struck her then that going away to school wasn't so much the issue; it was the fact that her little boy was no longer her little boy. He was growing up. Before her feelings had time to overwhelm her, she arrived at the train station and quickly pulled herself together.

As she reached the platform, she kept swallowing hard to force back the lump in her throat. Come on, don't act like a nut, she admonished herself, he can't stay a child forever. The train had already arrived. She darted along the platform, trying to find the right carriage. In the distance, she spotted Joyce's large frame with Shirley at her side, holding all the bags.

"Shirley, Joyce!" she called to get their attention. "I'm so glad you could both come." Ruth's composure had returned; she hugged her guests affectionately. What would I do without friends? she thought in between hugs; especially these two, they always make me feel happy.

"So they're watching the electrician install a television, eh? Little monkeys, I thought they'd be here to meet us."

"I tried, Joyce, but they were too engrossed, especially with the aerial going up on the mast."

"They grow up so fast these days, Ruth. Next thing you know, they'll be bringing boyfriends and girlfriend's home."

"Yes, I know, even Will wanted to stay behind." Joyce's comment made Ruth realise just how silly she had been. I should be glad he's growing up, she told herself; it means I've done my job. "Oh, well, I have the cotton, that'll keep me busy." Ruth laughed dismissively as if her children's rapidly developing independence had never occurred to her before.

"Never mind the cotton; you need to find yourself a nice man. What about Stewart's father? You ever thought of going back to him?"

"I used to, until I met Lachlan. Seems so far away now. Anyway, I'm sure he'll be married with a family after all this time."

"If they are such a good idea, Auntie Joyce, how come you don't have one?" Well used to Joyce's 'find-a-nice-man' advice, Shirley jumped in to rescue Ruth.

"Oh, I'm too old. Anyway, I've never come across any nice ones."

They all laughed. It was like old times, the three of them together.

"No, I'm joking, there's plenty around if you keep your eyes open; *nice* ones, I mean." The qualification being for Shirley's benefit.

The utility pulled into the siding at the homestead, followed by a cloud of brown dust. With no rain for weeks on end, the land was parched. Ruth's good fortune of timely rain the previous season wasn't to be repeated. Proudly, she pointed out the contrasting dark, sodden irrigation channels running between the cotton rows. The second crop was well underway and appeared far more robust than the first.

"Gawd, Ruth, it's bloody hot this year. Everything except your cotton looks dried out." Joyce's face glistened with perspiration.

"What do all those sheep next door do when the grass turns brown?" Shirley asked, noticing vast numbers of them scattered across Bry's faded beige paddocks.

"Well, if it has enough goodness left in it, they usually survive," Ruth said, "but he's overstocked at the moment; probably have to get rid of some."

"They're here!" called William, who ran out to meet the visitors followed by Jess and Stewart.

"I'm expecting an extra kiss off all you little gremlins for not coming to meet me at the station!" Joyce said sternly, before bursting into a hearty laugh and sweeping all three into a warm hug.

"We've got a television now, Auntie Joyce," Jessica said.

"And it's made of walnuts," added William.

"Well, I never, fancy that; you better take me in and show me,"

Joyce said as Stewart and Jessica rolled their eyes at their little brother.

They all went indoors out of the sun and after being suitably impressed by the new television, Joyce and Shirley made a beeline for their room to put on cooler clothes.

"I'll make some sandwiches and drinks to have out on the veranda," Ruth called after them.

"Mail for you on the table, the last until the new year," Joshua announced as he walked indoors.

"Where did you come from?" Ruth said, looking surprised.

"Had to go into town; thought I'd grab your mail for you. Anyway, I'm off home, can't stop."

"Oh, okay, thanks. You can say hello to Joyce and Shirl next time then," Ruth said, looking at her mail. Gran's Christmas card, she recognised, and another letter.

She scrutinized the envelope, noticing the Papuan postmark. The writing was unfamiliar. Deftly, she slit it open with the bread knife.

Dear Miss Madison,

Sorry to burden you with bad news at Christmas but I'm the only one who can write here at the moment and Essie said it can't wait. I have to tell you about Sally, she passed away last Wednesday. She turned eighty-six not long ago but had been ill for some months. She spoke about you a lot and used to tell us kids stories about when you lived here with Mr Madison and the rest of your family. Sally's things went to her sister, but I'm sending you a hanky she embroidered to send to you with a Christmas card, she never got to buy the card.

Sorry again for the sad news.

Miriam Ulu

The tears welling in Ruth's eyes cleared as she stared in shock at the writer's name, Miriam. Tommy's little sister who had died, the name he always said he'd give to his first daughter when he had one. Surely it couldn't be, she thought, could it? Ruth was besieged by a sudden yearning to be back home.

She shut herself in the bathroom so as not to cry in front of the visitors. Between waves of tears, she remembered her life while growing up in the lush Papuan hinterland, exploring the riverbanks and caves with Tommy; the workers' families with their dancing and singing; eating salty plums under Essie's mango tree; shopping trips to Port Moresby with her mother; and going to stay with Eliza. Everything possessed a vividness as if she were there.

"Are you right, luv? You've been ages." Joyce's voice broke Ruth's daydreaming.

"I'm coming now, Joyce." Ruth opened the door, trying unsuccessfully to disguise her distress.

"You've been crying, darl. What's the matter?"

"Some sad news from home. Sally, our housekeeper, passed away."

"Oh lovey, bad news at Christmas, that's no good." Joyce put her arm around Ruth, which made controlling her tears even more difficult. "Come on, I'll make you a cuppa."

Ruth was embarrassed, sitting up on a stool, teary-eyed, while her guest made her tea. "Let me do that, Joyce, you give your feet a rest."

"You know, Ruthy, Christmas can be one of the saddest times as you get older. We lose people along the way in life, people who have been special to us; then Christmas comes and they aren't with us, and it's like losing them all over again."

Ruth remembered Joyce's uncanny ability to pinpoint exactly what was wrong. It wasn't just Sally's passing; it was the loss of everyone with whom she had ever been close, and of a past for which she had never allowed herself to grieve.

The letter from Miriam had reignited buried memories. As Ruth lay in bed trying to sleep that night, images of her life back home flooded her mind. She tried to understand why life had suddenly fallen apart after her mother passed away. Her parents' marriage, though fractured, had been the glue which had held everything in place.

An annoying banging sound interrupted her train of thought. Looking out the window, she couldn't see anything, so she put on her dressing gown and hastily made her way down the hallway. Lifting her hand to knock on Matthew's door, she quickly withdrew it; she heard the sound of a muffled giggle. A woman's voice. Goodness no, she recognised the laugh, *Shirley!*

Surprised by her own shock, she hurried back to bed, not knowing what to make of her discovery. They are adults, she supposed, but how could Shirley do such a thing? Maybe she had too much to drink. Ruth tried to rationalise it away but couldn't. She hoped that no one else had heard and wondered what she should do, or say.

Matthew's absence from the breakfast table the next morning was conspicuous, but no one said anything, or they conspired to pretend everything was normal. Joyce disappeared into the kitchen and Ruth glanced across at Shirley, who stared into her cornflakes as if they were something of great interest. Ruth realised she was probably as embarrassed as she was and decided not to say anything. It was 1971 after all, but the silence became unbearable. She had to say something.

"Don't worry, Shirl, I was a bit surprised but it's none of my business. Just don't lead him on; he's been through a lot." The two women looked at each other with an expression of relief. Ruth wasn't sure that was what she wanted to say, but it would do.

"I won't, Ruth." Shirley smiled sheepishly.

"When we're finished, we can take Joyce into town," Ruth said, changing the subject. She wants to get her hair done. I'd do it for her but I'm out of setting lotion."

"Maybe we can have lunch at the Chinese restaurant you were telling me about," Shirley said, sounding normal again.

"Yes, that's a good idea. Although, I guess I could use some of Matthew's beer for Joyce's hair."

"I haven't had my hair set with smelly beer since the war and I'm not going to start again now, thank you, girls." Joyce re-emerged from the kitchen with a fresh pot of tea. Shirley disappeared to get dressed, leaving Ruth and Joyce to finish their breakfast and plan their Christmas shopping. Not that there was much to buy, just odds and ends and stocking fillers.

Christmas Day arrived at Derrigeribar with a fanfare of food and merriment. Ruth and her guests looked on with bleary eyes as the children opened presents at the crack of dawn. Visitors popped in and out, the turkey was stuffed, cooked and eaten, and within a few days, it was over. The days of long Christmas breaks and on-going celebrations ended when they left Bryliambone. The demands of the farm now ensured only two or three days' break at the most.

In spite of its brevity, the Yuletide had worked its magic. Everyone seemed more optimistic, rested, and their spirits were brighter. Christmas in the bush was a reaffirmation of the reasons why people toiled all year round under such harsh conditions: family, kinship and a strong sense of determined self-sufficiency.

Shirley and Joyce stayed for only two weeks because the railways couldn't spare Shirley for the whole month. Joshua had to return quickly to Gallerun to deal with a rush order for his orange juice, which left Matthew, Ruth and the children on their own. After agonising over what to say, Ruth decided not to mention anything to Matthew about what had happened with Shirley, but when the frequent letters started to appear, she found it difficult to hold her tongue.

"You're popular this month," Ruth said, looking expectant.

"Yes, seems so." Matthew didn't volunteer anything.

"All I get is rotten bills."

"Ah well, I won't charge you for my aerial spraying; you just buy the chemicals." Matthew had a smug look on his face; Ruth suspected he knew she wanted to ask about Shirley.

"That's only for the first year, of course," Matthew said, with his characteristic cheeky grin. A look Ruth hadn't seen for a long time.

"Then what? You'll charge me double to make up?" They laughed.

The urgent need to eradicate a new outbreak of Bathurst burr forced Ruth's attention quickly back to the cotton crop. Even her misgivings about Stewart's imminent departure to school were sublimated into fuel for another all-out attack on the invading herbaceous opportunists. Until the school holidays finished, that was.

"Can I come home if I don't like it?" Stewart asked, wanting to make sure he had a way out, should the adventure not turn out to his liking.

"Well, not unless you absolutely hate the place, but I'm sure you'll enjoy it once you meet some of the other boys."

"I guess it'll be okay. I'll get to do science."

"Of course you will, Stew. You're fourteen now; you have to start thinking about studying for exams so you can go to university. The little school in town won't prepare you for that and I certainly can't. Even Uncle Josh said..." Ruth became aware of herself talking incessantly, something she did when trying not to be upset.

In spite of Ruth's best efforts to make the trip to school cheerful, she and Stewart ditched the façade and lapsed into an apprehensive silence. Jessica, on the other hand, beamed with pleasure; she couldn't wait to get back to her friends after the long, seven-week break.

Their first stop was the girls' school and they barely had chance to say goodbye before Jess was off with her friends. The boys' college was only a short drive around the corner. William had fallen asleep, which left Ruth and Stewart free to endure a painfully long-winded headmaster's address. When the speeches ended, they made their way out to the quadrangle to say their goodbyes. Everyone, it seemed, had come out for fresh air or to see someone off. The crowd somehow robbed the moment of its emotional charge, and after a brief farewell, Stewart joined the other boys back in the hall.

The silence in the car driving home was palpable; the radio was out of range and William remained asleep. Ruth had only the sound of the engine for distraction. She hated the silence; her imagination tended to run out of control. She couldn't stop thinking about all the things that could happen to Stewart.

By the time the utility entered the gates of Derrigeribar, Ruth had begun to accept Stewart's departure and coaxed herself into a more positive frame of mind. The farm now felt like home, it had acquired that familiar, welcoming look. She pulled on the handbrake and surveyed the property with a feeling of contentment. She thought she had better go and see Matthew before she became miserable again.

"I heard a bit of a rumour in town today," Matthew teased.

"What about?" Ruth continued to open the mail.

"Someone told me Bry's going under, having to bring in feed for all those sheep and no rain in sight."

"They're fools. They should have sent them to the sale yards months ago and cut their losses." Ruth's focus shifted to the formal, typed letter from home.

"Oh no, God no! I was hoping to see her before..."

"What's up?" Matthew put down his newspaper.

"It's Gran; she's passed away."

CHAPTER 17

Ruth stared at the letter as if willing it to say something different. The news didn't seem real. Even though her grandmother's eventual demise had been at the back of her mind for some time, it was still a shock.

"I can't believe she's gone, Matt," Ruth said, trying to muster some sort of emotion other than startled numbness. "Jake obviously couldn't find the time to write and tell me."

"Poor old bird, I'm surprised she lasted as long as she did after having the stroke. She should have moved back to Okoro."

"She'd never have returned to live at Okoro; she loved the people of the village too much."

"Who wrote the letter?"

"Her solicitor, I'll read it to you."

14th January 1972

Dear Mrs McGrath (nee Madison),

I am writing to inform you of the wishes of our client, the late (Mrs) Eliza Rosemary Madison. It is our solemn duty to dispose of the deceased's estate in accordance with her last will and testament. As a beneficiary, your claim includes a fifty-one per cent share in Madison Holdings Pty. Ltd. and a parcel of land including a residence and outbuildings located in the Gulf Province of the territory of Papua & New Guinea.

I request that you contact me at your earliest convenience to provide instructions regarding the bequest.

I remain, your faithful servant,

Winston Barrett

"You want me to call Jake?" Matthew asked.

"What good would that do? The solicitor must have written to him too. I'm sure he'd know."

"I bet he's beside himself over you getting her share of the business."

"It's probably the reason why he didn't call and tell us anything."

"Jake's not as bad as you think, Ruth."

"I guess we'll never know, will we?"

Matthew's expression softened. "Are you okay? You were a lot closer to her than me."

"I will be once it sinks in. I might go and do some work."

Ruth went out to the chicken pen on the pretence of collecting eggs. Sitting down on an upturned oil drum, she stared off into the distance; no tears, just an overwhelming sense of loss. Eliza had been declining for a number of years; she wondered why she wasn't better prepared for the news. To make it worse, her grief was largely a private and solitary experience. Matthew wasn't close to Eliza and Stewart was only a baby when she had last visited.

By the following morning, Ruth was dealing with her sadness the only way she knew how, by working. Up at four, she had gone out to practise starting up the new irrigation siphons. She was angry more than upset, but wasn't sure who with, until her attention turned to Okoro. It had robbed everyone of a normal life, like an insidious cancer. Now it would make reparation; if not for this generation, then for the next. By lunch, she had taken delivery of her first ewes and worked out how to forge some kind of rapprochement with Jake. The fate of her grandmother's legacy wasn't going to be left to chance.

"I've been trying to raise someone at Okoro since last night and still no one's answering. I'm not sure what to do. The Sogeri operator's getting uppity with me calling so much," Ruth said, frustrated.

"Call the patrol office. They'll try and get him on the radio or send someone over." Matthew didn't seem concerned.

"I hate involving strangers."

"You could be calling forever, if Jake's away."

243

"Yes, I guess so." Ruth's voice brightened as she looked out the window. "Josh has just pulled up. I'll make us some lunch and try Jake again later."

Leaving Matthew and Joshua to enjoy a beer after devouring a mound of ham and cheese rolls, Ruth decided to ring the patrol office. Expecting there to be some problem with the lines or the new exchange, she was surprised when the call went straight through.

"Yes, my maiden name was Madison, Jake Madison's sister." She listened intently for a good five minutes before asking "Are you sure that's right? Yes, I heard what you said; I was trying to think…" Ruth hung up the receiver.

"What's the matter? You seem spooked," Joshua said, looking at Ruth with concern.

"I had to call home. My grandmother passed away." She didn't reveal the real reason for her distracted manner.

"Sorry, darl, I had no idea," he said awkwardly.

"I'm okay, Josh. Where did Matt go?"

"Out to the packing shed, I think he said."

"I'd better go and find him. I need to talk to him."

"You're right, luv. I'll be off now anyway, only called round to pick up Dave; he's finished fencing off the top paddock. We'll water the sheep and run them out for you."

"Okay, thanks Josh," Ruth said, aware her voice sounded as if it belonged to someone else. The shocking news continued to resonate in her head. As soon as Joshua disappeared across the paddock, she jumped into the utility and drove to the barn where Matthew was busily preparing for the arrival of his Piper Pawnee.

"Matthew!" Ruth called as she raced through the doorway. "I've just been on the telephone to the patrol office."

"What did they say?"

"I'm not sure how to tell you." She paused, struggling to get her words to come out right. "They said he's in Bomana prison, waiting for court."

"What?" Matthew threw his hammer down.

"He's been arrested following the discovery of something to do with Dad's accident."

"They suspect him of having something to do with it, you mean?"

"According to the patrol officer. I asked if he had his facts right and he said it was his job to get them right."

"What exactly do they think he did?" "Something to do with the car. It's too horrible to think about. I always suspected Jake wasn't right. You always stood up for him though; you said he wasn't capable of such a thing."

"Nah, I still don't believe it."

"Well what about the letter he kept from Dad? That was a peculiar thing to do. And what about Eliza, she wasn't sick like Mum; she wouldn't imagine things."

"What do you mean?"

"All the trouble between the two of them when Lindsay disappeared."

"What trouble?"

"Surely you heard the big argument they had before she left?"

"Yeah, but that concerned the route he took and not using proper trackers. She was livid."

"What about the rumours? The workers were talking as if they knew he'd done something, Sally told me."

"You know what they're like with gossip," Matthew said dismissively.

"They even said Mum's death was payback," Ruth added.

"All crap, Ruth, you shouldn't pay any attention to that bullshit."

"I don't know, Matthew; I can't deal with all this what with Gran going, the cotton almost due and Stew just gone away. Perhaps you can go up and sort things out?"

"Bugger that. When I left I promised myself I'd never return, and I've got no intention of breaking my promise."

"You hate the place that much?"

"Yep, the only reason you don't is because you were away at school the last few years. You missed all the fighting between Mum and Dad. Anyway, you can call in to the solicitor's if you go."

245

"Well someone has to go." It was a surprise for Ruth to hear of her parents' fighting being that bad. She guessed they must have called a truce when she went home for the holidays. Or just kept their distance, her father always found an excuse to be out of the house or away.

Sitting on her bed, she stared at the picture of her mother on the dressing table. They had had a difficult relationship, but there were fond memories. "I don't want to go back, Mum," she said aloud. "All those sad memories; I don't think I could bear it." After settling down in the country with Lachlan, Ruth had lost all interest in returning to Papua but now it seemed she had no choice. She couldn't leave Jake in prison if he was innocent. And if he wasn't, she needed to find out the truth.

"How are you feeling today?" Joshua had dropped by with the orange juice order.

"I'm miserable, Josh; I have to go home to sort out some family business now Gran's passed away."

"Well, if you ask me, going back will do you good, even if the reason for going isn't such a pleasant one. Derrigeribar won't go anywhere while you're gone, if that's what you're worried about."

"I wanted to take Stewart if I ever went back, to show him where I grew up and how we used to live."

"Is his father still alive?"

Joshua's directness took her by surprise. Stewart's father had never been mentioned before.

"I only ask because it's probably more important for him to meet his dad than just seeing places and things." Joshua's expression was one of genuine concern for Stewart.

"Yes, you're right. He needs to meet his father, and I guess if the truth be known, that's one of the main reasons why I've never wanted to go back. Everything was such a mess when I left."

"Going on your own now might be a good opportunity. You can sort things out and smooth the way for when you take Stew."

Ruth marvelled at how liberating it was to acknowledge her past rather than keep pretending she never had one. "You're probably right. There are a lot of loose ends to sort out. I guess once they're taken care of, Stew and I can go on a holiday without worrying about any complications."

Talking to Joshua dispelled much of Ruth's unease at the prospect of returning home. By the end of the week, she was almost looking forward to the trip.

Her last few days on Derrigeribar were hectic; the farm calendar had to be juggled, sheep jetted and stripping contractors booked for the cotton. Whenever a break in the work flow occurred, Matthew endured a barrage of instructions from his sister on how to run the property in her absence. One of her main worries was William, who couldn't travel with her; the risk of him contracting malaria was too great, the disease was rampant throughout Papua. After the incident with Stewart and the snake, she had rarely let the other children out of her sight until they were older. Now, the prospect of leaving Will caused an attack of nerves.

"You don't credit me with much sense, Ruth. You lecture me on how to run the property, even though I've run one of my own for years, and now you don't trust me to take care of my nephew."

"It has nothing to do with me not trusting you, Matthew, but Stewart could have died from the damn snake bite when I left him with Josh."

"I'm not Josh, Ruth."

"No, I know, but he's still little and I worry." Matthew grabbed his crutches and stormed out, leaving Ruth feeling annoyed and guilty at the same time. She sat in an armchair, stony-faced, trying to decide on a less worrying arrangement for William. After what seemed like hours of mental torment, imagining everything from goanna bites to wild pig attacks, she stood up with a triumphant smile. You'll thank me later, Matty, she thought, and walked over to the telephone and dialled...

Ruth spent the remainder of the week making the final arrangements for her trip, readying William's clothes and writing out easy to follow recipes for Matthew. He had been in a bad mood since she told him of her concerns about leaving William and hoped her news would cheer him up.

"I had a call from the post office yesterday; the new moisture meters are waiting to be picked up," she announced as she joined her brother at the kitchen table.

"So? Do you actually trust me to go and get them? They're made of glass."

"Now you're just being silly; besides, I've got another favour to ask if you go." She couldn't keep from smiling.

"What's that?" Matthew bent down to attach his artificial leg.

"Shirley needs picking up from the train station," Ruth gloated.

"Ahh, now that's a much better idea than me looking after Will!" His mood changed instantly. "I'd better go and put something smart on; can't disappoint one of your friends, can I?"

"Go on with you." They exchanged a knowing glance. It was sheer luck that Shirley had been available at such short notice. The railways had told her to take her remaining two weeks' holiday left over from Christmas, so she had no problem getting the time off work.

When Matthew arrived home with an excited Shirley by his side, Ruth knew her trip to Papua could now go ahead without her worrying too much over William's welfare. Shirley doted on Will as she had Stewart, maybe a little more. Ruth guessed that Shirley probably missed having children of her own, especially now that she was getting older. She thought it a pity that Matthew and Shirley hadn't met before he married Barbara; there was a certain naturalness between them, no coyness or games, just a comfortable ease.

The following morning Matthew had beaten everyone to the breakfast table and was avidly going through Ruth's list of urgent jobs. The cotton harvest was only a couple of weeks away. Shirley busied herself in the kitchen making Jonny cakes, and Will was tucking into Shirley's boiled eggs, as if they were some new, mouth-watering delicacy. With all the activity, Ruth felt in the way. The only things left for her do now were visit the children at school and catch her flight.

When the time came to actually leave Derrigeribar, Ruth's

optimism had waned a little. It was as though she had become physically and mentally fused to the property. The mere thought of going away gave rise to panic. Derrigeribar had been her salvation after Lachlan's death and she had devoted herself entirely to making the venture work. Leaving to go back to Papua, and to her past, brought forth a flood of apprehension.

Her mind went into overdrive on the trip to town: Jake accused of murder, her father's death under mysterious circumstances, Tommy's fate unknown, her mother's illness and suicide, now Eliza, gone; all these things to worry about as well as trying to look normal when she saw the children.

"Can I come with you, Mum?" Stewart pleaded.

"You can come next time; we'll go for a holiday. I need to sort out Gran's business now." She tried to allay his concern.

"When are you coming back?"

Ruth had never been far away from Stewart before; even as a baby, the longest distance was her bus ride to the pottery. Journeying overseas was something entirely foreign to him; he had never known anyone who had travelled so far, apart from his uncle.

"I'm only going for a week; I'll be back sooner if I get everything done." Ruth put her arm on his shoulder.

"I've got some news," Jessica announced with a defiant glare.

"What's that, Jess?" Jessica was full of surprises lately and judging by the look on her face, Ruth wasn't sure what to expect.

"In the holidays, I want to visit Uncle Bob. I wrote to him and he wrote back saying he'd love to have me come and stay."

Ruth now understood the significance of Jessica's expression, but resisted the urge to remind her of the fact that if Lachlan hadn't needed to borrow money to pay Robert, he wouldn't have been carting wheat and might still be alive. But that would be unfair.

Instead, she tried to be noble, "Jessica, you've already made up your mind, I think. If you want to go, then you should." In spite of his greed, he is Lachlan's brother, she thought. Perhaps it's his way of making up for what he did.

"He's still my uncle, and I always liked Aunt Evelyn."

"Calm down, Jess. You're old enough to make up your own mind about who you want in your life." Ruth thought Jessica looked as though she had been expecting a battle.

"I want to go back to class; we're playing netball against St. Martin's this afternoon," Jessica said, looking relieved.

"Okay, give me hug." Her annoyance with Jessica dissipated and she gave them both a hug.

Ruth and Stewart dropped Jessica back at the gate before walking together to the café near his school.

"Are you going to visit my real father?" Stewart asked.

Ruth masked her surprise by having another sip of tea. "My reason for going is as I explained; I wasn't intending to go looking for your father."

Ruth knew she had to deal with this carefully. She was the one who had erased the past from their lives in the misguided hope of it being in everyone's best interest. Joshua had helped her to realise that although Lachlan's ego might have been preserved by the obliteration, she had deprived Stewart of knowing the man who gave him life and, more importantly, of any connection to his roots.

"You've never called him your real father before."

"He is though, isn't he, my blood father?"

Something resonated in Ruth. She wanted to tell him how much she had loved his father. How Stewart, the only remaining evidence of that love, was the most beautiful part of her life and that everything she had ever done had been to ensure his life would turn out to be a happy one. But she didn't tell him.

"Yes, Stewart, he is; perhaps we should have spoken about him before now."

"We talk about home and our parents a lot in here."

"I guess everyone misses being at home."

"Not everyone; some have lousy dads, mean even."

"Well, you can rest assured, yours isn't mean. I loved your father, Stewart; things were very different then and we couldn't be

250

together." Ruth wondered if she had said too much.

"So you wanted to be together? Married?" Stewart sounded surprised.

"Yes, Stewart, but then my mother, your grandmother, died and I came back here to the mainland and everything changed. Anyway, I'll tell you more another time. Do you want me to pass on your regards to your father if I see him?" She wasn't sure exactly what to say.

"Yeah, you can say hello for me, and get a photo. I want to know what he looks like."

"You look a lot like him, Stew; you'd be surprised. You have his build and broad shoulders. Your eyes are my colour but your thick eye-lashes and eyebrows are your father's. Apart from looks, though, you're both very self-possessed; like a rock, stable and calm, even when the world around you is going crazy. Perhaps next year we can both go and visit him. I'll get you a photograph to tide you over if I can. He'd be proud of you, Stew, a big, strapping boy, and clever too."

After saying goodbye, Ruth made her way to the railway station. She felt dreadful leaving him but nowhere near as bad as the time when he had first started boarding school. That day she would never forget. It was like having her soul wrenched from her. Stewart never seemed to get overly upset or emotional; his rocky start in life must have equipped him with a certain resilience. And that can only be a good thing, she thought, satisfied that her turbulent past hadn't left any irreparable damage.

As on many previous occasions, the train shunted alongside the platform, but this time there was a definite poignancy. Train journeys had punctuated the various events in Ruth's life: boarding school, being sent to Sydney, running away from the nuns, moving to the country and now back to Papua. It seemed she had reached yet another juncture in her life, and it would probably all soon change again.

Time was too tight for social visits after the train arrived late at Central

Railway Station. Ruth caught a yellow cab straight to the airport. In spite of the rush, she was struck by how much Sydney had changed again; it was even busier and more crowded than on her last visit. Lovely, old, historic buildings had disappeared and modern skyscrapers had risen up in their place; even the flying boats had become an historical curiosity. More disturbing, was the fact that Papua was soon to become an independent country with its own government and borders, a foreign country in every respect.

No sooner had she checked her portmanteau through the luggage counter than the loudspeakers announced her flight. She hastily tagged onto the snaking procession out to the aeroplane.

"Do you prefer the window?" the man in the next seat asked.

"Not especially."

"Are you going to Brisy?" he wanted to know.

"No, Port Moresby." Great, a chatterbox all the way, she thought, trying to quell the rising anxiety in her stomach. The horror of her fated flight with Lindsay was indelibly imprinted on her psyche. She was annoyed that it should bother her now. It hadn't worried her when returning to the mainland, and that was soon after the disaster.

"I'm sorry, I always get nervous when flying and can't stop talking." The man smiled.

"Oh, that's okay; I used to be the same way." He wasn't as annoying as she first thought. At least he wasn't drunk, and he had a warm smile. "I'll swap seats if you'd be more comfortable in the aisle. We're going to be sitting next to each other for a while. My name's Ruth, Ruth McGrath."

"John Callahan, pleased to meet you."

"Are you going to Brisbane?" Ruth asked.

"No, I'm also going to Port Moresby, I'm a public servant, they're banishing me to the jungle for a year."

"Oh, it's not that bad."

"You've been before?"

"I was born in Papua."

"What do you think about independence?"

"To be honest, I was hoping it would become another state but Canberra doesn't seem to like the idea anymore."

"No, not a good move according to Barnes, our External Territories minister; I think he realised it would be political suicide."

"I must say, I can't picture the place as a foreign country, and I certainly can't imagine how everyone will cope; left on their own, abandoned."

"I'm sure we'll support them until they're stable and get themselves established. Should be a wealthy country someday, with all the resources."

All very neat and tidy, Ruth thought. Surely the fate of a nation can't depend on one politician's decision. But then again, perhaps it does; possibly everything fundamentally boils down to just a decision you make at the right, or wrong, time and then a whole way of life evolves as a result. In this case though, it's an entire nation which is affected by that decision.

Ruth enjoyed having someone to talk to; the distraction helped her to stop worrying about what may lie ahead and focus on what to do once she arrived. She hoped she wouldn't run into anyone she knew, Jake's arrest must have been scandalous when it occurred. With all her years away on the mainland, she decided it would be unlikely that anyone would recognise her. So feeling a bit more at ease, she put her seat into recline and closed her eyes.

Her respite didn't last long, the new 727 T-Jet, at almost double the speed of a flying boat, ensured the journey was over almost as quickly as it had begun. Just two hours from Brisbane, Ruth spotted the Torres Strait Islands below and knew the Papuan coastline would soon come into view. As the plane banked sharply to the right, she recognised the familiar last leg of the journey. Another thirty minutes and she would be on home soil.

The much acclaimed 'whispering' T-Jet certainly lived up to its name. The landing was the smoothest ever! Walking across the baked tarmac to the terminal, Ruth noticed how unattractive Jackson's Airfield was compared to the flying boat port. Apart from the litter, the heat rose up from the ground like vapour, distorting one's view into the distance. Dust spun in little whirlwinds across the tarmac and the dryness of the air could be felt at the back of your nose and throat. The terminal wasn't much cooler than the bitumen outside, a converted hangar with only two of the six ceiling fans working. To her relief, and in true island style, the administrative officials seemed happy simply to wave everyone through the gate. Within minutes, she was on a crowded minibus into town.

Little had changed, although most of the war wrecks had gone, or been covered by vegetation, but a few odd pieces of abandoned machinery remained. The density of expatriate houses on the hillside had exploded, and the number of highlands people walking the streets had increased significantly. This concerned Ruth; she had been taught to be wary around highlanders, they had a reputation for being more unpredictable than the coastal people.

The bus pulled up outside the Papua Hotel. She tipped the driver and wrestled her suitcase half into the foyer before being pounced upon by a rush of eager, native porters. Once inside, it was refreshingly cool. The stream of perspiration running down her back was like ice-water as the circulating air caught her blouse.

"Reservation for McGrath," she announced, walking up to the counter.

"Is Mr McGrath arriving later?" the receptionist asked, looking puzzled.

"No, Mr McGrath isn't arriving later." Ruth realised how little anything had changed. "I'm travelling alone."

The woman behind the desk motioned to a porter, who whisked Ruth and her luggage away to her accommodation on the top floor.

The room appeared to be the smallest and most sparsely furnished they could find. Punishment perhaps for going against custom and travelling unaccompanied. At least the fan worked. She turned up the speed and undid her blouse to allow the circulating air to cool her skin. Mixed with perspiration, the powdery dust that had gotten into her clothing had formed streaks of mud, which ran down between her breasts. Feeling grubby, she decided to have a shower and change.

The hot water was tepid, but it had adequate pressure. It would have been easy to have stayed under the shower all night, but tomorrow was going to be busy and she hadn't eaten.

On her way down to the dining room, she changed her mind about having something to eat. The heat and unfamiliar odours that met her on the stairs robbed her of her appetite. She bypassed the meals area and went out into the street for some air. A balmy evening once outside, with a golden, pink haze sitting along the horizon. A walk along Ela beach would be enjoyable, she thought, remembering the sensation of cool water over her feet and fine sand between her toes. But the capital had become unsafe for white women out alone at night. The disapproving gaze of a passing policeman convinced her that such a luxury would have to wait until the daytime. As she turned to go back to the hotel, a native woman tapped her on the arm. Ruth jumped.

"Excuse me, Misis, you from Okoro, eh, Miss?" The woman looked pleased to see her.

"Yes I am, well I was, I..." Ruth stopped in mid-sentence. "Surely not, you are, aren't you? You're Millie, Essie's daughter!" Ruth recognised the woman's face in spite of the deep scars and tattoos on her cheeks. Her family lived on Okoro; they had even played together as children. She took Millie's hands in hers. "I'm so glad to see a familiar face; I was beginning to feel like a displaced person."

"You come up to visit Masta Jake? He at Bomana gaol now."

"Yes, I've come to see Jake. Would you like to come in for something to eat or a drink?" Ruth wasn't ready to discuss Jake.

"Not in there. I've only been to the bottom pub before and I don't like being here at night; you can get arrested."

"Where are you working, Millie?"

"I work for the McMaster family, cleaning, and they eat early so I get home by seven. It's a good job, Miss Ruth."

"That's wonderful, Millie. Are you sure you won't come with me for a cuppa? You can tell me all about Okoro."

"No, I'm dirty from working. I must go anyways. If I'm not home, my husband, he come lookin' for me."

In her excitement, Ruth had forgotten about the uneasy relations between whites and the indigenous population. The colour bar had only recently shown any sign of relaxing. For native men, even being on the street at night had been an offence.

"Okay, Millie, I understand. I'll be here until the end of the week; we might bump into each other again." As Ruth waved goodbye, she realised how tired she was and decided to go back to her room to sleep.

The morning sun streamed through the window directly onto Ruth's face. She half opened her eyes and wondered why it was so hot. The electricity must have gone off over night, she guessed; the fan had stopped! As she lay on the bed, she tried to imagine in what state she would find Jake. Bomana had a fearsome reputation. She wasn't even sure whether she would be allowed in without an appointment. Well, there's only one way to find out, she thought, and forced herself to get up.

She decided to hail a taxi from the main commercial area of town, as it afforded greater anonymity than calling one to the hotel. In spite of both her parents being dead, she couldn't help wondering what their friends might be saying. Her mother would be turning in her grave with shame. Ruth recalled all the effort she used to put into appearing 'proper' and 'respectable'. Just look at us now, Mum, she thought guiltily, we've all gone and let you down. Finally, a taxi pulled up, much to her relief; the last thing she wanted was to bump into any of her parents' friends. Now out of the public gaze, she could relax a little for the drive to the prison.

"Not a bad place to live, luv, but there ain't much here for holidaymakers." The taxi driver was fishing for some tantalising gossip, but Ruth had no intention of divulging the nature of her business.

"Yes, you're probably right," she said, scrutinising her hotel brochure to discourage further attempts at conversation.

After what seemed like hours of awkward silence, interspersed with talk about the weather, the taxi pulled up outside the prison. Only a few years earlier, the gaol had been moved to new premises, according to the driver, so the building façade didn't appear as ominous as she had been expecting.

"I'm sorry, Madam," the surly man at the desk informed her, "visiting is on Saturday mornings only."

"I've come all the way from Sydney; surely you can make an exception?"

"Of course we can, Mrs McGrath. I'll authorise it for you myself," the softer voice of a gentleman cut in.

Ruth couldn't believe her eyes. She was standing face to face with the man from the plane. How embarrassing seeing him here, she thought.

"That's very kind of you, Mr Callahan," Ruth said, trying to appear gracious.

"You'll need to leave your handbag, Madam," the churlish clerk butted in, as he eyed her with a mixture of disdain and curiosity. Ruth wondered if he suspected her of having some sort of improper liaison with his superior. She blushed at the thought. He gave her a receipt for her handbag and led her out through a stark corridor which ended inside a covered courtyard. She kept taking deep breaths to quell her uneasiness. What a hideous situation to get myself into, she thought.

"Wait here," the guard ordered rather than requested, then disappeared.

Ruth could hear keys rattling and men's voices shouting obscenities. The boorish official soon reappeared with a dishevelled, dirty-looking man in ragged attire. Shock caused Ruth to wince. It was Jake.

"You finally came then; I wondered if you would," he said.

Jake looked like a wild man. They half embraced, but Ruth didn't know whether to be pleased to see him or angry and repulsed. Her immediate reaction was to fling her arms around her big brother but she stopped herself as she remembered her father and Lindsay.

"Yes, I had to come and find out what this mess is all about."

"Didn't they tell you? I'm a murderer."

"I heard that, but I want to hear what you have to say." Apart from the confused feelings, her reaction to him surprised her. As he was so much older, she had always been a little wary of Jake; now, he held no power over her at all. He looked beaten and pathetic.

"You think I did it?"

"That's what I want to know."

"Jesus, Ruthy, I didn't do anything; it's all some political beat up." Jake's tone was a mixture of resentment and anger.

"What do you mean, political?"

"Well, my dear little sister, when father had his accident, the natives brought him back to Okoro. No one bothered to retrieve the vehicle from the river. Then a few weeks back, some stupid patrol officer decided to have the wreck hauled out to inspect and found the brake lines cut through."

"I don't follow; how is that political?" Ruth tried not to imagine her father's horrific last moments of life, fighting for air in a submerged vehicle.

"In the current climate, they don't want to bring the natives to account, so they hauled me in." Jake laughed in mocking indignation.

"So you think one of the workers did it?"

"Jesus, Ruth, yes I do, a group of them, more like. Things are different to when you went away; they want their land back."

"I thought they respected Dad. You think he did something to upset them?"

"You're all grown up but still as bloody naïve as ever. Of course he did something to upset them. He rooted half the village."

Ruth reeled back in shock. She wondered if imprisonment might have triggered a delusional reaction in her brother.

"I don't follow you at all, Jake, what are you trying to say?"

"Ruth, he'd been with half the women in the village, been at it for years, since the war, I think. You and he were always too bloody friendly with the buggers and no amount of discouragement would stop you. Luckily there's only one child that we know of."

"You mean one of the women had his child?"

"Don't tell me after all this time, you still don't know?"

"Know what?" Ruth was losing her patience.

"Your fancy boy, Mister Tommy, is our half-brother." Jake looked at his sister, waiting to see her reaction.

"You mean Dad's son?" Ruth managed to say as her body reacted to the horror of what he had said.

"Yes, he's our brother. Why do you think I spent so much time trying to keep you two apart?"

Ruth could feel every word Jake uttered cutting into her heart and soul, as if some demonic monster were wrenching apart every element of goodness in her life.

"But that can't be, Jake! He can't be, no, not Tommy."

"You always thought I hated him, but that wasn't true. I just didn't want you getting too close. Dad never bothered."

"No, not Tommy, not Tommy, Jake. Tommy's the father of my son."

Jake's expression morphed into stunned bewilderment. "What? I always kept an eye on you, that can't be... when, Ruth?"

"What does it matter, when? It happened, oh no, Jake."

"Jeez, Ruthy, I hadn't a clue..." He held Ruth's hands within his.

"How could this have happened, Jake, how?"

"I'm so sorry, Ruth. We all thought you got pregnant in Sydney."

"That's what I told everyone, I wanted to protect Tommy. I had no idea he was my brother." As Jake held her, she wondered if Tommy had known.

CHAPTER 18

Ruth cut short her visit with Jake. Reeling from the shock of what he had told her, she needed to be alone to think. Not only was Tommy her half-brother, but she had borne his son. Outside the prison, a wave of nausea came over her; she ran to a tree near the kerb and vomited. After wiping her face with a handkerchief, she went back to wait for the taxi.

She knew now that her father had told Matthew and Jake about the impromptu liaison in Sydney and they had believed the ruse. Stewart, they all thought, had been the product of that indiscretion. Ruth's mind raced, going over and over every detail of what Jake had said. Was her father's inability to come to terms with her pregnancy out of wedlock the real cause of his unwavering disgust? Or, did he suspect the truth? she wondered. At least that would explain his behaviour more than simply moral indignation over some affair many years before. As the horror sank in, she felt faint; her knee joints were like jelly. She grabbed the taxi door, almost collapsing as she slunk into the seat. Her heart pounded; she felt like throwing up again.

"Do you want some water, Ma'am? You don't look well." The driver held up a grubby tin cup.

"Thank you, no; I'll be fine." Ruth just wanted to be alone. She wasn't capable of small talk and, to her relief, the driver didn't press her for conversation.

When the car dropped her back at the hotel, she went straight to her room. Complete solitude was what her mind needed to be able to process what she had discovered.

On entering her tiny, airless room, she flopped on the bed and buried her face in her hands. What am I going to do? How could I have done such a thing? She wanted to disappear into oblivion, to cease to exist. She stared at the ceiling, wide-eyed, as her mind dissected everything she remembered about Tommy: his light skin tone, his wavy rather than fuzzy hair, his smile and the shape of his fingers. Things she had wondered about, found attractive even, but had never connected to anything so aberrant. How could I have been so stupid? she kept asking herself. Surely Matthew had some idea; she wished she had told him the truth about Tommy. Self-recrimination and doubt wavered between infuriation until she began to accept her powerlessness over the past.

As the hours passed, her despair gave way to defeated acceptance. Like so many things that had happened in her life, all she could do was deal with them and try to minimise the damage. Damn this godforsaken place, she thought, it turns everyone into liars and misfits!

She awoke to the beeping sound of a vehicle in the street below and a man shouting at someone to get out of the way. The harsh light coming into the room had a golden tinge to it. Late afternoon, she surmised, not wanting to open her eyes. Keeping them shut somehow made her predicament less real. She knew that once fully awake, she would have to confront again the horror of what she and Tommy had done.

As dusky pink and yellow hues melted into a depressing blackness outside, Ruth began to accept the probability of having borne her brother's child. If Tommy's mother had given birth to her father's child, it would no doubt be Tom; he was clearly of mixed blood. The only thing that made the whole mess bearable was Stewart's innocence, and the need to ensure his life didn't change as a result.

Ruth had accepted that she couldn't change anything, but now agonised over what to do about it. The situation was just so damn horrible, she had no idea what to do. She knew she had to find Tommy now, but what would she say to him? And what about Jake? She immediately thought of Millie; she had to find her, she would know where to find Tommy. She jumped up from the bed and went to the wash basin. After splashing cold water over her face and neck, she hurried downstairs to the front of the building.

The evening air was unbearably close and sticky, what little breeze existed was warm and damp. By the time she had reached the pavement, she was desperate. I must find Millie, she thought, trying to remember where she worked. She walked up and down the adjoining streets before deciding that Millie probably took the same route each day; she waited outside the hotel. Nearly an hour passed and there was no sign of Millie.

Even more determined, Ruth made her way along Musgrave Street, trying to appear purposeful to avoid any negative attention. In the distance, she could make out a woman's silhouette. Her pace quickened. She started to catch up, but then the woman turned a corner and disappeared.

Ruth suddenly felt exposed and vulnerable under the poor street lighting. She hurried back to the brighter lights of the Burns Philp department store. She set off again in a different direction but within minutes became aware of footsteps behind her; soft shoes or bare feet, she wasn't sure. Quickly, she turned around in the hope of scaring off whoever it was; but no one was there. Her heart pounded; she wanted to run but didn't want to appear afraid.

"Miss Ruth!" A figure emerged from a gate opening onto the footpath.

"Millie! Oh my God, you gave me such a fright!"

"I just finished working; this is my husband, Kapi." Millie gazed past Ruth.

"Oh, I'm sorry, I heard someone behind me. I wasn't sure... Pleased to meet you, Kapi." The footsteps belonged to Millie's husband. "I was hoping to find you, Millie. I'm going to Okoro to sort out some business but wanted to find out what you knew first."They walked back in the direction of the hotel.

"Kapi and me were at home last year, then we come here. Everything changed now, Miss Ruth; the big men want to take over now Masta Jake in gaol." Millie stared at the footpath.

"No good place for you, Miss Ruth; you better stay away," Kapi warned.

"Shall we go for a coffee or milkshake? I want to find out as much as I can." Ruth wasn't put off by Kapi's warning.

They found a suitably concealed location, a run-down Chinese store-cum-milk bar. The wiry, grey-haired proprietor eyed them with a mix of curiosity and suspicion; a white woman out at night with locals was a rare sight. Ruth didn't care; she had to learn whatever she could about the situation at Okoro.

"What makes you think the big men want the plantation, Millie? It could just be talk."

"Essie and Miriam write me; she writes last month, eh, Kapi?" Millie glanced at her husband. "Sam and his *wantoks* say they will take Okoro when the gov'ment gets independent, but now Masta Jake in gaol, they want their land now." Millie swirled her milkshake around the glass, looking up only briefly to confirm that Ruth had heard.

"Millie, did you ever hear anything strange about Jake's arrest? Gossip, anything?"

"You mustn't say to anyone, Ruthy, but Essie tells me Sam did somethin' to big masta."

Ruth realised there must be some truth in what Jake had told her.

"So you mean Sam planned my father's accident, Millie?"

"That's what I been told, Miss Ruth."

"Didn't they know that Jake would take over Okoro if Father wasn't around?"

"Yes, they know, Miss Ruth."

Ruth listened, dumbfounded. "So getting rid of Jake was all part of the plan, Millie?"

"That's what Essie says."

"God, Millie; I don't understand anything anymore. Okoro was our home. I thought the villagers accepted us and wanted the plantation to prosper; the business brought good things to the village for everyone."

"Things changed a lot, Miss Ruth."

Ruth hesitated, but she had to find out. "And Tommy Ulu, do you know where he is or what he's doing?"

"He's in the struggle; he travelling round to get people to protest against New Guinea and Papua joining up to become one," Kapi said.

Ruth had been away a long time, but she understood that many Papuans regarded themselves as a race apart from the New Guinea tribes. It was an unfortunate situation, and a futile one with the joint administration now firmly established.

"Tommy's in Lae; he does shop business too," Millie added.

Ruth's hopes sank; she had hoped he wasn't too far away so she could see him before going to Okoro.

"You better go with *kiaps*, Miss Ruth, you be safer."

"I couldn't march in with patrol officers, Millie, it would make things worse. I'd be showing I don't trust them."

"Better you don't trust anyone, things bad now," Kapi cautioned.

"I'll come with you, Miss Ruth," Millie offered, looking excited.

Kapi, agitated, told her she wasn't to go. He hadn't paid any bride price yet and her family were unlikely to allow her to leave the village again. Millie reluctantly agreed; he was right, they might not let her come back with him.

Millie eyed Kapi. "You can go; you can take Miss Ruth."

Ruth wasn't so sure about taking Kapi; the last thing she wanted was to become involved in a bride price dispute. Such things had been known to lead to bloodshed.

"I couldn't expect you to come away at such short notice, Kapi." Apart from the bride price, she had only just met him and didn't know if he could be trusted.

"I want to come, I talk to Millie's family about bride price," Kapi said.

Ruth mulled it over; if things are as bad as they say, going with someone else would be safer. "How much do you have to pay?" she asked.

"Five pigs, *kina* shell and masta money," he replied, looking overcome by the seemingly impossible amount.

Ruth suspected he would have trouble convincing his clan to pay the price unless he returned to negotiate in person. "Are you happy for Kapi to come with me, Millie? I'll be going straight to Okoro and back, just a couple of days; we can take Essie some salty plums." Ruth and Millie had made themselves sick as youngsters when they stole a bag of salted plums from Essie's string bag.

"Yes, Kapi don't work, he can go. Essie always likes salty plums!" Millie laughed.

With her plans finalised, Ruth returned to the hotel to make the arrangements and to call home. Matthew needed to know what was happening. A trip to Okoro would add two or three days to her absence.

"G'day, Ruth! How's it all going?" Matthew sounded uncharacteristically happy.

"Not bad. I've been trying to get this call put through for ages but it kept dropping out. How's Will?"

"All going good. He's been a bit whiny of a night but is fine mostly. Shirley's good with him. Been treating me like a king too, big cooked meal waiting for me every night when I come in."

"Oh well, make the most of it, I'll be back soon."

"You still reckon you'll be home by Friday?"

"Actually, that's why I'm calling; I want to go to Okoro to check on a few things, so I'm going to be delayed a day or two. It'll be Thursday next week by the time I get back here and sort out Jake's mess."

"How is he?"

"Seems like he didn't do anything after all. And that letter he kept from Dad was more to keep the peace than anything underhanded. He used to go off his head if Jake ever mentioned me, so he decided to hang on to the letter until Dad had come to terms with things more."

"I told you he wasn't the nutcase you thought."

"I guess so. I'll have to find out exactly what happened at Okoro before I go to the police. I think Sam had something to do with Dad's accident."

"You be careful, Ruth. You've been away a long time, things have changed."

"I will, Matt, don't worry. I'm going to go; the beeps are sounding and I don't have any more coins." The telephone disconnected.

The following morning, Ruth felt more like her usual self, which she put down to a good night's sleep. She had somehow managed not to dwell on Jake's shattering news about Tommy by keeping herself busy with the Okoro plans. When she arrived at the bus stop outside the hotel, Kapi was already waiting. In spite of what they had agreed the previous day, she was having second thoughts about taking him along.

"Good morning, Kapi, I thought you might have changed your mind."

"No, I'm here."

"Are you sure you want to come? I was thinking that once I get to Okoro, everything will be okay."

"Maybe, but maybe not. The big men are angry about their land and want it back. I think they won't be okay, 'specially with a woman."

"We'd better get on the bus." Ruth's enthusiasm, and indeed her courage, was rapidly evaporating. "The coming of independence has changed a lot of things, Kapi; even the people at the hotel seem hostile towards the locals."

"They make a lot of money, and maybe soon they lose everything." Kapi's eyes fixed on the back of the seat in front. Ruth detected that even he might harbour some degree of resentment.

"Perhaps the way forward is to split the wealth, make partnerships," Ruth said optimistically, but at the same time recognising that not many of the white Australian expatriates would welcome such an arrangement.

"Maybe," Kapi said, as if he knew there were little prospect of such an egalitarian solution.

The plane was empty, apart from one other passenger, an old woman who fell asleep as soon as the plane became airborne. The islands were still experiencing the northwest monsoon and the further away from Port Moresby one travelled, the wetter it became. The smell of damp always filled Ruth with a sense of expectation, probably due to the circumstances of her previous trips: shopping in Port Moresby, holidays or going to school.

"We'll be in Woitape soon," Kapi reported, without turning his head from the window.

"Yes, I'd better have cup of tea." Ruth withdrew a shiny silver Thermos from her holdall. "You want a cup? I brought enough."

"No, I feel sick when I fly."

"How about some water?" She held up a bottle.

"Yes, water good," he said with a half smile, his first since the previous evening.

The clouds disappeared from view and Ruth leaned over to see how far the plane had descended. "Better put the belt on, Kapi."

Ruth braced herself for the usual scary landing. Mountain airstrips were frequently short and uneven; their remoteness ensured only the most vital of repairs were carried out. On this occasion her nerves were spared, everything went smoothly. Apart from a sharp jolt as they came to a halt.

"Come on, let's stretch our legs," she said, noticing the old woman getting off the plane and going in the opposite direction to the terminal, a tin shed propped up by poles. As Ruth came down the steps, she saw the pilot examining the right wheel. He had a worried look on his face.

"Everything okay?" she asked.

"Not good, I'm afraid. We hit a pothole about a hundred yards back; one of the wheels is buckled," he growled.

"You carry spares, though, eh?" Ruth expected they would.

"Only tyres; the wheel itself needs replacing." The pilot returned to the cockpit and picked up the radio handset.

"Great!" Ruth said under her breath.

"What's up?" Kapi had wandered back to join her.

"The damn wheel. The pilot said it needs to be replaced; he's on the radio now." They both studied the warped piece of machinery.

267

"Looks like we won't be going anywhere at least until tomorrow afternoon," the pilot declared with a look of resignation on his face.

"Can't they get one here today?" Ruth said, unable to conceal her annoyance.

"They have to locate one first. It'll be too late to fly it up today. We can stay in the terminal. There'll be provisions inside and the place will be dry if it rains." The pilot no longer seemed bothered by the inconvenience.

"When you say they have to locate one, is that easy to do or is there a chance they won't find one straightaway?" Ruth wanted to know exactly how long she was going to be stuck.

"Well, there are two more of these planes in the fleet, so there should be six spare wheels located somewhere. Once they find out where they are we'll be right; worse case, they'll have to fly one across from Popendetta."

"And if that's the case, how long?" Ruth was getting more and more frustrated; she'd forgotten how lackadaisical life could be in the territory.

"Should be here by tomorrow afternoon, or Friday morning."

"We only have to get over that ridge, Kapi, and we'd be home." Ruth surveyed the surrounding peaks and then the wheel again, as if to will it back into order.

"We can walk, Miss Ruth, only about twenty-five mile," Kapi said enthusiastically.

"It isn't far, Kapi, but I don't know if I'd make it through the jungle on foot." Ruth glanced over at the dense bush surrounding the airstrip.

"You'd be better to stay here, Ma'am," the pilot said, looking surprised at Kapi's suggestion.

"If I weren't in such a hurry to get back to Moresby…" Ruth stared over towards the ridge again. If it rains, the mud will be pretty bad, but Kapi knows his way, she reasoned; the locals walk everywhere. "Oh bugger it! Let's walk. I can't stay here for what could be another two and a half days."

Ruth found a piece of canvas inside the terminal and tore it into strips to make straps for her holdall. She then emptied out her spare clothing to make room for water bottles. The old, rusted machete that someone had left behind, she attached to her belt.

"You'll let the patrol office know I've gone on foot?" Ruth said, looking directly at the pilot.

"Yes of course but I'd rather you didn't go."

"Just tell them I wouldn't listen. That'll get you off the hook." She was eager to make a start.

The first few miles were down the side of the mountain and across the valley floor to the next rise. Ruth soon realised that her work at Derrigeribar had equipped her body with a high level of fitness; she had no trouble hiking through the rugged terrain. Kapi was an excellent guide, and she was grateful at not having to cut through the vegetation herself.

"You've been this way before then, Kapi?" she called ahead.

"A few times, long time ago," he replied without stopping.

"I wasn't expecting such a good track."

"It run out soon, Miss Ruth."

"Over there, you mean?" Ruth pointed to the shadowy jungle ahead.

"Yes, but don't worry," he reassured her.

The thick, verdant canopy had been a relief initially. The dense foliage provided shelter from the sun, but as they made their way deeper into the jungle, the rising moisture was suffocating. Perspiration soaked Ruth's clothing, which had become clingy and heavy. Her face throbbed from the heat, and her breathing quickened into a rapid rhythm. Birds of paradise, with their piercing calls, periodically interrupted the cacophony of unique insect sounds. She glimpsed the vibrant blue and red neck plumage of a cassowary darting in and out of a clump of sago palms.

"Aren't we a bit high up for cassowaries?"

"They wander up sometimes; lots of fruit this way." Kapi's intimate knowledge of the forest and its inhabitants reminded her of Tommy. Indeed, that was her earliest memory of him; he seemed to know everything about the mysterious forest beyond the safety of the homestead gardens. It was through Tommy's eyes and his love of the diverse jungle-dwelling animals and insects that she learned to appreciate the beauty of her surroundings.

As the hike progressed, her thoughts turned to Stewart at school, completely ignorant of the dark truth she had learned. The more she thought about him, the more her stomach contracted with waves of anxiety.

"You a'right?" Kapi called out, as he turned to check on Ruth.

"I might stop a while. I feel as though I can't breathe." Ruth slumped down onto a fallen tree.

"You need water." He passed Ruth a water bottle. "You shouldn't sit on logs without looking for snakes."

"I know, the heat's making me careless." She savoured every mouthful of the lukewarm liquid, it tasted sweet. "We'd better find somewhere to sleep soon." The jungle ahead had rapidly turned dark beneath the canopy; they would have make camp.

Kapi nodded and then motioned to a clearing. They both trudged over to the grassy patch and decided it would make a suitable camp. Where the canopy broke, Ruth detected a hint of cool breeze, which helped rid her of the feeling of suffocation.

"I didn't bring any food, you think there's any fowl around? I couldn't face anything else," Ruth said.

"I can find fowl."

The mere thought of eating snakes or couscous turned Ruth's stomach. Kapi set about cutting down a number of long bamboo stems and expertly fashioned them into spears.

"How much further to go, do you reckon?" She hoped they would arrive at Okoro before lunch the next day.

"Ten mile," he said, as he gathered up his spears.

"I can't wait to get there, do everything and then leave. We might even get the same plane back."

"Maybe." Kapi walked off towards the forest.

Ruth had slept rough on many occasions while travelling around the plantation with her father and brothers. This was different, having a strange man for company. She hoped she hadn't gotten herself into another predicament, but dismissed the idea and set about collecting bark and dead branches for the fire. The heat of the day was deceiving at these altitudes; the nights often became extremely cold. Retrieving the machete from her makeshift knapsack, she began harvesting armfuls of palm leaves.

Ruth jumped backwards and cursed. "Damn! It must have been on a leaf!" The giant birdwing butterfly fluttered past her head. Having lived on the mainland for so long, she had grown unaccustomed to the unusual and sometimes dangerous fauna. Luckily this was nothing more than a harmless giant.

When she returned to the clearing, she wove the leaves together to form a crude mattress, only to run out and have to go back for more. This time she found some broader banana leaves which, when strung together, provided good protection from the rain. By the time Kapi returned, Ruth had constructed a small, but serviceable, shelter.

"Bush fowl and mangoes." He plonked the decapitated bird on the ground.

"And I found some bananas," Ruth said, as she held up a hand of plantains.

"I'll fix the bird." He picked it back up and walked away to prepare the bird for cooking. Ruth set about starting a fire, thankful that she had the foresight to bring along a pack of the hotel's wax vestas.

The two trekkers finished off their barbecued meal with mangoes for desert. As they sat watching the night sky, Kapi asked, "You look for Tommy after?"

"Yes, I want to find him when I'm done here." Ruth wasn't sure what to say; her reason for finding him had now changed. She could barely bring herself to think about those reasons, let alone talk to a stranger about them. "I'm hoping he'll come back to Okoro to work with the villagers; we can't lose it."

"You lose Okoro?" Kapi looked puzzled.

"No, I mean to make sure the plantation keeps running and making money."

"What about Masta Jake?"

"Masta Jake will have to work with Tommy, Kapi. Too much has happened, too many people hurt and cheated, things have to change." Ruth stared into the fire.

"What about the big men?"

"The big men should understand Okoro can't be theirs; even a new government wouldn't agree to that. Besides, when we get to the bottom of this business with my father, there might not be any big men." Ruth wondered if she had said too much; Kapi was still one of the villagers, no matter how helpful he was being at the moment. "It's best you don't say anything to anyone in the village until I sort everything out, Kapi."

"I keep your secrets." He poked at the embers of the fire with a stick.

"Come on, let's get some sleep," she said, thumping her knapsack into shape to support her head.

As a grey, misty dawn broke, Ruth was already awake, staring up at the sky, trying to make sense of everything that had happened. The makeshift mattress had become increasingly uncomfortable, and her hip ached. She could put up with the discomfort no longer. As she stood up to walk around, she slipped on a wet banana leaf and woke Kapi. He appeared startled and went straight for the machete next to him; he was ready to pounce.

"Sorry, I slipped. Everything's okay." She noticed he didn't appear at all happy. "I'm really sorry, the leaves were wet."

He started to laugh. "We can go soon, before the sun gets too hot."

After a breakfast of leftover fruit, they made their way across the clearing and re-entered the forest. The jungle came alive just after dawn. The sounds of insects, strange bird calls and tree kangaroos rustling through the canopy overhead added interest to the tedious task of fighting though tangled tree boughs and razor-sharp vines. After taking a shortcut through a large puddle of water, Ruth stopped to examine her waterlogged boots.

"Hang on, Kapi, I've got leeches in my boots." She lit a match, aiming carefully at the slimy, bloodsucking parasites, and began to burn them off her leg. Kapi brought some *marasin* leaves, which she rubbed on the bleeding welts. The tribal remedy would congeal the blood and disinfect her wounds.

A little less adventurous now, Ruth remained behind Kapi for the rest of the trip. A blaze of sunlight glimmered in the distance, and within minutes, their expedition beneath the canopy had come to an end. Once out in the light, they found themselves in grasslands which extended all the way to the distant tree line. Ruth spotted blue-grey smoke coming from huts over to the east.

"I think we made it, Kapi. I can see Okoro village." She pointed.

"We made it a'right, Miss Ruth. Not far now," he said, looking no more pleased or displeased than he did at the beginning of the journey.

The walk to the village was easy compared to the irregularities of the jungle track. As they passed the round, thatched huts, children came running up to Kapi, many with not a stitch on, although some of the older girls wore dazzling floral *meri* blouses and *laplaps*. They eyed Ruth with suspicion. As they walked along the track at the side of the coffee rows, more people joined the procession. So many new faces, Ruth noticed, and very few of them appeared friendly.

"Where did all these people come from?" she asked Kapi.

"Kuru village. After old masta died they come and live here and help work with Masta Jake."

"I'd like to talk to Tommy's father before we go any further," Ruth said, pointing to a large hut set apart from the others.

Kapi remained silent.

"I want to hear what he has to say about things," she continued.

"Miss Ruthy!" Tommy's brother rushed towards her as she reached the doorway. "You come no long time, come sit down."

Ruth noticed he had aged. His mouth was bright red from chewing betel nuts and many of his teeth were missing. She tried not to look shocked by his appearance.

"How are you, Pups? I've come home to see how everything is going. I was hoping to find Billy here." She wondered where Tommy's mother was, but chose not to ask.

"Old man, he dead. Many changes now, Miss Ruth, maybe you no belong here."

"Oh, I hope I do, Okoro's my home, Pups." Ruth almost questioned her hearing; no one would have dared say such a thing in the past. She told Pups how sorry she was to hear about his father and excused herself.

"Did you know Billy was dead?" Ruth looked at Kapi.

"We all knows," he said without meeting her gaze.

"You should have told me," she said, annoyed, but thought she had better not say too much.

As they passed a grove of lofty sago palms, the homestead came into view.

The once well-maintained buildings looked run-down; broken trellises littered the gardens and weatherboards were missing from the side of the house. As they walked towards the steps, a man's voice called out.

"You lookin' for me, Miss Ruth?"

There was Sam, looking defiant with his legs apart and arms folded. He appeared twice the size he used to be and was wearing an old ragged white business shirt over his laplap. Probably one of her father's, Ruth guessed. An almost overpowering surge of anger came over her, but she managed to stay calm.

"I was actually looking at the state of my house, but what a nice surprise to see you, Sam." She noticed his posture relax; her feigned friendliness had disarmed him. "It's lovely to be home again, but I must have a shower now. I'll come to visit you and your wives later. Are you still over by the silos?"

"Yes, Miss Ruth, I still by silos. We talk *bisinis* when you come."

274

"Yes, lots of bisinis to talk about, Sam." Ruth turned and opened the door. Until she knew the extent of Sam's involvement in her father's death, there was no point in confronting him. She went inside.

"No one has been here by the looks of things," she said to Kapi. "It smells musty, and look at all the mould on the walls." She was about to open the windows when she heard a loud thud on the door behind. "What was that?" she said, turning to Kapi.

Kapi had already rushed out to see. Within seconds, he returned. "Someone threw this," he said, holding up his arm.

Ruth stared in disbelief. It was a dagger.

CHAPTER 19

Ruth's reaction to the dagger was more one of intense sadness than fear. Happy childhood memories of life at Okoro had, until now, provided her with a mental refuge, a place where she could escape when real life became unbearable. She realised those days were now gone.

"I guess you were right, Kapi; they don't seem overly pleased that I'm here. I must be as naïve as Jake says. I really expected everything to return to normal when I arrived."

"Mistakes are easy to make, Miss Ruth; memories of children never come to life again," he said, sounding more profound than his years should allow.

"I promised the pilot I'd call Moresby when we arrived. I'll book us a return flight at the same time."

To Ruth's annoyance, the telephone was dead, and the radio's valves had been pulled out and smashed across the floor. "I wonder who did this?" she said, rummaging through the desk drawers only to discover there were no replacements. "We'll have to walk to Sogeri if the radio at the airstrip doesn't work."

"We be right, Miss Ruth, walking is good," Kapi said, unperturbed.

"Are you hungry?"

"I've got meat in my bag," he offered, opening his bilum to reveal the remains of last night's fowl.

"I might give that a miss, Kapi," she said, trying not to sound repulsed. "You want Ox and Palm with rice? That's all I can find, but I'll get an onion from the garden, that'll add some extra flavour."

"I like that. I'll get onions," Kapi volunteered. Bully beef fry-up had become a favourite of the locals.

Ruth started to prepare the meal while she rehearsed the conversation she intended to have with Sam. She had to be sure of her facts before broaching the subject with him. Her intention was to ask around the village first, but after the dagger incident, she wondered whether it would be safer simply to tell the police.

Kapi returned with the onion. Ruth thought it wise to make conversation. Even though she trusted him, having witnessed the hostility of some of the villagers, she didn't want to take any chances. She guessed her imagination was probably working overtime, but you could never be too sure; his people may force him into taking sides.

"Kapi, what's happening with the bride price arrangements? Are you going to visit Millie's family?"

"Maybe I go after we eat," he said, without looking up from his meal.

"I might go and talk to Tommy's mother before I tackle Sam."

"He's probably gone now he knows you here."

Ruth decided that if she couldn't find him, she'd still ask some of the older villages about what had happened. At the back of her mind, though, she suspected that anyone with any information would probably clam up if questioned.

From the veranda, the plantation appeared deserted. It used to be such a busy place, Ruth lamented: farm vehicles coming and going, native children playing, women in and out of the house borrowing household items or helping out in the gardens. Ruth found the complete absence of activity disconcerting so she walked down to the workers' camp, a small settlement of demountable buildings and native huts. Approaching the women's vegetable gardens, she called out. No one seemed to be around; apart from the chatter of friarbirds, there was only silence.

"They be at the river, Missie," a voice called out, making Ruth jump.

"Oh, I was hoping to find Meka Ulu. Essie!" Ruth immediately recognised the old woman.

"Ruthy, you come home!" They embraced.

"Yes I'm home; you seem to be the only one pleased to see me!"

"Come to my place, we talk. I tell you about what happens here, too many bad things now."

They both sat down on a faded wooden bench, shaded by a large mango tree weighted down by green fruit.

"You remember this tree? I lose count of the times I chase you and Millie for pinching my mangoes."

"Life was good then, eh?" Ruth said, experiencing an overwhelming sense of sadness.

"They were good days; we were happy people with no worries and the white bosses were happy with their coffee gardens; no trouble in those times."

"Tell me, Essie, what happened? I even had a knife thrown at the door after I arrived this morning."

Ruth had to fight back tears as the old woman told her about Sam's cousin, Hiri. She explained how he came from Kuru village to Okoro with other members of his clan; Jake had brought them in because he needed extra workers. Essie told Ruth that no sooner had he arrived, he began stirring up the men over the ownership of land and disputed the right of white families to be there.

"They bad mens, Miss Ruth," Essie added.

"I heard a rumour that father's death wasn't an accident."

"They shouldn't tell you, Ruthy, they tell you too much; they forget you white sometimes because you grow up with them." The old woman looked away, but Ruth pressed her to tell what she knew.

"Sam and Hiri fixed everything; Hiri work on trucks before, he good mechanic. Sam is stupid, he follow what Hiri says."

"So it's true, and after they killed father, they made it appear as though Jake was to blame." Ruth noticed tears glistening on the old woman's cheeks.

"I'm sorry, Ruthy; yes they make Masta Jake go with patrol officer."

"What I don't understand is why they waited so long after father's death to go to the police."

"I think they plan to kill Masta Jake too, but he went away. When he come back, old Billy Ulu threaten to tell kiaps if Hiri do anything to Jake. Then things change with politicians and everyone think they get their land back from the bosses. Then things change again, and they got told they won't, so they get angry, more angry than before."

"That's when they decided to lie to the kiaps so Jake would be blamed for my father's accident."

"Billy try to stop them, he fight with Hiri. He a weak old man and shouldn't get involved; I think his heart stop with shock a few days later."

"He had a heart attack?"

"He died before kiaps take Masta Jake away."

"Does Tommy know how his father died?"

"Maybe he does. Miriam was with Billy, she used to be here all the time."

"Miriam is Tommy's daughter?"

"She his daughter, his woman die birthing her. Meka sent Miriam away, she safer if she's not here."

Ruth had suspected Miriam to be Tommy's daughter when she wrote her about Sally's death. He obviously had kept his promise to his mother that his first daughter would take the name of his little sister who had died. Even Tommy's life, it seemed, had been touched by sadness.

"Yes, she probably is safer away from here."

"Hiri is a bad man, Miss Ruthy, but he clever, he got the village peace officers in his pocket, they his wantoks."

"What a mess, Essie. I guess I hoped there might have been some mistake."

"No mistake, Ruthy. Better you go back to Moresby; too dangerous here."

"I can tell no one wants to talk to me. Perhaps you're right, Essie, I should just go."

"They shamed, Missie; they can't look at you without shame, knowing about what happened. They frightened of Kuru clan too."

"Where are Hiri and Sam now?"

"Hiri gone back to Kuru; Sam went hunting after he see you at the house."

At a loss for words, Ruth had trouble comprehending how all this could have happened. She stared at the bough of the tree, trying to make sense of the emotions surging through her: sadness, anger, disillusionment and fear, all combined.

"Maybe you fix it up, Ruthy?" The old woman's eyes pleaded.

Ruth wondered how she could possibly fix anything now. "What's the village doing for money? I notice the coffee hasn't been picked."

"If they pick coffee, what they gonna do with it? No fellas here can sell, that the masta's business."

"Makes no sense; they want the land but do nothing with it when they've got it."

"All they see is the bosses having good life on their land; they don't care about the coffee so long as no one else have it."

Ruth understood the unfairness of the situation. After being away, and viewing everything from a visitor's perspective, the problem was blatantly obvious. Not only had these people been cheated out of their land, but they were paid a pittance to work it. Even her own half-brother had missed out on what was rightfully his. The situation had to be put right. Enough had been taken; the time had come for something to be paid back.

Ruth stood, satisfied that her brother Jake had no part in their father's death. "Thanks, Essie, you always were good to talk to about problems."

"Just a toothless old woman, Miss Ruth."

"A wise old woman, Essie. I better go and find Meka. I need to talk to her about something." Ruth suspected Essie could answer all her questions, but she had to hear the words from Tommy's mother.

Ruth followed the path down to the river. It struck her how everything looked the same; very little had changed while she was away. She remembered individual trees, trees she had climbed as a child; even the windy, uneven path was the same, with its dense hibiscus and frangipani bushes on each side. The intense floral perfume of the flowers mixed with the aromas of green leafy vegetation and damp earth, reminded her of walks she had taken with her mother and with Tommy. She experienced a sudden rush of anxiety as memories of her romantic involvement with Tommy came to mind. Unable to shut out the shame and guilt, she felt dirty and to blame for the whole situation. She even feared her own reaction to seeing Stewart again and wondered if he would sense how appalled and ashamed she was about the act which gave him life. Would he feel the same sense of shame when she told him? She tortured herself with such questions until distracted by the sounds of women's voices and splashing water.

"Excuse me," Ruth called as she approached the water's edge. The two women looked up; one was quite old and the other in her early twenties. They gathered up their washing and walked over to Ruth.

She recognised the older woman: Tommy's mother. "Meka, I've come back. I must talk to you." Their eyes locked. Ruth knew the answer to her question immediately, without asking. But she had to go through the process of asking. Meka had to say the words to make it real.

Their reunion was cool, no hugging or animated smiles. "I want to talk to you about my father."

Meka waved towards the village. *"Yu go long haus!"* The younger woman was sent home.

"I've been away a long time; so much has changed." Ruth wasn't sure where to start.

"Some things changes, Ruthy, but not everybody change, some always the same." Ruth got the impression that Meka had expected this visit. Her manner indicated little surprise.

"You come looking for Tommy?" Meka asked.

Ruth wasn't expecting the question, but it broke the ice and provided her with the opening she needed.

"No, Meka, I haven't come to find Tommy. My reason for coming home was to help Jake. When I spoke to him, he told me something

281

that I must ask you about. That's why I came. It's to do with Tommy, with you and my father." As the words came tumbling out, Ruth thought her voice sounded as though it belonged to someone else; what she was saying seemed crazy and unreal – made worse by Meka's silence.

"In the days gone, many things different to now. When your father send home your mother before the war, he all by hisself, he got no womans for company."

Ruth's immediate reaction was a nauseating revulsion, not at Meka, but at the thought of her father acting like some lascivious animal.

"Your husband, Billy, he allowed you to be with my father?"

"Ruthy, you understand our ways. I was third wife of Billy; your father make him boss while he go south for war. He give him kina shell and nice things, he look after us."

Ruth knew about the trading of women for goods or favours but the thought of her father being part of such an arrangement filled her with disgust. Her father had always treated Billy and Meka differently to the others. She recalled her last Christmas at home when, against her mother's protestations, her father had left the family breakfast to give Meka supplies.

"He good to Billy, Ruthy, and I loved Billy so it all a'right."

Ruth's contempt for her father didn't extend to Meka. She understood how powerless the woman must have been in the deal. Such abuses of power used to be common, one would often hear of white men taking advantage of their workers, especially to gain access to their women.

"I understand, Meka, but I am angry with my father, even though he is dead. I don't understand how he, of all people, could have done such a thing."

"No point having anger. Anger will eat you and make you sick. It happen long time ago, different times."

"They were different times, Meka, but what happened then has consequences now. I have a son. He is Tommy's son, your grandson."

Ruth watched Meka's face change, but couldn't discern the emotion. More awkwardness than shock, then tears welled in the woman's eyes. Ruth put her hand on Meka's arm. "You knew about us, didn't you?"

"We try to make him lose interest. Billy send him hunting and fishing when you come. Masta John want to give him money to go away but it too late." Meka put her hand to her mouth as if to smother the words she had just uttered.

"My father knew? He knew about us?"

"My mother, Hoku, saw you and Tommy at the river. She tried pleading with Masta John to send Tommy away, but he didn't believe what she said about the two of you. Then after you went, he comes looking for Tommy with money to go away, but he a'ready gone to Moresby." Meka lapsed back into Motu, which Ruth didn't understand. "You won't tell Tommy about your boy, Ruthy? He thinks another man give you baby."

"I must tell him, Meka. He has a right to know he has a son, and my boy must know his father. I'm not sure when I'll get to tell him but I must; there have been too many lies. Too many things weren't said that should have been said. I want to put an end to it; there has been too much hurt." More determined than ever, Ruth vowed that there would be no more cover-ups, especially as far as her son was concerned.

After thanking Meka for telling her the truth, she made her way home in a daze, trying to piece together the effects her father's deception had had on everyone. His behaviour towards her and the guilt he spoke about in his letter made complete sense now. He had guessed the baby belonged to Tommy. Even her mother's misery and suicide made sense, her bitter attitude towards Billy and Meka at Christmas, everything fell into place.

Unsure of what exactly she should do, and becoming worried about her own safety, Ruth decided against confronting Sam on her own. Essie's testimony of what had happened was sufficient; she would tell the police and let them take the necessary action.

Ruth reached the side of the storage silos. The place where she and Tommy had gone to be together on that dreadful night. She remembered how in love with each other they were as she appraised the now battered door, which hung off its hinges; the one they had tied shut on the night they had made love. If only they had known the consequences of what they were doing at the time, she mused. And now Stewart was going to be burdened with the fallout.

The only thing that made it bearable was their own innocence; both of them unknowing parties in the incestuous mess caused by her father. Her feelings towards Tommy were still feelings of love, albeit without the fire of sexual longing. Those feelings, she acknowledged, had long been extinguished. How she felt about him now was entirely different, more like the brother he was. In fact, she realised, he always had seemed like a brother in so many ways. Always willing to listen, always there for her, he was her confidant and would cheer her up when she was miserable. Perhaps if she hadn't been so cut off from everyone else, life would have turned out very differently. Still, too late now to worry about what might have been, she thought; there's no going back. She briskly walked away.

Arriving back at the homestead, it looked in even greater disrepair on this second approach. The vegetable garden was full of weeds, three of the sunroom windows were broken, and a sheet of iron from the roof had either blown away or been taken.

"Your house needs paint," Kapi said, as he emerged from the back door.

"I think a stick of dynamite is what it needs," Ruth said, feeling defeated.

"I brought something to eat." Kapi held up four ripe coconuts.

"Save the water for cooking. Meka gave me some fish, and I found *maniota* and taro in the garden. How did you go with Millie's clan?"

"The men are away, I'll go back later."

"Come on, *me kookim kai kai*." Ruth's English was increasingly giving way to pidgin.

284

Returning to Okoro had turned out totally different to how Ruth had imagined. Apart from seeing Essie and Meka, everything about the place depressed her. The house looked dilapidated, the villagers had become surly and distant, the heat was unbearable, and they had no proper supplies.

"Is your village like Okoro, Kapi?" she asked, trying to make conversation while they ate.

"Yes but we have no white boss."

"No, I think Okoro is unique in that regard. After the coffee started, the village just sort of expanded in this direction."

"Maybe I go out to find the men now."

Ruth guessed he had become bored with her attempts at conversation.

"Sure, Kapi, I'm going to have a shower and go to bed; I feel a bit off-colour."

After he had left, Ruth went outside. She walked to the end of the garden to her mother's grave. Even the plot had become overgrown. She crouched down and tore away the overgrowth of weeds and grass then placed two red hibiscus flowers on the vandalised headstone.

"Well, I came back, Mum. I didn't think I ever would. My life's a complete mess, and so is everyone else's. I can't imagine how you survived here for so long. You knew about Dad, eh? I suspect you did. God, this place must have been hell for you. I guess I was lucky in a way. I got out."

Ruth sat in silence for the best part of an hour. Being close to her mother again was comforting. Ironic, she thought, she seemed to understand her mother better now than when she was alive. She wiped the tears from her face and stood up. "I'll come back before I leave." She lightly patted the headstone, as if comforting her mother. "I'm going for a shower," she whispered and walked away.

The shower was the only good thing about Okoro, a syphon hose running from a black, painted rainwater tank which retained heat from the day's sun. The water was lukewarm and gentle on her skin. After drying herself, she went to her mother's room and stood outside the door. It was as though she had been transported back in time. Resisting the impulse to knock, she turned the handle and gently pushed open the door.

Apart from the dust and mould on the walls, the room looked exactly as it always had. Ruth remembered finding her mother dead. Nothing had changed; even the cretonne bedspread was the same. She wondered if her father had ever slept in the room afterwards.

From the dressing table, she picked up a faded photograph of the family and some of the workers. The picture was taken not long after they had returned after the war. Smiling, happy faces stared up at her, all looking forward to a bright and prosperous future. Ruth could tell from her mother's expression that she had come back to Okoro more out of duty than love. "What a sad life, Mummy." Placing the picture back on the dressing table, she went to the spare room; sleeping in her own room would have been too unsettling.

She lay in bed, thinking. It was like watching a movie of her childhood. In her mind's eye she could see quite clearly her life before she went away: Sally cleaning the house, her brothers being abominable, her mother sitting on her favourite velvet-covered chair, sewing some beautifully-coloured material. Being back in the house after all this time was a peculiar experience. Any sense of it having been a home had gone; it was a mere shell now, a remnant of some past reality.

Kneeling down, she checked under the bed for snakes or lizards, a habit left over from childhood, when she inadvertently discovered a python in her bed-springs while hiding from Jake. The walls were also scrutinised; spiders were frequent visitors, especially after rain.

It had been an exhausting couple of days and Ruth relished the cool cotton sheets against her body as she slowly sank into the centre of the mattress. Her mind drifted home to Derrigeribar. She missed Stewart and William intensely and longed to give them the biggest hug. She wondered if Jessica had contacted Bob and his wife and if they had arranged her visit. Stewart was mentally strong in spite of his years, she thought, but would that be enough to help him cope with this dreadful mess? Discovering he was conceived as a result of incest would be likely to affect him forever, she agonised. Somewhere between thoughts, sleep intervened.

She bolted upright, wondering if she had been dreaming; was that shattering glass? She put on her mother's old chenille dressing gown in case Kapi had returned drunk or under the effects of betel nut.

The generator had gone off so she groped her way through the house in darkness. The kitchen curtain flapped outside the window. She remembered closing all the windows but thought, even if she didn't, the fly screen should be there. Grabbing the torch, she noticed that the edges of the broken window had some dark splattering running down.

In a panic, she dashed out to the veranda and slammed on the generator. Back inside, her eyes fixed on the object at her feet. At first she thought it was some kind of animal and bent down for a closer inspection. She reeled back in horror, too shocked to scream. Staring up at her was Kapi's severed head, lying in a pool of blood.

CHAPTER 20

Ruth's eyes were transfixed on the gruesome mass of hacked flesh at her feet. She didn't notice Essie walk in.

Essie gasped at the horrific sight before covering Kapi's face with a tea towel. "Ruth, you must go; the men are back!"

Ruth remained frozen. Her brain refused to comprehend what had happened; her body wouldn't respond.

"Come on, Ruthy, look at me!" Essie shook her until recognition registered in her eyes.

She stared at Essie, unable to look at where Kapi lay; she began to hyperventilate until a coughing fit ended in vomiting. Essie pulled her by the arm towards the door. "You come with me now." The old woman manoeuvred Ruth out of the kitchen, down the steps and up the path leading to the drying huts.

"Where are we going?" Ruth said, still overcome with horror and shock.

"You must hide. The men are back with drink, you not safe in the house."

"Kapi, they've killed him," Ruth said as she turned away, still dry-retching and trying to catch her breath.

"Come, Ruth, you go to my fishin' hut by the river, next to Meka's washing place on left side." Essie led her up behind the huts and past the storage silos until they reached a path. "I better go back in case they guess we're together. Can you find the hut yourself?"

"Essie, this is madness. Yes, I can find the place." Ruth began to grasp the danger.

"I come in the morning. You can sleep there, it's woman's place so men won't go." Essie gave her a quick hug. "Go now," she said, before disappearing back down the path.

Ruth continued towards the river, wondering if anyone was following. Looking back at the homestead, she saw nothing but could hear shouting. Men's voices; they sounded wild and crazy. She hurried to the place where Essie had directed her, grateful for the bright, full moon to see by.

The hut was exactly where Essie had described, a short way along the bank to the left of the washing pool. Thick bushes covered the area; it appeared sufficiently hidden and protected. She pushed through the grasses covering the opening and slunk inside. With nothing to sit on, she crouched down on the dirt floor, oblivious to any natural dangers that might be lurking in the dark.

The riverbank possessed an eerie stillness, apart from the occasional frog or fish causing ripples on the water's surface. As time passed, Ruth's initial sense of relief began to wane. In her distraught state, the pitch darkness caused her mind to play tricks. She saw images of Kapi's blood-covered head staring at her from out of the blackness.

The dizzy, sick sensation she had experienced before going to bed had returned, worsened now by the recurring horror that kept playing itself out in her head. At first she thought she would try to sleep, but after hearing a twig break, she decided to stay awake. Thoughts of never laying eyes on Stewart and William again began to torment her. She panicked. Her breathing became shallow and frequent. Please don't let it end like this; oh God, please let me see them again! She tried to block out the fear, but it began to overwhelm her. In desperation, she scrambled outside to make sure no one had followed.

The quietness of the jungle did nothing to quell her terror. Unsure of whether she was imagining sounds or actually hearing them, she left the safety of the hut and ran along the riverbank – the more distance between her and the village, the better. She came across a large hollow tree and thought no one would find her there.

After checking for snakes, she squeezed her body through the split trunk and crouched down inside. As she surveyed the water's edge, she became convinced that pairs of dim, pinkish lights were observing her – the tell-tale sign of crocodiles. In her distraught state, she couldn't remember whether crocodiles had ever been seen in the river, but you couldn't be certain of anything, the odd one or two could have made it up stream.

The terror of being caught by the villagers, or being eaten by crocodiles, became too compelling to simply stay put any longer; she crawled out of her damp refuge. She hurried further along the river, hoping to find a track away from the water. Crawling up the muddy bank, she became nauseous and dizzy. As she grabbed a branch to steady herself, a burning sensation filled her mouth and throat; she could feel her saliva increasing. She swallowed quickly to prevent herself from vomiting again. It didn't work; she vomited so violently that she couldn't catch her breath and feared she might faint. Clasping onto vines, she pulled herself to the top of the bank, where she lay briefly to recover her breath. Even more exposed now, should she pass out, she forced herself to get up and walk. Only feet away, there was a path which seemed clear of vegetation. Her pace quickened in anticipation of greater safety.

Within only a short distance, the forest became thick again and completely blocked her way. The canopy obliterated the moonlight, which hampered her vision. What little she could make out was obscured by stinging perspiration running into her eyes. Tying up her hair with a piece of vine, she realised her thirst had become acute.

"Damn! Now I have to drink!" she swore, and climbed back down to the river. Crouching over the embankment, she splashed the ice-cold water on her face and neck.

She pulled her hands out of the water and listened. Men's voices; it seemed they were coming from the women's washing pools. In a state of renewed panic, she ran further along to another clearing. Miraculously, secreted between a clump of bushes, someone had hidden their dugout. She hauled the heavy canoe into the water and climbed in, pulling a broken branch with her to use as a paddle.

Paralysing fear dissolved into a sense of relief as she pushed the craft out into the river, but her nausea persisted. She began to retch over the side of the canoe. As she washed the watery vomit from her face, the vessel started to keel over. She flung herself back to the other side to prevent it from capsizing. As she glanced upward towards the moonlight, everything began to spin, or fall, or sink, or... there was a crash. Ruth had collapsed backwards into the boat. It continued on its journey down the river.

The canoe drifted along with the water until it became ensnared on a wayward vine. The current propelled the wooden craft into a muddy bay along the bank, where it stayed until late into the afternoon.

"*Wantok com pas tim!*"

Ruth was vaguely aware of a male voice, calling to his friend to come. Her pursuers had caught up and were grabbing at her clothing.

"Get away! Get away, how dare you touch me!" Her cries went unheeded. The men persisted.

"I will tell my father; he'll have you shot! Let go!" She struggled and thrashed out at her abductors before passing back into unconsciousness.

"*Mi ting meri em long long,*" one of the men suggested.

"*No gat, em sik meri.*" The older man explained she was delirious, not mad. The men deftly tied Ruth between two bamboo poles then carried her towards a small outcrop of thatched buildings.

"Rogi, who is that?" a woman's voice called to one of the men as they approached the hut.

"Misis come in canoe, she sick," the older man answered.

"Take her up to the house. Sister Rose, go with them, I'll get the medicine bag." In a flurry of activity, the men whisked Ruth away to a long wooden hut set apart from the others.

"*Yu pela* go now." The older nun returned with her medical supplies and dismissed the two men.

"We need to clean those cuts before they fester, Sister," she said to the younger nun.

Ruth discerned the softer voices of women and realised that the men must have gone. "Essie, *yu me go now kisim kiap*, he won't get away with this!" Ruth shouted, alternating between Pidgin and English. She wanted Essie to go with her to fetch the police.

"God knows what she's been through; she's delirious. Let's get her on the bed." The two nuns washed mud and leaves from Ruth's body and disinfected the deep scratches she had acquired from brushing against razor-sharp lawyer vines. As the nuns worked, Ruth's taut muscles began to relax; her eyes shot open and stared at the wall, then she tried to sit up.

"What are you doing?" Ruth demanded, looking at the two nuns staring down at her.

"I'm Sister Benedict, this is Sister Rose. You're very sick dear; you've contracted cerebral malaria." Unlike the sisters at school, these nuns were dressed entirely in white. Ruth wondered how they kept clean. *Or maybe they aren't real.*

Ruth must have looked as though she understood because the nuns didn't explain any further; she just closed her eyes and drifted back to sleep.

The malaria had been like a small death, Ruth recalled later. She remembered nothing of the ten days spent swearing, calling for help and fighting with the sisters, who she imagined were her native captors. Until one cool morning, her eyes opened, her fever had spontaneously remitted and she was lucid.

"How did I get here?" she asked.

"Two of our boys pulled you out the river. Well, from a canoe," Sister Rose explained.

Ruth vaguely remembered the canoe and running away from Okoro. And Kapi, God no, poor Kapi, she thought, remembering their journey on foot through the jungle to Okoro and the horror of his murder. It's all so terrible, he's dead.

"My family will be worried sick, they expected me home days ago. I must get back to Port Moresby."

"You're still too weak, Ruth. Sister Benedict sent word to the patrol officer. He's been in touch with the police and your hotel." The nun explained how they had found a box of hotel matches in her pocket. "Sister Benedict gave instructions for them to contact your people."

Ruth could imagine how worried they would be at home. "I must call them," Ruth pleaded.

"I'm sure they'll understand you'll need some time to recover," Sister Rose said.

"Where are we? I don't recognise anything."

"This is St. Joseph's Brown River Mission. We started the hospital about fifteen years ago.

"I've never heard of a hospital out here."

"Well, we're here," she smiled. "We only treat Hansen's disease though."

"A leper colony, like Gemo Island you mean?"

"Like Gemo Island, but a lot smaller of course. Don't worry, you won't catch it. Everyone's receiving treatment and you're a long way from the patients over here."

"I must get in touch with Millie. Her husband's been killed." Ruth's head began to clear.

"You certainly have a lot of things on your mind, Ruth. I'll ask Sister Benedict to come and visit you. She'll know what to do next."

Ruth tried to get up but had to lie back down. Her head pounded as though her skull were about to burst. She lay immobilised, until the pain started to subside.

"Well, well, Mrs McGrath, you are on the mend!" Sister Benedict came bursting into the hut. "There'll be a plane on Friday, but it doesn't come here. We'll need to get you back across the river to Tegora Station."

"Back to Moresby?" Ruth asked.

"Yes, but you'll be taken to the hospital directly."

"I've got things to do; I have to call my family."

"You'll be able to do that from hospital, but see what the doctors say first. You're over the worst."

Friday seemed a long way off, but Ruth knew that in her weakened condition she would just have to wait. At least someone has called home, she thought, resting her head back on the pillow.

After a couple of days of eating and drinking normally, Ruth was able to get up and walk around. The mornings dragged, but Sister Rose visited after lunch each day and they would go for leisurely strolls through the gardens. In spite of the mission's isolation, patients had cultivated large tracts of land and a wide variety of fruit and vegetables grew neatly in rows. There were pigs in pens, and chickens roamed freely; the mission was entirely self-sufficient.

"Is that a cemetery?" Ruth pointed towards an area of well-kept flower beds.

"Yes it is. In the early days people would often end up staying here permanently. We had to battle to get the villagers to accept their relatives back. We've been educating them about the disease over the years, so things are a little easier now. They usually go home when they're well."

"I notice a number of sisters buried here too." Ruth walked over to a group of more elaborate headstones.

"Yes, our founder died here as well as two of the early sisters who helped establish the mission."

"Who's this?" Ruth pointed to a plaque inscribed, 'A Lost Gentleman'.

"Villagers brought him here a few years ago, from Kigoryu village. Quite insane he was and had become violent. As it turned out, he was an Englishman who had met with a terrible accident and suffered brain damage."

Ruth immediately thought about Lindsay. Could this man be him? It wasn't unheard of for local villagers to adopt shell-shocked soldiers and other 'lost' people.

"How old was he?"

"Probably in his late sixties, early seventies, why?"

"One of my uncles disappeared after a plane crash. He was never found." As fantastic as it seemed, Ruth thought it had to be Lindsay. "Would anyone have more information about him?"

"Well, Sister Benedict nursed him; he came down with pneumonia. That's what he died from."

Ruth couldn't wait to talk to the nun to find out what she could remember. The riddle of Lindsay's disappearance might finally be solved.

Sister Benedict described the old man's features very clearly. Her description of his eyes matched exactly how Ruth remembered Lindsay's: the brightest blue, like her grandmother's. She told of the man's delirious ranting, as if defending a criminal in court. This was enough to satisfy Ruth. But the only way to be sure, she realised, would be for the police to examine the remains.

She wondered if they would bother after all these years. As comforting as it would be to know, finding out seemed less important now; Eliza had passed away, and other matters were more pressing. Still, his family in Scotland should be told of the discovery.

Friday had arrived; Ruth could hardly contain her excitement about returning to Port Moresby. The few days of enforced recuperation while waiting for the flight had seen her strength return almost to normal. Headaches and tiredness in the afternoons were the only remaining symptoms, but the nuns had assured her that would eventually go.

The same two men who found her ended up with the task of taking her to Tegora. Ruth figured Tegora must be about ten miles from the mission on the other side of the river but separated, it appeared, by a local taboo to do with the mission, or the disease that they treated. The two escorts took her only to the perimeter of the large tea plantation before returning to their canoe.

When she reached the homestead, she was expecting to be greeted by the owner. The taboo extended to the white plantation owner too, it seemed. One of the native workers had been given the unenviable task of transporting the 'misis from the leprosarium' to the plane. No sooner had she arrived than the man whisked her away by jeep to the airstrip. She guessed they were probably as ignorant about leprosy as she used to be. So much for the sisters' notion of greater acceptance for sufferers of the disease.

Ruth recognised the aircraft and pilot immediately. It was the same one who brought her and Kapi out to Okoro, which seemed like such a long time ago.

"I hear you've been sick," he said, as she climbed into the cabin.

"Malaria. I thought I'd die," she explained, making sure he understood it wasn't Hansen's disease that ailed her.

"I heard there was trouble at Okoro."

"Yes, a lot of trouble."

"Someone murdered over a bride price, the kiaps were saying."

"A bride price?" Ruth exclaimed. Essie had told her that Hiri and Sam attacked Kapi because he had brought her back to Okoro. It was clear they expected to cover up another murder. This time it won't be so easy. Ruth resolved to bring them to account, one way or another.

It was a quick journey back to Port Moresby. It always amazed Ruth how in just seventy miles, life went from primitive hunter-gatherer villages to the modern suburban communities of the capital.

The sisters, it seemed, had sent instructions ahead, even down to the taxi driver, who took Ruth directly to the hospital. He refused to go to the hotel first, in spite of Ruth's protestations. In the end, she gave in and decided to plead with the doctor that she didn't want to be admitted. The examination revealed that the Larium treatment she received at the mission had been effective. The doctor downgraded her status to outpatient.

"I wonder where they get their supplies," the doctor said, looking intrigued. "It's only been available to the forces so far."

"Well, whatever their source, I'm glad I don't need to be admitted. I've been away for nearly three weeks and have things to do." Ruth thought she would impress on the doctor how dire her situation was in case he changed his mind.

"I understand, Mrs McGrath, but if you notice the return of any symptoms, you must come straight back. And don't forget to keep taking the medication."

"I will, of course." All she could think about was returning to the hotel and calling home.

When she finally got through on the phone, Matthew sounded more angry than pleased. They had received no word from the police after the initial call, and had she not called today, Matthew was ready to leave for Port Moresby the following afternoon. The children had to be told about what had happened. Stewart's school wanted to send him home because he was upset and unable to focus on his school work. And Shirley had been beside herself with worry. Ruth suspected he was relieved underneath his anger, a bit like she was when Stewart had been bitten by the snake.

"I'll be home within the week, Matthew. The doctor said I've got to stay here and rest. Besides, they're more used to treating malaria here." Ruth hated telling lies, but there was no other way to buy enough time to finish all she needed to do.

"No more idiotic trips. You've got kids to think about. Jake can sort out his own business; he can't expect you to be risking your life. I'm going to call the school now. Make sure you keep in touch."

"I'll call you Wednesday. Give Will a big hug for me."

The first thing Ruth had to do was call on Millie. Then the police. The thought of breaking the news to Millie about her husband made her sick. She didn't want to be the one to tell her, but hearing about Kapi's death from officials would be worse. She quickly changed and made her way to the bus stop.

It was only after getting on the Koki market bus that she realised only native locals seemed to travel by bus. With the driver looking down his nose at her and stares and giggles from the passengers, she found a seat near a window. The bus was stuffy and overcrowded. Ruth thought she would pass out but wasn't sure if it were the malaria returning or the prospect of telling Millie about her husband.

As she alighted from the vehicle, she found herself at Koki

settlement, a shanty town with rows of tin, board and wooden houses. She wondered if Millie would be easy to find. All she knew was that she lived in the area, somewhere.

After pretending not to look lost, Ruth gave up. She decided to ask someone. A small group of women sat on the ground under a mango tree. They had betel nuts, lime, ginger and sago laid out for sale on a brightly coloured rug. "Hello, I'm looking for Millie Dikana. I don't have her address."

One of the group stood: a tall, solidly built woman with a shiny dark complexion, whose features almost disappeared against her vibrantly-coloured floral dress. The whites of her eyes were red and she looked angry. "Why you want Millie?" she asked then spat out a gob of red masticated betel nut just inches from Ruth's foot.

"She's a friend," Ruth said. "I must speak to her. I have news from the village." Ruth fished in her handbag for money. "I'll take two mangoes too, please. You can keep the change"

The woman stared at the five dollar note in disbelief then she softened. "That too big money, I give you extra mangoes."

"They look lovely," Ruth said, watching the mango stalks being deftly tied together.

"You find Millie over that way." The woman pointed to a shack about a hundred yards away. The dwelling appeared to be made from a mixture of tin, tar paper and sheets of asbestos cement.

"Thank you," Ruth said, glad to be on her way.

When she arrived at the house, she spotted Millie lying on a grass mat outside. The children played quietly in the sand, watched by an old woman sitting cross-legged and holding a banana leaf for shade.

"She sick, Misis, she don't talk to anyone," the woman warned, as Ruth made her way over to Millie's side. Millie didn't look up.

"Oh Millie, you've heard already. I came to tell you, I'm so sorry." Ruth held Millie tightly in her arms.

After a few minutes, Millie began to sob. Ruth never relaxed her embrace but held her like a child; they cried together. For Ruth, it was a cry she had stifled for weeks, emotions she had to disown to ensure her survival.

"He was a good man, Miss Ruth." Millie looked up at her.

"He was Millie, a very good man. I'm just so sorry." Ruth had never known such wretched feelings of guilt. If she hadn't gone to Okoro, Millie's husband would still be alive. "I'm so sorry, if I hadn't wanted…"

"Don't, Miss Ruth, don't blame yourself. He wanted to go about my bride price," she reassured Ruth, in spite of her own devastation.

"I promise you, Millie, I'll make sure they don't get away with it."

Ruth had difficulty extricating herself from Millie's pain as she made her way back to the hotel on foot. Walking in the heat and dust didn't seem like such a good idea once she had started on her way. Apart from an incredible thirst, she wavered between intense shortness of breath and uncontrollable bursts of crying. Everything in her life had gone wrong, and now she had caused another human being untold grief and sorrow.

A good three hours later, she arrived at Ela beach. She had blisters on her feet, and her knees threatened to give out from under her. The salty sea breeze on her parched skin was cool. The urge to go into the water was too hard to resist. Maybe the coolness of the sea would cleanse away not only the dust and heat, but also her pain and the intolerable guilt.

By the time she reached the hotel, her feelings of wretchedness had transformed into determination; she would finish what she had set out to do, as well as bring Hiri and Sam to account.

After a quick shower, she changed her clothes and went straight to the police station. Entering through the large double glass doors, she experienced a sense of relief. Not only would Jake's difficulties be solved, but justice would soon prevail and Kapi's murderers would be caught. At least that might give Millie some peace of mind.

"I can understand your frustration, Mrs McGrath, but I have every confidence in the patrol officer who attended the scene; his reports are always accurate and well corroborated."

"I don't care what he says, I was there. It was no accident. His head was hacked off! And what about my father's death? How can you simply dismiss what I say?"

"As I said, Mrs McGrath, I do understand your concerns, but with the investigations conducted to date, everything seems in order."

"If you won't listen to me, I'll take the matter to Canberra. You can't just dismiss what I say and accept the villagers' account of what happened."

"Look, if you believe we've overlooked something during our investigation, I'll refer it on to one of the senior inspectors to review, but at this stage, that's all I can do."

Ruth marched out onto the footpath; she was fuming. Once outside, she began to question whether it really happened, or whether she had gone insane and didn't know. Maybe the malaria has come back. She sat down on a metal bench, trying to work out whether she was going mad or whether everyone around her was insane. Surely what Jake said can't be true, she thought. That can't be how things work; even if it is political, that's just not right.

The next morning, she was up and dressed before daybreak, ready to catch the early flight to Lae and to find Tommy. She had to talk to him about what she had found out from Jake and hopefully, once over the shock, he could be persuaded to help find witnesses to her father's and Kapi's murder. She wanted to call home to tell them where she was going but Matthew wouldn't understand. He was likely to call the hospital and cause all sorts of problems. She reasoned that if she found Tommy straightaway, there would be enough time to sort everything out and return to Port Moresby ready for her flight back to the mainland. Matthew needn't know anything until everything was fixed.

Luckily, there was a non-stop flight. It would take the quickest route, which more or less shadowed the Kokoda track before veering off to the northwest. Her nerves about flying seemed to have been cured thanks to the police; she was still furious at the dismissive way she was treated, and now she was determined to get them to listen.

As the plane droned towards its destination, she became restless. The reality of seeing Tommy after all this time, coupled with the knowledge of his bloodline, caused her to feel quite ill. Looking out of the window in an attempt to distract herself, she noticed that the coastline was already in sight. She recognised the half-submerged bow of the *Tenyo Maru*, a converted Japanese liner sunk by the Americans. Within just an hour, the Electra was descending rapidly towards the Lae airstrip.

When the plane touched down, the prospect of coming face-to-face with Tommy became more real, and unnerving. She tried to focus on the things she had to do, rather than trying to imagine the actual meeting. I need to find him quickly, she thought; tell him about Stewart, Kapi, the death of his father and Jake's wrongful arrest. She reasoned that if she kept the pending encounter straightforward and business-like, her emotions would survive the ordeal and his reaction would be easier to cope with. She knew she had to be careful, the last thing she needed was for him not to want anything to do with Stewart.

As she tried to force herself to keep thinking rationally, she could feel her whole being gradually succumbing to a force she could barely control. The thought of seeing him again after fifteen years, and having to tell him that he was her brother, and the father of her child, was too much. Perhaps he even knows by now, she thought, someone must have said something during all this time. She tried to calm herself, taking deep, slow breaths and imagining Stewart at home, totally unaware of the events soon to unfold. Tommy's response to the news would have significant consequences for Stewart; it was imperative that she said everything in the right way. Regardless of what had happened in the past, Stewart must never be made to feel tainted in any way, she told herself, Tommy *must* acknowledge him. She walked down the steps onto the tarmac.

Panic started to set in, she was feeling as though she couldn't breathe, but she took more deep breaths and walked purposefully. Damn! she thought. I'm just going to say what I need to say and worry about it afterwards! She got into a taxi.

The Hotel Cecil was a large white building set against a picturesque backdrop of native vegetation interspersed with blossoming *ohi'a lehua*. Ruth wondered how long it would take to find Tommy, or if he was even still there. Millie said he had some sort of business, but in the rush to leave, she had forgotten to ask what sort. Lae wasn't anywhere near as large as Port Moresby so she reasoned most of the locals should know each other.

"I'd like to find one of our former workers while I'm here, his name is Tommy Ulu," Ruth asked the porter, as he unstrapped her portmanteau.

"I don't think I know him, Madam, is he in trouble?" His eyes remained on the port.

"No, not at all, I just want to speak to him." Ruth realised he probably wouldn't tell her, even if he knew.

"Maybe you ask for him at George's Café," the porter offered. "It's on Fourth Street, opposite the chemist. Small place but easy to find." He smiled.

Ruth guessed he did know something. She gave him an extra tip.

It was imperative that she remained as inconspicuous as possible. An unknown white woman walking the streets alone would draw attention. The best route, she decided, would be through the back of the hotel to Huon Road. Fourth Street was then just a short walk. Lae had grown since she had visited as a child with her mother. The town had suffered more damage during the war than Port Moresby so a lot of new buildings had appeared.

The café was easy to find; a good start, she thought, crossing her fingers.

"Excuse me, I was told you might know where I can find Tommy Ulu."

"He one of your boys?" the man asked.

"Yes, he used to work for us, and as I was visiting, I've brought news from his family." She decided that sounded believable.

"He in any trouble?" The man seemed hesitant and suspicious.

"No, no trouble. In fact, the news is important, so I must find him before I leave."

"You go ask over the road, the Highlands' Grocer."

"Oh I see, thank you very much."

Ruth walked across the street to the greengrocer's. A well-stocked oasis of every imaginable fruit, grain, seed and vegetable grown in the highlands. She gently manoeuvred herself past two shoppers and went up to the man at the counter.

"Hello, the gentleman from across the road said I might be able to find –" Ruth stopped in mid-sentence.

The shopkeeper looked astonished as she stared at him, trying to absorb and process every aspect of who he was.

"Ruth?" Tommy's voice strained; his eyes opened wide in disbelief.

"Tommy?"

CHAPTER 21

There he stood, in front of her, the man she had loved so blindly that nothing else in the world mattered. She hesitated, trying to work out what her body should do: hug him, shake his hand or kiss him. It was difficult to understand how she had been so in love with him. He looked so ordinary. Apart from his having aged, his shiny black hair had become dull, and his jowls had begun to sag.

"Tommy, how are you?" Ruth said, immediately recognising, and responding as always, to the softness in his expression. He had the same open and engaging eyes possessed by her grandmother and Lindsay. She hadn't noticed this resemblance before.

"I can't believe you're here. I never thought I'd see you again," he said wonderingly, holding her gaze.

"So much has happened, Tommy. I didn't intend to come back but I had to; we need to talk about things." She searched his face; the more she studied him, the more she saw the Tommy she remembered, but the burning desire to possess and be possessed by him had gone.

"Let's go down to the beach," he said, calling behind him, "*Yupela*, come look after the shop." A young boy ran in from the back of the shop and sat down at the counter.

Ruth's mind wrestled with all the things she had to say: where to start, what to tell him first and whether she should leave Stewart until last. Once he knows about Stewart, she thought, he might be too shocked to think about anything else. Perhaps it'll be too much to take in. She tried to second-guess his reaction. Maybe I should tell him only a couple of things and save the rest. Her mind was ready to explode.

"There's no right, wrong, or easy way to tell you... you have a son... we have a son. His name is Stewart... it was that time in the packing sheds." The words came tumbling out, not at all in the way she had planned.

Tommy remained silent and kept walking, his gaze focused on the ground. Ruth wondered if he had heard, but then realised his mind must be grappling with what she had said. He always used to go quiet when trying to understand something.

"He's a wonderful boy," she continued, "good-hearted and sensible. We had a difficult time in Sydney to start with, but everything worked out in the end. He's a happy boy." She wondered if she should wait and let the news sink in, but Tommy's slowness to respond compelled her to keep talking.

"Jake's been arrested for father's murder. I went to Okoro to find out what happened. Hiri and Sam were the culprits, but they told the police it was Jake. Your father stood up for Jake and got into a fight." Ruth hesitated. "Essie said he died a few days after the fight."

Tommy turned towards Ruth. "I know my father is dead. I know about everything at Okoro. Let's go over by the trees; it's more private." He pointed to a clump of coconut palms.

He always remained calm in the face of calamity, she remembered, a trait Stewart seemed to have inherited. "There's more to tell you, and it won't be easy." She glanced at him, trying to gauge how he might react. "You'd better brace yourself. I wasn't sure if it was true when Jake told me, but I asked your mother, I had to know, I had to hear her say it." Ruth paused to think how she might make what was to follow less shocking. But there was no way of lessening the blow, the truth was ugly and there was no way to make it sound anything less. "You're my brother, my half-brother."

Ruth expected something catastrophic to happen when she uttered those words but having now told him, the secret spontaneously lost some of its potency. The horror was no longer solely hers to grapple with; they could deal with it together.

"Let's sit down," Tommy said, smoothing a patch of grass. "I knew about your father and my mother. Not at first, not when we were together. My grandmother, Hoku, told me. Remember, she came to the house after your mother died? She was the one who spotted us at the river. I told you that in my letter when you went away. I didn't know what to do. I hoped nothing would happen. I had to get away, so I decided to go to Moresby.

"Your father – my father – sent me money when I was in Moresby. He said, in exchange I wasn't to return to the village. I took his money. I figured if he was my father, he owed me something. That's how I bought the store. I hadn't heard anything about how you were going. I guessed everything was okay."

Ruth interrupted, "He told me not to write to anyone until my situation had been 'taken care of'. He meant giving Stewart up for adoption. I couldn't give him away, so I never wrote."

"We were all told you had married someone and wouldn't be home," he said with a wistful look in his eyes.

Ruth thought back over all the misery of the past and responded ruefully, "It seemed no one could tell the truth about anything. I think half the problems in this damn place would disappear if everyone told the truth." Ruth remembered the day she had left Okoro to return to the mainland, she thought Tommy hadn't turned up because he didn't like saying goodbye. Now she realised that he must have been going through hell, after Hoku told him that John Madison was his real father.

"Maybe they had to lie," Tommy said, "too many standards to maintain." Tommy and Ruth both understood the hypocrisy of white 'standards'.

The day slipped away, and within what seemed just an hour or so, the sun was sinking into the sea along a blazing, red horizon. In talking over the past and their current situations, they had rediscovered the special bond they shared while growing up. Ruth realised how easy, or inevitable, it had been for them to mistake their shared feelings and deep connection for romantic love.

"I think a lot will change when we get our independence," Tommy said. "Our people will be able to say no to the white bosses, and our children won't go through this sort of thing." He appeared angry, as if a smouldering rage existed beneath the surface. "Tell me about my son."

The day had passed them by when Ruth finished telling Tommy every last detail about their son. The salt-laden breeze blowing in from the sea had turned chilly and damp. They could easily have gone on talking through the night, had Ruth not started to shiver uncontrollably. Tommy reached across and put his hand on her forehead. Years before, his touch would have been electric; now, it induced a feeling of reassurance and understanding.

"You've got a fever; better you go back to the hotel. I'll take you to the side door. No one will notice us at this hour." Tommy was acutely aware of the dangers of being seen at night with a white woman – to have disclosed their shared parentage would have made things even worse.

"If you aren't any better when you get in, call the doctor and send me a message through Mualu; he's the night porter." Tommy's eyes lingered. Ruth observed his frustration at not being able to help any further.

"I will… I'll come to the shop tomorrow. I want to talk to you about Okoro. When all this business with Hiri and Sam is over, I need to sort out what will happen to Okoro, but that can wait." Ruth surmised her feverish chills were probably just hunger. Tomorrow she would be rested and fed, and more able to explain her plans for Okoro. And, hopefully, for Tommy.

The hotel was stuffy and hot inside. Ruth's shivering showed no sign of abating. As she went up the stairs, she had to grasp onto the banister to stop herself from falling. The staircase seemed as though it were moving, and the patterns on the gaudy, embossed wallpaper became blurred. Distorted voices came from somewhere, then nothing. Ruth had collapsed onto the floor.

"You're very naughty, Mrs McGrath, you haven't been taking your medication." Ruth could hear a disembodied voice reprimanding her. She tried to open her eyes long enough to see where she was, but the lights were too bright and painful. She closed them quickly, and the comfortable darkness began to consume her again. She sank back into unconsciousness.

"You mustn't stay for long. She's still in a coma," a woman's voice interrupted a man saying something about seeing someone.

Why are they talking about me as if I'm not here? Ruth wanted to shout at them, but her leaden body wouldn't respond.

"I'll come back tomorrow," the man said.

When Ruth managed to force open her eyes, no one was there. Then she remembered. She was at the river alone today and thinking how Stewart would love to be here swimming. The lagoon looked spectacularly beautiful, with the overhanging branches, every shade of green vegetation imaginable, interspersed with the vibrant, electric reds and orange of the dendrobium orchid. As she swam further upstream, the water was cool against her skin; refreshing at first, but it gradually became colder and she started to shiver violently.

"Careful now, honey, you've dribbled your drink." Ruth recognised the same voice that kept telling the man to leave.

"Who are you?" she said, forcing her eyes to stay open, but this time she saw a woman. A nurse, sitting on the edge of the bed next to her, holding a beaker of water.

"You've been unconscious, sweet; come on, drink some more."

"Am I in Lae?" Ruth couldn't work out if she was back at the hotel or still at the leprosarium.

"No, honey, you're in Port Moresby Base hospital. We shouldn't have let you leave so soon the last time."

"I went to Lae. Where's Tommy?"

"Yes, that's right; you had to be flown back. Don't know about any Tommy, but Joshua has been here with you."

"Joshua? From the mainland?" Ruth thought she was still dreaming. "Joshua, you say? It can't be, he's at home."

"Yes darling, Joshua. I'll send him back in once you've had a wee

308

for me." The nurse deftly manoeuvred the cold bedpan into place.

"He must have flown up here," she said, bewildered.

"I'd say so, luv, unless he came by boat. I'll send him in."

Ruth stared in disbelief as Joshua came through the swinging doors. A familiar face from home, taller and trimmer than she remembered, and handsome too, with his clean-shaven face and slicked black hair. I'm sure he wasn't that attractive, she thought, deciding the drugs must be affecting her brain.

"Josh! What are you doing here?"

"Hello, Ruth! Someone had to find out what was going on."

"How are the children? I've missed them so much."

"They're fine. They send their love and say they can't wait for you to come home."

"I miss them so badly, Josh. At times, I wasn't even sure if I'd see them again."

"You just take things easy. You'll be home with them soon enough."

"God, I've been so sick with this damn malaria, I'm not sure if I'm awake or dreaming."

"The doctor said you've been admitted twice. I don't think Matt knew you'd gone bush again after your last admission to hospital."

"No, I didn't tell him. You know what he's like. It was my own fault; I forgot to take the tablets with me when I went to find Tommy. The last thing I remember is talking to him on the beach and coming over dizzy. Or maybe that happened in the hotel. I can't remember exactly."

"Well, don't go worrying too much until you're stronger."

"How did you find me?" Ruth asked.

"I went to the hotel, they told me I'd find you here. Flown in from Lae, they said."

"Yes, I went looking for Tommy."

"How was he?"

"Okay, I think. I had so much to tell him, ghastly complicated stuff mainly; then this happened."

"Ghastly stuff?" Joshua said, sounding concerned.

"You wouldn't believe what's been going on here, Josh. I had no idea until I arrived. It seemed like everything, and everyone, had gone crazy." She tried as best she could to explain about Jake's false imprisonment and her journey to Okoro, but she fell back asleep.

Joshua returned to visit each day and evening over the next few days. By the fourth day, Ruth was staying awake for longer periods and feeling more like her usual self.

"You're quite a fighter, the doctor tells me," Joshua said.

"Case of having to be; Derrigeribar and the children need me to be well. I want to finish off here and get back. I've been away too long."

"What's left to do?"

"I have to see Jake and try to get him released. He shouldn't be in prison; he had nothing to do with Dad's death."

"You know who did?

"Yes, but the police weren't interested in what I had to say. That was one of the reasons I went to find Tommy. I can't remember everything we spoke about though. I'll try to get hold of him by telephone."

Joshua explained how the doctor had said Ruth could be discharged the following day, as long as someone stayed with her. "I told him I'm booked into the room next to yours. I can help you finish up here, if you like. Two heads are better than one when things get complicated."

"If you're going to be helping me, I'd better explain something to you."

"Sounds serious."

"I would have been too ashamed to tell anyone earlier, but the last couple of weeks has changed that, especially after seeing Tommy."

"You don't need to tell me anything, Ruth, I'm here to make sure you're okay and to get you home safely; I don't have to know all your private stuff."

Ruth knew that if anyone could understand what had happened in her past, it would be Joshua. He was always understanding and supportive. And since William was born, she had grown used to talking to him about her problems.

"I know, but I want to tell you. You've been close to me and the children over the last few years so I feel you should know."

"Okay, let's get it over with, then we can make plans for tomorrow," he said, not looking the least bit perturbed.

As with Tommy, talking to Joshua about her father's affairs and Stewart's parentage was nowhere near as difficult as she had imagined. He was sympathetic more than shocked and said his own grandfather had a reputation with the local aboriginal women, something Lachlan had never mentioned. Sharing your troubles with people who cared about you, Ruth was discovering, made them seem much less ominous and daunting. It somehow robbed them of their power.

Once discharged, Ruth wasted no time. She returned to the hotel with Joshua after unsuccessfully trying to call Tommy on the telephone. Having Josh around bolstered her confidence and helped restore her usually high spirits. Chatting and laughing together, it was just like being back at Derrigeribar. He gave her strength; nothing seemed too hard. The following day, she had booked an appointment with the solicitor.

They set out early to avoid walking around too much in the sun, but already, the air was stifling. As they made their way to the solicitor's office, Ruth realised how happy she was that Joshua, and not Matthew, had come up to find her.

"I just can't get over you coming all this way. It's lovely having you here."

"I'm glad to be here, but I have to admit it wasn't a totally selfless act on my part."

Ruth wondered what he was about to say.

"I've always wanted to visit the islands; my uncle came here during the war."

"Oh," Ruth said a little awkwardly, and thinking herself silly for even imagining he was going to say it was her he wanted to see. "Yes, it is a fascinating place but still backwards in many ways."

"That's an understatement. It's like stepping back into colonial times. The way people live here, with the locals calling everyone masta and misis; wouldn't get away with that back home."

"True, but things aren't that progressive back on the mainland either. They've only just recognised the aborigines as people in the census."

"Yeah, I guess so."

"Here we are, Barrett, Barrett and Baine Solicitors. How do I look?"

"Oh, very much the business memsahib," Joshua smiled wryly.

"Cheeky; come on."

The waiting room possessed only one seat, a large chesterfield settee. The dark wood panelling halfway up the walls made the place seem small. Antique ornaments were carefully placed on locally-made hardwood tables, and portraits of what appeared to be English gentry hung on the wallpapered section of wall. Ruth marvelled at the contradiction. The room could easily have been transported here from another world.

"Good morning, Mrs McGrath. Would you like to come through? My secretary tells me of an additional matter you'd like to deal with today."

"Yes, I would like to finalise my grandmother's business, but I want to gift my inherited share in Okoro to my brother."

"So, you want to sign everything over to Jake? Are you aware he is…"

"Before you go on, yes, I am aware he is in prison, wrongly so, and that is something I'm hoping to correct in due course. But I want my share of Okoro to go to Tommy Ulu. He is my half-brother."

"I wasn't aware of any other siblings apart from Matthew."

"My father had a liaison with a local woman which resulted in the birth of my brother, Tommy."

The solicitor looked nonplussed and a little embarrassed before quickly regaining his professional demeanour. "This is highly irregular. Have you considered the implications of Mr Madison sharing ownership with a person of native origin?" He addressed the question, not to Ruth, but to Joshua.

"I'm sure the lady has considered the matter very thoroughly."

"Can we move on please? I have other business to attend to." Ruth was almost ready to explode with anger but managed to restrain herself.

"Yes, of course, but I must tell you it will be against my better judgment."

"I'm not here to seek your judgment, Mr Barrett, favourable or otherwise. Now may we proceed?"

The papers were drawn up while Ruth dealt with the receipt of Eliza's bequest. The atmosphere in the solicitor's office was tense; Ruth couldn't wait to leave. It was a relief when the secretary returned with the completed paperwork.

"If you would initial each page and sign at the end of the document, you will then no longer have any interest in your family's coffee operations."

"And that interest has been duly transferred to Mr Ulu?"

"Precisely," the solicitor said curtly, as if the deed had caused a bitter taste in his mouth.

Pompous old fool, Ruth thought, and with the swirl of a pen, she made good decades of injustice brought about by her father.

Stepping out onto the footpath, she experienced an overwhelming feeling of relief. "I can't tell you how good I feel having done that. I don't think I've ever done anything before that felt so satisfyingly right." She guessed Jake probably wouldn't agree, but he would have to get used to it.

"Are you angry with your father?" Joshua asked.

"I was, but not now; after speaking to Meka, I can understand what he did. Well, what a lot of white men did, and probably still do. Not that I condone it, of course; I think it's a vile misuse of power. I might understand, Josh, but I'll never be free of the predicament he's created for Tommy, Stewart and me. In a way, I'm glad he's dead. If he were alive, I'd be angry and bitter; I'd want him to know about the pain he has caused."

"I guess we all have to make the most of the deck life deals us, eh?"

"We do. Now, how are you coping with this heat?" Ruth had noticed his profuse sweating.

"I've never been so bloody hot. There's no break; it's just as hot at night as through the day."

"You should get some lighter clothes. We'll go and look in Steamships, if you like; mother and I used to shop there when we came to Moresby. That and Burns Philps are the only two proper shops here."

"Fair enough. Do they have air conditioning?"

"Well, they have fans. The climate is a lot cooler where we used to live; Okoro is higher up above sea level."

After buying a couple of short-sleeved cotton shirts and shorts for Joshua, along with a box of food for Millie, they returned to the hotel. Ruth reluctantly agreed with Joshua that she needed to rest, although finding Tommy and visiting Millie was uppermost in her mind. She agreed to stay in her room and rest so long as Joshua went to Koki to drop off Millie's food parcel. She realised the food wasn't much, but maybe some treats for the children would cheer them up a little.

When Joshua left, Ruth realised just how much she had come to depend on him. She smiled. He's a good, kind man, she thought.

Having promised to rest, she found it impossible to relax no matter how dark she made the room. Her blouse was sticking to her from the humidity, and her feet had sandal-strap marks from the dust. She decided to treat herself to a bath before lying down. She turned on the taps full blast and watched the tepid water foam as she sprinkled in the luxuriously fragrant lavender bath salts.

As she slithered into the relaxing, perfumed cocoon, she realised how positively ghastly she felt. With the trip to Okoro, Kapi's murder, the malaria and finding Tommy, she had been functioning like an automaton. Now her body ached and felt fragile. Examining her nails, she noticed they were jagged, with scabs in the corners of two on her right hand; her legs hadn't seen a shaver for over a month and her hair was greasy and coarse. The soothing, perfumed water seeped into every crevice and fold of skin, salving and cleansing the pain of the past few weeks. She scrubbed her skin with a heavily lathered loofah, trying to rid herself of any remaining traces of the jungle, and the memory of the terrible things she had seen. Even more, she wanted to wash away the ugliness she had witnessed, the depths to which humankind can stoop, and the shame brought about by her father's lascivious acts.

The bath made her feel tired rather than refreshed, so she lay on the bed and placed the fan so it blew directly on her; it felt like a refreshing coastal breeze drifting off the ocean. The sheets beneath her were cool and smelled of the sun and fresh air. She thought of her children and how she longed to be with them. A single tear made its way across her cheek and disappeared into her hairline. I'll be home soon, Stew, Jess, little Will. I'll never go away and leave you again.

CHAPTER 22

Startled, Ruth's eyes shot open. She sat upright. It took a few seconds to get her bearings and realise that she was safe in the hotel. I must have dozed off, she thought, while registering that someone was frantically knocking at the door. "Damn!" she cursed as she jumped off the bed. "Wait, I'm getting dressed!" The banging continued. She put on her dressing gown and went to the door.

Standing in the doorway was Jake, clean-shaven and wearing whites, almost unrecognisable as the same person that she had seen in the prison. "Jake!" she exclaimed, noticing his familiar rakish grin. "What are you doing here?"

"I've been released, thanks to Tommy. Can I come in?"

"Of course. Tommy?"

"Yes, he and some of the men at Okoro took Sam to the patrol office and he confessed to everything. He's being flown to Moresby this afternoon. The kiaps have gone to bring in Hiri."

"So Tommy went back to Okoro after I left," Ruth said, experiencing a surge of gratitude and relief.

"I guess so, must have done."

"Where is he now?" She wondered if Tommy would come to Port Moresby or whether she would have to go looking for him again. There was still a lot to sort out, including the fate of Okoro.

"I don't know; they didn't say."

"I tried to tell the police about everything before I went to find Tommy; they treated me as though I had made it up, or that I was hysterical. Useless lot they are; in the state I was in, they had me wondering whether I'd imagined everything."

"Well, they can't say that now with the culprit confessing." Jake's expression softened as he took his sister's hand. "Thanks for going in to bat for me, Ruthy."

"I could hardly leave you in prison once I knew the truth."

"So how are you, Sis? I heard you were at the leper's mission. How on earth did you get there?"

"I had to go to Okoro to find out about what happened with Dad, and ask Meka whether what you told me about Tommy was true."

"You asked Meka? I bet that went down well," he said wryly. "They don't talk about things like that, sort of taboo."

"Well, she did talk, and you were right. Tommy is our brother. And my son's father."

Jake had an 'I-told-you-so' look on his face, which annoyed Ruth. She guessed it wouldn't last long once she told him what she had done with her share of Okoro. Before doing that, though, she wanted to savour having her big brother back just a little longer. She recounted the horror of what had transpired at Okoro and her escape along the river before being struck down with malaria.

"And I think I saw Lindsay's grave at the mission. They said locals had brought in an elderly white fellow; he'd gone completely mad apparently, and didn't make any sense. The Sogeri people found him wandering in the bush years earlier."

"Sure sounds like him. Didn't he carry any identification?"

"Well, he'd been living with the villagers for years so I'd imagine any documents were lost. The nun who nursed him said he had nothing on him which gave any indication as to his identity. She did say he kept ranting about some criminal activity, as though in a court of law. I'm going to let the police know anyway. They might be able to bring the body back for testing or something. Although, after my last run in with the local constabulary, I'm not sure they'll bother doing much at all."

"Might be best to let sleeping dogs lie," Jake said.

"You're probably right. It's all such a long time ago now, although his family in Scotland will want to know." Her thoughts drifted to what Lindsay must have gone through, wandering around trying to make sense of his surroundings. That alone was probably enough to send him over the edge. She paused momentarily before plunging into her carefully planned spiel.

"I guess now is as good a time as any, Jake. As you know, Gran left me her share of Okoro, but I've got my own life on the mainland. I wouldn't be able to come back here all the time to keep an eye on things. Besides, after what I've learned about Dad and the village women, I don't think I want anything to do with the place anymore."

"I can understand that," Jake said pensively.

"I also have to consider Stewart. I don't know what he'll want to do in the future, but I want to make sure he has choices, the chance of something here with his father if he chooses. We must try to put things right as best we can after the mess Dad made of things."

"I don't mind giving Tommy a cut of the profits, if that's what you want," Jake offered.

"With the current political situation and bad feeling in the village, you won't get anyone to work for you, or for me, after what I've seen. Not to mention the danger you'd be in if you tried to force everyone back to work. We'd lose Okoro, and Stewart would have nothing here. I've signed my share of the plantation over to Tommy." She waited for his reaction.

"I thought you'd do something like that."

"It's the only right thing to do when you think about it." She studied his face, there was no sign of anger.

"Perhaps, if you think he'll understand the business side of things."

"He's not stupid, Jake. He just didn't get the opportunities you and I had. The only difficult part is dealing with buyers, and the place is still half yours; you'll need to stay involved."

"I had time to think while locked up. I want to spend some time at Garua. I have commitments."

"At Gran's village? What sort of commitments?"

"I've got two children," he said with a sly smile.

"What do you mean? Your own children?" Ruth said.

"Yes, I had a woman, but she got killed in a fight."

"So you had a relationship with a local woman?"

"Yes, Ruth, a local woman. Didn't you ever wonder why Gran hated me?"

"Yes, I did." So that was why Gran disliked him, she thought, remembering how her grandmother detested white men who preyed on village women. "I assumed it had something to do with Lindsay."

"No, that was just her thinking she knew the mountains better than me; thought I didn't look properly."

"The way you used to talk about the Papuans, I would never have guessed you'd take a native mistress." Ruth couldn't imagine her brother romantically involved with a Garua woman. She then realised their relationship probably wasn't anything particularly romantic, like with her father and Meka.

"Gran wanted me to acknowledge them as mine and take the woman as my wife. Could you imagine Mum, if I had?"

"How old are the children?"

"Alisi's nineteen now and my boy, Daniel, is twenty."

"I don't know, Jake, I really don't. My brain can't take it all in, the sooner I leave this place and get home, the better. How long will you be at Garua?"

"A week, a month; perhaps I'll stay."

"You know we have land there, eh? And a house."

"I know *you* have land."

"Well, if you're serious about wanting to acknowledge them…"

"Of course I'm serious; what else have I got?"

The sincerity in his voice caught Ruth by surprise. The initial disgust she had felt at the thought of him following in her father's footsteps diminished slightly. She had never imagined him caring about anyone other than himself or the plantation. What do any of us truly have apart from our children? she thought, realising that he had probably lost as much as she. They had both learned of the precarious nature of life, and of relationships especially. There was a certain vulnerability about her brother now, she noticed, maybe it had always been there. She realised he must have had it hard too, living at Okoro with their father's womanising and mother's crazy carrying-on.

"I'll sign the land over to the three of you. It's undeveloped, so you'll lose it if you don't do something by the time the government changes."

"I'll give it some thought; perhaps we could grow tea."

Ruth knew Jake would take advantage of the offer. It was pride preventing him from appearing too enthusiastic.

"Anyway," he said, "I need to go and buy some clothes and book myself into the Moresby Hotel; I'll stay in town until you leave."

"Are you mad at me?"

"What, for giving away your share?"

"Yes," Ruth nodded. She didn't want him to leave feeling resentful. If the arrangement was to work, he had to think of Tommy as a partner, not just tolerate him.

"I was mad at Eliza when I heard, but I got used to the idea of sharing Okoro with you while I was in prison. Working with Tommy will be easier, he knows how everything works."

"You be good to him and remember, I'm only a plane trip away."

"Jeez, you've turned into a proper *bos meri*, Ruth."

"Case of having to be with a family like mine. Anyway, you can't talk, you used to be the worst of all of us, telling everyone what to do." They laughed and embraced briefly. "I'm thinking we should meet up for dinner tonight. You can meet Joshua." No sooner had she mentioned his name, there was a knock on the door.

"Josh! Come in and meet my brother, Jake. He's just got out of prison."

"She makes me sound like a bloody criminal. Pleased to meet you, mate." The two men shook hands.

"How was Millie, Josh?" Ruth asked, still reeling from guilt and concerned about how the woman was going to manage without Kapi.

"As well as can be expected, I think. I met Tom too," Joshua said.

"He's at Millie's?"

Joshua hesitated, "Yes, he was, he came back with me. He's outside."

"Why didn't he come up?"

"I told the bloke at the door he couldn't wait outside, but he said he wasn't dressed properly."

"It's a wonder they don't still use the damn *taravatu* signs."

"What are they?" Joshua asked.

"Motu for 'keep out', but the signs only applied to the locals. And in case they didn't understand Motu, they had Pidgin ones as well, *itambu*, with a picture of a big black hand barring entry."

"Why not bring him over for dinner tonight?" Jake said.

"Yes, the four of us will be nice," Ruth agreed. "We'll make sure our plans aren't disrupted by their dress code though, Tom will need a jacket to wear. I won't have him refused entry again. Look, I'd better go down; I can't leave him waiting outside." She left the men to arrange pre-dinner drinks at the bar of their hotel.

Jake's apparent change in personality had come as a surprise. He was his old self again, the big brother she had always idolised, until he went away to school. She reasoned that the changes at Okoro, along with his stint in prison, must have caused him to experience some kind of epiphany. Or is it just me? she wondered. Maybe we just lost touch with each other amongst all the chaos at home. Ruth came to herself with a start and rushed downstairs to find Tommy.

"Tommy! I thought I was going to have to fly back to Lae to see you."

"I had to sort things out at the village," he said stiffly.

The tone of his voice was gruff; she couldn't tell whether he was uncomfortable at seeing her again or annoyed at having to wait outside. "You did us all a huge favour; I couldn't get the bloody police to believe a thing I said. Come on, let's go for a coffee. There's a Chinese place up the road."

As they walked towards the café, Tommy began to relax. He was bursting with questions about Stewart.

"Are you going to tell him about our father?" he asked.

"Yes, I want him to know the truth. I want him to understand the circumstances; how it was, how we were. He deserves the truth."

"He should know," Tommy agreed. "Growing up with lies can hurt you." He pulled out a piece of bark from his pocket. He had painted a picture of a *kumul*, the bird of paradise. "This is for my son."

"Oh, Tommy, it's beautiful! You always could draw birds better than me. I'll get him to write to you." Ruth wondered what Stewart would think of the place when he eventually came to visit, or whether he would even want to visit.

Sitting opposite Tommy at the cafe table, Ruth studied his face in between sips of too-hot coffee. His features had softened over the years; he had a comfortable look about him. She puzzled over why she hadn't noticed her grandmother's eyes before. The same quirky smile lines around his eyes, they were one of his most striking features. Those same eyes, which had once ignited her passion, now only elicited a warm affection. She would always love Tommy; nothing would change their unique bond, but now she loved him as a brother.

"I didn't get a chance to talk to you about Okoro when in Lae," Ruth said, feeling it was safe now to raise the subject of the plantation. "The villagers are angry. They don't trust Jake. We'll lose the place, if we don't do something."

She went on to explain how she hoped he would build some sort of partnership with the village. Okoro would pay rent for the land and proper wages to the workers.

She thought for a moment. "It would have been easy just to forget about the place, but I can't now. Even though I'm happy on the mainland, I've come to realise this place is still part of me; it made me who I am. It's part of Stewart too." She paused, trying to judge his reaction to what she was saying. "I want you to take my share of Okoro and make it work again; for you and the villagers, Meka, Essie, Millie and all the others. And for the children, especially the children."

Tommy stared into his coffee. Ruth wondered how he must feel, disowned by his father, having a son by his sister and now being told he can have half the plantation where his people had spent their lives working for bully beef, rice and trinkets. She had always admired his ability to weigh things up thoroughly before arriving at an answer, but his hesitation was killing her now. If he wasn't prepared to partner-up with Jake, everything at Okoro would be lost, and Stewart would lose part of his heritage.

He finally spoke just as she was about to give up hope. "If I were alone, I'd say no," he said, then stared back into his cup. "But I have children, and my people will be lost once we gain independence. They've nothing but their huts, pigs and the fish in the river. We can't go back to the way we were. I'll take your share."

"If anyone can do this, Tom, you can. I'm so glad; I hoped you would." She wanted to give him a hug but caught herself, unsure of how to be with him physically now, so she hit his arm like she had done as a child.

"Ha! If you're going to be my sister, you'd better start being nice to me."

"Go on, you big booby. Let's go, Jake and Josh will be waiting at the Moresby for you, and I need to get my things sorted out."

Ruth arrived back at the hotel with plenty of time before dinner. She decided to start on her packing. Joshua had managed to get two tickets for an early morning flight back to Sydney the next day so she was beside herself with joy at the prospect of going home.

As she emptied the contents of the wardrobe on the bed, her excitement suddenly vanished. She remembered Millie and her children. The devastation of losing a husband and having no family around was bad enough on the mainland, but here, women had nothing without their men. Ruth hoped Tommy would take them back to Okoro; they needed family now. Images of her own children flashed through her mind, it was easy to picture them sitting at home on tenterhooks, waiting for her to turn up. Not long now, she thought, and I'll be able to hold them again.

Ruth was glad of some time alone; she was able to do all the personal things she had neglected. She even found time to get her hair done, which made her feel so good she splashed out on one of the new maxi evening dresses for dinner.

Dressed to the nines and looking uncharacteristically glamorous, Ruth took the Brownie camera from the pocket of her vanity case and loaded the film. "Oh well, Stewy, at least I can bring you the photograph you wanted," she said, as if he were listening. "Things are different now, but he is still your father." She pushed the camera into her new Glomesh clutch and went down to dinner.

The three men were waiting when she arrived in her elegant new dress, complete with halter neckline. They all looked pleasantly surprised, as she thought they would, never being one to bother much with make-up and fashionable clothes. Ruth thought Tommy looked uncomfortable, sitting all stiff in his new white jacket. When their eyes met, she too felt uneasy, or embarrassed. She wasn't sure what the feeling was exactly, but knew she had to push it to the back of her mind. If we're going to make the best of things, she told herself, dwelling on the past isn't going to help us. She took a deep breath and smiled.

"Good evening, gents. Don't stand up." She sat down next to Tommy. "I'm glad you came, Tom. I suspected you weren't that keen."

"He'll soon get used to all this," Jake said. "Once Okoro is back on its feet, he'll have more money than half these bastards sitting around here staring."

"Shh, Jake. I know, but for the time being let's not upset anyone. I want our last night together to be special."

"Will you come back again, Ruth?" Tommy asked.

"I want to bring Stewart up here; maybe we'll come back next year." It then occurred to Ruth, what would Jessica think about Stewart suddenly getting his father back? It would probably remind her of her own losses again. Maybe Bob and Evelyn were the answer, she hoped, making up her mind to invite them out to Derrigeribar. Jess would enjoy that; they'd both have new people in their lives then. "Sorry, I was just thinking about Jess."

"She'll love it here. Always been fascinated with foreign places. I'll tag along too," Joshua said.

Of course, Ruth thought, we can all come; no one needs to be left out.

The conversation turned to farming and the government. With Joshua and Jake debating the possible introduction of tariffs once the country became independent, Ruth asked Tommy if he would take Millie back to Okoro. He said that had already been arranged, Essie was on her way down to take Millie and the children back to the village.

"So what's going to happen about the grave you found, Ruth?" Jake asked in between mouthfuls of crab.

"I'm going to inform our wonderful Mr Barrett, he can follow it up."

They raised a toast to Okoro and the soon-to-be self-governing Papua New Guinea. Ruth couldn't think of a time when she had felt more positive about the future. Everyone now had a chance to start afresh; it was as though all the bad in her past had been shaken out of her life. Even Jake seemed content with the new arrangements for Okoro.

"I just hope you two get along," Ruth said, looking at Tommy and Jake.

"We'll be all right, Ruth; you worry too much. We've already planned some changes for Okoro while we were waiting for you."

"If you both get it right, you can show the way forward for other businesses."

"We'll be right; stop worrying. Now let's eat this dessert. I haven't had a decent meal for nearly four months," Jake said, as his attention turned to the baked Alaska in front of him.

The men seemed to have everything worked out, Ruth decided, with a sigh of relief.

"Looks like we'll be catching that plane in the morning, Ruth, unless you want to change to the later flight?" Joshua asked.

"No, I don't want to stay any longer. I can't wait to return home. I'm going to keep the children home from school for a week as soon as I get back. I've missed them so much."

"Will was okay after the first few days, but Stew got into a bit of a state."

"Yes, he'd be worried. It's a good thing Jess is close by."

"Matt took him up crop-dusting which took his mind off things for a while."

"Oh my goodness, good job I wasn't there to see that. Which reminds me, have you heard any more about Bry going under?"

"Only what Matt told me, that they eventually want to move back Molong way."

"If they want to get out, I'd be interested in taking it off their hands. If the bank will lend me the money."

"Bry?" Joshua said, looking intrigued.

"Yes, I want to get it back. I don't think Jess has ever forgiven me for selling up."

"Perhaps we can do a deal. I could use some of the land and the bank would be less likely to say no if you had a partner."

"A man, you mean?"

"Well, yeah I guess so."

"I'd put it under cotton for the first few years to get the loan down," Ruth said, sounding excited.

"Lighten up, Ruthy. Stop talking shop." Jake seemed determined to assert his older brother standing now that everything was getting back to normal. Ruth didn't care; he was welcome to it.

"Oh, okay bossy boots. I'll take some snaps instead." She took out her camera and fiddled with the flash attachment. "These are for the children, so nice smiles please."

It was the first time Ruth could recall feeling so completely in control of her life. As horrible as coming home and confronting her past had been, she now possessed a new sense of confidence in who she was and what she was capable of doing. It had turned into a journey of self-exploration as much as one of tying up loose ends. As she turned over in bed to sleep, she realised she was happy. Things have turned out well enough, she thought. At least for now.

Early the following morning, spirits were high on the minibus to Jackson airfield. Tom and Jake had dragged themselves out of bed to see Ruth and Joshua off on their journey home. The sun had just peaked over the horizon and the air rushing through the open bus windows felt cool as it hit their sticky, perspiring skin.

Sitting squashed up next to Joshua and her two brothers, Ruth remembered the many times she had taken this trip in the past. She had always felt sad as the bus hurtled its way along the rough road out of town to the airfield, but this time was different. The country she had once called home was no longer a wonderland of vibrant colours and complaisant people. No longer did it possess the familiar, safe feeling of home. It was a land and people waking to the call of independence and self-determination. Ruth had witnessed the mounting discontent, the pain of subjugation, exploitation and the malevolent depths to which humanity can reach in its attempt to cast off the restraints of a colonial past. Ruth herself had changed; no longer a girl with dreams of faraway places and a naïve trust in human nature, but a woman of strength who had managed to rise above what life had put in her path. She decided that saying goodbye to Jake and Tommy wasn't going to be a sombre affair.

"It's like a new beginning for everyone," she said, looking at Joshua and realising for the first time what an important part of her life he had become.

"For sure, darl," he said, gently ushering her forward with his hand on her back. "No looking back now."

47

Lightning Source UK Ltd.
Milton Keynes UK
UKOW051807071011

179950UK00001B/54/P